WOLVES AND ROSES
FAIRY TALES OF THE MAGICORUM — BOOK 1

CHRISTINA BAUER

First Published by Monster House Books, LLC in 2017
Monster House Books, LLC
34 Chandler Place Newton, MA 02464
www.monsterhousebooks.com

ISBN 9781945723070

For My Husband

CHAPTER ONE
BRYAR ROSE

I wait in the bottom level of the Denarii League in Midtown Manhattan. As basements go, it's not too bad. The space is snug and clean with concrete block walls, a linoleum floor, and hardly any cockroaches. For New York, that's a big deal. I fidget on my chair. The plastic seat is so cockeyed my left butt cheek has gone numb. And that's not the worst part of this situation.

Any minute now, my Magicorum Teen Therapy Group will begin. Yay.

The metal door slams open, and our group facilitator, Madame Grimoire, swishes into the room. As always, Madame looks like she fell out of a kitchen appliance ad from 1952. She's middle-aged with wavy brown hair and perfect makeup. Her A-line dress is sky blue and stops mid-calf. She tops off the look with pearls, red lipstick, and white gloves. No, I am not kidding. White gloves.

I hate her. So much.

"Greetings, children."

No one answers her. *Looks like I'm not the only one who hates Madame.*

After slipping onto her chair, Madame folds her hands neatly on her lap. "I am Madame Grimoire, your facilitator. If you were assigned to this group, that means you're part of the Magicorum."

I inwardly groan. *Here she goes again.* It doesn't matter how many times we've heard this spiel, Madame always gives the same speech.

"That means you're one of the three magical races: shifters, witches, or fairies. In addition, you could be a non-magical human in their immediate family. But however you came to be classified as such, being a member of the Magicorum makes you a very rare commodity. Magic is disappearing from our world, and the Denarii League is committed to saving it." Madame pulls a tablet from her pocket. "Now, let's begin with roll call. Bryar Rose?"

I raise my pointer finger. "Here."

"Cinderella."

"I've told you a million times. It's Elle."

I scope out Elle and smile. Today, she came to group dressed like a street urchin, complete with ratty blonde hair and rags. *Huh.* Elle must be working a new con that involves dressing like she's homeless. All her scams are for good causes, though, so I shrug it off.

"Scarlett?" asks Madame.

"Present."

Scarlett gets her name from the Red Riding Hood fairy tale. She's got ebony-dark skin, a punk-rock wardrobe, and a firm commitment to avoid talking in group. That's typical for werewolves, though. Weres are notorious for being silent, grouchy, and fashion forward.

"And last but not least, we have a new girl here." Madame slaps on the fakest smile ever. "What's your name?"

A long pause follows. When the girl speaks, the word comes out as a peep. "Avianna." She has straight black hair, brown eyes, and pale skin. Considering her long dark dress and the crow perched on her shoulder, Avianna is definitely a witch.

"You're new to group, Avianna."

"I am."

"How much do you know about what we do here?"

2

"Nothing." Avianna's big brown eyes seem to take up half her face. Poor thing is terrified.

"Why don't I give you an example?"

"Sure."

My shoulders slump. *Oh, damn.* Madame always chooses me as her "example of why we're here." It's super-embarrassing.

"Now." Madame's face beams with a sick sort of glee. "All the Magicorum have lives that follow a fairy tale template. Since you're here, that means you're failing miserably at that template. Now, who should I choose as an example?" Madame scans the room while tapping her chin.

Don't say Bryar Rose. Don't say Bryar Rose. Don't say Bryar Rose.

Madame points right at my nose. "Let's use Bryar Rose."

She said it.

I raise my hand. "Maybe someone else wants to be the example this time."

Madame keeps right on going like I haven't said a word. It's super-irritating. "Bryar Rose is a non-magical human who should follow the life template for Sleeping Beauty." She eyes me from head to toe. "There are some ways in which Bryar Rose is an excellent illustration of that template. To begin with, she's the adopted child of three fairy aunties who named her Bryar Rose. Also, she's an attractive girl with brown hair and blue eyes, so she does somewhat look the part. And finally, she's afflicted with a magical illness that makes her fall asleep whenever she's overexcited. Show them your inhaler, Bryar Rose."

This is so humiliating. "No."

Sheesh, does she ever listen? "Bryar Rose is embarrassed about her condition, so she keeps an inhaler close by to help her stay awake. The easiest way to explain her ailment is that it resembles a disease where you spontaneously fall asleep such as narcolepsy. However, Bryar Rose stays frozen—usually while standing—with her eyes wide open. It's odd, but still very much in accordance with the Sleeping Beauty life template."

"Did you get permission from my doctor to tell everyone my medical history?" I'm just speaking to hear myself talk at this point. The whole "legal permission thing" has never shut up Madame before. Even so, you can't blame a girl for trying.

"According to her life template, Bryar Rose should reach her happily ever after by the age of eighteen, which is almost here, isn't it? Today is Wednesday, and your birthday is…?" She stares at me expectantly.

"Saturday."

"So your birthday is only three days from now. And according to your life template, you should be marrying your handsome Prince as the sun sets this Saturday, shouldn't you?"

"According to the template." *And that's a bunch of crap.* I don't want to be Magicorum. I want to be a regular human. Who cares if I don't match up to their idea of a Sleeping Beauty?

Madame sighs. "Alas, your happily ever after is nowhere in sight, is it?"

Answering Madame isn't helping today, so I keep quiet and check my manicure instead. *Yup, still there.*

"Let's review the key ways that Bryar Rose fails her life template. Her aunties have found her a wonderful Prince in the form of Philpot; I'm sure you've all heard of him. The papers call Philpot His Highness of Hedge Funds."

I'd explain that we're all seventeen and don't give a crap about hedge funds, but that would only make her launch into a speech on how important money is. *I'll pass.*

"In any case, Philpot is a darling, yet Bryar Rose hasn't warmed to him."

Translation: I can't stand Philpot. The man is the definition of a douchebag.

"He offered to marry you this weekend," says Madame.

"I remember. I was there when he proposed." *And I said no. Talk about awkward.*

Madame's voice turns all dreamy. "Any woman would kill to marry Philpot."

I roll my eyes. Madame is always going on about how super-awesome Philpot is. It's super-creepy. The way she talks about him, you'd think she was the one marrying him. Only, you know, willingly.

"Enough about Philpot." Madame clears her throat. "We need to discuss Bryar Rose's other shortcomings."

I hold back a moan. *More shortcomings?* "I thought we were here to learn how to follow our life template."

Madame keeps right on ignoring me. Instead, she continues talking to Avianna like I'm not even here. "Bryar Rose also fails to show any interest in birds and woodland creatures."

Now I won't admit this out loud, but Madame is spot on about this part. Birds do nothing for me. The only thing I really care about—of all things—is finding papyri from ancient Egypt.

I know. *Strange.*

"Because of all this, Bryar Rose has been declared unfit for a typical school with normal humans. Instead, she receives a combination of home tutoring and group therapy."

In other words, my life is the fairy-tale equivalent of the Island of Misfit Toys, and it's all thanks to a spell cast on me by the powerful fairy Colonel Mallory the Magnificent. *Jerk.* He's the one who gave me this sleeping condition. I hate him even more than Madame.

As Madame drones on about all the ways I suck, I force myself to focus on the bright side. With any luck, my sleeping condition ends in three days. *June the first.* That's when I turn eighteen and the spell from Colonel Mallory goes buh bye. Come the fall, I could be caught up on normal human stuff and should pass for a typical non-Magicorum girl. I might even attend the exclusive West Lake Prep School, so I can spend my senior year with other non-magical teens.

A normal high school. I want that so badly, I could scream.

Madame clears her throat, which is a sure sign that she's done with her speech. I catch the tail end. "And that, my children, is why Bryar Rose is a total disaster. Any questions?"

No one responds. Elle starts yanking bits of string from her frayed skirt. Since she's my best friend, I know what that means.

She's pissed for me and planning to derail Madame the first chance she gets. I love Elle.

Madame keeps glaring at Avianna. "So, my child, if you're here, you're a reject. A failure. Do you understand?"

Avianna's lower lip quivers. "Yes."

"Excellent. I'm glad I made that so clear for you all." Madame is a spiteful woman, but she's the gatekeeper of my future. I can only attend West Lake Prep once she signs off that I'm no longer magically challenged. She turns to me again. "And one more thing."

Don't let her pick on my clothes. Don't let her pick on my clothes.

"Bryar?"

"Yes?"

Madame's nostrils flare as she looks me over. "Your outfit this week is slightly improved."

And there, she did it. Nothing like a half-compliment, half-insult to cut someone down while you're seeming to be nice.

I keep my face calm. It's important not to let Madame see that she got to me. "Thank-you for sharing."

Here's what that final bit of nastiness was *really* about. In some ways, Madame and I are similar. We're both what my aunties would call "put together." My long brown hair is styled in fashionable waves. My clothes are tailored black pants along with a fitted cashmere sweater. I even have funky jewelry to jazz things up. What can I say? I like to shop. However, Madame thinks we're in some sort of fancy-pants competition.

Whatever. I cross my fingers, hoping Madame is done fixating on me. Unfortunately, she keeps right on going.

"Since Avianna is new to our little group, I have an idea." Madame turns to acknowledge me once more. "Why don't you tell her about your strange dreams? Get the conversation started."

"Like I said, maybe someone else wants to share." Madame always dives into my dreams as soon as she has the chance. It's a little weird.

"But I'd like *you* to talk," says Madame. "Or don't you want to go to West Lake?"

And here comes the great challenge of my life. On the one hand, we have normal high school. On the other hand, we have the satisfaction of mouthing off to Madame.

Guess what always wins?

I lower my voice, which is a sure sign I'm about to kick some verbal butt. "As a matter of fact—"

"Nah, I'll go first." Elle raises her hand, silencing any further discussion. She's trying to save me from another verbal run-in with Madame. Elle is awesome like that.

"I asked Bryar Rose," says Madame.

"You sure did. I'm answering, though." Elle glares in Madame's direction. When Madame backs down, it's only because Elle made her do it. Some days, I wish I were Elle. Instead, I settle for being her best friend.

"Fine." Madame lifts her chin. "After you're finished, I have big news to share with you, *Cinderella*." The way she says Elle's fairy-tale name, I know it's trouble.

Elle shrugs and turns to Avianna. "I'm watched over by an evil fairy godmother. Other humans get too close and—BAM—she takes them down. That's why I'm on the streets instead of in a regular high school."

Avianna's brown eyes go wide. "Did you say *other* humans? Madame just said you're a member of the Magicorum."

"Sure, I'm a member. It's like Madame said—you can be human and still be a member of the Magicorum. You just have to be related to a fairy, wizard, or shifter. In my case, I live under the watchful eye of my fairy godmother." She elbows me in the ribs. "It's the same deal for Bryar Rose, only she lives with three fairies."

I lean back in my chair and kick my legs forward. "Yup, three magical kooks and a penthouse overlooking Central Park. That's my life."

Madame's nostrils flare again. "That's quite enough sass, you two." She focuses right on me. "Especially you."

There's almost an audible twang as my restraint finally snaps. Madame has gone too far. "Technically, I was being sassy, and Elle here was just sharing."

"Oh, you both think you're so clever." Madame rounds on Elle. "How about we discuss what I found out about you, Cinderella—or shall I call you Abigail?"

I roll my eyes. "So, we're having this conversation again?" *Bring it on.*

"Once again, my name is Elle. E-L-L-E. No one calls me Cinderella."

"Cinderella is the name on the forms you submitted to the Denarii Institute in order to join this therapy group," says Madame. "Perhaps it's even your criminal moniker. But all this talk about a Cinderella life template is just that: talk. There's never been any evidence of a fairy godmother in your life."

Elle picks some chunks of dirt off her raggedy dress. "Says who?"

"My research." Madame lifts her small handheld and scrolls through various screens. "I just obtained some additional back records. Your birth name is Abigail Smythe. It seems that Cinderella is your outlaw nickname." She taps the screen with her long pink fingernail. "Rumors abound that you're an expert jewel thief and con artist."

"Not sure where you're getting that load of garbage," says Elle. "I'm just plain old Elle, or in a pinch, Cinderella. Got the evil step-family to prove it."

"She does," I offer. "They suck."

"You're both lying." Madame folds her arms over her chest. "I'll have you expelled from this group, *Abigail.* You belong in a regular high school."

"You belong in a regular high school." How much would I love to hear those words? Unfortunately, Elle hates the thought. Living on her own means she can hide from her stepfamily. Which is a good thing, considering how they treated her like a servant until she ran away. Now, if Elle attended a regular school under the name Abigail, she'd get dragged back into servitude in a heartbeat. For some reason—Elle won't give any particulars—her family thinks Elle can only go under the name Abigail. I'm sure some kind of magic is involved, but I don't push for more information. Like I

said, Elle's family is bizarre. And if it protects my friend, I'll call her whatever name she wants.

Fortunately, Madame has brought up the whole Abigail thing before. Elle flicks her hair, sending a cascade of dirt to the ground. "Per the Magical Preservation Act, as long as I have a Magicorum witness to my fairy relation, I can keep my official classification. Therefore, I am protected as an endangered species." This is one minor benefit of being part of the Magicorum. Since magic is disappearing from the world, humans are trying to preserve it. They passed a bunch of cool laws too, like the one Elle's citing.

Madame straightens in her chair. "That would be true, if such a Magicorum godmother existed. Who has seen this mysterious fairy?"

I raise my hand. "I've met her. Tons." Not sure if this is part of the Sleeping Beauty template, but I'm a really good liar. Seems to go along with my sassy mouth.

Madame glares at me like I just threatened her kittens. "What?"

"We've been over this before. I've absolutely met Cinderella's fairy godmother." I pretend to need to lick my lips. In reality, it's just an excuse to semi-stick out my tongue at Madame.

"You do realize that lying to me means you'll never go to West Lake Prep?"

How like Madame to keep threatening me with the number one thing I want. Well, I'm salivating to attend a regular school, but not enough to screw over Elle. "I do. And I'm telling the truth." *Not.*

Elle and I bump fists. We so have each other's backs.

"Really?" asks Madame slowly. "If that's the case, then what does this fairy godmother look like?"

"Same as the last time you asked me," I say. "Blackaverre is a small blue fairy with pink wings and pointed teeth." I smile sweetly. "Any other questions?"

"I suppose not." Madame looks disappointed. *Good.*

In truth, I've never met Elle's fairy godmother. I can't get a straight answer out of Elle if the woman even exists. Still, I need to protect my best friend. And since Elle is a master at the long con, she coached me on what to say when people press for information. Mostly, it's Madame who asks. Honestly, I worry about how much these two hate each other. But Elle needs Madame, same as I do. Every so often, my bestie gets noticed by the cops. They wonder why she isn't in school. That's when Madame can verify that Elle is part of her Magicorum Teen Therapy Group and therefore can't attend a regular school anyway. Long story short, Madame is a Get Out of Jail Free card for both Elle and me. In my case, I eventually want out of the jail of home tutoring and into West Lake. Elle just needs occasional help avoiding an actual lock-up situation.

Madame returns her focus to her favorite victim. *That would be me.* "Let's circle back to my original request. I asked you to share with the group. Are you still having those bizarre dreams?"

"Shouldn't Avianna and Scar go first? I mean, Avianna is new and has a bird on her shoulder. I think she should share. Plus, Scar is a werewolf who hasn't shifted yet. Unless she takes her wolf form by her eighteenth birthday, her inner animal could…" I lower my voice. "You know…"

"Die," says Scar. She doesn't seem too upset by the prospect. She never does, really. Elle and I have a theory about that. We both think Scar has already shifted, only she doesn't want anyone to know for some reason. Otherwise, the girl would definitely be freaking out about her eighteenth birthday and all. I mean, I've seen shifters who have lost their inner animals. They all have this thousand-mile stare and act like robots. It's really sad.

Elle leans forward. "For the record, I'd also like an update on Scar's life."

"Exactly," I say. "Everyone is sick of hearing about me and my dreams."

Madame taps her high heel against the concrete floor. "We've had enough interruptions for one afternoon. Bryar Rose, you're talking. Now."

I take in a long breath. *Remember West Lake Prep.*

"Fine. I had the dream again last night. I'm in some crappy hotel room in New York, but the window looks out over the pyramids of ancient Egypt. Across the room, there's a table covered in papyri."

"And the boy?" asks Madame.

"Oh, yeah." I can't help the dreamy tone that enters my voice. "He's there too. He has black hair and ice-blue eyes. There's a scar along his jawline and through one eyebrow." He's not necessarily pretty, what with his all his scars and leather. Still, there's no denying the guy is crazy attractive. I think about him a little. Okay, a lot.

"Anything additional to share?"

I glance around the room, and the other girls seem so open and interested, I can't help but keep going. "Last night, I saw something else, too."

Even Scar is intrigued. "What was it?"

"A golden jackal."

Madame frowns. "You saw dogs?"

"Not all jackals are dogs. Some are actually wolves, like golden jackals. They're native to Egypt." Everyone looks at me like I'm crazy, so I decide to clarify. "I looked it up on Google." That seems to settle things. No one questions Professor Google.

Madame frowns. "A wolf? Why would you see a wolf? Even if it is one of these jackal things?"

"How would I know?"

Madame's cheeks burn red. "You're a Sleeping Beauty template. You should see the woods somewhere in Germany, along with bluebirds, mice, and chipmunks. Maybe even a few badgers."

She lost me there. "Badgers?"

"My point is, this is all wrong."

"You think I don't know?" I gesture around the room. "Isn't that why we're all here?" I raise my finger as if an idea was just occurring to me. "Hey, how about this for a concept? Maybe you come up with some helpful hints instead of grilling me about my dreams all the time?"

Madame lifts her chin. "I will not be spoken to in this manner. You're clearly getting worse. That's all the time I have for you today." She rises.

My mouth falls open. "But what about everyone else? They haven't said anything. Scar's situation is pretty dangerous."

Scar leans back in her chair and smacks her lips. She still doesn't look too worried, but even so, Madame should be freaked out for Scar's safety. After all, the girl is were and she could lose her inner wolf! I've heard of shifters whose inner animal has died because they didn't turn. It's really sad and tragic. Madame should be concerned about that. For that matter, Madame should be concerned about all of us, really.

Madame starts typing away on her handheld with her thumbs. "I'm making a note about your disobedient attitude, Bryar Rose. Don't let it happen again." She quickly pulls some brochures from her skirt pocket and hands them out. "Here's some reading material for next time."

I check out the brochure. The headline reads "Mysterious disappearances in the Magicorum—what you need to know to stay safe." Madame slips out another sheet from her pocket, along with a pen. "All of you must now sign here and acknowledge I gave you a pamphlet."

Elle and I exchange a confused look. *This is weird.* Even worse, it isn't the first time we've gotten the safety brochure and a "cover your ass" form to sign. The last time this happened, someone from our group went missing. It was Blanche, a girl with a Snow White life template. I jam the brochure into my purse and stare at Madame. "Are you worried about one of us?"

Considering she just lost it over my wolf story, there's a short list of who she could be worrying about.

"Of course not." Madame gives me that 1950's smile, the one that says, *I just love cooking rump roasts in my new electric oven.* She makes sure everyone signs the form in quick succession. I watch her every move with interest.

Madame is totally lying. Something about my dream set her off.

Elle rests her hand on my shoulder. "You know, Bryar Rose here is home tutored. One of her teachers is a master in mixed martial arts."

"Plus I can handle a gun." For some reason, it seems very important to add that fact into the conversation.

Madame's fake smile stays firmly in place. "In that case, I'm sure our dear Bryar Rose is perfectly safe." With that, Madame picks up the sheet of signatures and simply walks out the door. Even for her, that's a strange thing to do.

CHAPTER TWO
BRYAR ROSE

Long after Madame is gone, I find myself staring at the closed steel door. When I finally become aware of my surroundings again, I realize that Elle and I are the only ones left in the room.

My best friend gives my shoulder a gentle squeeze. "Madame is weird. Don't let her get to you."

A twinge of fear tightens my insides. "I can't stop thinking about Blanche, though. Remember how she told the group that her dreams changed, too? She saw pelicans or something."

"It was falcons."

"Yeah. And right after that, Madame gave out brochures and sign-off sheets. Then Blanche disappeared."

Elle's blue eyes fill with understanding. "So, what do you want to do? I can stay at your side as a bodyguard."

I chuckle. "Last time that happened, you picked the pockets of my aunties and all their friends from the Summer Fairy Court."

"What? They had too much stuff. I was just trying to show them what was really important in life."

"To fairies?" I try to all-out laugh, but I can't. Instead, my pulse speeds up. *Blanche's body was never found.* My eyelids droop. Silver spots cloud my vision. The walls seem to move in closer. Deep inside my soul, I feel that familiar sensation. It's as if someone placed a lockbox in the core of my being. Inside that impenetrable safe sits the spell from Colonel Mallory. Right now, that lockbox is shifting inside me. It wants to break free. That can only mean one thing.

Another episode is coming on.

Elle grabs my purse and pulls out my inhaler. "Quick, take your medicine."

I uncover the top of the small device, set it in my mouth, and give myself a puff of medicated air. This stuff tastes terrible, but I start feeling more alert again. "Thanks."

Elle narrows her big blue eyes. "You shouldn't be alone. I'm staying in my condo this week. Why don't you hang with me?" Elle has her own apartment in the Village under an assumed name. "We can do some recon work on my latest target. I'll even give you access to my good computer. You're a way better hacker than I am." My aunties might not have let me attend a regular school, but they did get me a computer with high-speed Internet access. Over the years, I've become quite good at being a bad girl online.

"It's tempting." I worry my lower lip with my teeth. "But I'm supposed to join Philpot later at his Wednesday night soiree." I make little quotation marks with my fingers when I say *"soiree."*

"Blow him off. Philpot is a total tool."

"I know, but it's just easier if I pretend that I'm still considering marrying him someday. Don't judge. You know my aunties."

"I've met them." Elle sighs. "No judgment." She doesn't need to mention the real reason why I do whatever my aunties say. They're the only ones who can make my magical meds. Trust me, I've tried to find alternate sources. No go. My aunties are it. Until I'm eighteen and don't need meds any more, I have to deal with them. But once my birthday is over, so is my curse. There will be no more sleeping sickness, no more Philpot, and best of all, no more aunties.

My breath catches. *Crap, I forgot all about my aunties.*

I stare at the metal door. No doubt, all three of them are waiting in the hallway outside. If I don't leave soon, they'll barge in for sure. I have to finalize plans with Elle—and fast. "Want to go with me to the party tonight? Philpot's penthouse is right next door to the LeCharme Building." LeCharme is only the biggest and fanciest jeweler in New York. In fact, easy access to the LeCharme HQ is one of the only advantages of fake-dating Philpot.

"I'll pass."

"What? You've always gone with me before."

And by *"gone with me,"* I mean breaking and entering. Elle and I have hit the LeCharme Building a ton of times. The bottom floors have jewels galore, many of which fit Elle's theft profile. You see, Elle specializes in reacquiring jewels that have already been stolen. She returns them to their rightful owners and collects the reward. She calls the entire process "un-stealing," which is total Elle-think, but I don't judge. After all, a girl's gotta eat and avoid her evil stepfamily. For my part, I'm interested in the top floors of the building. That's where the LeCharme family lives and keeps their offices. Their eldest son, Alec, likes to collect rare papyri from ancient Egypt. Super-unusual stuff, too. Whenever we break in, Elle gets jewels while I take photos of rare hieroglyphs. It's always been a win-win.

Elle sighs. "Don't get me wrong; I'd love to break and enter with you. Just not tonight."

I shake my head. "I can't believe you're taking a pass."

"Let's just say I've been spending too much time with the LeCharme inventory lately. I need to give them some space. Plus, I have another huge job I'm working on. It's—"

"I don't want to know."

"Probably for the best. Still, you should totally skip the Philpot soiree. Come hang with me at my place. Like I said, you'll get to use my good computer."

Which is no small gift. Elle's so-called good computer is tricked out with every hacking app the black market has to offer. The only system that beats it is the one I built in her cabin in the Adirondacks."

"It's tempting." I worry my lower lip with my teeth as I think about the papyri that are supposed to be in Alec's office right now. "Sorry, I have to pass. Alec just got a new shipment of papyri. You know his system. He only keeps them around for a few days before sending them someplace even I can't find. There's no way I can pass up the chance to make copies."

Elle picks at some stray threads on her torn dress. Her normally bright features droop with fear. "I don't the idea of you going there alone."

My eyebrows lift. "Don't tell me you're afraid?" Elle's scared of nothing.

"I'm protective of you." She puffs out her lower lip. "There's a difference."

Now, if Elle told me everything would be fine, I might have skipped the party, hung out at her condo, and hacked the night away. But since Elle worries that I can't handle this alone, it makes my rebellion-reflex kick in. All my life, I've been told that I can't do stuff because of my episodes. Sure, anything I do is a risk, but staying home and hiding out? That means missing out on my life. Not an option.

"Don't worry, Elle. I'll be fine."

"If you say so."

"I do. Will you have my back?"

Elle perks right up. "Always."

"Thanks. In that case, can you be on phone duty tonight? Say I'm sleeping over at your place?"

This is all part of a scam that Elle and I worked out years ago. I have two phones. My aunties bought me the first cell, which has GPS software on it so they can trace my location. I loaded the app myself and showed them how to use it. As fairies, they aren't what you call tech savvy. Looking at my location on a computer gives them an unreasonable sense of comfort about me going places without them. Plus, with magic draining from the world, they have to save their spells for extreme situations. The second phone is my latest burner. Only Elle gets that number.

"No problem." Elle hands me her cell, and I program in the number of my temp phone. These are pretty much untraceable, and I get a new one every week. Once the new number is entered, I give Elle my "official auntie phone" for safekeeping.

Elle slips my main phone into her raggedy pocket. "After the party, are you going to the cabin?" This is Elle's place in the Adirondacks. She lets me keep my master computer setup there. It's mighty sweet. I even added a wall of monitors that are perfect for looking at papyri.

"Where else? I'll want to look through the latest hieroglyphs. Besides, the quiet will be good. My aunties are making me crazy." I stare at the closed door. Any minute now, they'll burst through.

"Do you need anything to break into the LeCharme Building? Access cards? Codes?"

"Nah, I've got all the stuff from last time. Those should still work, right?"

"Oh, yeah." When it comes to acquiring tools for breaking and entering, Elle has the best underworld contacts in the business.

"In that case, I'm all set." I pat my purse, where I carry all my goodies.

Elle doesn't reply, though. Instead, she winds a strand of filthy hair around her finger. She's still worried. "If you still insist on going—"

"I do."

"Just promise me that you'll take your meds. You can't have an episode while you're driving."

"I always take my meds. You know how careful I am."

Suddenly, the door flies open, and my aunties rush in. Like many fairies, they are petite with quick, bird-like movements. First, there's Lauralei. She's got light gray hair and a body that reminds me of a flamingo: skinny with long legs, a short torso, and a nose that can only be described as beak-like. My second auntie, Fanna, looks pretty similar to Lauralei, except her hair is black and streaked with gray. And third, there's Mirabelle. To continue with the bird analogy, Auntie Mira always reminds me of a plump red hen. She's got a round body, small black eyes, and red hair that's pulled back into a bun. Mostly, she and Fanna cluck about in the background while Lauralei does all the talking.

Speaking of Lauralei, she's the first to rush into the room. The woman is a flurry of movement with her long legs and pink Chanel pantsuit. "You're still in here. We were gravely concerned."

"Nothing to worry about." My voice sounds fake-calm, even to me. "I was just talking to Elle."

Lauralei freezes. Since Fanna and Mirabelle were following closely behind her, they almost slam into Lauralei's back. "You." Lauralei points to Elle. "You're in rags."

Elle grins. "Isn't it wonderful? I got the lead in the Magicorum Academy production of *Oliver*." For the record, Elle has my aunties convinced she goes to a high school for elite Magicorum kids. Don't ask. "I'm just practicing getting in character."

Elle is so awesome. I'm sure she made that up on the fly.

"How clever!" Lauralei gasps and turns to Fanna and Mirabelle. "Don't you both think so?" My other aunties agree, but Lauralei doesn't stop to listen. "Now, what are you two girls doing tonight?"

"Going to Philpot's party," I say.

Lauralei keeps staring at Elle. "I assumed that part, but what about after?"

"We'll stay at my family's condo in the Village," explains Elle. In this case, Elle is her own family—not that my aunties know that. "We'll watch TV. Maybe indulge in low-fat frozen yogurt. The usual."

Lauralei shrugs. "That's fine. So long as she's back to the penthouse by Saturday at midnight, that's all I care about." My aunties are throwing me a birthday party of some kind. Those always start at midnight and end with the penthouse being trashed. Say what you want about my aunties, but fairies know how to party.

"Queen Nyxa is coming and everything," adds Fanna.

Elle and I share a long look. Queen Nyxa leads the Fairy Summer Court, or what's left of it, considering how magic is dying and all. But what Nyxa lacks in power, she more than makes up for in crazy. Mostly she asks odd riddles with bizarre consequences for getting the answers wrong. I've made it an art form to stay out of her way.

Ugh. But she'll be at my birthday party again this year. What a disaster.

I lift my chin. Still, it's a disaster that I don't have to worry about until Saturday, and that's all thanks to Elle. Without her vouching for me, I'd be locked in my room to read *Alice's Adventures in Wonderland* for the hundredth time. It's the only book that calms me when my aunties are near. I suppose that's because it's the story of a typical girl who gets pulled into a land of madness. Alice is my soul sister.

I stand up and stretch my arms. "Guess we better get going. I need to spend a lot of quality time getting ready for the party. Elle's loaning me a dress and doing my makeup."

"Good." Lauralei exhales. "You'll look presentable, then."

Anger tightens up my spine. Those kinds of comments always get to me. It's bad enough that I have no freedom and a fake boyfriend. But the constant sniping about my appearance pushes me over the edge. "I always look presentable."

Lauralei narrows her tiny eyes. "I'll be the judge of that. I still don't understand why you won't marry Philpot on Saturday. It would fulfill your life template."

"Not happening, Lauralei. I'm trying to date him. That's all. We'll see how it goes. If I like him, then *maybe* I'll marry him. But that's someday far off in the future."

Lauralei looks down her long nose at me. "As you say." There's a gleam in her tiny bird-like eyes that I don't like at all. *She's up to something.* That said, she's given me that look for years. With only three days left before my birthday, I can't start letting it get to me.

"And do you have your phone with you?" asks Mirabelle. Actually, it's more like she clucks out the words from behind Lauralei.

"Always." It feels good to lie to them. Not sure what that says about me as a person.

"We have to go," says Elle brightly. "Lots of work to do."

Elle marches me out the door and away from my aunties. The three fairies watch us leave in awed silence. If there's any proof that Elle is part of the Magicorum, it's how she can con anyone, anywhere, and at any time. She's the best.

As we head out of the Denarii League, all my previous worries melt away. Midtown Manhattan is a bustle of movement as office workers stream out of their skyscrapers and trudge across the sidewalk. The scent of hotdogs and sausage wafts toward me from a nearby pushcart. Big white clouds roll overhead in a deep-blue sky. A sense of calm washes through my soul. *What a great night this will be.* I'll get digital copies of some new papyri, which is always good reading. And after that, it's only three days before my birthday and freedom.

I smile. After Saturday, I'm an adult. No more Philpot. No more aunties. And if I wanted to, I could even move in with Elle. She invites me often enough. I just haven't wanted to jinx anything by making solid plans.

But who knows? With so many choices opening up, maybe I will find my happily ever after—and soon. At this moment, anything seems possible.

⚘

CHAPTER THREE
BRYAR ROSE

I'm seventeen. By rights, I should be spending my weekends at parties playing Seven Minutes in Heaven in someone's basement closet. I should *not* be wearing a black cocktail dress and standing in a Manhattan penthouse with a bunch of adults who talk about nothing but banking. It's so boring I want to cry.

"And that's why the markets became so volatile. Am I right?" That's Philpot speaking. He's handsome and chiseled, what with his dark eyes, pale skin, and wavy brown hair. Sometimes he reminds me more of a mannequin than a person. It gives me the creeps. "I said, *right*?" Philpot looks at me as if I haven't been paying attention. Which I haven't. So I smile instead.

For the last hour, I've stood around and tried to seem cordial to my fake boyfriend. *Three more days. I promised my aunties I'd give it a try, but after Saturday? Once my curse is over, you are toast, Philpot.* After my eighteenth birthday, this is over. And in the meantime, no touching.

"Did you hear what I said?" he asks.

"Absolutely, Philip."

"It's Philpot."

"What?"

"My name. Philpot Herbert Utrecht the Third."

"Right." He's lucky I didn't call him by his unofficial name, Philpot the Turd. It's not pretty, but neither is fake-dating someone.

Philpot sips his cocktail. "Honestly, Bryar Rose. You need to remember my name. Any girl would be thrilled to date *the* Philpot Herbert Utrecht the Third."

Here he goes again. Philpot is forever finding ways to work his full name into conversations, including the bit about being the Third. Like inbreeding is a selling point for the upper crust of Manhattan society.

What am I saying? I'm part of that society, too. I live in a penthouse, drive an awesome car, and enjoy an unlimited shopping account. I just can't go anywhere on my own without lying my ass off.

Come on, Saturday.

Philpot leans in. "Soon, you'll agree to be my wife. I can't wait for our wedding."

Ugh. Philpot is laser-focused on marriage. For a guy his age, it's weird. But then again, everything about Philpot is weird.

I take a half step backward. "Not happening. Look, I promised to give dating a try—emphasis on the word *try*—until Saturday."

Philpot's eyes take on an evil gleam, but the look is gone so quickly I'm not even sure it was there. I scan his features carefully, searching for any sign of dark intentions. *Nope, nothing.* I shake my head. How could I imagine Philpot is anything other than a money-grubbing loser?

"Let's not argue." Philpot lowers his voice conspiratorially. "Do you want a martini, babe?"

"I'm seventeen. You're twenty-five. And don't call me babe."

"Hey, I'm cool."

Ah, no. "I'll have a Diet Coke."

"You should learn more about wines and mixed drinks. Cocktail parties are a big part of my life."

And there it is. The two words of his that I hate.

You should.

I'm about to tell him what he *really* should do when I spy the thing I've been waiting for all night—a clear shot to the back door. The staff have been barring access to the freight elevator, what with all their rolling around food on stainless steel carts. But now, the door is unblocked and unwatched.

My breath catches. *This is my chance.*

I'm now on the twenty-eighth floor. From here, I can take the freight elevator to the basement and use the connecting tunnel to reach the LeCharme Building. With all my IDs and access cards from Elle, I can then sneak into LeCharme, get pictures of the new papyri, and return before Philpot notices anything.

So I lie again. "You know what? I'd totally love a martini. What an awesome idea." *I'll never drink a drop of it, though.*

"Right." Philpot purses his lips. This is clearly an attempt at a sexy face. *Ugh.*

"Just don't rush. I have to hit the bathroom and freshen up."

"You got it, babe."

I let the second babe comment slide. As he heads off to the bar, Philpot spots one of his investing buddies. *Perfect.* They'll blab for hours about how to make more money in the markets. Because, you know, they clearly don't have enough already, for some reason.

After I slip out the back door, I take the freight elevator to the basement and use my key cards to get into the LeCharme Building. Once I'm inside the bottom level of LeCharme, I find the private elevator for the family floors. There's an access keypad by the elevator doors. I quickly enter my special code. These digits are ones that I hacked myself. They shut down all security cameras in private areas for the next hour or so. Turns out, the LeCharme patriarch has a thing for the ladies. He created the code to sneak the ladies in whenever he likes. In my book, it's poetic justice that Elle and I use it to rob him and make copies of his stuff. Dude should stop fooling around.

Soon, I'm riding the family elevator upward. It only takes you to the top levels, where the LeCharme family lives and works. Alec's office is number 14B on the fortieth floor.

The elevator doors slide open with a mechanical hiss. I step out and make a quick scan of the hallways. The place looks mostly deserted. Only a few workaholics type away at their desktops. I saunter down the halls, and no one says a word. Fun fact: you can get away with a lot when you wear a little black dress with Louboutin heels.

In no time, I find a heavy mahogany door with gilded letters that read *"Alec LeCharme, Vice President."* What he actually does is a mystery. The kid's my age, so I'm guessing he uses the office to buy papyri and goof off.

I pull out another handy ID card from my bag and swipe it through a nearby control panel. The door swings open with a soft click.

Here it is. Alec's office.

Inside, the place looks like the showroom for a high-end corporate furniture catalog. It's dark now, but when the lights are on, you can see tons of couches made from strips of leather on chrome frames. I'm not going to lie. Elle and I have jumped on them a few times. They have good spring action.

Alec's desk sits against the far wall. Only one ceiling fixture is lit up, and it casts his desktop in a small pool of brightness. Other than that, the rest of the office sits in the dark, which is fine with me. No one needs to wonder why the lights are on in the VP's office this late on a Wednesday night.

I get right to work. Alec always leaves his papyri shipments out in the open. I rush over to the desk, and sure enough, there they are: two small wooden crates, each one about the size of a shoebox. I dig into my purse and pull out the handy leather zippy-bag that contains my copying kit. It's got all the basics, including a magnetic staple remover, camera, and X-Acto blade. In a matter of minutes, I open the crates, take digital pictures of the papyri, and close everything up again without leaving a sign.

Mighty slick, if I do say so myself.

I'm feeling really good about my badass-ness when it happens. The hair on my neck stands on end.

Someone's here.

I slowly turn, and there stands Alec, the heir to LeCharme dynasty himself. He's a handsome guy, in that clean-cut, laid-back, surfer-dude kind of way. He's all tanned skin, blue eyes, and sun-lightened hair. Even though he's wearing a black suit, Alec still rocks a young and casual vibe. I've spent enough time with Elle to know my best move is to play it cool.

I give him a little wave. "Hey."

"Hello. I'm Alec." And he smiles. There's no calling the guards. No yelling his lungs out.

Interesting. I'm not sure if that's good or bad. Either way, I should get out of here.

"I came here to take pictures of your papyri. I'll just leave now."

The smile disappears. "I was waiting for the jewel thief. Normally, she comes here with you."

My spine straightens. *He's after Elle.* Even worse, he knows who we are and what we've been up to. That leaves one option. *Lie my ass off.*

"I don't know what you're talking about."

Alec holds his hands up, palms forward. "Your friend isn't in any trouble. I've started running checks on the pieces she takes, and they're all stolen jewels with a bounty on them. LeCharme would have returned them if the company were aware."

If Alec knows this much, I figure there's no point holding back. I set my fist on my hip. "Your parents totally knew."

I heard all about this from Elle. When she started off, Elle tried to inform LeCharme of the thefts and split the reward. Alec's parents wouldn't hear of it.

"You're right. My parents knew. But I didn't."

"And?"

"I'm ready to work with her."

Sure, he is. "And why would you want to do that?"

"Every time she steals something, she leaves a little pile of cinders on my desk. The cleaning staff have been complaining." He works that surfer-dude smile again. I'm not buying it.

I step toward the door. "This is me leaving."

Alec moves to block my path. Another creepy sensation seeps up my scalp. Alec isn't the only one here. *Damn.* One guy I can handle in a fight, especially if I can see him coming. But two people, and with one of them hidden? Not so easy.

I glare at Alec. "Back off. I said I was going."

Alec rakes his hand through his sandy-blond hair. "How come you want to steal my papyri anyway?"

"I make digital photos of them. There's a difference."

"Why not ask my office for access?"

"I did. Many times."

"Let me guess. Your requests got routed through my parents."

"That they did."

"Well, ask me this time. You'll get a different answer."

A growly voice sounds from the shadows, making me jump. "No one else should look at those papyri. They're ours."

The tone of voice sets off alarm bells through my brain. I scan the darkness, trying to see something, anything. I don't get so much as an outline of this man.

"If we're having a group discussion, why don't you come out of the shadows?" I ask.

Alec hitches his hand into the right pocket of his black suit. It makes him look like he fell out of a menswear catalog. He eyes me carefully. "Oh, I like her. We should work with her directly." The way he says the word "directly," it's like he knows everything that Elle and I have been up to.

The growly guy growls again. "No."

That voice. It makes me a little crazy, I guess. I glare at the darkness. It's really my only option at this point. "Quiet, you. I'm talking here."

Alec chuckles. "Oh, we're definitely working together."

Part of me wants to run for the door. More of me is interested in getting access to papyri. I can't help but ask the obvious question. "Working with you on what?"

"The papyri, of course. There's a code in them. We're trying to break it."

"A code?" *Whoa, I thought I noticed a strange pattern in those hieroglyphs.* They all start off telling the history of magic and then go into a bunch of nonsense sentences. Could you rearrange those words and get a secret message? *It's possible.* Suddenly, my burner phone starts ringing. *Crap.* It's Elle, and Elle never calls unless there's an emergency with my aunties. I raise my pointer finger. "One sec. I have to get this."

"You're taking a call?" asks Alec. "Right now?"

"You always this fast?" I say it with a smile and a wink, though. Another fun fact: you can get away with a lot of insults as long as you have the right delivery and outfit. After pulling out my burner, I take the call.

"*Hey, Bry.*" Elle's voice sounds all crackly on the phone.

"Hey."

"*Your aunties are on hold right now. I told them you're in the shower at my place. Normally, that would make them hang up, but they wanted to stay on the line until you got out. I said I'd take them off hold once you were done. You ready?*"

"Sure. Patch them through."

"*You got it. Oh, how's it going with the heist?*"

"It's going."

"*That good, eh?*"

I look over to Alec, who's grinning from ear to ear. Somehow, I have no doubt he realizes I'm talking to Elle. "I'll explain later. Patch them through now, or they may actually be tempted to use magic." That could get ugly.

"*You got it.*"

On the other end of the line, my aunties are all on speakerphone and chattering at once. I make out the words "episode" and "homework." Alec is still smiling in my direction. Who cares if he looks all sneaky? As long as he doesn't say a word, I can handle this.

"Look, aunties. There's no need to freak out. I was just in the shower. I haven't had an episode. Plus, my homework is done already, so drop it. Elle and I are late for the soiree."

Next my aunties start going off on Miss Chang, one of my tutors. They're all yammering at once again because apparently,

Miss Chang trains one of their friends in jiu-jitsu. Now they're all freaked that she's teaching me street self-defense, too. Which she totally is. Not that they know that. I groan. This is just what I did *not* need. Their voices rise to ear-splitting levels.

"Guys...guys...GUYS!" Finally, they quiet down. "Miss Chang is not teaching me mixed martial arts. We're working on table etiquette."

"That's a relief," says Lauralei. "Where are you, anyway?"

"Right where I said I'd be. Over at Elle's, getting ready. We're leaving for the party any second now."

With that, Lauralei launches into a lecture on how irresponsible I am. For what, I don't know, but it seems like she needs to hit this speech at least once a day. Listening to it always gets me worked up. Without realizing it, I pace the floor. Evidently, I get too close to Growly Guy because he lets out another unhappy rumble. I pause.

"What's that noise?" asks Lauralei.

"Oh that? We're watching *Animal Planet.*"

"It was terrifying."

"I know. We'll turn down the volume." As long as I listen to them complain for a few minutes, they'll leave me alone. And—happy me—those two minutes are now up. I can end the call with abandon, so that's just what I do. "Love you all. Buh-bye." After hitting the End Call button, I turn to face Alec. I still can't see Growly Guy at all. "Sorry about that."

Alec remains very amused. "Can't they trace you?"

"Duh. This is a burner. My friend has the real phone."

"Your friend named Elle."

Okay, I shouldn't have let that slip. Still, it's not as if he wasn't aware anyway. "Like you didn't know." I slip my hand into my purse and pull out my mace. "I'm going to leave now. This is the last time I'll say it."

"Please. I waited patiently while you rifled through my things. I didn't even call security. The least you can do is answer a few questions before you mace my face off." He stares pointedly at the bag. "I can see it in your hand, you know."

Oh, that. "Fine. Ask your questions."

"How old are you?"

"That's rather personal. How old are *you?*"

"Eighteen. And you are?"

I shrug. "I'm eighteen."

Alec doesn't seem convinced. "You're eighteen?"

"That's what I said."

"Right now?" That's Growly Guy again.

"My birthday is in three days."

Growly Guy steps into the light. He stands only a few feet to my left and—oh damn—this is the man from my dreams. Literally. He's over six feet tall with black hair, ice-blue eyes, and scars along his brow and chin. He's wearing low-hanging jeans, a fitted black T-shirt, and a long leather jacket. And yes, there's that raw magnetic *something* that seems to vibrate around him. I want to throw my arms around his neck and rub myself all over him. It's really disturbing, actually.

I was pretty calm before, but now? I'm starting to lose it. I drop my mace back into my bag and swap it out for my inhaler. Sure, I don't feel an episode coming on, but it doesn't hurt to be prepared.

"What…what's your name?" I ask.

"Knox." He steps closer. His scent wraps around me. It's a mix of sandalwood and musk. Delicious. Dangerous. In fact, I should leave.

This is me, going for the door.

Any second now.

Nope, my damn body won't do anything but stand around and inhale more of his yummy scent. Dumb limbs.

"Knox. Like the gelatin?" *Leave it to me to make a bad joke at this point.*

"Like the fort."

"Oh."

Eloquent, Bry.

He takes in a long breath, and I swear he's sniffing me as well. Which brings me back to the question: why does this guy smell so good? That just shouldn't happen.

"What's your name?" Knox asks.

"Bryar Rose."

"You're not safe here, Bryar Rose." Knox's voice goes growly once more.

Did I mention that I hate it when people tell me I'm helpless? *Well, I do.* "I can handle myself."

"No, you need to leave." Knox points to door. "Don't ever come back. You got me?"

That settles it. I turn to Alec. "You wanted to talk?"

"Yes, I did."

Does this guy ever stop smiling? "Well, I'm listening."

"When you were on the phone just now, you said something about tutors. Are you one of the Magicorum that can't go to a regular school?"

Well, that little question has me interested. "Why do you ask?"

"I attend a school called West Lake Prep. Heard of it?"

"Maybe." *I'm obsessed with it.*

"I'm a student there. Going into my senior year, as a matter of fact."

"And?" It's an effort not to start salivating. This is everything I've wanted.

"My parents are on the school's board. You want in? You're definitely accepted, so long as you join the summer internship program at LeCharme."

Knox rounds on Alec. "You don't have a summer internship program."

"Quiet, Knox." Alec maintains his perma-smile. "I just made it up. But I assure you, my parents will do this for me. They're dying for me to take an interest in the business. They'll be thrilled if I organize some interns."

"But what if someone says I'm not qualified for West Lake?" *Like Madame.*

"We have ways around that. We're a private institution and not subject to all the government rules and regulations. Plus, if you were awarded a scholarship..." He allows the logic to hang out there. And I must admit, I like where it's hanging.

31

Knox's face darkens. "You don't have a scholarship program, either."

"I said, quiet." Alex focuses on me again. "So, what do you think?"

"If I take your internship, are there more papyri I can read?"

"Sure, I'll even give you everything we have on the code."

I want to cheer, but I keep my face calm. "How will you do that? You ship all the papyri away."

"They're shipped, but to another floor. All the original samples of my papyri are stored right here in this building."

Huh. "I thought you sent them somewhere else." I'm having a hard time processing this for some reason. Mostly because I thought the sources I hacked on this were pretty solid.

"You thought wrong. In fact, I hereby declare that your internship job will be to research all the papyri in our archives and work on breaking the code."

"What's the code about?"

"That's a good question, isn't it? Once you break the code, you can tell us." Alec's grin becomes strained. *He's totally lying.* This guy knows damned well what that code is about.

That should make me want to run for the door, but it only increases my interest in what he has to say. "What do I get in exchange for all this?"

"LeCharme will pay you a wildly inappropriate salary, whether or not you crack one word of the hidden code. We even have furnished apartments here in the building. You could work round the clock, if you wanted to. That's what interests you, doesn't it? The papyri in our collection and being independent?"

"Possibly." *Totally.* Some small part of me wonders how he knows that I'm obsessed with papyri, but I'm way too excited about uncovering the hidden code to focus on that. Plus, having a place in the city where I can crash without mooching off Elle all the time? Even better.

"So, consider it."

Knox steps between Alec and me. He spies the edge of Madame's brochure and plucks it out of my bag. "You really think you're in the Magicorum, yeah?"

"I know that I am." I snatch the brochure back. "Don't touch my stuff."

Knox rubs the scruff on his chin. "If you're in the Magicorum, then what's your fairy-tale template?"

"I'm not answering that."

But Knox keeps staring at me with his big ice-blue eyes, and my mouth moves on its own. "My template is Sleeping Beauty." *I think.*

Knox steps even closer. Now I have to notice how good he smells yet again. Plus, I can't help but catch how he has one of those "broad shoulders to small waist" deals that look especially good in leather. It's so attractive it's annoying.

"Then why are you after all these papyri?" asks Knox. "Shouldn't you be out in the woods looking for your Prince?"

"I have other interests." It's an effort, but I stop looking at Knox and address Alec once more. "I'd like to find out more about your internship."

"No," says Knox. "She wouldn't."

"Yes." I counter. "*She* would. Don't order me around." For emphasis, I poke him in the chest. Bad decision. The guy is ripped, and that's super-distracting. I take a big step away. Maybe it will help me focus.

Nope. Doesn't help.

I flick my hair in what I hope is a casual move. "Like I said, *Alec.* I'll be in touch."

Alec moves into another one of those men's catalog poses, this time by leaning against his deck. "Stop by my office anytime… Only preferably during working hours. I'm here every day during the summer and bored to tears. All they do is pay me to dress up and surf the web. I'd love some good company."

"Hey, I'm here with you," growls Knox.

Alec winks. "Like I said. I'd love some *good* company."

"I'll stop by." I shoot one last glare in Knox's direction before I hustle myself out the door. I can't believe my luck. An opportunity for papyri, independence, and West Lake Prep…what could be more perfect?

There's no point in sneaking around anymore, so I leave the LeCharme Building via the front foyer. The guards wave me through and add, "Mister Alec said to wish you a good evening, Bryar Rose."

He's something else, that Alec.

By the time I step outside, I'm feeling downright giddy. My Land Rover is stored in a garage not far from here. I look forward to the short walk to reach it. It's a warm night, and the darkening streets look magical. As I step along, I start to second-guess my commitment to Alec. This whole situation is pretty insane. I mean, who breaks into someone's office and ends up with a pretend internship? How does that happen?

The whole thing has got "bad idea" written all over it. And I'm a failed Sleeping Beauty template with an inhaler and three crazy aunties.

I nod once to myself, the decision made. I'll just have to pass on the fake internship with Alec. Instead, I'll drive to Elle's secret cabin, look through photos of my ill-gotten papyri, and forget any of this ever happened. In the long run, that's more than enough weirdness for my already strange life.

CHAPTER FOUR
KNOX

I can only stare at the closed office door. My chest feels so tight, I can hardly breathe. Bryar Rose just walked away. Her silky voice still wraps around my thoughts.

"Don't order me around."

Damn. I want to do more than order her around. I want to build my life around this girl. Know her thoughts. Touch her skin. Bring her into my world and never let go.

How can one woman upend your entire existence so quickly?

I scrub my hands over my face. There's no way Bryar Rose should be able to get under my skin. I'm a werewolf. She's human. Which means she's just sexy and tempting, that's all. And I haven't hooked up with anyone in too long. Too much of my time is spent hunting Denarii on the sly.

"An internship." Alec leans back on his desk. "Tell me that wasn't brilliant."

"You can*not* hire her."

"Why not? I like her. And if she can get something new of out those papyri, we need to try."

"We'll figure it out on our own." Inside my soul, my inner wolf is pacing with frustration. The moment he scented Bryar Rose, he wanted me to shift into wolf form so she could pet him. *Talk about crazy.*

Alec folds his arms over his chest. "If there's some secret in there to taking the Denarii down, our people haven't found it in the last—*what is it again?*—oh yeah, that's right. Two thousand years. I don't see the harm in giving Bryar Rose a chance. Besides, she'll just keep trying to copy them illegally otherwise."

"No."

"No?"

"You heard me."

"Then what about our little issue?"

There's no question what "issue" Alec is talking about here—he and I are both wardens of magic. At any point in time, there can only be three wardens in total, one for each category of Magicorum. Alec is the warden for witches and wizards. I'm the warden for shifters. We have no idea who's the fairy warden, but we're not too broken up about that fact. The fae are crazy. Our jobs are to police and protect our people, which is why we're super-powerful for our kind. That's the nice side of this gig. The awful part is that we're supposed to guard the fountain of all magic. The trouble is, no one knows where the damned fountain is hidden. So until that thing is found, our powers prevent us from getting married or having a family. Consider it extra motivation to get our asses in gear.

Not that it's worked, though. No one's found the damned fountain for the last two thousand years.

"I mean it," says Alec. "We can't get married or have a family until we find the fountain. That's an issue for me."

I shoot him a sly look. "Don't pretend you want a wife. You're seventeen and like sleeping around."

"That is *not* true for either of us, and you know it."

I grit my teeth. Alec's right. We've known each other since we were kids, and yeah, we both want families. Maybe it's because everyone always told us it was impossible because of the warden thing. But for whatever reason, having a wife and kids is important to us both. Still, I see right through Alec's plans here. He just wants to pull Bryar Rose deeper into our crazy world, and I won't let that happen.

When I speak again, I let a little growl into my voice. "Leave Bryar Rose alone."

"What is it with you and this girl?" I don't like the over-curious look on Alec's face. "Is it because she's so different from your regular werewolf ladies?" Alec isn't a werewolf, but he tilts his head to bare his neck, which is the shifter sign of submission. After that, he lets out a high-pitched whine. "Bite me, big boy."

"Shut it."

"You're a warden, and that means your wolf is a megabeast. Everyone rolls over and submits to your awesomeness."

"Really? You don't."

"I'm a wizard. We don't let the furry little creatures get to us." As a point of fact, Alec is a senior wizard. Usually, wizards and werewolves can't stand each other. But since we make up two out of the three wardens, we've been friends for ages. Long story.

Alec bobs on the balls of his feet. "I'm right, aren't I? You've never had to hustle for a girl before, have you?"

"Screw you."

"Hey, I'm not that kind of dude."

"I mean this. The internship is a crap idea. Let Bryar Rose go."

Not that I can. My inner wolf is aching to break free and track her.

"We'll drop the subject...for now."

I grunt. Dropping the subject isn't agreeing to back off Bryar Rose, but it's the best I'll get out of Alec at this point. I've been friends with the guy since we were kids. I know how to get what I want out of him. Eventually.

"In the meantime," says Alec. "I've another area of interest." He rocks on his heels, a smug grin still stuck on his stupid face. He reaches into his pocket, pulls out a handful of rubies, and stares at the gems on his palm. "Cinderella, Cinderella."

"You gonna cast a spell on her?"

"I was toying with the idea."

"Toying? Those gemstones contain more magic than I've seen you handle in months. Why are you pulling out the big guns?"

Alec eyes the gems. "Guns?"

"You know what I mean. Have you been trying to cast spells on her before?"

"If I had, it's none of your business."

I pinch the bridge of my nose. "Alec."

"Fine. I've been casting spells on her. None of them have worked. This girl has a null zone around her when it comes to magic."

"Is she a witch?"

"I don't think so."

"Fae?"

"Maybe. She said she has a fairy godmother."

"That's bad news, Alec. Fairies are crazy."

"I'm a tough wizard. I can handle crazy. But if I want to find out more about her, it means I have to call in extra power." He raises his fist high. The gemstones gleam until red light shines from between his fingertips. The temperature dips a few degrees, too. That means Alec's starting to cast a spell. No way.

A protective instinct stiffens my spine. "Stop it right now. Elle is Bryar Rose's friend."

"So? I'm not going to lure her here to have my wicked ways with her. I just want to talk to her soul without her knowing anything about it."

"Liar. You've nailed every Cinderella template girl in the state. You're all about wickedness when it comes to any girl like her. Leave Elle and Bryar Rose alone."

Alec taps his cheek. "Now, you have me curious." The red light inside his closed palm grows brighter. The room gets downright chilly.

My hands ball into fists. "You have some serious listening issues, you know that?"

"What?"

"You're casting a spell on Elle."

"False."

I know how Alec thinks. If he's not casting on Elle, that only leaves one option. "Don't you dare cast a spell on Bryar Rose."

"It's only a soul speak." That spell pulls out part of someone's soul so you can talk to them while their body stays somewhere else. It requires tons of power to pull off.

"Stop it. You'll hurt her."

"False again."

"Hey, I haven't forgotten the frog incident from third grade." After school one time, I dared Alec to pull the soul out of a frog. The thing exploded all over the driveway.

"That only happened because I pulled out the soul from the frog while it was right in front of me. If I'd picked one farther away, it would have been fine." He bobs his eyebrows playfully. I want to tear them both off his head. "Bryar Rose is far enough away, dummy. From a distance, she's in no danger. I'm not a murderer."

"Find some other way to get your answers."

"I'm merely curious. Besides, you won't let me find out more about Elle. This is the next best thing."

"Damn you, Alec."

"Too late, my fellow warden." The light glows brighter inside his palm. This is a rare sight. Alec keeps his magic on the down-low, as a rule. Neither of us advertises that we're part of the Magicorum. There's no point in attracting attention—you just end up another casualty to the Denarii.

Alec opens his hand, and his spell takes shape. The glowing red gems fall to the floor, where they multiply until they look somewhat human. Within a few seconds, the glittering form settles into the shape of Bryar Rose. The sight makes my chest ache.

When Alec speaks again, his voice resonates with magic. "Bryar Rose."

The gemstone version of Bryar Rose turns to Alec. "Yes?" The way this spell works, the real Bryar Rose has no idea what we're doing. Alec has summoned an echo of her soul to get some answers. I'd complain, but it won't hurt her. Besides, I'd like a few answers myself. My wolf is still going nutso inside me. I've never seen him this bad, but I've witnessed this kind of thing in other weres. You don't grow up in a pack and not know the signs of a werewolf finding his mate. The thing is, your inner animal doesn't care how old you are or what else is happening in your life. When it wants a mate and cubs, that's it.

Me. Having a mate. How could that work?

Werewolves only mate with their own kind. And the werewolf warden, like me? I don't mate with anyone. Sure, I can sleep around. But this bone-crushing desire to center my life on one person? It's just not right.

"What template are you?" asks Alec.

"Sleeping Beauty."

"You don't have any werewolf blood in your family?" I ask.

"I wouldn't know. My aunties adopted me when I was a baby. But they've tested me a million times. I always come back human."

"Do you have any magic?" Alec asks this one, which makes sense. The occasional human can gather magic into them. It's rare, but it happens.

Her glowing face turns to me. She's so beautiful it knocks the breath from my lungs. "No, no magic at all."

I step closer. *This girl.* "That's good. The Denarii won't want anything to do with you."

She frowns. "What do you mean? The Denarii League is one of the only places that actually tries to help me."

"What do they do for you, exactly?" My claws come out on instinct and press into my palms. The Denarii are sneaky as hell. They run all sorts of pretend charities that really screen for members of the Magicorum. If they think you have real power, then you wind up missing or dead. I shake my head. Humans wonder why magic is missing from the world. The Denarii are the reason why, only they're too good at hiding their tracks.

"They run my Magicorum Teen Therapy Group," says Bryar Rose. "If I ever want to attend a real high school, then I need to deal with them."

"Wait a second." I ball my hands tighter until my claws break through my skin. The coppery tang of blood fills the air. "That brochure you had. Who gave it to you?"

"Madame Grimoire. She leads my Magicorum Teen Therapy Group. We always meet at the Midtown Denarii League."

"You get near the Denarii?" I absently rub the scar along my jawline. I got this fighting a Denarii in Brooklyn. They may be able to hide their true nature from the world, but I hunt them down all the time. Except for their leader, Jules. That guy has been hard to track. "Promise me something."

"What?" she asks.

"You'll never go near them again."

"Trust me, none of us want to be in that group."

Alec actually stops smiling for once. "You said 'us.' Is your friend in that group, too?"

"Elle? Sure."

My eyes widen. "That brochure talked about Magicorum teens going missing."

"Yes." Bryar Rose nods. "It's very strange. Madame gave out that brochure once before. Afterwards, one of the girls in our group went missing."

"Blanche." I'd heard about that.

"Yes. She's the one."

"Does Elle have any magic?" asks Alec.

"I'm almost certain of it. The way she cons people?" Bryar Rose sighs. "It's not of this world."

Alec races closer to Bryar Rose. He reaches out to grasp her shoulders, but his hands slide through her gemstone body.

"Watch out," I warn. "You'll break the spell early." Alec is a high-level wizard. He should know better. But when it comes to Elle, it seems like the guy is a little off his game.

Glad to know I'm not the only one. My inner wolf is howling up a storm. He never wanted to let Bryar Rose out of our sight.

Alec heaves in rough breaths. "Where's Elle right now?"

Bryar Rose's gemstone eyes flare brighter. "I'm not telling you that."

"If she has magic, then she might be in danger." Alec rummages in his pocket for more gemstones, ignites them, and then pours more stone power into the spell. Deep circles of fatigue appear

41

under his eyes. All this casting is pulling on his life force. "Where is she? Where is Elle?"

A dreamy look takes over the magical version of Bryar Rose's face. "Elle has a place in the Village. That's all I'll say."

"Please," begs Alec. "I won't hurt her." I've never seen my friend so worried. But if Elle has magic, he's got reason to be out of his mind. We've known for years what the Denarii really are: a bunch of extremists out to destroy magic.

The gemstone version of Bryar Rose shakes her head. "Fine. She lives on Seventh Avenue between Perry and Charles. It's a brownstone called the Barrow Arms. You can't miss it. Apartment 6D."

Alec turns toward the door. "I'm out of here."

"Wait, Alec. Bryar Rose could be in danger, too."

"You know the drill," says Alec. "The Denarii only set up stuff like that therapy group so they can screen potential Magicorum for power. If anyone proves to have magic, then they kill them. Bryar Rose has no magic. No one is after her. It's Elle that they want."

My voice lowers to a growl. "Call it a protective instinct. You're not going anywhere until I find out where Bryar Rose is."

Alec rakes his hand through his hair. "Fine." He glares at the gemstone version of Bryar Rose. "Where are you?"

"I'm heading to Elle's cabin in the Adirondacks. It's at Six Old South Road, right at the foot of Mount Marcy."

"Got what you need now?" asks Alec.

"Yup. And you're loaning me your Mustang."

"Take whatever car you want from the garage. I'm getting a driver to the Village anyway." He pauses. "You sure you can find her?"

"I'm a werewolf, and she's heading to the mountains. Once I get out of the city, she's all mine." And the way my wolf is howling inside me, I mean that in more ways than one.

CHAPTER FIVE
BRYAR ROSE

I steer my Land Rover up the dirt path that leads to Elle's cabin. The night sky sparkles with a crazy number of stars. Pine trees loom on either side of the road. I drive past the Thornhill Arms, a deserted hotel that sits high atop a forested hill. I can't help but grin. Seeing that old wreck of a hotel means that my drive is almost over. Elle's cabin is only two minutes away now. I glance at my smart watch.

2:13 a.m.

I didn't make bad time, all things considered.

A ratty log cabin appears through the trees. My headlights reflect off the darkened windows. It's a three-room deal with a fireplace and an outhouse, but it stores my computer setup well enough.

When it comes to analyzing my papyri data, no place is better than Elle's cabin.

I pull the Rover up to the cabin, grab my bag, and step outside. This moment is one I always savor—that first rush of fresh air. It stings my lungs with its purity and reminds me of all my plans for the future. A typical high school. Regular college. A normal life.

But until then, I have my papyri to focus on. I hoist my bag higher on my shoulder and trek up the short flight of stairs to the cabin's front door. This far out in the wilderness, a lot of cabins aren't locked. That said, a lot of cabins aren't owned by a thief, so Elle's place comes complete with a full set of keys and deadbolts. It takes me a minute or two, but I'm soon inside.

The cabin is a rustic-looking place with a small bedroom, smaller kitchen, and sizable living room. Most of the furniture is shabby stuff that Elle and I picked up at garage sales in the village. The bedroom roof leaks, and all the walls are filled with mice. The place is a total dump.

That is, except for the living room. That's completely high tech. I have stainless steel tables in here and a half-dozen wall monitors. My heart lightens. I can't wait to get to work.

Now that I'm inside, I have a system for how I set things up. Generator first. Fireplace second. Third, I make a humungous pot of tea and change into my fave jammies, which are a combination of boyshorts and a cami. Only then, when all the prep work is done, do I fire up my computer, flip on my wall of monitors, and check out my latest ill-gotten papyri pics.

All of which brings me to the present moment. Right now, I'm sitting in my favorite rolling chair, sipping my tea, and waiting for my latest hieroglyphs to appear on the computer screens before me. The monitors flicker with blue light before—YES—there they are. New hieroglyphs.

I can't believe it. These are the best ones I've ever gotten.

Like always, they're only fragments. At one time, they were full papyrus sheets, and together, they made up the ancient *Book of Magic*. There were about five copies of this book, and they were all stored in the Library of Alexandria. But when Julius Caesar invaded, he burned the library to charcoal. If the papyri hadn't been infused with magic themselves, they would never have survived. But they did.

Now, I'm rebuilding the *Book of Magic*, piece by burned-up piece. It's even trickier because it's written in a special kind of hieroglyphics called the Code of Isis. Only a few high-level priests and priestesses could read it. Carving any of it into rock was forbidden. I find burned-out fragments and put them together like a giant jigsaw puzzle. As hobbies go, I've heard of worse ways to spend your time. Not that I had much choice about the whole thing. I kept dreaming about assembling one hieroglyph in the *Book of Magic*, over and over. It was so boring I thought I'd go insane. Once I started doing my research, the dreams finally went away, only to get replaced with dreams of Knox. We laugh, talk all night, and work on papyri. I can't remember much of what happens in the morning, but I do know this: it's anything but boring.

I click through pic after pic. Finally, I run across some glyphs that are definitely from the Code of Isis. Hieroglyphs are pictograms, so every word is represented by an image. The Code of Isis uses totally unique images—nothing you'd find elsewhere in ancient Egypt. I run across a fragment with the unique hieroglyphs for "wizard," "fairy," and "shifter."

Bingo. I found another puzzle piece. Now I just need to figure out where it fits.

I gulp down my tea and get to work. This is where the fun begins: finding the right home for each new fragment in my master copy of the *Book of Magic*. Back in ancient times, about twenty scrolls made up this particular book. Each one was about five feet long when unrolled. To see each page fully and still be able to read it, I must span all four of my computer monitors.

With a few button clicks, the first scroll-page appears on my screen. I drag the new hieroglyphs onto different parts of the image, trying to find where these three pictograms fit into my master puzzle. Normally, this task consumes all my focus, but tonight? I can't seem to stay on track. My attention keeps wandering to another image entirely.

Silky black hair.

That scar along his jawline.

The haunting look in his ice-blue eyes.

Knox.

And that scent. Sandalwood and musk. Why is the very thought of it hypnotizing?

I press my palms onto my eyes. *Forget growly men. Tonight is about the* Book of Magic. It's taken me years, but I've got one quarter of the thing put together. Sure, it's a compulsion to complete the task I saw in my dreams, but that doesn't mean I'm not proud of what I've done. And there's no way I'll stop now.

A mechanical buzz fills the air. My monitors flicker and turn dark. The only light in my cabin comes from the fireplace in the living room. The sound of my own breathing seems incredibly loud.

I freeze. *This is so weird.* The generator sometimes dies in the winter, but never in May. I pull open my bag and take a deep breath of meds from my inhaler. It never hurts to do a preemptive strike against a possible episode. After that, I open the top drawer of my desk, where I keep my favorite gun—a seven-millimeter Glock—and its leather shoulder holster. Miss Chang is more than an expert in mixed martial arts. She also taught me about guns. After slipping on my Glock and holster, I head outside to check the generator.

What can I say? I'm a cautious girl.

The moment I step outside, I'm hit with cool air and a cacophony of insect noises. I stare back at the cabin door. It's wide open. *Crap, I forgot to grab the keys as well.* Maybe I should go back inside and hunt for them.

I debate the idea for all of two seconds before giving up. *Fiddling with locks in the dark isn't my idea of a good time. I need to get the generator back up and working.* Besides, I won't be gone long.

I pad barefoot over to the hefty metal box that sits around back of the cabin. It's hard to find my way, but there's a little light from the moon. I stub my toe on a rock.

Too bad I thought of a gun before a flashlight.

I make it to the generator, and sure enough, one of the extension cables fell out. Usually ice weighs these things down in the winter, but I suppose a raccoon or something might get to it at this time of year. I plug the line back into place. Brightness flickers inside the cabin once more.

I hug my elbows—and not just from the cold. The idea of having lost everything I was working on sends a chill through my bones.

When did I last save my file? I can't remember.

Crap, if I lose my work, I'm going to freak. When you have files as big as mine, autosave can take a while to finish. If you lose power mid-save, it can corrupt everything.

Damn.

I rush into the cabin and hustle over to my mega-desk of computer gadgetry. After pressing a few buttons, the monitors come back to life. I scan them carefully and exhale. *Whew.* I lost a few little things, but not too much. In fact, I'm about to redo the work when I feel it.

The cool muzzle of a gun against the back of my head.

What. The. Hell.

"Hands up, *Cherie*."

Oh, no. It's Madame Grimoire. And she's holding a gun to my skull.

Lessons from Miss Chang race through my mind. Unfortunately, I don't have a good way to disarm Madame from this angle. I need to buy some time. It's an effort to keep my voice casual. "What are you doing here?"

In reply, there's the unmistakable sound of her cocking the gun. Miss Chang taught me all about that stuff, too. A jolt of worry zings through my limbs. Blanche disappeared, and now Madame is in my secret cabin with a gun. Not a great situation.

I raise my arms. "Fine. My hands are up."

Madame's arm darts around me. In a flash of movement, she pulls my gun out of its shoulder holster.

Great. My weapon is history.

"Turn around," she orders.

With shuffling steps, I slowly spin about. Madame still looks like she did in our group session today. Her brown hair is frozen into a perfectly curled bob. Her A-line dress is without a crease. She's even wearing her white gloves, although now they make a little more sense. If she's been shooting people, the gloves might help to hide any evidence on her skin. Which is not a comforting thought, really.

Madame raises her free hand. My burner phone is gripped in her fingers. She tightens her grip, and the device gets smashed to bits. That's a shocker. I mean, it's already overwhelming that she found me and broke in here. But that's a pretty solid object. Who goes around smooshing things with their bare hands?

"Who are you, really?" I ask. "What do you want?"

Madame smiles, and it's not the nice kind. "Answer some questions, and I'll kill you quickly."

I glance around the room, searching for any kind of weapon.

"Don't bother trying to escape," says Madame. "You made the mistake of warning me about all your battle training. That's why I sabotaged your generator; I knew you were experienced and would require a sneak attack. When I kidnapped Blanche, I merely knocked on the door and asked her to let me in."

Every inch of my body seems to go numb. *Wow. Madame really is planning to kill me.* Not that the loaded gun wasn't a tipoff. But the fact that she confessed to going after Blanche? Not a great sign for yours truly.

Madame keeps right on talking. I guess she wasn't expecting any response about the whole kidnapping Blanche thing. "Let's begin. How long have you been in love with Philpot?"

"What?" Of all the questions she was going to ask, I did not see that one coming. "I am not in love with Philpot at all. He's a loser."

"No, he's wonderful." Madame motions to the monitors with her gun. "You've been trying to impress him with this research, haven't you? Show him that you're more than a pretty face, am I right?"

"Philpot doesn't know anything about my work here."

"Liar. Someone like you doesn't deserve to live. Besides, you look delicious."

"Delicious?" The word tumbles from my mouth before I can stop it.

Madame stares at the monitors, her eyes narrowing. "What are you doing here?"

A plan forms. If Madame is curious about the papyri, I might be able to use that to my advantage. "I'm translating the *Book of Magic*." She seems really fixated on my work, so maybe that'll be somewhat interesting to her.

"No, that's not possible. The Denarii have been trying to reassemble that text for ages without success."

My mind races through the few things I've learned from the *Book of Magic*. "I know about the three wardens and the fountain."

Her eyes widen. "You know who the wardens are?"

"Sure." In truth, I have no idea who they are. It's a closely guarded secret.

"And where the fountain is, too?"

"Absolutely." Another whopper of a lie. "It's all right here on my monitor screen. Come take a look."

And get close enough so I can disarm you.

Madame takes a half step nearer. That's an improvement, but it's not close enough for me to take her gun. "What does it say about the fountain?"

I point to the monitor right behind me. "The location is clearly written out. Do you know any hieroglyphs?"

"A few." Madame squints, trying to see that corner more clearly. "Do you have any idea what would happen if someone found that fountain?" She takes another half step closer.

My heart pounds so hard, it feels like it could burst through my chest. Only one more step, and Madame will be close enough for me to disarm her. "The glyph for the fountain is four wavy lines in a circle. You can see it here, in the bottom left corner." Which is the truth. The glyph is in that corner. But it's also true that she'll need to step closer than ever to see it properly.

"Four wavy lines in a circle…ah, I see it now." Madame's gaze stays locked on the monitor as she finally takes another step.

Gotcha.

My training from Miss Chang comes back with a vengeance. I step to one side, grab the muzzle of the gun, and twist hard. A snap of bone sounds as Madame's finger breaks. From there, I grab Madame's arm and flip her onto her back. A few moves later, and I have both guns again and Madame at my mercy. Triumph flares through my soul. I can't wait to tell Elle about this one.

I reset one gun into my holster. Using both hands, I point the other straight at Madame's head. "Now it's your turn to talk. Who are you, really?"

"Why, I'm one of the Denarii, of course."

"The Denarii are good people. They're humans who are trying to save magic." I pull back the hammer on the gun. "That's not you."

"Oh, I'm a true Denarii all right. And you, my dear, are ridiculously naive." Madame slowly rises to her feet.

"Stand still, or I'll shoot."

The crazy lady steps closer to me. "I don't doubt it."

"Stop!" The room starts to go hazy around me. Silver spots appear in my vision. All my limbs turn rubbery. That locked-down container inside my soul rattles. It's that damned spell from Colonel Mallory trying to break loose.

Oh, damn. My last dose of medicine wasn't enough. Now, on top of everything else, I'm about to have an episode. If that happens, I'll really be dead.

It's an effort to keep my eyes open. "I said, stop!"

"Never." Madame moves closer.

"Don't take another step!"

She does just that.

The world seems to move in slow motion as I squeeze the trigger on my Glock. BOOM! Once I start, I can't seem to stop. BOOM-BOOM-BOOM! Spine-wrenching blasts echo through the cabin. A small hole appears in the center of Madame's forehead as she gets thrown backward. Crashes sound as bullets ricochet around the room.

With trembling hands, I set the gun aside. "I told you to stop!"

Madame lies at my feet, lifeless. *This is terrible.*

The next thing I know, silver spots start clouding my vision again. Inside my soul, the lockbox that holds my curse begins to fracture. *No, no, no.* I cannot have an episode with a dead Madame on my floor. I race over to my bag, pull out my inhaler, and suck in a few breaths. Every breath feels better than the last.

The medicine tastes like hell, but it soon does the trick. My vision clears, but my body still feels like a wet noodle. I slump onto the floor by Madame's feet and force myself to look at her. The odd thought occurs to me that for a head wound, she really didn't make too much of a mess on the carpet.

She didn't make too much of a mess? What is wrong with me?

I just killed a fellow human being. Sure, Madame called herself a true Denarii and came after me, but that didn't mean she deserved to die. I just…panicked. My skin chills with shock and fear. What do I do with a dead body anyway?

One name appears in my mind. *Elle.* I need to contact my best friend. She might know someone who specializes in this kind of thing. I set my hand on my chest, trying to force my breaths to slow.

That's a good plan. Call Elle.

My stomach sinks. I would call Elle, except for one fact. My cell phone got destroyed. Madame crunched the thing to bits.

I glance over my shoulder at my computer setup. The monitors are all dark. A huge bullet hole peeps out from the hard drive. Damn. The system was damaged when I shot the gun at Madame so many times. That sucks. I could have used the computer to patch through an IP line and get to Elle's phone.

Suddenly, Madame twitches. Now, I've read about how bodies do strange things during rigor mortis, but that takes a long time to set in. There's no way Madame should be moving right now.

She flinches again. *Huh.* It actually seems like Madame is still alive.

In one single movement, Madame rises to her feet. Although, it's more like she's levered up by some invisible board, rather than actually shifting her weight like a normal person would. Shock charges through my nervous system. I scream my head off.

Madame is alive and coming for me, even though she has a bullet hole in her head and everything.

My mind blanks. *How do I kill someone who's already dead?*

I watch her approach and think through all my lessons with Miss Chang. Madame may be magical, but I'm stubborn. Whatever's going on, I won't go down without a fight.

CHAPTER SIX
KNOX

My throat tightens with another held-in growl. For the last ten minutes, I've done nothing but drive up and down this same damned road. All I've got to show for it are a lot of trees, darkness, and frustration. No sign of Bryar Rose and her cabin. Yeah, my GPS app tells me that I'm at the right address, but there's nothing here. I grip the steering wheel of Alec's Mustang with extra force.

Get a hold of yourself, Knox. Chances are, Bryar Rose is fine. Whatever feelings you have for this girl are just hormones, pure and simple.

That thought should make me feel better, but it doesn't. I can feel my wolf inside me, pacing the inner walls of my soul. He wants his mate, and he thinks Bryar Rose is it. *What a shit show.* Not to mention that the marks on my back—marks that every warden has—are now pulsing with power. It's what happens when my wolf is really upset.

Well, my inner wolf may be losing it, but my mind is still intact. There's no way Bryar Rose is my mate. She's human. Weres only mate with our own kind. And then, there's the fact that I can't mate with anyone.

I'm one of the three, just like Alec.

But my wolf is having none of it. He howls inside me, calling for me to find her. I punch the roof instead.

"Shut the hell up, will you?" Sometimes yelling at my wolf helps. This isn't one of those times. He only howls louder.

I slam my skull back against the headrest. "Come on, man. You know who we are. Wardens never find a mate." I scrub my hand down my face because, damn it, my wolf is freaking out worse by the second. I jam on the gas and pull over into a clearing. It'll be a bitch getting the Mustang out of here, but my wolf is howling for me to stop.

I kill the ignition and step out into the night. The air's crisp and still. *Good.* If Bryar Rose is anywhere nearby, then I'll scent her easily enough. Normally, I strip down before making the change to my animal form, but my wolf isn't having any of that. The second I step away from the car door, he rips through my skin.

Damn, this part always hurts.

My bones snap and realign. Fingers stretch into talons. Muscles contort, and every inch of me hurts like hell. Within seconds, I'm a huge badass black wolf with golden eyes. This was *not* how I planned to spend my night. I snort in a deep breath, checking to see if my wolf is right or crazy.

There's no scent of Bryar Rose on the air. *Crazy it is, then.*

"See?" My logical self rails inside my head. *"Told you there was nothing. We were just going to drive past her place, and now I'm all wolfed up, you freak. Don't get any ideas. I'm not chasing rabbits around just to placate your sorry ass."*

My wolf's guttural voice echoes through my thoughts. *"Danger,"* he growls. My wolf isn't one for long sentences as a rule. *"Mate."*

I'm about to launch into a long lecture about how we can never have a mate when it happens. A scream breaks the quiet. My wolf-strong hearing knows the voice instantly.

By the three. It's Bryar Rose.

I speed off in the direction of Bryar's cries. Whatever control I was trying to wrest back from my wolf, I hand it all over to my animal side. Everything becomes sensation and instinct. Rocks jut into my paws. Low-hanging branches scrape against my fur. Bryar Rose's yells grow louder. A guttural growl escapes my throat.

Whoever makes her scream, they will bleed.

A small cabin appears through a clearing of trees. Figures move just beyond the windows.

Bryar Rose.

The door's shut, but that means nothing to me. I leap high into the air and slam my bulk against the barrier. In my wolf form, I'm twelve feet long from snout to tail, not to mention tall as a horse. The door shatters like kindling. I land on the cabin floor with a thud.

Bryar Rose is here. Her skin is all scratched and bloody. Some fucking Denarii is parked on her chest and trying to choke the life out of my girl.

Oh, hell no.

I leap forward, grip the Denarii by the throat, and toss her through the air. She lands against the wall and slumps to the floor.

Bryar crab-walks backward, staring at me with wide eyes. "She won't die. I shot her in the head."

My wolf huffs out a growling laugh. His rumbling voice echoes inside my head. *"Strong mate. Good for pack."* Damn, my wolf is in deep.

Not that I can worry about that now. I have a Denarii to kill.

I round on the undead freak who's lying motionless at the bottom of the wall. Her head sits at an odd angle, which means I snapped her neck. That won't stop her from coming back, though. The Denarii are easy enough to down, but unless you chop off their heads, they always return to life. And to be absolutely certain they won't regenerate, you need to burn them in a bonfire. I should know. I've destroyed hundreds of them and have the scars to prove it.

I prowl back and forth in front of the prone woman. I don't kill the Denarii unless they attack. And they always attack.

Sure enough, the woman's eyes pop open. She lets out a howl of rage and leaps toward me. I jump up, grip her head in my jaws, and extend my razor-sharp talons. With a few swipes of my claws, the Denarii's head is separated from her body. I fling her skull far from the corpse. I've seen heads reattach if you leave them too close to their bodies. Like I said, the best solution is to burn the corpse. Even so, things are safe enough for now.

I round on Bryar, who stands against the far wall. She holds her gun straight at me. It's not likely that she'd kill me with a Glock, but she could make things pretty uncomfortable.

"Out the door, wolf." Bryar Rose wiggles the gun toward the busted-open doorway. "Now."

Before I can stop myself, I let out a whine that would make a hungry dog proud. *"Mate,"* whispers my wolf inside my head. *"Want mate."*

Now, I'd like to punch my wolf in the muzzle, but I can't. So I settle for mentally reminding him of a few unpleasant realties. *"You can't have her."* I don't even get into the fact that a true mate bond with a human is impossible for anyone, let alone me. Instead, I go with logic. Sometimes it works. *"A half-ton black wolf just burst into her cabin. How about we back off?"*

"We go human. For now."

My body realigns once again. Agony tears through my limbs as my muscles reform. Bones shrink. Fur disappears. Claws retract. Soon, I'm back to my human self. And buck naked.

Bryar Rose's hand pops over her mouth. "Oh, my God. Knox."

"Hey." Werewolves spend a lot of time naked, so it isn't a big deal to us. Humans, however, can get a little freaked.

She stares at the ceiling, clearly averting her gaze from my nakedness. It's cute. "Watch out for Madame."

"The Denarii?"

"Yes, she could wake back up."

"Nah. Once their heads are off, they stay down. We do need to burn her body, though, just to be safe. If her head reattaches, then she could regenerate."

"Oh." Bryar Rose glances down from the ceiling, and her gaze spikes right to my waistline. After that, her cheeks burn bright red. It's even cuter. "You want to—" She clears her throat. "Put something on?"

"Other than this, yeah?" I'm such a smartass, I lift the pendant around my neck. It looks like a black opal shaped like a wolf claw. Alec gave it to me ages ago as a failsafe. It's an all-purpose escape spell from wizard attacks. It's a long story, but witches and wizards infight like crazy, and Alec and his family have their enemies. He gave this to me to protect me. But right now? It's just a fun way to tease Bryar Rose.

"No." She starts staring at the ceiling again. "A necklace doesn't count as clothing."

"It's a pendant." *I'm not a necklace kind of guy.* "How about you set that gun down first, and we can talk about it?"

"The gun?" She looks at the firearm in her hands. "Oh, the gun. Right." She places it on a nearby table and turns to face me. "So… well…um…clothes?"

"Yeah. You got any?" I look around. "I didn't bring stuff with me." I point at the dead Denarii. "Unless you want me to…" I leave the logic out there for her to catch up.

"NO!" She clears her throat again. "I mean, no. Don't touch Madame's things. This is Elle's place. She's got some disguises here—" Bryar face-palms herself. "I mean, she's got some clothes around that might fit you. Don't move."

"No plans to." I lace my fingers behind my neck. Bryar is so shy and blushy, it's totally adorable. My wolf likes it, too.

No mates. No cubs. In the logic of my wolf, he thinks Bryar's awkwardness is a sign that she hasn't dated much, if at all. *No mates to compete with, no previous cubs to parent.* He's still stuck on that crazy idea that she and I belong together. He's nuts, but I'll deal with it later. Besides, it's easy to ignore my wolf when Bryar is still standing there, trying not to stare at my dick.

"You gonna get me something?" I'm smiling, which is a somewhat bastard move, but I can't help it.

"Right. Clothes." Bryar steps off to the bedroom. She rustles around in there for a minute or two before coming out with a pair of loose sweat shorts and a T-shirt. She tosses me both.

I pull on the shorts and read the wording on the shirt. "FBI Secret Operation: Domino?"

"It doesn't really say that." Bryar Rose steps closer.

I hold up the shirt as evidence. "Last time I checked, the FBI doesn't do theme shirts for their secret ops."

"That's Elle. I'm sure there's a reason." Bryar Rose looks away. "Why don't you get dressed, and we can talk about the decapitated body on my floor?"

"What? I've got on shorts." She's too easy to tease, this one.

"Knox. This situation is tough enough without nakedness being brought into things."

I slip on the T-shirt because even I know my limits on giving pretty girls a hard time. Now that I'm clothed, I can't help but notice that Bryar Rose is almost naked herself. She's wearing these mini sleep shorts and a camisole that leaves little to the imagination. *Man, is she ever gorgeous.* Wolf likes the way she looks, too. I'm not dumb enough to tell her to put anything on, though.

I nod toward the dead Denarii. "You know her?"

"She ran my Teen Magicorum Therapy Group."

"Denarii, yeah?"

She nods. "They're evil. She told me." She tilts her head. "But you know that already, don't you?"

"Yeah."

Bryar hugs her elbows. "Why was she coming after me?"

"You don't have any magic, right?"

"None."

"Then I don't know." I rub my chin. "It's also strange that you know her. She must have been acting alone. Assassins are almost always strangers. Did she have any reason to carry a grudge against you?"

"Her? Tons. We don't exactly get along. The only person she might hate more than me is—" Bryar Rose's eyes widen. "Oh, no.

Elle! If Madame came after me, maybe someone else went for Elle, too."

"Don't worry. Alec went to check on your friend."

Bryar Rose gives me the side-eye. "Somehow, that doesn't make me feel any better."

"He's good people. I could call him and find out what's up. You've got a phone around here?"

"I did, but Madame broke it. There's my computer, but—" She turns to the wall of computer monitors. All of them are dark. She rushes over to them. "Oh crap, I forgot. My system got shot."

"Like with a gun?"

"Yeah. It happened in the fight. I save everything in a private cloud, though, so I can get it back."

My wolf doesn't understand what she's saying, but I do. And as much as I hate to admit this, I like that Bryar Rose can fight the undead *and* geek out on computers. Alec sure was right about Bryar being different from werewolf women. Female weres are rare. Many get so spoiled they act like pretty princesses. Lots of demands. Not a lot of self-sufficiency. In the long run, that behavior is the definition of "turn-off."

I take another long look at the setup Bryar has here. It's pretty impressive. "You a hacker, too?"

"Let's just say that I've had a lot of free time on my hands."

I nod. There's a story to this girl; that's for sure. I might even want to hear it. Still, we can't hang out at this crime scene. I glance around the room. "You got anything in here you need, you should box it up."

Bryar Rose tilts her head. It's a canine move, which I like. "What do you mean?"

"Even if she went rogue, her superiors will figure out that she came here to kill you. They'll expect a fire. It's standard procedure after they kill a non-Denarii. If we burn her body here, it will buy us some time." I brace myself, waiting for the whining about all the things she needs.

"Sounds like a plan." She grabs her bag. "I'm ready."

My brows lift. "Really?"

She rolls her eyes. "Really and for truly. Everything of mine that's important is online, and that's—" She points to the ceiling. "All in the cloud."

"Because you're a hacker. Right." I shake my head. *This girl.* "You got any kerosene around?"

"It's by the fireplace. Matches, too."

I can't believe what I'm hearing. "Matches, too."

"What?"

"It's just… You're handling this really well."

"I live with three fairies and got cursed by Colonel Mallory the Magnificent. I'm used to crazy." She sets her fist on her hip, daring me to disagree.

I lift my arms and flash her my palms. "I get it. You're tough. Just get yourself ready. I'll see you outside."

"You're going to get rid of the body?"

"That's the plan."

"Well, I can help."

I like that she's tough and all, but getting rid of bodies is a nasty business. I've done it before, but Bryar? Living with fairies doesn't prepare you for everything. "Look," I say. "You can help by double-checking that there isn't anything here that you or Elle need. I'll take care of your dead friend here."

"If you're really sure."

I use her own line back at her. "Really and for truly."

Bryar Rose chuckles, and I like the sound. "Okay, fine." She checks all her drawers and finds a few other trinkets that she'd like to keep. While Bryar Rose waits outside, I drag the body onto the couch and douse it with kerosene. The head goes into the fireplace. I also find some matches and pocket them.

Soon, we're both standing outside. Bryar Rose is still in her cami and mini shorts. Not that I'm complaining, but regular humans usually get chilly this late at night. I check out the horizon. The sky is starting to lighten behind the trees. *It's early morning.* All the more reason for her to be cold.

"You sure you don't need a jacket or something?" My wolf hates this idea of Bryar Rose getting dressed. He wants our so-called mate as close to naked as possible. Nut job. I tell him to shut up, and for once, he listens.

"No, I'm always a little on the warm side."

"If you're sure."

"I'm sure." She bites her plump lower lip, and that makes me crazy in all sorts of ways that I don't want to think about.

"Something wrong?" I ask.

"I should have said this before, but I was just overwhelmed." She looks at me with her big blue eyes, and I'm a dead man. "Thanks for saving my life."

"Oh, it was nothing," I say quickly. "Alec got a tip; that's all."

My wolf hates this. *"No lie to mate. We hunt her, protect her."*

I have had it with my wolf. "Shut up." I meant to say that in my mind, but I basically growl it out loud.

"Shut up?" asks Bryar. Her eyes glisten, and I feel like a total ass. "I was just saying thank-you. You don't have to be rude."

It's on the tip of my tongue to explain to her that I was talking to my wolf, not her. But that would just mend fences—and honestly? It's better if those fences stay broken. After all, she's a human. I'm a wolf. And I'm one of the three. Even if we could be mates, the mating ceremony would kill her. It's not worth considering.

"Let's get back to my car. You can call your friend from there."

Bryar Rose lifts her chin. "That's not all. Once we get there, I want some answers, too. Madame said some strange things to me. I have a suspicion you know what they mean."

Madame's the Denarii we're about to roast. Something in Bryar Rose's voice sets me on edge. Denarii love to blabber when they're going in for a kill. "What did she say?"

"She saw the papyri I'm reconstructing and asked me if I knew the location of the fountain."

My protective instincts go through the roof. "That freak was talking nonsense at you. The fountain is nothing."

In truth, the fountain is everything, at least to me. But Bryar's in enough trouble without bringing her in on all my crap.

"I don't think so," says Bryar. "I'm reassembling a full copy of the *Book of Magic*. I've run across the fountain a few times already. It's important."

I can't believe what I'm hearing. The damned *Book of Magic*? Why doesn't she wear a blacktop costume and lay out on the street—it's just as dangerous. I knew she was stealing papyri and assembling things, but I didn't know it was the damned *Book of Magic*.

"You're what?"

"Assembling a copy of the *Book of Magic*. You have a problem with that?"

Yeah. Everything.

My wolf doesn't like this either. "*Stop her,*" he says. For once, I agree with him.

I move to stand toe to toe with Bryar. I'm tall even in my human form, and it usually intimidates the crap out of people. "Here's the deal. We're burning down this cabin, going back to the car, and calling your friend. That's it. No questions and answers. No gossiping like a pair of girls at a damned slumber party. Do you understand?"

Bryar glares at me, and the hurt in her eyes tears right through my soul. "I understand. You're an ass."

I shrug. "That's right." It's a total douchebag thing to say, but it's the truth. I'm one of the three wardens, which means that I'm cursed to carry the magic of my people. Alone. No mates. No cubs. No home. And no matter what my wolf feels for Bryar, I can never be anything to her but a distraction. Much as it kills me, she's better off without me.

CHAPTER SEVEN
BRYAR ROSE

⚘

I slide into Knox's jacked-up Mustang and worry my thumbnail with my teeth. *Please let Elle be okay.*

Knox slips into the driver's seat. Instantly, his massive frame overpowers the car's snug interior. It's more than that, though. The guy has some kind of energy vibrating around him. It's hypnotic and irritating all at once.

He pops open the glove compartment, pulls out a phone, and hands it to me. "For your friend." *Meaning he wants me to call Elle.*

Those are the first words either of us has spoken since Knox agreed that he's an ass. I swipe the phone out of his hand. "Thanks." But the way I say that word? It sounds more like a version of *screw you.*

I dial Elle's number and drum my fingers on my kneecaps. Knox revs up the engine and peels out onto the darkened street.

The line rings five times before Elle picks up. "Hello?"

"Elle, it's me."

"Hey." She has a lazy, happy tone in her voice.

"Are you okay?"

"I'm great. Why?"

"Well, some bad things happened tonight." *Specifically, I killed our group therapy leader and burned your cabin down.* "Maybe it's best if I come over and we talk about it face-to-face."

"Sure." There's a voice in the background. A male voice.

"Is someone there?"

"Oh, that." There's a rustle as Elle places her hand over the microphone. A muffled *"Be quiet. I'm on with Bryar Rose"* sounds in my ear. "It's nothing."

"It sounded like something." That particular male voice registers in my memory. "Is Alec there?"

"Him?" She's acting super-suspicious now.

"Yes, him. Alec LeCharme, the guy you've been not-stealing from for years. Knox already told me that he was going over to your place."

"Um, sure. He's here." She makes a humming sound, which is something Elle only does when she's really happy.

"And?" I know I shouldn't have a snippy tone in my voice—especially since I just killed our group therapy leader (the first time, anyway) and burned down her cabin—but I can't help it. An evasive Elle is an annoying Elle.

"And what?" asks Elle. *More evasiveness. Grr.*

"What's going on?"

"He's giving me a backrub."

"Oh." Elle is getting busy with Alec right now. I can't believe it. Mostly because Elle is in the same club as me: the "sweet seventeen and never been kissed" club. We were supposed to tell each other the minute we smooched someone. And now I have to drag it out of her that she's getting backrubs? This is not good.

"Oh?" Elle asks.

"Oh." It's another single word that I say in my screw-you tone.

"Don't 'oh' me." Another rustle sounds as Elle cups her hand over the mouthpiece of her phone. "It's not like that. We've been talking. That's all. He and I have some big things in common. We haven't...you know."

"Oooooh." This time, my word is laced with relief. I've had enough shocks for one day. I don't need to add my best friend holding out on me to the list. "You can tell me all about it when I get there."

"I'll try."

That's another totally evasive answer, but at this point, I'm done attempting to figure out what Elle is up to. This is the kind of conversation that's best had face-to-face. "See you soon."

"Bye."

I end the call and hand the phone to Knox. He nods toward the dashboard. "You can put it back in the glove box."

"Say please." I'm still not done being testy with this dude.

Knox looks at me over his shoulder and, damn it, he's smiling a little. That melts my heart a touch, which is something my brain did not authorize. He follows it with a sincere reply. "Please."

That gets me right in the ticker. I toss the phone into the glove box, fold my arms over my chest, and turn to Knox. "We need to talk."

The headlights of an oncoming car highlight the chiseled planes of his face, a detail I wish I didn't notice. He sighs. "Sorry about being an ass before. You got questions. Let's talk."

A little more of my resistance slips away, damn it all. "What happened back there? Who are the Denarii really?" I'm starting to think my initial impression of them protecting magic wasn't exactly accurate.

"Denarii are coins from ancient Rome."

I roll my eyes. "You know what I mean."

Knox huffs out a breath and runs his hand along his jawline. "How much do you know about the *Book of Magic*?"

"I've been collecting bits of it. I've got about a quarter of it put together and translated."

"You do?" Knox stares at me.

I make shoo fingers at the windshield. "Eyes ahead, Knox."

Slowly, Knox turns his attention back to driving. "That's why Alec and I have been getting those bits of papyri. We've been trying to do the same thing."

"You mean, put together the *Book of Magic?*"

"Yeah. We haven't gotten anywhere near assembling a quarter of the text. We just got a small part put together."

"About what?"

"Nothing." He stares at me again like I hung the sun and moon. "You really assembled a quarter of it? I mean, the way you talked in Alec's office, I thought you were just putting together bits and pieces of Alec's papyri. Maybe you knew a phrase of two. I didn't think you knew all about the *Book of Magic.*"

"I did, I do, and eyes front." I point at the windshield again.

"What does your part say?"

"Nuh-uh. You answer me first. I asked you who the Denarii really are. The woman who attacked me in the cabin—she called herself a true Denarii."

Knox sighs. "There's no way to tell you about the true Denarii."

I roll my eyes. "Sure, there isn't."

"You've assembled part of the *Book of Magic.* So you know about wardens and the fountain?"

"Yes. Wardens guard the three types of magic, all of which come from the fountain."

"The stuff about the wardens and fountain, that's all in the first half of the book. It's easier to read and translate. What's hard is the second half. It looks like—"

"A bunch of words strung together with no rhyme or reason."

"Yeah. Alec thinks that if you rearrange the hieroglyphs in a certain way, then the words will make sense. It's a hidden code. Whatever is hidden in those glyphs, that's the most important part of the *Book of Magic.* It's what the true Denarii want."

I sink into the leather chair and contemplate this bit of news. "So, we've both translated parts of the book. If we merge our stuff together and then run it through some decoding programs, I might be able to find the pattern quickly enough. What does Alec think the code is about?"

Knox grips the steering wheel tighter. "It's about how to find and activate the fountain. And how to bring back magic, or at least stop it from disappearing."

I don't like the way he's grabbing that steering wheel for dear life. "Why do I get the feeling you're holding back on me?"

"Because I am. Look, I don't know you all that well, and this stuff, it's between Alec and me. I'm telling you all I can."

This is disappointing, but I get it. We've known each other less than a day, and he's told me a lot. "I understand."

A long minute passes before Knox speaks again. "Take the internship job with Alec. There's a room in the LeCharme building that explains the Denarii."

"Okay, I will."

"Good."

"Just answer me one thing. Am I still in danger from the Denarii?"

He frowns. "Yeah."

I tap my lower lip with my pointer finger. "I lied. I have another question about the Denarii. Are all of them evil? Because the girl who works the front desk of the Midtown League seems really nice."

"No. Someone that low level is probably fine." There's a world of experience behind that answer, but I get the feeling it will need to wait until I start my internship. All of which is cool with me. This night has been far more than I bargained for already.

"Okay. Thank-you." And this time, there isn't even an edge to my voice. "Not that you still aren't an ass."

"I get that a lot." Knox tilts his head like he's listening to someone else speaking.

I look around the car. "Do you hear someone?"

"Sort of. Sometimes my wolf..." Knox huffs out another breath. "He talks to me."

"Oh. I didn't know they did that."

"Not all of them do. I'm lucky, I guess."

I stare out the window and watch the lampposts fly by. The city-scape appears on the horizon. We aren't far from Manhattan now. I think through everything Knox said. The fountain…the *Book of Magic*…and the three. I can't wait to get back to my papyri with all this in mind.

But first, I have to tell Elle that I burned her cabin down. That won't be easy.

CHAPTER EIGHT
KNOX

I pull up to the curb before the Barrow Arms, a five-story brown-stone in the Village. *Nice.* "This is Elle's place, yeah?"

Bryar Rose shifts in her seat. "This is it."

Her scent turns bitter, which means that Bryar Rose is unsure how to act around me. Not that I blame her. I've been a dick to her ever since I met her. Sure, it's because I don't want her to get hurt by my semi-insane wolf, but she doesn't know that.

"You good getting inside? Want me to walk you up?" Just because my wolf is crazy doesn't mean I'm not feeling protective myself.

Bryar Rose grips the door handle. "No, I'll be fine." She starts to pull down the handle, but I don't want her to leave.

On instinct, I reach over and grab her wrist. "Wait."

Touching her skin is nothing less than electric. It's a warm jolt that I feel down to my soul. The warden marks on my back start to pulse with power. Meanwhile my inner wolf howls with glee.

"Mate! Mate!"

I tell him to shut up while I keep staring into Bryar Rose's blue eyes. Her voice comes out all silky again. "What is it, Knox?"

What is it, anyway? It's a good question. I guess I'm still feeling protective. There are too many questions out there when it comes to Bryar. "What are you going to do about your therapy group?" I force myself to drop her hand.

"Oh." Her eyes cloud over. "I hadn't thought about that."

"Alec has contacts. We'll find some way to assign you to a new group that has nothing to do with the Denarii. Maybe he can get you out of it altogether."

"Are you sure?"

"This is the kind of thing Alec specializes in." She gives me a small grin, and I want to see more of that. In fact, I want her smiling all the time and only at things that *I* say and do. It's crazy. "And what about your aunties? You talked to them when we were in Alec's office. Are they going to cause trouble about what happened tonight?"

"They won't suspect a thing. They thought I was going to some party and then staying over at Elle's. They won't expect me back home until Saturday at midnight for my birthday party."

"You're having a birthday party at midnight?" I frown. "I thought you said your birthday was Friday."

"I suppose it would make sense for the party to be at midnight on Thursday or Friday night." She shrugs. "I don't know why my aunties insist on Saturday. I'd say they're up to something, but the three of them are always scheming. You know...fairies."

"Right." *The fae are nuts.* Case in point: they're the only group stupid enough to go out in public in their Magicorum forms. Humans love seeing anyone with magic. If Alec ever cast a spell in public, he'd get mobbed for photos and autographs. I've seen weres in their wolf forms get asked to pose for pictures with human babies.

Bryar shakes her head. "This is too good to be true. Alec and his internship, the therapy group, everything... It doesn't seem real. Alec can't really do all of this."

"Oh, he can. Alec's parents are super-wealthy, and he's their only child. That family will do anything for their heir."

"That doesn't explain all the papyri. His parents have to know that he's collecting that stuff."

I shrug. "They do."

Bryar stares at me for a moment. "Oh. I get it."

"Get what?"

"Alec. He's a warden, right?"

My mouth falls open. This girl is sharp. "I can't talk about that."

"You don't need to spill his secrets. I hadn't heard that any wardens officially existed, but it makes sense. They can't have families and kids. Alec's parents probably want him to have the papyri so he can find and activate the fountain."

Hell yeah, that's what they want.

My breathing gets tight. Damn, I'd forgotten she knew about the fountain and the wardens. Why wouldn't she put it together? Bryar read and translated the damned *Book of Magic*. I sigh. There's no point lying now. "Yeah, Alec is a warden. That's why he'll help you."

She slumps back in her seat. "Wow."

"Don't say anything to Elle, okay? It's Alec's story to tell."

"I won't." She shakes her head. "Poor Elle. I think she's falling for him a little."

My mouth thins to an angry line. "Don't pity him. Not everyone has to have a family. He's young and having a good time." Bryar stares at me for a long minute, her eyes getting larger. My heart starts beating at double speed. "What?"

She leans in closer. "You're a warden, too. Aren't you? That's why your wolf is so huge."

"That is none of your business." The words come out far sharper than I intended.

"I'm sorry; I didn't mean to pry. I mean, you're right. You and Alec are young and want to have fun. I'm sure it's no big deal that you can't take a mate."

My inner wolf goes berserk inside me. *"Bryar Rose mate. Bryar Rose maaaaaate!"*

I find myself snarling words at both him and Bryar. "What can you possibly understand about mates and werewolves? My kind won't even consider hooking up with something that's human."

All the blood seems to drain from Bryar's face. "Forget I said anything."

"No, that's not what I meant—"

Before I can come up with a decent excuse, she bolts from the car. I feel like a first-class ass. My wolf growls inside my soul.

"Not be mean to Bryar Rose."

"I have to. She's getting too close. This is for the best."

I put the Mustang into drive and speed away. *Absolutely, this is for the best.* Maybe if I keep saying that over and over, I might just convince myself that it's true.

CHAPTER NINE
BRYAR ROSE

I race up the stairs to Elle's apartment door. One thing about living in New York, you don't need a StairMaster. With every step, my conversation with Knox runs through my mind, like it's stuck on repeat. How can someone be so cool at some moments…and then such a jerk two seconds later? It's not like I was hitting on him in the car. There was no reason for him to be such an ass about the warden thing.

Or maybe there was. I mean, I'm not forbidden to get married or mated or whatever. What do I know about how that feels?

I pause outside Elle's door. I hadn't known that werewolves saw humans as disgusting. But if that's true, then why are there times when I really think that Knox likes me? Am I going crazy?

I set my palms on my eyes and try to regroup. *Now is not the time to worry about Knox. It's the time to tell my best friend that I killed someone and burned her house down.*

Yipes.

Straightening my shoulders, I knock on the door.

"Who is it?" That's Elle.

"It's me. Bryar Rose."

A chorus of locks clicks before the door swings open to a very smiley Elle. It's on the tip of my tongue to say that Alec is a warden, but I hold back. "Hi, Elle!"

"Hey, girlfriend." She's wearing her terrycloth robe and a look of confusion on her face. "What's wrong?"

I'm about to say everything, but the words just don't come. "I… uh…uh…need to take a shower."

Nice bravery, Bryar.

"Sure. Go ahead. Alec left a few minutes ago." Elle steps back and lets me in.

Like the coward I am, I make a beeline to the bathroom and proceed to take the world's longest shower. An hour passes before I step back into the main part of the apartment. It's a huge, single-room deal with super-high ceilings and a bay window that looks out onto a brick wall. For New York, that's a nice view. On the main floor, there's a futon, television, mini-kitchen, and bathroom. Cool posters of old monster movies hang on the walls. I'm talking *Creature from the Black Lagoon, Bride of Frankenstein,* that kind of thing. Elle sleeps in a small loft that's reached by a ladder. It doesn't have enough space for anyone to stand up, but we still squeezed a mattress in there. For the Village, that's luxury.

I pull my own terrycloth robe tighter around me and head into the kitchenette. Sure, it's still early morning, and I haven't slept in more than twenty-four hours. But I'm too wired to think about resting.

I mean, who can rest when you have to tell someone you burned their house down? Not exactly a soothing conversation.

I root around the kitchen while Elle sits on her futon with her feet on the coffee table and a pint of Ben & Jerry's on her lap. She's watching *Animal Planet,* of all things.

"You feeling better?" asks Elle. She's wearing pajamas with ninja penguins on them. I may have to borrow those.

I open her freezer, grab myself a pint of mint Oreo double chocolate, and plunk down onto the couch beside her. "That depends."

"On what?" Elle jams an inhuman amount of ice cream into her mouth.

"On how you take my news."

Elle speaks through a mouthful of ice cream. "Hit me."

"Some members of the Denarii are downright evil."

"Evil? You're talking about the Denarii...the same ones that run our group?"

"Yup. Those are the ones."

"But they're squeaky clean, according to everything I've researched." Elle rolls some more ice cream around her mouth as she thinks. "Although, come to think of it, that's super-sketchy."

"What do you mean?"

"Everyone has something to hide. I asked for a full rundown from my street sources before I joined the group. They came up with nothing. After that, remember when we tried to hack into Madame's life?"

"Sure, we did that when she started over-focusing on my dreams."

"Right. We broke into every system we could find, looking for something suspicious on her."

I crack a smile at the memory. "We wanted to blackmail her so she'd leave me alone in group." It wasn't our best plan. But in our defense, it was a long weekend, and we'd watched too many detective movies.

"Let's face it," says Elle. "We're pretty good hackers. We turned up a ton of information, but all of it was squeaky clean. And that is what's truly fishy about the whole thing. Everyone has something at least a little sketchy out there."

"You don't."

"And that makes my point. I'm totally bad news."

I nod slowly. "You may be on to something."

"Of course, I am. You only get squeaky clean when you've been up to bad things and had them wiped away." She taps her spoon on her chin. "So, what did she do to you?"

I debate whether to break the news slowly, but this is the kind of thing that's best to get over with fast, like ripping off a

Band-Aid. "Last night, Madame broke into the cabin and tried to kill me."

Elle drops her spoon. "You're kidding me."

"I wish."

After that, Elle launches into multiple choruses of "what" and "I don't believe it" as I explain how Madame attacked me and I killed her, only to have her rise from the dead...only to get killed again by Knox. By the time I'm done telling the tale, Elle has finished her first pint of ice cream and cracked open a second.

"Wow. I can't believe that. I mean, I knew Madame was a witch-with-a-B, but a murderer? And the Denarii are really some secret cult? Yow." She shakes her head. "And coming back to life like that is amazeballs. What kind of magic is that, anyway?"

"No idea." I wince. "You still haven't heard the worst of it, though."

"Worse than Madame being a freaky killer?"

I turn to Elle and raise my hand. "Pinky swear you won't lose it."

Elle wraps her pinky around mine. "I swear."

"Okay." I take in a deep breath. "To really get rid of the body, we had to...you know..."

"Just spill."

"Burn the cabin to the ground. Maybe."

"Huh." Elle's face takes on an unreadable look. "Did you burn it to the ground, or didn't you?"

"Knox did the burning, but yeah. It's totally gone."

Elle gives my pinky a squeeze. "In that case, it's fine."

My mouth falls open. "What? You're not mad at me? I got your house burned down."

"For the record, I'd have been much angrier if you'd gotten hurt. I have other safe houses, and that one was a dump anyway. It had no electricity other than that sketchy generator thing. This way, I can get it rebuilt and have insurance pay for it."

I keep staring at Elle with my mouth open. "Really?"

"Would I lie about scamming insurance?" She frowns. "Only, it's not *really* a scam since you two did burn it down without my knowledge." She shrugs. "Oh, well. I'll figure out how to scam insurance another time. Besides, I never liked that place. It's got that creepy hotel nearby."

"The Thornhill Arms."

"That's the one. It's all rundown and nasty and surrounded by those pricker trees." She shivers. "Maybe I should just sell the land instead."

"Whatever you want." I finally start to dig into my now half-melted ice cream. "As long as we're good."

"We're great." Elle bobs her eyebrows up and down. "Only I'm dying for more details about you and Knox."

"What?" I jam a bunch of ice cream into my mouth to buy some time. I know Elle's eyebrow-bobbing routine. She wants gossip and won't stop until she has it.

"Please. I couldn't help but notice how he just showed up at the end of your story. I want deets."

"There's nothing to say." I bob my eyebrows right back at her. "Unless you want to share about Alec first."

Elle's face turns pink. "Uhhhh…"

Now, I'm totally stunned. Elle is making *uh* noises? Whatever happened with Alec, it's got to be interesting.

Suddenly, a knock sounds at the door. "Elle, are you in there? Open up. It's Lauralei."

Elle and I share a shocked look. Although my aunties can track my phone to Elle's place, they've never actually gotten into a taxi to visit the Village. To them, the south end of Manhattan might as well be another country. Sure, they could use magic to transport over, but that would be a major spell. I've seen them cast like two of those in their lifetimes.

Elle sets her ice cream aside and goes to answer the door. Lauralei stands outside in all her gray-haired splendor. She's even wearing a pink pantsuit today, which makes her look even more flamingo-like. "Where's Bryar Rose? We've been calling and calling all morning. You answered the phone, but you could never get our sweet girl on the phone. We've been so worried about her."

"Bryar Rose is here. She's been here all night." Elle says that so innocently even I believe her. "Want some orange juice?"

"No, those are empty calories." Lauralei rushes into the condo. "Bryar Rose. You're really here."

"Where else would I be?" *Other than getting attacked in a log cabin.*

My other aunties stream into the condo behind Lauralei. Fanna is wearing an orange pantsuit, which should look weird, only it's Chanel, so it doesn't. Mirabelle is in a crimson muumuu thing that wouldn't be my choice for her.

And after all my aunties, there comes someone I'd really rather weren't here.

Philpot.

My fake boyfriend is wearing chinos and a rugby jersey with the collar turned up. That should be a cool look, only Philpot's jersey is yellow with a strange black stripe, which makes him look like a chiseled bumblebee or Charlie Brown. Tough to decide.

Lauralei stares at me. "You're here."

"You said that already." I plunk down on the futon and kick my feet onto the coffee table. Lauralei hates when I do this, but I'm at Elle's, so she can't say anything. You have to enjoy the little victories in life. "You seem surprised to see me."

"After looking for so long, we feared the worst."

"Why?" I ask. "It hasn't even been a full day since I last saw you all." Which is totally suspicious. I'd worry that my aunties are in cahoots with the Denarii, but the Denarii try to kill anyone with magic, so that seems way unlikely.

"It wasn't only me." Lauralei pushes Philpot forward. "Your Prince was worried about you as well."

Philpot beams. "Just because they call me His Highness of Hedge Funds doesn't make me a Prince…to everyone."

Mirabelle rushes forward to paw his forearm. "It does to us, Philpot honey."

"Actually, it's Philpot Herbert Utrecht the Third."

Not again.

Philpot scans the room. "You left the party without saying good-bye. It had me so worried. And then, you didn't answer my calls."

"I never answer your calls."

Philpot sniffs. "I was forced to reach out to your aunties and—"

"We're always happy to hear from you, Philpot honey," says Fanna.

I rise and clap my hands. My aunties are like schoolchildren sometimes. A good clap helps them focus. "Well, now, you've all found me, and I'm safe. So if you don't mind, Elle and I need some sleep."

"But it's early Thursday morning," says Lauralei.

Elle slaps on one of her most winning smiles and tosses her long mane of blonde hair. You can almost hear my aunties think, *Awwwwww*. "This is all my fault. I kept Bryar Rose up all night."

Lauralei pats Elle on the shoulder. "Whatever you did, I'm sure Bryar had it coming."

I raise my fist. "Thanks for the love."

"Hush now; Elle's talking."

I'd hate that my aunties like Elle better than me, but Elle only uses her powers for good.

"Here's what happened." Elle scans the room, drawing everyone into her tale. I swear, you can feel the energy sparkle around her. It's got to be magic. Not that I'm complaining. "Bryar wanted so badly to stay at your party, Prescott."

"It's Philpot."

"Right. But she started having a terrible episode, so I took her away." Elle clasps her hands under her chin, not unlike poses I've seen on prayer devotionals. "And I had another reason to want some quiet time with Bryar. I've uncovered an amazing opportunity for her."

"What is it?" asks Lauralei.

"You've heard of the LeCharme employee discount?" asks Elle. "Sixty percent off."

I want to suck in a gasp, but I stop myself. I know for a fact that there's no such thing as a LeCharme employee discount. We hacked into their finance systems on more than one occasion. I can't wait to see where Elle is going with this.

"Oh, my." Lauralei's beady bird eyes glitter with interest. "Sixty percent?"

Now, some fairies wouldn't care about retail discounts, but those would be the ones who can magic up whatever they want. My aunties aren't necessarily strong in the magical arena—and they do like bright, shiny objects—so this is of definite interest to them. I'm starting to see where Elle is going with this, and my girl is a genius.

"Our Bryar Rose has a chance to get that discount for her friends and family."

"How?" asks Philpot. He looks overly interested as well, which is somehow creepy. Who's he buying jewels for, anyway? Not that I really care if he disrespects our fake relationship, but still. It's the principle of the thing.

"Bryar has an opportunity to work as an intern at LeCharme. That's how she'd get the discount." Elle sighs dramatically, complete with setting the back of her palm against her forehead. "Only she doesn't want to do it."

Now all my aunties talk in quick succession. As always, Lauralei starts. "Why ever wouldn't you want an internship at LeCharme?"

"What do they want her to do?" asks Fanna. "There's no way she can be around other people. She could have an episode."

"Bryar Rose is not really ready to work with customers or anything." That's Mirabelle. "We'd be concerned about her getting a big head."

Or any sense of self-confidence, it would seem. I'd call them out on this, but I don't want to bust up whatever con Elle's working. Instead, I decide to step in and help out. It's a passive-aggressive way to get my revenge, but I'll take it.

I put on my most serious face. "My job would be maintaining the rose garden on the roof." This way, there are thorns and greenery involved, which fits with my Sleeping Beauty template. They should like that.

"A greenhouse on a skyscraper?" asks Fanna. "That sounds incredibly dangerous. What if you have an episode and fall off the roof?" On a positive note, Fanna is consistently considerate of my safety.

"Did Bryar Rose say gardening?" asks Elle. "That's not correct. Actually, she has to scrub toilets." Now, that's a more Cinderella template thing, but it just might work.

Lauralei grins. "That seems a little more her speed."

I shiver dramatically. "It's a skyscraper, aunties. There are so many disgusting, dirty toilets. That's why I'm so unsure."

"You'll do it." Lauralei turns to Elle. "How does the discount work?"

"I'm going to be interning, too, so I'll manage everything."

Actual tears glisten in Lauralei's eyes. "That's so kind of you."

"Hey, that's just who I am." Elle's huge blue eyes never looked larger or more innocent than they do in this moment.

Philpot steps forward. "What about me?"

"You're absolutely included, Protus."

"It's Philpot Herbert Utrecht the Third."

Elle shrugs. "That's what I said."

Lauralei rounds on me. "You must accept this opportunity, Bryar Rose. We simply can't have you sitting around all summer doing nothing."

I shiver again, just to look even more convincing in my fake uncertainty. "Well…"

"We insist," adds Fanna. "You owe us."

"You're right. I'll help out. After all, it's the least I can do. You know, after all you've sacrificed for me."

"Everything is decided then." Elle opens the door and gestures to the hallway beyond. "Now, if you don't mind, we're off to bed."

Philpot looks confused. "What?"

Lauralei steps toward the door. "Didn't you hear? Our sweet Elle has been up all night convincing Bryar Rose to take this internship. They both need their sleep now. Mostly Elle."

I yawn. "That's right." And in truth, I am feeling way tired.

"Shouldn't she come back to the penthouse?" asks Mirabelle.

"Nope, I need to keep her here." Elle grins again, and I swear I can hear another silent *awwwww* fill the air. "I'm not taking any chances with her chickening out. Can't be late for our first day!"

"Today is Thursday," says Lauralei, Mistress of the Obvious. "When would you start work?" Fairies always find it hard to remember that there are specific days for humans to earn wages.

"We start tomorrow. Friday." Elle says it with such conviction, I'm sure it's the truth. Or it will be, soon enough.

"Of course, Elle." Lauralei is so happy she almost skips out into the hallway. "You really are a marvel."

Elle winks. "This, I know."

Philpot starts toward me. "I need to give my girl a good-bye kiss." There's that predatory look in his eyes again.

Come on, Saturday.

"Not now," says Elle. My best friend knows all about the no-touching rule. "Bryar has a mouth full of cold sores. Long story."

I point to my lips and shake my head *no*. "Yucky, honestly."

"It's all right," says Philpot. "I understand. Happens to me all the time."

My stomach twists with nausea. *Happens to him all the time? Gross.* "See you later."

Elle says something about the markets opening in Asia and ushers Philpot out into the hallway. The minute they're gone, Elle leans against the closed door. "All the people in your life? They suck. Hard."

"I know."

"No, I don't think you *do* know. We keep having this talk, and you keep not wanting to see the full scope of the nastiness here. There's something wrong with that whole scene."

All of a sudden, I've never felt more exhausted. The last twenty-four hours with no sleep come crashing over me. "Look, I know you've got a point, but I'm way overwhelmed right now. Can we save this chat for later?"

"You aren't going to address the thing with your aunties and Philpot?"

"No."

"I won't drop this. You realize that, don't you?"

I point to the ladder set onto the wall. "Sleep first. Boy-talk second. Crazy aunties and Philpot a distant third."

"So, we'll talk eventually. Fine." Elle steps over to the ladder and pauses. "I love you. You know that, right?"

My heart warms with her words. "I do. And I love you, too. Thanks for lying your ass off to get me that internship." I grin. "Although I can't help but notice you got one for yourself too, along with another line of semi-illegal income. You know Alec will also pay you an insane salary, right?"

"It's a win-win. My specialty."

"Well, whatever it is, thanks. I really appreciate it." My voice shakes a little as I talk. *What would I do without Elle?*

"Sleep well, Bry. I wasn't lying about starting on Friday. I talked to Alec."

I shouldn't be surprised, but I am. "You already set this all up?"

"Sure, I did." Her big blue eyes narrow. "You don't have to do this if you don't want to, you know."

"Oh, I want to." Excitement zings through me. "I can't wait to start my internship." And the fact that Knox promised to show me something about the Denarii while I was at LeCharme? That has nothing to do with my level of happy here. Nothing at all.

"Cool." With that, Elle climbs up the ladder and into her loft bed. I turn, ready for some sleep action on the futon. That's not what happens, though.

A man now stands in the room. He's tall with a wide-brimmed hat and snarky smile on his handsome face. He reminds me of that guy from *Gone with the Wind*, but with salt and pepper hair. Clark Gable, that's it. The unlit stub of a cigar sits in the corner of his mouth. All of this is way surprising and even more alarming. But it's not the most dangerous part of this situation.

That would be the fact that this guy is surrounded by more fairy dust than I've ever seen in my life.

Now, I've seen my aunties cast a spell a few times in the past. When they do, they use a little sprinkle of silver dust. But this guy? He's positively surrounded by a cloud of it.

So. Strange.

Magic of that level? It isn't supposed to exist anymore. He could cause some serious damage. And that is definitely something to be worried about, especially when it comes to fairies. They aren't exactly known to be predictable.

That said, I haven't lived my whole life with fairies for nothing. I know you have to play it cool around them, so I give the stranger a casual wave. "How did you get in here? Elle had like a thousand wards on this place. No one is supposed to transport in without permission."

"I'm not no one." He grins, and I guess that answer is his way of saying that he's powerful enough to do whatever he wants.

"Who are you?"

"Forgive my manners, sugar." He's got a lilting Southern accent. "I'm Colonel Mallory the Magnificent. Call me Colonel Mallory."

Every inch of my body goes on alert. *Oh, no.* This is the same guy who cursed me with my sleeping sickness…the very spell that is supposed to end on Saturday when I turn eighteen. And now, he's here again?

I can't handle another curse, so I decide to call in the big guns. "Elle, you want to come down here and meet our guest?"

"Your friend can't see or hear me." Colonel Mallory flicks his fingers, and more silver particles tumble to the floor. "That's why I need all this fairy dust. Keep her asleep and happy, so to speak. She's a powerful one, you know that?"

"Powerful how?"

"Ah then, you *don't* know that." Colonel Mallory shakes his head. "I shouldn't have stayed away for so long. A mistake on my part, clearly." He straightens the lapels of his dark jacket. "That said, there's no point dwelling on the past. Right now, you and I need to have a little chat."

I can only stare at the guy. "What?"

"You caught my name, right? Colonel Mallory the Magnificent."

"Yes, you're the one they call Mallifi—"

"No, that's not me." Colonel Mallory flashes his palms in the universal gesture for *stop right there*. "And never, ever call a fairy by their true name. Well, not unless you want them to show up. You were about to summon my cousin. Take my advice. Don't." He lowers his voice. "Makes her peevish."

"Uh. Okay." *This is happening.* The fairy who cursed me is actually standing in Elle's condo. What should I do? I'm so stunned the words seem to form on their own. "You look like Clark Gable."

"No, sugar. *He* looks like *me*." Colonel Mallory pulls the cigar from his mouth. "You caught up with me yet? Gotten your sweet self over the shock? Because I got a lot to chat with y'all about."

The little wheels of my mind start spinning again. I'm on the ball once more, and I know the deal. This guy is a creep. "You ruined my life."

"Wrong."

"What? You cursed me with this sleeping sickness."

"No, I *saved* you, sugar." Colonel Mallory raises his hand. My inhaler is clasped in his fingers. He tosses it in my direction. "You'll need that."

The world is starting to look a little hazy around the edges, so I take a puff of medicine. *This definitely can't be happening.* I mean, how long does it take before sleep deprivation causes you to hallucinate? Not long, I'd guess, especially if someone tried to kill you along the way. I fold my arms over my chest. "This is a dream. A really, really bad dream. You, Colonel Mallory, are an illusion."

"I'm not, and you know it."

I take another puff of my inhaler, just to be safe. "In that case, I'm losing my mind."

"You're perfectly sane. I come here with good news for you, sugar. What I gave you is not a curse, but a blessing."

"Fairies don't do blessings."

"Not as a rule. But you and I, we're different. One of a kind. And I'm here to tell you that you're about to get back everything you lost."

"I lost something?"

"More like had it placed under my protection."

"Huh. Are we talking about how I lost my life because of the spell you cast on me?"

"No, sugar. Something else."

My mouth falls open. "Something other than being transformed into a freaky Magicorum when I should have been a regular human."

Colonel Mallory laughs so hard he tilts his head back and almost loses his hat. "You were never a regular anything. That's why I came to visit y'all tonight after so many years. Your life is about to turn quite strange. See, you're coming up on your eighteenth birthday, and your powers are starting to shine through."

A chill prickles across my skin. "Powers? I'm human. My aunties have powers."

"What a pretty pack of liars they are." Colonel Mallory sets the cigar back in his mouth and gives a white-toothed smile. "You wait and see, sugar. Those powers will show. Or more likely, break through."

Every cell in my body goes on alert. "Break through how?"

"I think you know that already. I locked up all your powers for you, good and tight." He taps the center of his chest. "Should feel like a lockbox deep in your soul."

A chill crawls up my neck. The container in my soul. I feel it every time I'm about to have an episode. I always thought it was Colonel Mallory's curse trying to break out and freeze me... But could I have been wrong? Did Colonel Mallory merely take my magic and lock it up to help me somehow?

I shake my head. Colonel Mallory is a fairy and a liar. There's no way I have magic. And I don't need to listen to any of this garbage. I've lived with his crazy curse my entire life. There's no way he can come in here and pretend that his freezing spell is some kind of blessing.

"I don't have any powers." My voice takes on a desperate edge. "I'm human. The only reason I qualify as Magicorum is because I was adopted by my aunties and cursed by you. Once I turn eighteen, the curse is over. I won't need my aunties to give me medicine. I'll be a normal human who has a normal life…normal high school… normal everything." My dream seems to be vanishing before my eyes. "You're totally lying."

Colonel Mallory only grins once more. "I see. Well, when you're ready to learn about your powers, you just say my name. I'll be close by." With that, he takes the unlit cigar from his teeth. When he breathes on the end, it ignites.

Wait…did he just light a cigar with his breath?

Of all the things that Colonel Mallory has done, that is by far the strangest.

I point right at his face. It's rude, but I can't help it. "How did you do that? Fairies do not conjure fire. That's a shifter skill for… for…" I can't bring myself to say "dragons."

"You're quite right, sugar. Think on it a spell. You'll figure it out." Colonel Mallory tips his hat. "Good night, sweet Bryar Rose."

The silver light of fairy dust slowly disappears. Along with it goes Colonel Mallory.

He's gone.

Vanished.

I shake my head. He was here. The man who cursed my life. For a long time, I can only stare at the spot where he stood.

What. The. Hell.

This situation has gone way over the edge. Clearly, I need some rest. I quickly set up Elle's futon and slip under the covers. It takes me a while, but I eventually fall asleep. By the time I wake up again, I've almost convinced myself that seeing Colonel Mallory the Magnificent was all a dream. *Almost.*

CHAPTER TEN
KNOX

Long after Bryar Rose is gone, I keep the Mustang idled at the curb outside Elle's condo. My wolf's voice keeps growling inside my head. *"Follow mate. Guard mate."*

I force myself to sound calm as I reply in my mind. *"Bryar Rose is fine. Did you see her take on that Denarii? She can handle anything."*

"Guard mate." That's a wolf thing. Male or female, we never leave our mates alone if we can help it.

Closing my eyes, I keep talking to my wolf in my mind. *"She's not our mate."*

My wolf replies with an inner howl that's so loud, it makes my ears ring. *"Maaaaaaaaaaaaaaaate!"*

I angrily thump my palm against the dashboard. This time, I speak out loud. "Cut it out. You're making me crazy."

His wolfy voice sounds all snippy this time. *"Mate."*

This is a cluster. Bryar cannot be my mate, although there's no convincing my wolf of that fact. Something's got to be done. And at this point, there's only one guy who might be able to help me.

Azizi, my adopted father.

Az taught me all there is to know about being a werewolf. He's also my only source of info on being a warden. Not that there's too much to know about that, considering the *Book of Magic* has been burned up for ages. Still, what there is to learn is all in Az's head. He lives at Lucky's bar in Brooklyn, so that's where I'll go right now.

I peel away from the curb with one thought. *Screw the speed limit. I need to get to Lucky's.* There aren't many shifters left in the world, which makes Lucky's bar incredibly rare. This place is werewolf-only.

It doesn't take long to reach Brooklyn, park the Mustang in a nearby garage, and get myself over to Lucky's. On the outside, the place doesn't look like anything special. The entrance is on a street corner with a small sign and a flight of stairs going underground. If you didn't know it was there, you might miss it. Once you get inside, though, that's when you see the difference.

Everyone's eyes glow with golden light.

Gold. That's the shade of shifter magic. It's what empowers us to change forms. Sure, we can tone the shine down—while either in wolf or human form—but that's only to keep regular humans from getting twitchy. Or cracking out their cameras for selfies with a real Magicorum, which is worse. Plus, keeping a low profile ensures that the Denarii stay off our backs. Those guys kill folks with magic like nobody's business. But in places like Lucky's, we can be who we are.

Once inside, Lucky's looks the same as always. I've been coming here for years. It's a dimly lit space with low ceilings. A familiar patchwork of small, round tables covers the floor. Random junk has been nailed to the walls. It's all stuff from New York mostly, like old bagel flyers and bicycle wheels. The back wall is lined with bottles of booze. This time of the morning, the place is relatively quiet. About a half-dozen regulars hang around, drinking coffee or finishing off some booze from last night's party.

I scan the floor, looking for "howlers," a.k.a. humans who've become werewolf groupies. As much as I complain about humans who see us as oddities for keepsakes and photos, the howlers are worse. They'll rip off their undies and chuck them at your face. Some weres like that, but it's not my thing. Last time the howlers found our place, I had to call in some favors with Alec to erase a bunch of memories and place terror spells by all the doors. Now, any humans who get near Lucky's should freak out and run in the opposite direction. I scan the bar carefully. There are no howlers around today. Looks like Alec's spell is still holding. He is one amazing wizard. Not that I'd ever tell him that to his face. Guy's got a big enough ego as it is.

The second I start crossing the floor, the room falls silent. *Not again.* This happens every time. It's the fact that I'm a warden. Power comes out of my pores or something. It's nice in a fight, but when I just want to find Az? It ends up being a time suck because I can't walk across a room without gathering a crowd.

Someone turns around, and I wince. A werewolf named Joy is here. She's someone whose attention I really don't want. Joy is pretty in a "big blonde hair" kind of way. I'm not sure she owns any clothing that isn't made of denim, either. Weres are fashion forward, as a rule, but Joy totally missed that memo. She dresses like a Bon Jovi groupie. Even worse, we have a history. There's no way I want to talk to her now, so I keep my head down and march toward the bar. Joy stays put, which is awesome. She's hanging in the corner with some other were. Hopefully, that won't change.

I hit the bar and wave over Thad, the bartender. He's a young guy with a baby face, freckles, and a buzz cut. He's also new, which is why he gets the crap shifts like early morning. He strides over with his easy grin.

"Hey, Knox. You here to see Joy?"

Damn it. "No."

Of course, Joy only hears what Thad said, not my reply. From the corner of my eye, I see her glance in my direction.

"Definitely not here for Joy." I say that a little too loudly, hoping she'll get the hint.

"What about Constance or Hope?" Joy's from a family of three werewolf daughters, which is crazy rare. Her parents gave them all straight-arrow names, so of course the girls turned out wild as hell.

If I ever get to name a girl cub, I'm calling her Killer or something. That way, she'll end up being a nun.

"Not here for the ladies. Is Az up?" Azizi always hangs out in his room out back. My parents died when I was a cub, so Az is the closest thing I have to a father. In fact, he moved here from Cairo to be near me and help. The reason? Az was the previous warden for shifters. Now that my powers are growing, he's getting weaker. There can only be one of us at full steam at any point in time. These days, Az is looking and acting older, which bums me out.

"Yup. Az is here. He's always here." Thad can be a little thick sometimes.

"I mean, is he awake and all that? I need to talk to him, but I don't want to bug him." When I was little, I'd crawl all over Az and we'd brawl for hours. Now, he rarely shifts out of his wolf form, and that's only to use the john before going back to sleep.

"Oh, I get it. Yeah, he's awake."

Joy starts to make her way over in my direction. *Uh, no.* I give Thad a quick wave. "I'll head back. Make sure we're not disturbed, yeah?"

"You got it."

I speed to the back door before Joy can intercept me. *Sweet.* That girl's like a homing beacon sometimes. Not that it isn't partly my fault. I hooked up with Joy once. We didn't get too far, but it was still a major mistake. Just one minute into kissing, and Joy licked the side of my face. Total turn-off.

Before Joy can reach me, I escape through the back door, head down the cramped hallway, and enter the third entrance on the right. Azizi's place.

Az's HQ isn't so much a room; it's more of a makeshift cave. Az had the paint stripped from the walls and floor, so everything is just concrete. I find him hanging out in his wolf form, per usual, and curled up in the corner. Other than the chipped black paint on the bathroom door, the place is totally bare. I wish he'd let me hang up a picture or two, but that's Az. He's gone wolf.

The door closes behind me with a soft click. Az opens his right eye. The iris is a milky shade of gold. "Good morning, my son."

Az has a deep rumble of a voice that I love. It totally reminds me of happy times as a kid. Az is also one of the few shifters who can talk in his wolf form. It's a side effect of being a warden. My wolf can talk, too, but I avoid it. I don't need anything else bringing attention to my powers.

"Morning, Az." I sit down beside him and run my fingers through the graying fur on his neck. Az is a massive wolf, like me. Sitting here next to him, I can't believe how much muscle he's lost. The guy is skin and bone. It kills me.

Az sniffs the air. "Something troubles you. I can smell it."

Here's where I should just up and ask him about whether he's ever thought someone was his mate. But it's hard. This feels too big. The words weigh on my tongue like stones. Instead, I find myself talking about something else that's usually too painful. "I was just thinking. I don't remember my parents."

"I shouldn't think you do. You were only a cub when they died." He doesn't add in the part about the Denarii killing them. It's been my life's mission to pay them back for that.

"I was placed with some random were family. They didn't want to raise someone else's cub. Then one day, you walk in, grab me, and go. How did you find me, anyway? You were from Cairo. I was in Manhattan. That couldn't have been easy."

Az chuckles. "You're avoiding asking me your real question."

I scratch him behind his ears. "I'm working up to it. How did you find me?"

"It wasn't as hard as you might think. The warden who taught me had passed on, so I knew you were out there somewhere. A cub. I asked around. Who's the biggest and blackest werewolf out there? Rumors led me to you."

"And Rui?" That was the warden before Azizi. The guy was from Manchuria. You never know where the next warden will come from, by the way. The magic finds the warden. No one really knows how it chooses.

"Rui did the same thing." Az lets out little cough. My chest tightens to hear it. Az gets weaker every day. "He asked around for a black wolf who fought well."

"You and Rui…were you guys close?" I guess it's a little weird that I don't know this, but normally when I'm with Az, we don't talk about his past. He doesn't like it, as a rule.

Az's heavy brows pop up. "What's this sudden interest in Rui? You ready to ask your real question yet?"

"Not yet."

Az gives me a milky-eyed look that says he knows I'm up to something, but he'll still play along. "Rui and I were very close."

"Okay. So werewolf wardens find each other, but none of the others do? I mean, Alec has never met his last warden. Whoever that guy or girl is, they're still out there somewhere."

Az sniffs, a sound that says, *Really?* It's the noise he often makes when he's talking about the other magical races. "Warlocks and fairies aren't like us. They aren't pack."

"True that." Werewolves are driven to attach to a group. We share power. Some mates even share thoughts.

Az twitches his ears. "Are you going to tell me why you're upset, my son?"

I rub my neck. *He's right. I can't stall forever.* "Here's the thing. Did you ever feel a mating call?"

"Never." Az's answer is swift and without hesitation. Not a good sign for whatever strangeness is going on with my wolf and me.

"Are you sure? Didn't your wolf ever get confused? Maybe it thought someone was his mate when it wasn't even possible?"

"No."

I try another angle. "What about Rui? Did his wolf ever think someone was his mate?"

At these words, my own wolf decides to get into the act. His growling voice echoes through my mind. *"Bryar. Mate."*

I close my eyes and reply in my mind. *"I know your opinion on this one, buddy."*

"No, no, no." Az's voice is getting more clipped, which means he's not fooling around. "Rui never felt the call for a mate." Az's eyes narrow. "Why, did such a thing happen to you?"

I rub Az's neck like my life depends on it. I have the option of lying right now, but that's a waste of time. Werewolves can scent an untruth. "Yeah. My wolf thinks so."

With these words, my wolf decides to go berserk in my head. *"Bryar! Yes! Mate!"*

"Quiet, you."

Az shifts to stare directly at me. "And?"

"It's impossible. Wardens don't get mates. And even if we did, the girl my wolf picked is a human."

Az's milky gaze locks with mine. "I don't care what she is. Do you know what I'd give for one hour of the feeling that you're throwing away? We're pack animals. We want cubs and a family. Don't ruin this for yourself."

"I get that we're pack, but going after this girl? It's just selfish. I could hurt her. You know wardens can't mate. And even if we could, the bonding ceremony isn't an option. Within a day after getting married, our spouses sicken and die." It's all part of being a warden. The magic finds you. It also enforces your job. If you aren't guarding the fountain, you don't get a family.

"Only if you do a full mating ceremony."

I shake my head. "If I let someone in my life, my wolf is not going to be happy until we have a mating ceremony. We can't have cubs without it."

Az's long tongue slides across his lips. That's his "thinking face." A long pause ticks by before he speaks again. "Let me see your marks."

Now, all wardens have marks on their backs. They're like tattoos, but they show up magically when we first get full use of our powers. As we mature, they darken. Mine are hieroglyphs, and they started to appear when I was six. The markings pulse as I get more power, and yeah, I've been feeling them more ever since I met Bryar. Still, I'm not ready for more evidence that I should enter into a doomed relationship, especially when it means Bryar could end up dead.

I glare at Az. "My marks are fine."

Az huffs out a breath, which is his version of a chuckle. "In other words, you won't show your marks to me because they *have* changed."

Again, I'd lie to him, but he'd sniff it out anyway. "They've been pulsing lately. That's all. This mate thing has got me all mixed up."

"And so, you've come to ask me for advice."

"Yeah."

"My guidance to you is this. You need to be with your mate. Hunt this girl down. Make her yours."

My wolf loves this idea. *"Yes. Bryar. Mate."*

I'm not so convinced. "Like I said, I'm not sure that's a good idea. Especially for her."

Az shifts his weight until he's sitting sphinxlike on his front paws. "Listen to me, cub. There are three wardens for magic. As of this moment, two of them are within a mile of each other. That's unprecedented. And I'll wager the third is near you too, although you don't know it yet. Whatever you think the rules are for wardens, they don't exist anymore. Our magic is changing."

"That's what Alec says, too. He thinks that the fountain can only be found once every two thousand years, and we're coming up on that time."

"Alec could very well be right."

"I've read the passages he translated in the *Book of Magic*. You could interpret them ten different ways. It doesn't mean the fountain is returning or magic is changing."

Az arches his brows. "And is that what you truly believe?"

Times like these, I wish I could lie. "I don't know what to believe, Az."

"Because you know Alec speaks the truth. The fountain will return to us. Magic will change. The fact that you're finding your mate is all part of that. You must go where it leads you."

I shake my head. "That's not so easy. There are risks."

Az lies back down, resting his muzzle on his paws. "Right now, no path will be easy for you. You have two choices. You can follow the magic on this journey willingly, or it will drag you to its chosen destination anyway. At least if you go willingly, there will be less pain."

"Less pain. Nice."

"You came here for the truth. Just think on what I said. That's all I ask."

"I will. I promise." Something Bryar said pops into my mind, raising another question I can pose to Az. And right now? Any change of subject seems like a great idea. "You still keep your contacts up with the were packs, yeah?"

"I do."

"Do you know if there are any werewolves who are going to those teen Magicorum groups run by the Denarii?"

"I know of one. She's a Red Riding Hood template." Az's scent changes. Whoever she is, this girl is important to him.

"Pass around the word. Time was, some lower-level Denarii could be trusted. But that's over now. Make sure everyone knows… Any groups run by the Denarii are unsafe."

"Are you certain? There has always been a core of Denarii who are evil, but they stay hidden away from the public. The underlings you'd meet in a league building are harmless. Many can be helpful to our kind."

"Not anymore. The human I was telling you about? She was in one of those groups. The leader tried to kill her."

"I see." Az's upper lip twists into a snarl. "I'll take care of it." And I wonder what he really means by that. Az might be old, but when he's riled up, he can be a badass in battle. "Anything else?"

"No. Thanks, Az." I give him one last scratch behind the ears. "I'll be going now."

"And I'll be napping until later."

With that, I leave Az's place and head back to the bar. My body is so wound up, it's like I could jump out of my skin. Who knows? Maybe I should find Joy and see if her kissing skills have gotten any better. At this moment, I need any distraction I can get.

With that thought, my wolf totally loses it. He instantly turns into a howling mess inside me. *"No Joy. BRYAR ROSE MATE!"* Then he lets out a long series of whining noises.

I reply in my mind. *"Okay, buddy, I got it."*

"We go. Bryar Rose mate."

I know what he wants. *"Fine, we'll drive by her place. But that's all we'll do. Better?"*

"Mate, mate, mate."

When my wolf starts repeating stuff over and over, it means only one thing. There won't be any peace for me tonight. I need to drive by Elle's place, since I know that's where Bryar is staying. There was a café across the street from her brownstone. Maybe I can put the Mustang in a lot, grab some java, and keep an eye on her place. As I contemplate this plan, I must admit, my wolf isn't the only one who's pumped for this idea. Once I'm closer to Bryar, I know I'll feel a lot better, too.

CHAPTER ELEVEN
BRYAR ROSE

I check my watch. Or, I check the amazing smart watch that Elle loaned me for this morning. It's now Friday morning, a little before 10 a.m., and Elle and I are off to our internship at LeCharme.

Strolling side by side, we stride along Sixth Avenue. Early morning sunshine glints off the skyscrapers as we make a beeline for the LeCharme Building. Around us, the city is alive with motion. Someone in a yellow taxi slams on its horn. Up ahead, a young guy plays drums on a row of buckets. A street vendor sells hotdogs for breakfast. I love New York.

Turns out, Elle and I slept most of Thursday away. When we finally did wake up, we spent the time watching old movies and avoiding too much talk about Knox and Alec. I told Elle the whole story of how Knox saved my life, followed by his nasty behavior on the drive back. We both agree that he's not boyfriend material. Elle says that Alec is a flirt who'll never commit to anything, although she did appreciate the backrub and general concern for her well-being.

We then spent a good chunk of time insisting to each other that we aren't into those guys. And we mean it, too. The only reason we're walking over to LeCharme right now is because of the internship. Not the guys. *Maybe.*

Elle and I approach the LeCharme entrance. The first floor of the building is all retail space. In other words, it's one huge jewelry store. The upper levels are the business offices, and that's where our internship will take place.

Pausing, I scope out our reflections in the outer plate glass windows and smile. Damn, we look good. Both Elle and I are dressed in black suits and heels. Luckily, Elle had a few Armani suits ready to go in her closet, and the two of us are the same size. I guess she got them for some scam that never took off. As always, I didn't ask too many questions.

I elbow Elle and gesture to the window. "Hey. We look totally awesome."

Elle glances up from her phone. No question what she was doing just now. Ever since they met, Elle and Alec have been texting nonstop, supposedly about the internship. Elle says it's all professional. Still, she keeps blushing her face off whenever they text, so I know Alec's flirting with her. By the way, Alec said for us to dress in jeans today, but I found a LeCharme fan site that said all the full-time employees wear black suits.

Elle and I want to look full time and badass. We're wearing black suits.

Finally, Elle looks up from her phone. "What?"

"I said, we look amazing."

She pauses and checks out our reflection, too. The black outfit sets off her big blue eyes, long blonde hair, and toned legs. In fact, we look a little like sisters, only my hair is brown. She links arms with me. "We're totally ready for this."

"You got it."

"Only…I wish I had a briefcase."

"Why? We don't have anything big to carry?"

"I know that. It's just I've seen some really cute leather ones that would totally go with this look. They even have little bows on them."

"Something for next time," I say, as I wonder how exactly Elle plans to get her hands on those particular bags. I've seen them in magazines. They run four grand a pop.

Again, something I'd rather not know.

We pass through the revolving door and enter the main sales floor of LeCharme. Everything here is pale purple—that's the company's signature color. A maze of waist-high glass cases stretches out before us. The place is pretty busy with customers, sales clerks, guards, and...

Oh, no.

One particular guard. We call him Comb-Over Guy.

I grab Elle's shoulders and point her toward a nearby wall. My death grip on her suit makes it clear there's a problem, so Elle doesn't fight me at all. When she speaks, her voice is barely a whisper. "What's up?"

"Remember when we came in here over the winter?"

"The time I took the tiara?"

"No."

"Emerald ring set?"

"No."

"Diamond jaguar pin?"

"No!" I frown. "Do we really hit this place that often?"

"Sha." She snaps her fingers. "The ruby chalice."

"That's the one. We were all dressed up for a party, but we ran into that guard we called Comb-Over Guy and then..." I leave it out there, as the memory should be obvious at this point.

"No, I don't remember."

"You thought he was about to grab you, so you maced his face off."

"Oh, yeah. Comb-Over Guy." Elle taps her chin. "He's here?"

"About four yards behind us."

Elle's big blue eyes narrow. She's scheming up something; that's for sure. "And where do we have to get to?"

"The employee elevators at the back wall."

"So why don't we just walk by him?"

"Because he said that if he ever saw us again, I quote, *'I'll call the cops first and ask questions later.'*" I lower my voice. "We're trying to look cool and make a good impression."

"Got it." Elle smacks her lips, which means scheming time is over. "Here's the plan. You're good with me setting the plan, right?"

"Please." I roll my eyes. "You always scheme when we're avoiding trouble. It's your gift."

"Right. So this is it. We walk casually toward the back elevators."

"Not a great plan. He'll see us."

"Wait, there's more. As we step on by, we just keep our bodies angled toward the wall, like we're looking at the décor or something. That way, we can waltz right over to the elevator bank without showing our faces to anyone."

"That would be a good plan."

"It's an awesome plan."

"But there's nothing on the walls here, Elle. We'd look totally suspicious."

"Ugh." Elle groans. "You'd think LeCharme would have enough money to buy a freaking picture. Sheesh."

"Maybe we pretend we're like, interior decorators, sizing the walls up for future artwork." Elle and I always pick out personas before we launch into a scheme like this one. You'd be amazed how useful it is.

"Perfect." Elle scratches her cheek and discreetly glances over her shoulder. "Let's go."

We start a slow stroll by the far right wall. Elle makes comments about how some impressionist paintings might look great here. I totally agree with her. My imagination starts to run wild. Is that guard following us? I don't want the cops to haul us out of the building on our first day. I mean, chances are it will happen eventually, but I'd like to ease Knox and Alec into the whole mania that is Elle and me.

Not that I care what those guys think, of course.

At last, we make it to the bank of elevators. There are four sets, all of which go up to the fortieth floor. I hit the Up button, try to look cool, and ask Elle a question from the corner of my mouth. "Is he coming?"

"Oh yeah."

I risk a glance over my shoulder. Sure enough, Comb-Over Guy is hauling ass in our direction, and he does not look happy. *Yipes.* Nothing like getting maced in the face to make an impression. The dude is within a few yards of us when the nearest elevator opens up. Folks in black suits spill out into the foyer. A second elevator slides open right behind it. Only one guy gets out.

"There!" I point to the second elevator. "Let's make like New Yorkers."

"Right."

Now, Elle and I are experts in the intricate dance of hip-checking and shoulder-bumping that makes life in New York bearable. Luckily for us, Comb-Over Guy isn't as aggressive. He gets caught in the crowd of workers while we slip into the second elevator and hit the button that's marked "Tenth Floor Reception."

The doors close with a metal hiss. I turn to Elle and give her a high five. "That was so awesome, girlfriend. We got totally lucky with that second elevator."

"It's not luck," says Elle. "It's human nature. People are sheep. Everyone gets on the first elevator that stops on their floor. They pack in like sardines while a second, totally empty elevator follows right behind."

"True that. Either way, I'm glad we missed Comb-Over Guy."

"Me too."

The doors open again, and we step off into reception. It's a huge, funky space with high ceilings, low tables, and leather couches. Everything is LeCharme purple. There's no one around except for a reception desk with a long line of people waiting in front of it. Elle marches right past the desk.

"Whoa, there." I pull on Elle's sleeve. "We have to visit reception, right?"

Elle's big blue eyes are blank for a moment before reality kicks in. "Yes, of course."

Here's what that was all about. Usually, Elle and I are here after hours, so we don't have to bother with checking in. But now, we have to play nice with others, so we get in line along with everyone else.

I scope out the reception desk and see two girls sitting behind it. They aren't much older than Elle and me. The first girl has cocoa skin, long hair, and a nametag that reads *"Tamara."* The other has exotic almond-shaped eyes and long straight hair. Her name tag says *"Cinnamyn."* They're both helping out the first person in line who's a middle-aged dude in a blue suit with a goatee.

This will be a long wait. We've got about eight people ahead of us, I'd guess. I turn to Elle. "When were we supposed to get here?"

"Ten a.m."

I check my watch. "It's five after. We're running a little late. Should we text him again?"

Elle scrunches her mouth. "I did text him. It still isn't going through."

"Maybe he turned off his phone or something."

"Maybe." Elle goes on tiptoe to check out the line. It's not moving. "Let's give it another couple of minutes and see where we are."

Tamara starts gabbing away to her coworker. There's nothing else to do, so I listen in. "Did you hear?" she asks.

Now, I know the opening salvo into gossip. And the way Tamara asked that question while raising her voice when she said *"hear?"* Something good is coming up.

"Hear what?" asks Cinnamyn.

"Alec came in early today." Tamara bobs her perfectly coiffed eyebrows up and down. She looks like a million bucks.

Elle and I share a side-eye glance. This look says, *maybe,* as in *maybe they aren't talking about OUR Alec.*

"How early?" Cinnamyn slowly pulls out a purple Sharpie and writes a name on a sticker badge with such care, it's like she's moving in slow motion. I know this trick. I use it in tutoring sessions all the time. Elle calls it the labor fake. I call it goofing around. Either way, I'm glad it's happening since it might be giving Elle and me some useful information.

Tamara pauses for dramatic effect. "Eight a.m."

"No. Way." Cinnamyn gasps. "The vice president of *who knows what* never saunters in before noon."

Elle and I share a knowing smile. Vice president of who knows what? Check. Sauntering around? Check again.

Oh, they're talking about our Alec, all right.

Now, you might think that receptionists wouldn't spend their time gossiping when there is a long line of people waiting for badges, but I've seen the LeCharme payroll. These ladies are sorely in need of a raise. It's something I plan to bring up to Alec one of these days. So, a little gossiping is like a makeshift bonus, really.

Tamara sets down her Sharpie. "Why was he in so early?"

The Goatee Dude pulls on the neck of his dress shirt. "Aren't you done with my name badge yet? I have a very important appointment."

Tamara glares at him. "One moment, sir. I'm almost done."

I think I like Tamara.

After that, Tamara writes the guy's name so slowly you can barely tell she's alive. It reminds me of those people who pose like statues in Central Park.

"Well." Cinnamyn looks around, probably to see if any LeCharme employees are milling about. It's just us and the other badge-needers, so she keeps right on going. "He showed up with a specific list of rare and unusual jewels, *and* he asked that they be brought up from the vaults to his office."

"Why would be do that?" Tamara keeps staring at Cinnamyn, the finished name badge held between her fingers. Goatee Dude snaps it from her hand and marches off in a huff. The next person in line steps up to the counter, and Tamara holds up her pointer finger. "One sec." She lowers her voice. "So, what was that all about?"

"I don't know," answers Cinnamyn. "But he also asked for fresh flowers to be delivered to his office. And he's having lunch for two being brought in today from Chez Monique, which is only the most romantic restaurant in Manhattan."

Tamara gasps. "No."

Elle grabs my hand so hard she digs her nails into my palm. That's her "holy crap" move. Alec arranged jewels, flowers, and a fancy lunch? I swear, if Alec isn't doing all this for Elle, I'm going to take a baseball bat and smack in his surfer-dude face.

Suddenly, the lobby fills with dozens of stylish men and women, all in black suits. Folks stand around tables, lounge by the windows, and talk in small groups. Tamara and Cinnamyn immediately stiffen in their chairs. It's like someone jammed a cattle prod into their backsides. The two of them start tearing through the line of folks waiting to get badges. In fact, they go so quickly it's like watching a movie on fast-forward.

Seconds later, Alec strides into the lobby. Instantly, it's clear why everyone just so happens to be hanging around right now. The crowd swarms Alec the moment he shows up. As always, he looks very handsome and surfer-guy smiley in his black suit. He's no Knox, but Elle's panting up a storm.

Not that either of us care about those boys.

The suits start to move in and out of Alec's hearing range. It's like some complex dance as they call out different requests and greetings.

"Good morning, Mr. LeCharme."

"Mr. LeCharme. It's Lou in Purchasing. I'd like to show you my proposal for Asia Pacific." Lou then whips out said proposal and flashes it in Alec's direction. "Maybe you could put in a good word with your parents?"

"Hey, Al. Don't know if you remember me. Paulie from Sales. Some of the guys are going out to a club tonight, if you want to go."

It's amazing how Alec absolutely ignores them all. I'd think it was kind of rude except his gaze is locked on Elle, and she's blushing her face off. He raises his arm. "Elle, Bryar! I was wondering where you were." After sauntering up to the reception desk, Alec gives Tamara and Cinnamyn his best surfer-dude smile. "They don't need badges."

Tamara and Cinnamyn only stare with their jaws open. Eventually, they nod. After that, Alec and Elle go back to staring at each other but don't actually go anywhere or say anything. *Awkward.*

Finally, Alec leans forward to give Elle a quick peck on the cheek. "Good morning."

She blushes an even darker shade of red. "Hi."

I shoot him a wave. "Hey, Alec."

"I'm so excited you're both here. I can't wait to show you your new workspace. I got it all set up."

"Thanks." Elle frowns. "So we're not…going to your office?"

"No, you're here for the internship, right?"

Elle's frown deepens. "Oh. Yes. Sure."

"Then, follow me."

Alec leads us through a maze of hallways until we reach a huge storage room. After entering in the longest key code ever, he lets us inside. Everything here is bare concrete. Wide filing cabinets line the left-hand wall. Along the right is the biggest computer setup I've ever seen. My fingers itch to get on the keyboard. This thing makes what I had at Elle's cabin look like crap on a cracker.

Alec rubs his neck. "This room isn't too big, but you know real estate in Manhattan."

"I don't know, Alec." I step around. "It's pretty big." Three of Elle's condos could fit in here.

"It's not furnished, though. This is where Knox and I have been working on our papyri stuff."

At the mention of Knox's name, my stomach decides that now is a great time to do somersaults. *Stupid stomach.* After that, my mouth comes to the decision that it should move on its own. "Is Knox around?"

"Mister Moody?" Alec does another one of his men's catalog poses where he sets his hands in his pockets while rocking back on his heels. "I don't know. Haven't seen him in a while. Why do you ask?"

"No reason."

Elle shoots me a look that says, *I know the reason.*

I stick out my tongue at her, just a little bit. "Actually, I was wondering if he knew the computer system and where the images of the papyri were stored." *So there.*

Alec rubs his chin. "He does know this setup better than me. I'll send him over when I see him."

"Sure. Or don't. I really don't care either way."

Shut. Up. Mouth.

After that, Alec shows me all the papyri images stored on the computer system. It's pretty sweet. They even have a high-speed web connection with badass encryption, so I can download all my old images from the cabin as well. Perfect.

I sit down in the high-back roller chair before the wall of computers and monitors. "I can't wait to get started."

"Great." Alex motions to the far wall. "There's a photo station over there. We've got a hi-res camera hooked up with a FireWire to your system." He turns to the wall of long cabinets. "All the *new* papyri are in the first four cabinets."

My brows lift. "That many have just come in?"

"Well, let's just say they're new to you. You'll find them on your hard drive marked with 'NB' on the file name."

I'm still not following. "NB?"

Alec winces. "No Bryar."

"Wait, what? I thought I got all your shipments."

"Not exactly," says Alec. "I always got photo evidence before I made my final payment for papyri. I've been letting you find all the shipments that I was sure Knox and I couldn't decipher."

"You're kind of a dick." I set my fist on my hip. "You know that, right?"

His surfer-guy grin is back. "It's one of my best qualities."

"I'm so not commenting on that one." Instead, I sit down before my new supercomputer, and I click through the NB folders on my desktop. My eyes widen so much, I'm surprised they're still in my head. This is like seeing another half of a sheet in my treasured five-foot-long papyri puzzle, only with a bunch of the missing pieces filled in. "Wow. These are amazing. I can already see a few scraps that will really help."

"Great." Alec turns to Elle. "And as for you..." He rakes his hand through his wavy blond hair. "There's some stuff I want you to see in my..." He opens his mouth, but no words come out.

Elle smiles sweetly. This really is one of her best faces. "Yes?"

"This might seem over the top, but maybe you could come to my..."

Enough already. At this rate, it will take them an hour to leave, and I have papyri to investigate. "Why don't you two go to Alec's office?"

"Yes." Alec exhales. "I mean, if that's all right with Elle. You see, I found some more jewelry pieces that might be stolen. Thought you might want to take a look."

"Sure. I'd like that."

Alec beams. "Good."

They do that thing again where they stare at each other without moving. I've just about had it with this. I point toward the door. "The exit is that way."

Now, I'd worry about my best friend and Alec, who's a warden, player, and clearly not boyfriend material, but I happen to know for a fact that she is not interested in him at all. Just like I don't care about Knox. So there.

At last, Alec and Elle leave the room. I dive into my papyri work. Hours fly by. At some point, my stomach starts growling, but I ignore it. The information I'm turning up is simply amazing. And Alec is right about there being a pattern to the glyphs. If you use a repeating sequence of choosing every fourth symbol, you come up with an entirely different set of messages.

My pulse speeds as I link together my first sentences from his hidden code. "In using this magic, you will be able to achieve eternal life by becoming a..."

I stare at the glyph. That can't be right.

Nope, it's right.

"I mean, your body *can* achieve eternal youth by becoming a mummy. Sort of." I scrub my hands over my face. This must be a mistake. Sure, in ancient Egypt, it was believed that mummies gave the spirit a place to return, but that was only the spirit. No one thought the body actually stayed alive.

I look at the glyphs again. Retranslate. It still says the same thing. I lean back in my chair, ready to give up for a little while and take a break. There has to be a snack machine around here somewhere.

That's when the small hairs on my neck prickle with awareness. Someone's here.

I slowly swivel in my roller chair, and there he is. *Knox*. He looks badass in blue jeans, boots, and a black T-shirt. I wave, which is dumb, but I can't think of anything else to do. "Hey."

"Hey."

"How long have you been watching me?"

"A while. You looked too engrossed for me to bug you." He holds his hands up with his palms forward. "I'm not a stalker; I swear."

"I believe you. Maybe." With that, my head gets a little swoony, which means one of my attacks is coming on. "Can you excuse me for a minute?"

"Sure."

I head for the nearest bathroom at warp speed. Luckily, there's one in the workroom, so I don't have to go outside, meander the halls, and then figure out that complex key code to get back in. Once I'm safe inside the ladies' room, I pull out my inhaler and take about a half-dozen deep puffs of medicine. Then I fix my lip gloss, fluff my hair, and try not to look like I just freaked out because Knox walked into the room.

The whole experience takes less than five minutes, after which time I'm back at my work chair, trying to look casual. "So, why did you stop by?"

"First, to apologize for being an ass. Again." He rubs the scruff along his chin. "You drive my wolf a little crazy."

"I do?" The question comes out as a squeak, so I force my voice down an octave. "I mean, I do. Is that normal?"

"Not for me. But it's cool. I'm getting the hang of it." He gives me a lopsided smile that melts my insides. "I also came here to show you the truth about the Denarii."

"The truth?"

"Remember, I promised you that in the car ride back from the Adirondacks."

"Yes, I remember." *I was just freaking out too much to access any memories.*

"That's why I came by." He tilts his head, a move I've seen him do before. "But now, I'm thinking that may have been a bad idea."

"Is something wrong with your wolf?"

"Why do you ask?"

"When you tilted your head in the car, it was because your wolf was talking to you." *Not that I memorize every little thing you do or anything.*

"Yeah, about that." Knox grits his teeth. "I need to change."

I hop to my feet. "Now? This very minute?"

"Yeah." Knox laces his fingers behind his neck. "My wolf wants to see you. Know that you're safe. It's how we shifters are. Touch is really important."

"Touching."

"Yeah. If I don't change now, I'll need to go." Knox takes a few steps away. I step into his path.

"No, you can stay." I walk toward the door. "I'll wait outside."

"No!" Knox winces with pain. "No. Wolf wants you here. Just…" He keeps wincing and not talking, so I decide to offer up a plan.

"How about this? I'll turn my back." I turn myself toward the computer monitors, but I can still see some of Knox's reflection. *Oops.* For some reason, I decide not to share that fact. "We all good?"

"That works. Thanks."

"Oh. What about the door?"

"Only Alec has the key code, and he's seen everything before." After that, I hear the swish of fabric and the hum of a zipper opening. And yes, I see lots of muscly muscles reflected in the computer monitor. *I am a very bad person.*

Suddenly, Knox hunches over. Loud cracks sound. I wince in sympathy. Those are his bones breaking and taking a new form. *Yow.* The reflections in the computer monitor disappear. A few seconds later, something wet nudges my hand.

Looking down, I see a huge black wolf at my side. His upper haunches reach my shoulders. His muzzle is angled low to touch my palm. That scent I smelled before—sandalwood and musk—becomes overpowering in its yumminess.

I gently stroke along the wolf's neck. "Aren't you beautiful?" Wolf-Knox wags his tail, so I guess I'm doing this right. "I didn't get a good look at you when you were killing Madame."

Mentioning the attack from Madame seems to set off Wolf-Knox's protective instincts. He prowls around me in a circle before setting his paws on my shoulders. They're big as dinner plates and super-heavy. After that, Wolf-Knox moves in to nuzzle my cheek. A sense of warmth blossoms through my chest.

On reflex, I stroke Wolf-Knox's fur. It's both feather-soft and warm. "There we are." My voice is gentle. "I'm safe."

Wolf-Knox nuzzles me some more, and we stay like that for a while. A sense of contentment washes through me like nothing I've ever felt. Warmth pulses through my veins. Our eyes meet, and Wolf-Knox's irises turn from gold to blue. I don't know why, but I feel certain that's a good thing.

I pat his neck again. "Better now?"

In reply, Wolf-Knox nuzzles my neck one last time and turns away. The crack of bones sounds again. His body contorts at painful-looking angles. Some little part of me knows that Knox is changing back into his human form, and I should turn away. However, that little insight isn't making it from my cerebral cortex to any other part of my body. I can only stand around and watch him make the change.

Knox's limbs stretch and shrink. The fur disappears, and his bones realign. I thought the sight would be frightening, but it's oddly beautiful.

Within a few seconds, Knox is crouched on the floor. I can see his wide shoulders and the sculpted muscles of his back and legs. When he looks up, his ice-blue eyes lock with mine. "Thanks for seeing my wolf."

"You're welcome. Your wolf is sweet."

"He likes you too."

A long pause follows in which I try not to keep staring at how ripped Knox is. I'm not sure I do a good job.

Knox is the one who breaks the silence. "Hey, I gotta..." He looks at me as if the rest of his thought is obvious.

"You gotta what?"

"Change, Bryar."

My mind isn't working so well for some reason. Too many muscles, maybe. "You want to change into a wolf?"

"No, into my clothes." A sly look brightens the hard lines of his face. "So unless you want to watch..."

"I got it. No problem." I quickly turn around. A swish of fabric and more zipper noises follow. This time, I'm not standing in the right position for the monitors to let me cheat and take a peep, though. That shouldn't make me as sad as it does.

"Okay, I'm ready."

"Really? It's only been a few seconds." I turn around, and sure enough, Knox is totally dressed. I guess being a werewolf makes you an expert at this kind of situation.

"So, now you get the answers I promised you, yeah?"

I hug my elbows. "The truth about the Denarii."

"That's the stuff. It's easier if I show you than tell you. Are you sure you want to do this?"

Not at all. Still, this is something I need to know, so I mentally pull up my big-girl panties and meet Knox's gaze head-on. "Absolutely."

"Then let's go."

As Knox and I head out the door, I get the feeling like I'm passing across a different kind of threshold. Behind me, there is the Bryar Rose who didn't know what the Denarii really were. In the near future, there will be Bryar-the-badass who has faced something terrible. I force my breathing to slow.

I can do this. I have to.

⚘

CHAPTER TWELVE
BRYAR ROSE

Knox and I take the employee elevator to the basement. After that, he shows me to an old broom closet. He opens the door and gestures for me to walk inside. I give him the stink eye.

"That's a broom closet."

"No, it's not. There's an elevator in there."

"Are you sure? I hacked up the architectural plans on this building myself. There's no elevator in this spot."

Knox gives me another lopsided smile. "Hacked up? Is that a real phrase? I mean, unless you're a cat."

"Ha-ha. I'm serious." I set my fists on my hips. "I am not walking into a sketchy broom closet with you, even if you are handsome."

Crap, I said that out loud, didn't I?

His black brows jet up. "So, I'm handsome, yeah?"

I'd face-palm myself if it wouldn't make things worse. "You know you are."

Knox chuckles all low and sexy-like, which is super-distracting. "Okay, fine. Get closer. I'll show you."

I take what can only be described as mincing steps to stand in the doorway. I prop the door open with my shoulder as Knox strides inside and flicks on the light switch. The room is a small concrete box filled with mops, buckets, and brooms. Knox steps to the back of the space where the far wall is lined with cleaning supplies. Gripping the wooden frame, he heaves the shelves to one side. They slide away with ease. It reminds me of those haunted house movies where you pull on a wall sconce and a secret passageway appears.

I lean in closer. "What's back there, exactly?"

Knox flips another switch, and an ancient lightbulb flickers on, revealing what looks like an old-fashioned elevator inside the wall. Huh. I definitely didn't know that existed, and Elle and I have been snooping around this particular building for ages. I take a few tentative steps into the broom closet. Sure enough, there's definitely an elevator in here. It's one of those ancient thingies with a gate for a door.

"The elevator leads to the basement. What I need to show you is there."

"That doesn't sound sketchy."

"Trust me, if there was an easier way to do this, I'd take it." Knox hauls the gate open and gestures past it. "Are you still in?"

"Sure." I tiptoe around the maze of buckets and brooms until I reach what was once the back wall. I stare into the small elevator. This thing is an ancient and dusty mess. When was the last time anyone inspected this monstrosity? Or even cleaned it? My stomach gets all flooey. It's like I'm riding a Ferris wheel at top speed. I may be a little afraid of falling. Elle says I'm a wimp when it comes to heights. I always tell her I'm wise and cautious about vertically challenging situations.

"Are you sure this is safe?" I ask.

"I'm pretty sure it isn't. Why? Are you scared?"

That pushes my buttons in a big way. I refuse to let anything stop me from discovering the truth, even if that something is a scary-ass elevator that looks like it was assembled with Popsicle sticks and glue. "Not at all." I stride inside. The elevator rocks wildly the second my heels touch the floor. Grabbing onto the dusty metal grid that serves as the elevator's walls, I let out a very unladylike "Yipes."

"The floor wobbles," says Knox.

"You think?" I'm grabbing onto the metal grid so tightly, it's cutting off circulation to my fingertips.

"Don't worry. This won't take long." Knox steps into the elevator and pulls the accordion-style doorway shut.

Nothing in this thing is solid metal. The grid-like walls seem about as sturdy as a chain-link fence. And that door looks like it could crumple any second. My pulse races. Knox starts pulling on some levers along the ceiling, and the elevator lurches to life. I'm not going to lie; at this point, I freak out like a total sissy.

Without even thinking about it, I wrap my arms around Knox's waist, bury my nose in his neck, and squeeze my eyes shut. "Tell me when it's over."

He lets out a rumbling chuckle. "I will."

A few seconds pass during which I dig my nails into Knox's back. "Why aren't we moving?"

"We're, uh, stuck."

Something about his words just smell off to me, although I can't imagine why I'm smelling sentences. "You're totally lying."

"Well, yeah." He wraps his right arm around me, resting his heavy palm on the small of my back.

Uh-oh. I'm in a broom-closet-elevator thing with Knox. My body is pressed against his very firm and super-rugged self. Worst of all, he smells unbelievably amazing. I try to firm up my resolve. This is the part where I tell him he's a jerk and I step away.

Maybe I slap him on the cheek like in an old-time movie.

Or, I could at least yell at him to start the stupid elevator again.

But I do none of those things. Standing here and being held really is simply way too nice.

Knox lowers his left arm from the levers in the ceiling. His fingertips brush along my jawline while his thumb runs across my lower lip. My insides flip-flop at his touch, and it's not necessarily a bad feeling.

Little by little, Knox guides my face upward so I'm no longer nuzzling his neck, but staring into his eyes. He has these ice-blue irises. I never noticed before, but there's a lot of gold in them as well.

"I want to kiss you, Bry." His voice is a deep rasp that's so strong I feel it in my chest, too.

I try to think of something romantic and magical to say. After all, I'm pretty sure I'm about to have my first kiss. It feels like there should be some ceremony. Instead, all I can think about is how Knox has a really yummy-looking mouth. So all my plans for verbal fireworks go out the window.

I only whisper a single word. "Okay."

Our lips meet in the barest touch. Excitement zings through me. I fist the fabric of Knox's T-shirt. Someone growls, and I think it might be me, which is super-weird. Although I've never done this before, so maybe growling is totally normal. I could not care less either way because now we're both opening our mouths as we move past the gentle brushing stuff. I'm not going to lie. It feels amazing. Knox angles my head, and I go with his lead. His tongue licks along my bottom lip, and my knees turn wobbly beneath me.

For the record, I really wish I had started kissing earlier in life. Because if this is what I've been missing out on? I'm downright nuts. Some kind of connection forms between us. It's so intense it could even be supernatural. My blood heats in ways I never imagined.

A voice echoes up through the elevator shaft below our feet. "Knoxie, poxie, my sweetest little doxie."

I break the kiss. "What was that?"

Knox shifts his stance, moving until our foreheads lean together. "Sorry about him."

The nasal voice sounds again. "Knoxes, boxes, munch, and scrunch. Who is coming to bring me lunch?" That's a grown man, and if I'm not mistaken, he's also very, very insane.

"Let me try again. *Who* is that?"

"He's who I'm bringing you to see." Knox raises his arm to grab another lever in the ceiling. He brushes a gentle kiss across my mouth. "Sorry we got cut off." He stares at the floor. "I didn't realize

Reggie was awake." Knox yanks down on a lever, and with a lurch, we start to descend.

"Where does this elevator go?" As the words leave my mouth, I realize that was maybe a better question *before* I got into the elevator in the first place.

"Sub-basement. It's where we keep our resident Denarii."

"Reggie?"

"That's the one."

The elevator floor shimmies beneath my feet as we descend even lower. "Why is he down here?"

"I'll let him explain. It's easier that way."

The elevator stops with a thud. Knox turns to me. "Whatever you do, don't get too close to his cage, yeah?"

I nod, mostly because my throat closed up at the mention of the word *"cage."* Am I right that there's a Denarii person down here who's locked up, possibly against his will? What exactly have I gotten myself into?

Knox takes my hand and leads me out of the elevator and into a long corridor with doors on either side. No, these aren't doors. They all have bars over them. These are cells.

"What exactly is this place?"

"Are you bringing me a girl, Knoxie? Girly, twirly, pretty little swirly."

"Can it, Reggie." Knox turns to me. "This used to be an underground prison back in the 1900s. Technically, the city closed it down. But Alec's family cleaned it out and built an elevator to it. That happened some time in the 1930s."

"That long ago?"

"Warlocks and witches live for a long while. Alec's parents didn't start a family until they were well over a hundred."

"But their bios online say they're both only in their forties."

"Yeah, well. Let's just say that's not exactly accurate." Knox glances at me over his shoulder. "You aren't the only one with criminal skills, Bry."

I shrug. "It makes sense, actually. Changing your birthday and life history isn't a big deal, so long as you have the money for a good hacker and forger." I try to ignore the fact that the muscles in my back are bunching up with fear. This Reggie guy sounds terrifying.

Knox stops in front of one of the cells. "And here we are."

The place is a prison cell like all the others. A single lightbulb hangs from the ceiling and illuminates a pool of brightness on the center of the stone floor. A figure sits in the shadows just beyond the circle of light. Reggie. All I can see of the guy are his shiny wingtip oxfords.

Wait a second. *Oxfords?*

"Come on out, Reggie," orders Knox. "And no singing."

"If you insist." There's a long squeal as Reggie's metal chair slides behind him. He stands up and strides toward the wall of metal bars that mark the edge of his cell. I can't believe what I'm seeing. I don't know what I expected Reggie to look like, but this wasn't it. The guy is wearing a three-piece suit made out of gray wool. It's the high-waisted kind that was popular back in the 1950s. He's topped off the look with a matching fedora. I take a half step backward.

He's dressed just like Madame. They both could have fallen out of the same 1950s ad for toothpaste.

"I'm Reginald Winston the Second. Reggie to my friends." He extends his hand through the bars.

Knox sets his palm on my stomach, guiding me farther toward the opposite wall and away from Reggie. "She's not touching you."

"Pity." Reggie has that clean-cut mannequin-like quality, which also reminds me of Madame. He has brown hair, blue eyes, and skin that's so porcelain-smooth, it's downright creepy. There are a few flecks of gray at his temples. "She looks delicious."

"She's here to find out what you Denarii are. Nothing more."

"Is that all? Well, most Denarii are fine, upstanding citizens."

"You're not, and you know it."

"I won't say a word."

Knox's voice lowers to a growl. "Then you don't eat."

"You're a beast."

"Absolutely."

"Fine." Reggie rolls his eyes. "If you insist. I was born Regius Paullus Agrippa, Lieutenant of the Aegypti Legion. I served under none other than Julius Caesar." He gives me a toothpaste-fresh smile. "Does that surprise you?"

My mind whirls at this information. "You've been alive for two thousand years."

"Correct."

"No, that doesn't totally surprise me."

He half lowers his eyelids in a move that says he thinks I'm full of crap. "And why is that?"

"Julius Caesar burned the library at Alexandria. That's where the only full copies of the *Book of Magic* was stored. Whatever is keeping you alive for so long, it must have to do with the spells in that book."

"Quite right. You're not as infantile as you look."

Knox bares his teeth. "Watch it, Reggie."

My curiosity about this situation seems to overpower any fear about who Reggie is. It certainly short circuits any worries about him insulting me. I give Knox's forearm a pat. Touching him feels so natural I don't even think twice about it. "It's okay, Knox." I refocus on Reggie. "Were you with Caesar when he burned the library down?"

"Yes, and together, we saved the *Book of Magic*."

I straighten my shoulders. Here comes the big question. My skin prickles with gooseflesh. "How exactly have you stayed alive so long?"

"That *is* the mystery, isn't it? The answer was in those papyri. Julius had to torture the priests for hours to get them to translate it for us. It was all hidden in code and special hieroglyphs. Coding, boding, hiding, and reloading."

"Enough, Reggie," warns Knox. "Just answer her question."

Reggie grins, showing a mouth of inhumanly perfect teeth. "If I could have answered that, I would have already. Truth is, I don't know how the process of immortality works. I just know that it does. I wasn't awake when they did it to me."

My fear comes back with a vengeance. My pulse thumps so hard I feel it in my skull. "What did they do to you?"

"It's easier if I show you." Reggie tips his hat to Knox. "Do I have your permission?"

"Ask her," snarls Knox.

Reggie resets his hat and turns to me. "I'll need to remove my jacket and shirt to show you. Is that acceptable?"

"Yes, it's fine." I'm proud of how calm my voice sounds, because inside? My fight-or-flight response has kicked in, big–time.

"Then I shall show you." With calm movements, Reggie slips off his jacket and matching vest. After that, he loosens his tie, unbuttons the top of his shirt, and pulls them both over his head. With that done, Reggie steps right under the light and lifts his arms wide. "Behold my perfection!"

I set my hand over my mouth to hide my gag reflex. I've seen chest wounds like his before. The zigzag incisions are unique to a certain kind of mummy-making from ancient Egypt. I always thought that only the priests of Isis made cuts like these, but I could never be one hundred percent certain.

Not until now, that is.

Images appear in my mind: the coded message from the papyri that I translated today.

Living forever as a mortal, only in mummy form.

And this guy is doing just that.

"You're a mummy." My words come out as a whisper.

"Yes, I underwent the process back in 48 AD." He touches his various body parts as he speaks. "I've no heart, stomach, or lungs." He taps his temple. "My brains are gone as well, at least in physical form."

Enough of my researcher instinct is left that I don't scream and run. "So, how are you alive?"

"I should think that's obvious." An evil smile rounds his mouth. "But if you can't guess, I'll tell you."

With that, my researcher instinct dies a quick death. That creepy smile is all I need to know, really. I raise my hand in the universal sign for shut up. "You know what? I'll pass."

But Reggie keeps right on going. "I must consume organs from someone else. Preferably another human. An animal will do in a pinch, however."

Yuck, yuck, a thousand times yuck.

I turn to Knox. "Is this true?"

"I'm afraid so, yeah." He sets his hand on the back of my neck. The touch is warm and centering. "Is this too much? Want to go?"

My head is spinning, but I don't feel an episode coming on, so it seems safe enough for now. Plus, if I leave here? I'm not sure I'll ever come back and ask more questions. Best to get it all done now. I make myself look at the living mummy again. "Why are you here?"

"Why, sigh, try, sky...why does the pretty girl ask me why?"

"No playing around," orders Knox. "Tell her how you ended up here."

"I'm a little unbalanced. My fellow Denarii decided to put me out of my misery." He cups his hand by his mouth and speaks in a fake whisper. "They wanted to kill me."

Knox rubs his thumb in calming arcs on my neck. "I run a sort of sideline killing evil Denarii. I ran across Reggie in Africa. He was slated to be killed, so we made a deal."

"I receive these fine accommodations," says Reggie. "In exchange, I'm delivered regular meals of raw animal organs. I also provide information and demonstrations when they are required. As they are right now."

I force out my next question. "What happens if you don't eat?"

"Then I'll look like the typical mummies you see in movies. But that's rare. My kind are very good at finding sustenance."

Gross.

"And you don't remember anything about how you were changed?"

Reggie starts dressing himself, which I totally appreciate. "I wasn't exactly a willing part of the process, originally. Someone batted me over the head, and when I woke up? Immortality. If you truly wish the answer to that question, you'll need to find the *Book of Magic* and read it yourself."

"And why are you called the Denarii?"

"We follow Julius Caesar, and his face is on the Denarii coin. Although he goes by the name of Jules these days."

"Jules." My mouth falls open. The coin part I somewhat expected, but the fact that the man himself is still running around? Not so much. "He's alive." I can't seem to wrap my head around this fact. "Julius Caesar is alive." I look to Knox. "Really?"

"Yeah. I've been hunting the guy for years. Never seen him, but he's out there. The man is hard to pin down."

I'm still stuck on my history lessons from forever ago. "I thought they stabbed him to death."

Reggie resets his fedora. "Oh, they most certainly did. After that, Jules ate some brains, and all was well again. The Senate did him a favor, actually. Our lifestyle requires a public death every fifty years or so."

"How many of you are there?"

"That, I wouldn't know. Jules makes as many Denarii as he wants. And he's the only one who can. The *Book of Magic* was the sole place that held the information. After Jules learned the tricks of the trade, as it were, he burned the book. Jules, tools, pretty little fools." Reggie races forward until his body slams into the bars of the cell. It makes me jump.

"Cut it out, Reggie. You're scaring her."

But Reggie keeps right on going. His eyes seem to bug out of their sockets, he stares at me so hard. "Bye, sigh, pretty little cry, your wedding day is when you DIE."

Every muscle in my body tenses. According to my life template, I'm supposed to get married by sundown on my birthday. That's Saturday, which is a little over 24 hours from now. "I'm not marrying anyone."

Knox's voice lowers to a menacing growl. "That's enough, Reggie. Say one more thing, and you won't eat for a week."

Reggie tilts his head back and lets out a laugh that can only be described as maniacal. "I don't speak. Jules does." He flaps his arms up and down. "We're all little puppets on his strings."

"That's it, Reggie. No food for a week. Want to suffer longer? Keep it up."

Knox says other things to Reggie, but all I can focus on is the name he just shared. "Jules. Julius Caesar." The concrete walls start to press in on me. My chest tightens. Silver pulses flash on the periphery of my vision. It's there again… That damned locked-down container inside the deepest part of my being. The magical box of Colonel Mallory's curse.

I'm going to have another episode.

I reach for my bag. There's nothing there. I left my purse behind. I grip Knox's shoulder. "Need my bag…at desk…episode… inhaler…"

After that, the world turns hazy. I'm vaguely aware of Knox's arms around me as I fight to stay awake.

CHAPTER THIRTEEN
KNOX

Damn that Reggie. What a sick creep.

I want to open up his cell, race inside, and beat that Denarii's face in. How dare he frighten Bryar Rose? There's no time to worry about Reggie, though—I have bigger problems. Bryar Rose's eyes are starting to roll back into her head. She grips my black T-shirt, curling her fists into the fabric. Only a few minutes ago, she did the same thing as she kissed me. Now, she's having one of her episodes. Her scent turns acrid with panic.

At that smell, my wolf loses his freaking mind. He howls inside my brain. *"Mate hurt! Help!"*

"Don't worry. I got this."

Leaning over, I scoop Bryar Rose into my arms and pull her tight against my chest.

Reggie keeps smiling, the freak. "Eyes and lies, that one's Jules' special prize. Watch it now, or soon she dies."

I'm so concerned about Bryar Rose that I don't hear half of what Reggie's babbling about. Not that it matters. He's always going on about his "special connection to Jules." Right now, I don't need to get distracted by his crazy. "Shut the hell up, Reggie. She's fine." *I just have to get her to her medicine.*

Bryar moans against my chest. She forces her eyes to open a crack. "My bag."

"I'll get you there." I stride away from the cell. Within seconds, I reach the elevator, kick the gate open, and step inside.

"Inhaler..." Bry's trying hard to stay awake, but she's losing the fight.

"We'll get it. I know what you need." I run my nose down the length of hers. "But first, I have to set you down so I can flip the elevator lever. Can you stand up for me?"

For a moment, I think about the pendant that Alec gave me. It's an all-purpose "get out of jail" spell that I can use just once, either to fight a wizard or to cast one of their spells. Right now, I could activate it and cast a transport spell to reach Bry's inhaler. The onyx pendant presses heavily against my chest. I'm tempted to reach for the thing when Bry starts to move.

"Don't worry. I can stand." Bry curls forward, trying to stand on her own. She doesn't have enough control over her own body, though. Instead of staying upright, she tumbles forward in a jerking motion. I gasp as she hurtles toward the floor. Good thing we shifters have strong reflexes. Right before Bry hits the ground, I pull her back onto her feet, careful to keep my arm firmly clasped around her shoulders. "Not much longer." I yank down the lever that sets the elevator in motion. With a lurch, we start to move.

I lift Bry back into my arms once more. Damn, this elevator takes forever.

My wolf starts in again. "*Mate hurt.*"

"*I get it, buddy. But she's not really hurt. She's just falling asleep.*"

"*HURT!*"

I know what he's feeling because I have the same emotion, too. Everything about this situation is setting my shifter instincts on fire. Not only does she give off a smell of fear, but her natural scent has never been stronger. *Honey, cinnamon, and sunshine.* My need to protect her sends adrenaline racing through me.

At last, the elevator stops with a jolt. I boot the stupid gate open again with such force it snaps in two. Still, that's nothing compared to what I do to the broom closet door. I kick the thing down and tear out part of the wall with it. After that, I sprint my way back to her office, and yeah, that door gets crushed in as well. *Fine with me.* In my opinion, this is one of the benefits of being a shifter. Doors don't stop you.

I rush into the room and over to her desk. Bry's black bag sits on her chair. Crouching down, I set Bry into my lap. My left hand holds her firmly against me while my right rifles through the bag. Damn, she has a lot of crap in here. I start throwing stuff out until I find a small plastic inhaler. I slip off the cover and set it by her lips.

"Are you with me, Bryar?"

Her head lolls against my shoulder. "Mmmm?"

"I got your inhaler. Now open your mouth and take a breath."

Bryar keeps her eyes shut, but opens her mouth. The moment her mouth opens, I set the inhaler on her lips. I've never used one of these before, but there's an arrow and a button, so it doesn't seem too complex. I push down, and mist goes onto Bry's tongue. She breathes it in and instantly seems to perk up.

Thank heaven.

That's when the scent hits me. It's a subtle, almost unnoticeable smell, but then again, I'm a werewolf. This close, I can catch the scent, no problem. It's sickly-sweet, like rotten berries. And it can only be one thing: a fairy spell called Predator's Bane, which is incredibly illegal. It's also a spell that only works on werewolves. That's why I know the scent. I've had others try to gas me with it before. It forces werewolves to instantly change back into their human form, even in the middle of a shift. The Denarii tried it on me once. I turned human and naked in the middle of a huge battle. If Alec hadn't shown up and cast a ton of kill spells, I'd be dead right now.

But why give Bry doses of Predator's Bane? She's human. It doesn't affect her...or does it? Bry insists the stuff helps to her "wake up," as she calls it.

My wolf starts freaking out. *"Medicine bad."* He's clawing inside me, trying to break free. *"Protect mate. Medicine bad!"*

Bry moans in my arms. I curl her closer to my chest. My mind races through every kind of magic that could be related to Predator's Bane.

That's when I remember it: the Slumber Beast spell.

It's a curse that Az told me about. Centuries ago, the Shifter Council would give it to criminals as punishment. The Slumber Beast spell makes your animal fall asleep every time you start to shift. But with magic draining away, no one could cast the spell any more, so the Council moved on to other punishments.

And Bry isn't a criminal, so what's happening here?

The answer appears in a flash. Suppose some fairy cast a Slumber Beast spell on Bry. If that's true, she'd freeze whenever she started shifting into her werewolf form. But if she took some Predator's Bane, then she'd instantly become human again. No more shifting, no more Slumber Beast spell. Bry would wake up.

I shake my head. It's all too extreme to be real. Only a handful of folks even know about the Slumber Beast spell. And I'd never even heard about Predator's Bane before the Denarii sprayed some on me.

Bry opens her eyes to the barest of slivers. With shaky movements, she goes to take the inhaler from my hand. It's some kind of reflex, but I hold it away from her. She frowns. "Knox, I need more medicine."

At this point, I've got two choices. First, I can give Bry the medicine and pretend nothing happened. Second, I can ask to see her irises. If her eyes are glowing with a golden light right now, then she *is* a werewolf. The difference between the two options is this: how much do I want to know if Bry is a were?

The moment the question enters my mind, the answer is clear. If Bry really is a werewolf, then I absolutely must know the truth. I lean in closer. "Look at me, Bry."

Her eyebrows raise, but nothing else. "I'm trying."

"No, I need to see your eyes." Nervous energy twists through me. "Please."

Little by little, Bry forces her eyes to open fully. What I see knocks my world over. Her irises are golden.

Bry really is a werewolf.

A line of memories falls into place. Back at the cabin, Bry wore a tank top and shorts in freezing weather without so much as a shiver. Werewolves always run warm. Plus, she's always sniffing and tilting her head, which are total wolf moves. And when Bryar Rose began to pass out, my wolf went nuts inside me. Her animal must have been fighting to get free, and mine could sense it.

Speaking of my wolf, he's none too happy. *"Mate has wolf."* I feel him clawing inside me, wanting to blab everything. *"Tell her now."*

Great. My wolf wants me to announce to Bryar Rose that she's a shifter only seconds after she almost passed out. *"Give me a minute, buddy. She still thinks she's a Sleeping Beauty life template. This isn't going to be easy."*

Bry nuzzles into my shoulder. Her eyes are at half-mast now, but they are definitely still golden. I can't believe it. She's really a werewolf.

"Tell mate now."

"Bud, I've got to take this slowly, or we'll scare the hell out of her."

A long moment passes. Finally, my wolf grunts his agreement. That's as good as I'll get at this point. When I talk to Bry again, I take care to make my voice really gentle. It isn't easy, especially because my wolf isn't the only one who's worked up at this point.

Bry moves to take the inhaler from my hand. "I need more medicine, Knox."

"Not yet, I need to take a look at the inhaler. Is that okay?"

"Sure." She curls into my lap and rests her head against my shoulder. "I shouldn't take more than three or four puffs a day anyway. I took a ton before we left for LeCharme this morning, just to be safe. Something about you…" She yawns. "It brings out the worst in me."

I angle the device for a better look. It's got one of those pharmacy labels on it. "They call this Narconium. Never heard of it. You know what it is?"

"It's a fake label for humans. The medicine is something my aunties make for me out of fairy dust. It's the only thing that helps with my episodes. Otherwise, I'd freeze."

"Your aunties." Rage boils up my spine. Those crazy fairies have been in on whatever scam is being pulled on Bry. It's an effort to keep my voice level. "Your aunties give this to you."

"Sure. They don't have a lot of magic. It's nice of them to cast it for me. It's one of the few times they ever use magic at all."

"You know anything about Predator's Bane?"

"No."

"How about fae attack spells on shifters? Ever hear how those work?"

"Why would I?"

I can't believe what I'm hearing. Everyone knows the spells that fairies use when they attack. Then I think of those scheming aunties and the brochure in her bag. If Bry is in a Magicorum Teen Therapy Group, that means she was home tutored. Maybe those aunties of hers controlled her social life too. Bry wouldn't learn anything that could be really useful. My blood runs hot, and my body aches to shift.

I force myself to stay calm. "How much do you know about other magical races?"

She opens her eyes again. *Still gold.* "Why are you asking me all this?" She reaches for the inhaler. "I should keep taking the medicine until I'm wide awake. It could be dangerous."

"You'll be all right." I brush some strands of hair from her cheek. "Just tell me how much you know about other magical races."

"Not much. Most of my tutoring is about manners, history of human society, that kind of thing."

"So you can marry that Philpot?"

"I'm not getting married." She gives me a sleepy smile. "Are you jealous, Knox?"

I shouldn't get flirty, but with Bry, I can't help it. "Maybe. I mean, I've kissed you and all. My wolf thinks you're my girl."

She yawns again. "That was a great first kiss, even if it was in a creepy elevator."

Those words take my breath away. I'm her first kiss? Bry's aunties have basically hidden her away. Sure, she's not stuck out in a cottage in the woods like it says in the Sleeping Beauty story, but she might as well have been. Bry's certainly stuck to the whole "growing up isolated" part of the tale. Where do I even begin to explain all this?

My wolf is a step ahead of me. *"Help mate."*

The second his words ring through my mind, I know what he means. I need to settle her wolf, and without that damn Predator's Bane.

"Look, Bryar. I can help you wake up without the medicine. Can we give it a try?"

"Will it hurt?"

I run my nose along hers. "No. It won't hurt."

"Okay."

"Give me your eyes again."

We lock gazes once more. As a warden, I'm an alpha wolf. That means I could lead a pack if I wanted to...but I haven't wanted to. Still, I have the alpha's power to connect to other wolves. So far, it hasn't had a ton of uses. But right now? I'm thrilled I have this skill. Keeping my gaze locked with Bry's, I picture my energy flowing around and through her. Suddenly, I can sense her wolf's heart beating a mile a minute inside her. Her animal is beautiful and strong. A fighter. My chest aches with longing to call her animal forth into physical form. I hold back, though.

First things first, and what I need to do right now is calm Bry's wolf. I speak to her in my mind. *"Calm. Peace. You're safe."* After those words, I give the order to Bry's wolf to retreat. Her animal is cautious, but it obeys.

Bry tilts her head. It's such a wolfy movement. I can't believe I didn't suspect she was a were right away. "I'm safe."

"That's right."

Bry's eyes lose their golden glow. She's all human again. "How did you do that?"

I set her on her feet. If I keep touching Bry, I'll be tempted to call her wolf again. "That's a tough question to answer."

"Tougher than the Denarii? Come on, that was pretty terrible."

I step back and take a few seconds to calm my head. This is one of the worst things I have to tell anyone. Not only is Bry a werewolf, but she's about to lose her animal. Unless she shifts by the time the sun sets on her eighteenth birthday, her inner wolf dies.

Her eighteenth birthday is tomorrow. Damn.

There's so much I need to tell her, but I have to give it to her slowly. "I'm so sorry."

"About what? Answering my question? Honestly, what could be worse than Reggie?"

"What I have to tell you? Yeah, I think it might be worse."

"Look, you don't have to worry about me and my episodes. Once I turn eighteen, they'll be over. That's when the spell from Colonel Mallory the Magnificent will end."

Every muscle in my body stiffens. "That's right. Everything changes when you turn eighteen." How many lies have people been telling this girl? And why are they hiding so much from her?

"What's wrong, Knox?"

I shake my head. There's nothing for it but to just tell her. She has a right to know. After all, today is Friday. Tomorrow is her birthday. If she doesn't shift, her wolf will die before sundown. "You better sit for this one."

A voice sounds from the smashed-in doorway. It's one of the security guards. "Excuse me, Knox?"

I glare at the guy, but I'm not really looking at him. Rage streams through me. I can't believe we're being interrupted. *Not now, of all times.* "You got a question, you need to find Alec."

"But we can't find Alec, and it's not really his problem anyway."

My mind starts to think through the haze of anger. I know this guard. He's a total whiner with a bad haircut. Elle maced him in the kisser once. Alec and I watched it on video replay like twenty times.

"Is it a problem in LeCharme?" I ask.

"Why, yes, sir."

"Then it's Alec's problem."

"No, it's the problem of your new employee there. The intern who works in this office. Miss Bryar Rose."

Bry steps forward and straightens her suit. "What seems to be the trouble?"

"Well, I don't mean to interrupt you and Knox…"

I don't like the tone in this scumbag's voice. "Get to your point," I warn.

"Fine. There's a man on the first-floor sales area who's causing trouble. Says he's Philpot Herbert Utrecht the Third. Claims we have his fiancée hostage, and if he can't speak to her right now, he'll call his cousin on the NYPD."

I turn to Bry. "Is this true?"

"Philpot is a little possessive. And yes, his cousin is on the NYPD."

The guard shifts his weight from foot to foot. "I tried to find Alec, but he's not around. And when it came to the interns, he ordered us to speak only to him or you." The guard squints at Bry. "Have we met?"

Bry steps back to her workstation and starts typing away. "Nope, never." She angles her body away from the guard.

I wave the guy off. "We'll be down shortly to handle this situation. You aren't needed anymore."

The guard sets his hands on his hips. "What if this Philpot gets dangerous?"

I glare at him. "If Philpot causes trouble, then Bry and I will kick his ass."

That seems to convince him. The guard stares at the shattered door. "I'll tell maintenance to bring up a fresh door."

"You do that." I have rage issues, so this isn't the first door I've smashed in. I point toward the exit. "Really, you can go."

That seems to do the trick, and the guard walks away. Once he's out of earshot, I turn to Bry. "Are you sure you want to do this? I can go down to the lobby and see him alone."

"I don't want to, but I need to." She grins, and it's like my birthday and Christmas rolled into one. "Maybe it's when you calmed me down instead of my medicine, but I can't remember ever feeling this good. It's like I fit in my own skin." She blushes, which is adorable. "That must sound crazy."

"Hey, I'm glad to help." And by *"help,"* I really mean to help get rid of Philpot so I can tell Bry the truth. She doesn't know she's a werewolf, and she's never shifted. Worry coils through my stomach. Her eighteenth birthday is almost here. If she doesn't shift by then, her animal will die.

No question about it. Once we get rid of Philpot, I'll let Bry know the truth.

We walk side by side toward the main elevator bank. I try to focus on how to confront this Philpot loser, but I can't stop thinking about the fact that Bry is really a werewolf.

What if my wolf is right? Could Bry be my mate?

A weight of sadness settles on my shoulders. I'm a warden. We don't have mates. And even if we did, I couldn't risk the mating ceremony with her. No one's lived past that. Plus, what kind of ass would I be to lock someone as amazing as Bryar Rose into my crazy life? I roam the world hunting Denarii. She deserves so much more than I could ever give her.

No, I'll let Bry know who she is, and then, I'll let her go.

With that decision behind me, I focus on facing the dead man who claims to be her fiancé.

CHAPTER FOURTEEN
BRYAR ROSE

Knox and I walk toward the main set of elevators. The hallways around here are all deserted. The offices are too. The ones with open doors only hold a few sticks of furniture.

"Where is everybody?" I ask.

"Alec doesn't let anyone work near our papyri."

"Makes sense."

The place is so quiet I can hear my own breathing. A heavy sense of worry fills the air. I really don't want to deal with Philpot right now. I'd rather think about how Knox just made me feel better without my inhaler. What was up with that?

I sigh. Much as I'd like to contemplate Knox, there's no way to avoid Philpot when he's in a snit. I'll just have to deal with my fake boyfriend now and think about what happened with Knox later.

Once we reach the elevators, Knox cups my face in his hands. "You ready?"

The more I see Knox's face close-up, the more I love the scars on his eyebrow and chin. I reach up and run my pointer finger along the one on his brow. "Did you get this fighting Denarii?"

Knox closes his eyes and leans into my touch. "Yeah."

I gently brush the one along his jawline. "And this too?"

"Same." He opens his eyes, and the intense flash of ice blue makes my breath catch. "You're not answering my question."

"You noticed, huh?"

"What can I say? I'm smart like that." A small smile rounds his full mouth while his thumbs make little arcs on my cheeks. It makes my stomach flip-flop with happiness.

"Look, I appreciate your offer and all, but I think I should go alone."

"Absolutely not. I'm going with you." His eyes flash with specks of gold. That must mean his wolf is getting riled up.

All the more reason for me to face Philpot solo. If my fake boyfriend is already making enough of a scene to drag in security, then adding a wolfed-up Knox into the mix isn't a good idea.

I give Knox my most casual smile. "I won't be alone. I've texted Elle about a million times today." I carefully avoid sharing how she hasn't replied yet. "She'll show up and help."

Here's the real deal on this one. I know Elle is a lost cause. My texts aren't even going through. Still, I do not want to have Knox around while Philpot's having one of his hissy fits. Plus, if I know His Highness of Whine-ness, I'm sure he's called my aunties in as well. If those three show up, that's even more humiliation. I'd rather Knox never saw any of it.

Knox slides his hand down to entwine our fingers. "Look, Bry. I'm in this now. You're strong, beautiful, and smart. And all the work you've done on the papyri? You could have been hanging with Philpot or listening to nonsense from your aunties, but you've chosen to do something with your life. I respect the hell out of that. I'm guessing this guy is downstairs and acting like an ass."

I nod. Nothing else to say to that, really.

"So, you're walking into a tough situation. There's no way I'll allow someone as amazing as you to walk into the line of fire alone. I will be at your side."

I open my mouth, ready to clarify who exactly will be in that line of fire. "Um—"

"Hey, I get where you're going with this. You're all worried that your aunties will show or Philpot will be a freak, but you have to give me more credit than to be turned away by something like that. Please know this. Whatever happens, I will fight with everything in me to stand at your side right now."

Well, okay then.

That was quite the awesome speech. In fact, I can't stop the huge smile that spreads across my face. "Just don't break down any more doors."

Knox chuckles. "That's between Alec and me. Over the years, he's learned to buy them in bulk."

I give his hand a squeeze and then let go. I'm glad that Knox is offering to help out, but it's a little scary how much I've come to rely on him in just a few short days. I have to be cautious. My feelings for him are growing too strong and too fast.

Taking a big step away from Knox, I hitch my thumb toward the door. "I know a shortcut to the lobby."

"Somehow, I never doubted that." He lowers his voice to a sexy growl. "Alec and I have seen you two on the security tapes, you know."

"Oh. The first time I met Alec, he knew Elle and I had, uh, *visited* LeCharme before, but you've been watching us?" *Come on.* I specifically hacked up a special security code to avoid video, not that I'm sharing that with Knox.

"A little." He gives me a lopsided grin.

"Oh." I can't seem to stop saying that over and over. The urge to kiss Knox hits me again, so I decide to do the mature thing. Walk away—and fast.

With quick steps, I lead us on the fast path to the elevator banks and press a button for the reception floor. Once we're inside and on the move, I can't help but notice how much fancier this elevator is than the last one that Knox and I just rode in to see Reggie. Also, I can't help but think about the kiss we shared there, too.

Focus, Bryar.

Less than a minute later, the metal doors slide open to reveal the main sales floor of LeCharme. This morning when Elle and I walked in here, the place was abuzz with activity. Now, it's absolutely quiet. Everyone stands around staring. Some buyers are leaning over display cases with half-finished purchases in their hands. All eyes are fixed on Philpot.

Nightmare, table for one.

The quiet is broken as Philpot marches around the sales floor while waving his arms. "Who's in charge here? Where is my fiancée? Someone is holding her hostage!"

Wow. He looks like a total loon. That's an achievement, too, considering that he's wearing a blue banking suit with a red power tie. But he's hitting the crazy-guy vibe and then some. A few people have their cell phones out and are taking video.

Shoot me now.

Philpot sets his hands on his hips. That's his *I'm important, and I'm in charge* pose. It usually works. But I hate it. And I hate him, really. Funny how that thought is just hitting me right now.

I loathe Philpot Herbert Utrecht the Third with all my soul.

Philpot steps up to a random guard. He hasn't seen me yet. "I won't say it again. I'm here for my fiancée, Bryar Rose."

I roll my eyes. That was my name right there, and he said it really loudly for all the phone cameras. *Great move, dickhead. Why don't you give out my Social Security number while you're at it?*

Philpot scans the room. His gaze quickly stops on me. "My love! They wouldn't let me see you. I've been so afraid!"

I shake my head. "You've been so afraid. You." *Because, of course, this is all about Philpot Herbert Utrecht the Third.*

My fake fiancé starts to make his way through the maze of display cases. For the record, everyone is still totally quiet and watching his every move.

This sucks.

Well, I've come this far, and I won't slink away. I march up to him and speak in a loud voice. No point whispering; they're all listening intently anyway. "I am fine. I am not your fiancée. As of this moment, I am not even your fake girlfriend anymore. I want nothing to do with you ever again. Please leave."

A zing of happy energy moves through my limbs. Saying that out loud makes me feel like a million bucks. And there's some little part of me that got extra-energized by doing that while standing a few yards in front of Knox. It's something primal inside me, and it's super-happy that I finally broke it off.

In front of a crowd of people.

With all their cell phone cameras locked right on my face.

I. Am. Awesome.

Like always, Philpot ignores what I said. Instead, he goes right on being the star of his own drama. "Bryar Rose!" He points to Knox, who is hanging a respectful distance behind me. "Who is this man?"

That does it.

Now, my rebel-reflex kicks in, and how. I stride over to Knox, grip his face in my hands, and kiss him. Hard. Whatever we did in the elevator, that was like sissy-hot compared to the smooch we share now. A few people in the crowd whistle. I've never felt more free.

Leaning back, I break the kiss and look at Knox. "Sorry for using you like my boy toy, but I'm trying to make a point."

"What?" A sly grin rounds his full mouth. "I wasn't done being used."

Philpot steps over. "How can you do this to us?"

"There is no us. I just broke up with you. Not that we ever kissed anyway, which is technically, I think, an official requirement for dating. So the fake relationship is over."

More people have filtered onto the retail floor. I'm pretty sure word is getting out through the building that there's a scene going on. *Fine with me.*

Somehow, Tamara ended up not far away from us. She raises her hand. "The girl is right. If you haven't kissed her, you haven't dated her."

"Thank-you, Tamara." I'd offer her a fist bump, but she's standing too far away.

All of which calls to mind the fact that Elle still hasn't showed up yet. It's getting on my nerves. If I should be fist-bumping anyone at this point, it should be Elle. I'm torn between irritation and worry. *I sure hope she's okay.*

Philpot runs his fingers along his chiseled jawline. "You haven't been taking your medicine, have you?"

With that, Knox steps right between Philpot and me. Waves of rage positively roll off the guy. "Leave Bry alone."

Philpot points to Knox's eyes. "You're a werewolf."

"No kidding." I like how Knox adds a nice level of snarl to his voice.

At these words, a chorus of gasps sounds around the room. The two people who hadn't yet cracked out their cell phones now dig around and bring them up. Even the guard's taking video. It's a big deal to spot a real werewolf these days. *Great.*

Philpot's face turns pink with rage. "You're the one who should leave. I've been working this girl for months. You can't sweep in and fill her head with lies. You're not the only one who's powerful."

For a few seconds, I can only stare at Philpot. Working me? Who says that? It's like I don't know him at all. Plus, the way he says Knox is "sweeping in," it's like I'm a sack of potatoes on the shelf. And that powerful stuff? Philpot invests in hedge funds; he isn't a superhero. A creeping sense of dread oozes up my spine.

There's something wrong with Philpot. Way wrong.

But there's no time to analyze my ex-fake-boyfriend. At last, Elle pushes her way through the growing crowd in her classic New Yorker style. "Bry, I found you. Are you okay?"

"I'm maintaining." I give her the side-eye. "Where have you been? A guard came and found Knox and me. No one could find you or Alec."

"Oh." My guilty friend looks totes guilty.

I know that look on Elle. She won't blab the details here, which is fine. I can be patient.

All of a sudden, Alec steps onto the sales floor and raises his arms. His right hand is clasped into a fist. Red light oozes out from between his fingers. I don't know much about wizards, but I'd bet that Alec is casting a spell right now. And considering the fact that no one is noticing that fact? I'd bet that he's casting a cloaking spell, too, which makes him one powerful wizard.

"Hello, everyone! We're closing down LeCharme for a few hours for some unexpected maintenance. Please follow the guards and leave the lobby. Anyone with purchases, we will finalize your transactions at a later time with a steep discount. Thank-you!"

As he makes this announcement, Alec is all surfer-boy smile and charm. His spell works, and how. The crowd simply marches toward the front door in an orderly line. Knox told me that Alec was a wizard who keeps his powers under wraps. He wasn't kidding. In less than a minute, everyone's gone.

Everyone, that is, except Philpot. *What is it with this guy?* He stands by the revolving door and glares at me. "This isn't over."

"Yes, it is over." I point toward the street. "Go away. And for the record, I never want to see you again."

Philpot makes a growling noise, which is super-weird. After that, he finally marches out of the building. I've never been happier to see someone leave in my life.

Once the retail floor is emptied out, Alec turns to me. "You've had a busy time of it. Why don't you and Elle take the rest of the day off?"

I could kiss Alec for offering me an out here, but it would be weird on multiple levels. Instead, I try my best to look unconvinced.

"Are you sure?" I don't want to look like a wimp, but between Knox, Reggie, and Philpot, I'm already over quota for overwhelming experiences.

"Positive," says Alec.

At this point, Elle's smiling so hard, it's like she's surrounded by a halo of happy. She tugs on my elbow. "Let's go to my place and catch up." One guess what she wants to talk about: Alec. I wonder if we both got our first kisses on the same day. That would be something.

"I'd like that, sweetie." I turn to Knox. "I know you wanted to tell me something serious, but I really need some downtime. And food." *Let's not forget the fact that I skipped lunch.*

Knox steps closer. "What I have to talk about with you is important. It can't wait."

People talk about having an inner child, but I never really met mine until this moment. Inside me, my inner two-year-old sticks her fingers in her ears and screams, *La la la, I can't hear you.* In other words, whatever Knox is talking about? It doesn't really register. All I want is to take a break.

"Look, Knox, in the last few days, I've been attacked by my ex-group leader, had a conversation with an undead nut job from Julius Caesar's army, and broke up with my fake fiancé. I really need a few hours to regroup."

Knox frowns. "But this is about your safety." Our eyes lock, and that warm sensation happens again; it's like my veins heat up from the inside. Tendrils of connection wind between us. It feels beyond awesome.

Then it all goes to crap. The lines of connection start prodding at the lockbox inside my soul. I freeze. What is THAT all about? It's more overwhelming stuff, and my inner toddler is having none of it. With every cell in my body, I push back against whatever is happening.

Knox blinks and looks away. "I'm sorry." Instantly, the sensation of warmth and connection ends. I miss that part. But the prodding at my inner lockbox has stopped. That's the good news. It raises a question, though.

I focus on Knox. "What were you doing just then, exactly?"

Elle steps forward. "Did he hurt you?"

Alec sets his hand on Elle's wrist. "No, he was testing to see if she was ready to talk. Werewolves are sensitive like that. Isn't that right, Knox?"

"That's it." Knox rubs his neck. "And you're right, Bry. Now is not the time for all of this." He meets my gaze again. "I was wrong to push you. How about I stop by Elle's place in a few hours? Bring you something to eat, yeah?"

I nod hesitantly. "Sure."

"But we need to talk then. Do you think you can do that?"

I hug my elbows. "I'll try."

"Enough is enough." Elle drags me toward the door. "Bry is going on a break. See you later, guys!" Once we're out of earshot, she lowers her voice. "What have you two been up to?"

A ton of things. But nothing that I want to discuss within earshot of the guys. "I don't know," I say, careful to use my full sassy voice. "What have *you two* been up to?"

"Let's get some ice cream and greasy food first. After that, I'll explain everything."

And with those two little sentences, the world seems a lot more right. Elle and I are going to eat bad-for-us foods at her condo, where we'll rehash everything that happened. There's no better way to deal with a bad day. Or even, after what happened to me this morning, a crazy day.

Whatever this is, Elle and I can figure it out. I remember Knox's saying that he needed to explain something else to me. Something worse than all the other nasty revelations that have come before.

All of a sudden, I'm not feeling so confident that ice cream and girl talk will do the trick. I need some supernatural advice. Maybe it's time for me to call on Colonel Mallory the Magnificent. It's a long shot—after all, I'm pretty sure I imagined him—but it might be worth a try.

As Elle and I head toward the subway, I cup my hand by my mouth and speak in a loud voice. "I summon you, Colonel Mallory the Magnificent."

"What?" Elle's huge blue eyes almost bug out of her head. "That's the guy who cursed you."

"About that." Since we're New Yorkers, we can weave through a packed sidewalk of bodies while having this conversation. "He visited me before. I was hoping it was a combination of sleep deprivation and nerves. In fact, I'm pretty sure it was, but he offered to help and give advice. It's crazy to try to summon him, but my life has gotten so strange so quickly. At this point, I'll try anything." I scan the sidewalk. No one appears, outside the ordinary stream of New Yorkers.

"I don't see anyone supernatural, hon. Are you sure you saw him?"

"In the interest of full disclosure, I could just be having a breakdown of some kind."

"Look, I know my Bryar Rose. Drop this Colonel Mallory stuff. You need some food and ice cream. In that order. Then we can talk about everything and make it right, okay?"

"Sure, let's go." For some reason, a weight of disappointment settles into my bones. I knew that Colonel Mallory thing was a total bust. Still, the fact that he didn't show bums me out for some reason.

It's just that kind of day, I guess.

CHAPTER FIFTEEN
KNOX

I stare at the front door of the LeCharme building. Bry just took off through there. My hands ball into fists. Was I wrong to let her go? She needs to know the truth, and soon. Unless Bry shifts at least once, her wolf could die by sundown tomorrow.

Trouble is, she needs to be willing to shift.

When we looked into each other's eyes, I reached out with my alpha power and probed into her soul, testing to see if her animal could come out. If Bry had seemed in the least bit ready, I'd have insisted we talk right then and there.

That's not what happened, though.

Bry pushed back on my powers in a big way. In fact, she shoved my alpha consciousness out of her head with so much energy, it felt like a fist to my chest. I've sensed stuff like that before, but it always came from Alec. And that makes zero sense. Bry is a werewolf, not a wizard. I set that aside for later, when I'm not losing my mind because Bry just left.

I speak to my wolf in my head. *"We should follow her."*

"Her wolf not ready. You stay here."

I can't believe my wolf isn't with me on this one. *"She needs me now. I'm going."*

"No scare mate."

Alec sets his hand on my shoulder. "You having a fight with your inner wolf?" Over the years, Alec's seen enough of my mental wolf battles to know when one is happening.

I growl out a single word. "Yeah."

"Tell him to back off. Bryar will be fine."

"He's not the one that wants to go after her." I keep glaring at the door.

Alec eyes me for a long time before speaking. "Why don't we go to my office and chill? I rigged up a PlayStation to my work computer. It's sweet."

Normally, that kind of an idea is a slam-dunk. "No."

"Dude, you can't just stand here and glare at a door. Your eyes are gold and everything. You'll frighten away the customers."

"You already cleared out the sales floor. And humans would love to see me going wolfy. Would make their damn day on Facebook."

"Well, you're scaring the crap out of me. Let's go to my office. I'll order up some raw meat and a chew toy for you."

I round on him. *Chew toy, my ass.* I have six inches on Alec, which means I can easily loom over him. Not that he cares, but the chew toy comment is out of line. "I am not a dog."

"That's my grumpy buddy." He tugs on the shoulder of my T-shirt. "Now, let's go hang out in my office because, sooner or later, we are going to reopen our front doors, and I can't handle you looking this way to customers. They're here to buy jewelry, not take selfies with a werewolf."

Mentioning customers triggers a memory. "People had their cell phones out before. They took video of Bry."

"Please. I'm not some greenback wizard from the corner of nowhere. I wiped all their electronics before I brainwashed them all to leave quietly." He opens his right hand to show a bunch of blackened diamonds.

My brows lift. "Nice work."

"What else do you expect?" He tugs on my shoulder again. "Let's start with some basics here. Walking is a simple movement. You raise your right foot and then your left."

"You're a dick."

Alec wags his eyebrows. "Bigger than yours."

"Dream on, douche." Even so, I finally step toward the elevator bank. Alec grins like he won the lottery.

Within a few minutes, we're doing exactly what Alec wants. In this case, it means hanging out in his palatial office with the door locked and snacks on the way. Part of being a werewolf is that I'm perpetually hungry. In fact, I can't help but notice the lunch spread that Alec has on his desk, which is now totally eaten over. No doubt he ordered in for him and Elle. And that gets me thinking. Why did the guard have to come after Bryar Rose and me when Philpot showed up? How come he couldn't find Alec, anyway?

I plunk down onto one of Alec's funky couches. "Where were you earlier today? No one could find you."

Alec takes the chair across from mine. "When?" He asks the question innocently enough, but the acidic scent of guilt oozes all over him.

"You know what I mean. Why couldn't anyone find you when Philpot the Douchebag showed up?"

"Oh, that. Elle and I had some lunch in my office. After that, we went for a walk. Elle wanted a coffee, and our machine here is junk, so we went to this little café I know. And along the way, you know." He gets a dreamy look on his face. That part in itself is a stunner. Alec does not go gooey over women.

"No, I don't know."

"I kept getting texts, and Elle was teasing me about it, so we both decided to shut off our phones for a while."

"Your phone. Off." This is unprecedented. If Alec could get his phone surgically implanted in his cranium, I think he would in a heartbeat.

"Yeah, sure. Why not?"

I sniff. "You've got it bad."

"What?" Alec rolls his eyes. "She's a friend. I like her. That's it." After that, he starts going off on how much he isn't into Elle, and honestly? I start to tune him out. Normally, I'd give him crap about all the lying he's doing. The man reeks of a rotten garbage scent that means he's telling untruths left and right. Normally, I'd call him on this, but I'm just not in the zone today.

Instead, I'm still thinking about how Bryar Rose is a werewolf. How is that possible? Why would her aunties try to hide something like that from her? And most importantly, how can I get her comfortable enough to tell her the truth and get her to shift before it's too late? I picture that fool, Philpot. Somehow, he feels like a bigger part of this whole thing. Only I can't imagine how. Still, sometimes it's the dumb-looking ones who are the most dangerous.

I don't like this. At all.

Alec keeps blabbing for a while, and then he snaps his fingers. "Hey, Knox."

"Yeah."

"I've been talking to you. Have you heard a word I said?"

I lean back on the couch. "No."

"Let me get this straight. You're not going to ask me a million questions about anything I've been saying? Nothing about Elle?"

"Nah. It's obvious that you're crazy about this girl. Why ask questions about that? You'll just get all misty on me, and I'd rather keep whatever manly image I have of you intact."

"You're a true humanitarian."

"That's just how I roll. And another thing. Don't think I didn't notice how you're holding back about Elle in general. She told you something important."

Alec gives me one of his patented *I can't believe you* squints. "What?"

"Give it up." I tap my nose. "I can smell a lie, you know. And right now, you reek."

"I'm not lying."

"Well, you're withholding truth, and that smells the same."

Alec leans forward, braces his elbows on his knees, and stares at the floor. "It's not my secret to tell, Knox."

This is another situation where I'd usually press Alec for answers. Not that he'd ever say anything. The man is like a rock when he wants to stay quiet. Even so, I've got enough to worry about without trying to crack that block of granite. "Fine. Keep your secrets."

"What?" Alec looks up. "You're letting me off the hook?"

"You catch on quickly."

"You'd only do that if something big was going on." His blue eyes widen with concern. "What happened?"

"Something bigger than you can imagine." I speak really slowly so Alec won't miss a word. "Bryar Rose is a werewolf."

Alec leans back in his chrome chair and laughs. "Come on, man. You scared the crap out of me there. Stop playing around."

"I'm not playing you. She is a werewolf."

"Knox." Alec shakes his head. "She's a Sleeping Beauty life template, not Little Red Riding Hood."

"I saw her eyes, Alec. Golden. And that medicine she has in her bag? Predator's Bane."

All the blood seems to drain from Alec's face. "Predator's Bane? Are you sure?"

"I'm sure. Remember that fight back in Mexico City? I got stuck as a human and couldn't shift."

"They hit you with Predator's Bane. I remember. So why would anyone give that to Bryar Rose?"

"I think they're doing it because she's under a Slumber Beast curse."

"Slumber Beast? No one's cast that in a hundred years. I don't think there are any fairies left who are strong enough to do it."

"Colonel Mallory the Magnificent might." I lean forward. "Think about it. If Bry is under a Slumber Beast curse, then whenever she tries to shift, the spell would freeze her up. She takes a few whiffs of Predator's Bane, transforms back to all human, and the sleeping spell stops."

"Predator's Bane." Alec scrubs his hands over his face. "I mean, Elle told me about Bryar Rose taking medicine, but I thought it was for her Sleeping Beauty sickness."

"It was."

"And you really saw eyes turn golden?"

"Oh yeah. Her eyes turned golden, and then she started to fall asleep."

Alec frowns. "Has she shifted before?"

"No, I reached out to her wolf, and it's never been set loose." I shake my head. "And her eighteenth birthday is tomorrow."

"That's terrible, Knox." Alec doesn't seem too upset, though.

"But?"

"Honestly, what can you do about it? She's got a spell on her that knocks her out before she can shift. You know how powerful magic like that is?"

"I don't, actually. I was hoping you could tell me." Alec loves to study all kinds of magic, including fairy stuff.

"Maybe if you had a dozen wizards or fairies working at it for a year, you could break a Slumber Beast spell. But that's a long shot."

"Come on, how can you know it's unbreakable?"

"Please. How often have I wanted to knock out your werewolf ass, even for a second?"

How I hate to say this. "You've tried that a ton." When we were kids, Alec used to try to stop me all the time. And the spell he wanted to cast was the same general kind of thing that happens to Bryar Rose, too. He wanted to freeze me in place like a statue. It never happened, though. Eventually, he gave up.

Alec grins. "Exactly. And you know how strong I am. That's how I know that there's no way to fix this in the next twenty-four hours."

"Thanks for giving up like a pussy."

"I'm a man of magical science." Alec rolls his eyes. "There's a difference."

"Maybe if she stops taking that damn Predator's Bane..." I leave the thought to hang out there.

"No."

"Right." Alec never gives up this fast. *There's something else at work here.* "Talk to me. The truth now."

Alec sighs. "Fine. We can't lose her skills. Did you see how much of that papyri she translated? She downloaded her stuff to the mainframe, and I took a look. That girl is a machine."

"I knew it." Anger tightens up my spine. "You selfish bastard. You just want her to keep translating for us."

"Come on. Our people have been looking at those papyri fragments for two thousand years. Everyone's been trying to translate them. We got some of the easy bits done, but no one's come anywhere as close as Bryar Rose. Whether or not she has a wolf, she can always work on papyri."

I rise to stand. It takes everything I have not to punch Alec in the face. "You haven't met people who've lost their animals."

"I've seen them. Sure, they aren't chatty, but they can still work. And if we give Bryar Rose enough time, I know that she'll decode the full papyri. That means she'll find out how to stop the Denarii. If you scare her off with wolf talk, then that may never happen. It's too much of a risk, man."

"This is her *wolf* we're talking about. Have you seen what happens to shifters who lose their animals? They lose all their personality. It's like turning a human being into a robot."

Alec taps his chiseled chin. "And what happened back there on the sales floor, huh?"

"Nothing."

"Now who's lying? You tried to use your alpha mojo to see if she wanted to shift… And she didn't. The girl doesn't want this. And if we keep shoving werewolf stuff at her, she could bolt. Like I said, we can't take that chance. She's here and working on the papyri. We need to leave Bryar Rose right where she is."

My voice comes out a low growl. "That's not an option."

"This is bigger than one person. You know the Denarii master plan. They're taking down all of the Magicorum because we're all that can stop them from turning human beings into a never-ending buffet. We need to stop them, and that means translating every hieroglyph in the *Book of Magic*. It will tell us how to end the Denarii. Hell, it may even give us the keys to finding Jules. Can we really put that at risk?"

"Not at the expense of her wolf."

"Come on. Our people are being wiped out."

"And what about you? What if this meant stripping a witch or wizard of their power?"

Alec folds his arms over his chest. "You're not going to like this. If the question is whether to sacrifice one wizard to save all of the Magicorum? Hell yes, I'd do it. Your feelings for Bryar Rose are getting in the way of your judgment."

"No, my feelings are based on judgment. Bryar Rose is smart and strong. She'll keep working on those papyri because that's who she is. And what if she finds out we let her wolf die because we wanted her as our papyri bitch? No way. Then she'll really disappear on us."

"On us?" Alec has his future CEO face on. I hate it when he does that. "Or on you?"

"Fine, I do have feelings for this girl. I believe in her, Alec. Nothing you say can change that." I stalk toward the door.

Alec moves to stand in my way. "Don't leave. You convinced me."

I glare at him. "I'm still going."

"Look, there's a lot at stake. I had to know how serious you were."

My wolf is tearing it up inside me. It takes all my self-control not to howl with rage. "Right now, I want to go wolf on you and rip out your throat. But I won't. Instead, I'm going for a run in the woods so I can calm the hell down. After that, I will see Bry and tell her the truth." Alec opens his mouth, but I cut him right off. "And you're going to shut up and let me do that. Got it?"

Alec motions across his mouth like he's zipping his lips. He's trying to be cute, but it only makes me want to kill him even more. And since I only have one best friend, I'd really like to keep Alec around. Gritting my teeth, I stalk away without saying another word.

My wolf starts speaking in my head. *"We run?"*

"That's right. We're getting out of this city and going for a run."

"After we run, we see mate?"

Again, he's calling her "our mate." Frustration tightens up my shoulders. Bryar Rose is a great girl, but she's not our mate. No one is. Wardens don't have mates, end of story. Eventually, my wolf will have to accept that. For now, I'm just going to avoid the topic.

I take the elevator down to the main shopping floor and stare at the front door. Do I go for a run or chase after Bry? The more I think about it, the more I realize that there's only one answer to that question.

"Change of plans," I tell my wolf. *"We're going to see Bry right now."*

"Her wolf not ready. We run in the woods."

That's a crap plan. Running in the woods won't fix my mood. Only seeing Bryar Rose can do that. She needs the truth, and fast. I check my watch. *Damn.* Friday commuter traffic has already started.

"Tough. We're going now."

My wolf doesn't say anything in reply. He's pouting.

"It'll be hell if we drive over to the Village. Better if we take the subway. Even then, it'll take a while to reach her."

"We see mate." He says that with even more pout in his voice, as well as a special emphasis on the word *"mate."*

"Yeah, we'll see her." Now, it's my turn to emphasize the word *"her."*

With that, my wolf is on board for the trip to the Village. For now, that's the best I can expect out of this crap situation. Later on, I can break the news to him that Bry will never be our mate.

We're wardens, and that's just how this goes.

CHAPTER SIXTEEN
BRYAR ROSE

I've grabbed my favorite spot on Elle's couch. Chinese takeout sits on the coffee table before us. Sure, Knox said he'd bring over food, but I'll just eat that too. In my life, carbo-loading is an essential form of therapy. That said, our supplies for the evening go far beyond Chinese takeout. Elle and I also have three pints of Ben & Jerry's in the freezer, along with a binge-watch fiesta of *Stranger Things* ready to go on TV. After all the craziness with Philpot at LeCharme, it's time for some fun with Elle. I grab an eggroll and stuff my face.

Meanwhile, Elle sits at the far end of the couch, staring at her hands and looking super-guilty.

"What?" I speak through a mouthful of food. "Aren't you going to eat?" I also can't help notice that Elle is still wearing her suit while I've taken it upon myself to borrow a pair of her skinny jeans and a long sweater.

"I just need to clear the air."

"No you don't. Eat."

"I'm so sorry I wasn't there for you back at LeCharme." Elle holds up her phone. "You sent me like a million texts."

I keep stuffing my face, but I don't correct her. It was totally annoying that we couldn't get in touch. "What happened? Why'd you go off the grid?"

"Alec and I decided to take a walk and get some coffee. I was teasing him, and we decided to both shut off our phones and, well, that's it."

"Don't worry about it."

"Are you sure? Just so you know, I got you a first edition of *Alice's Adventures in Wonderland* for your birthday."

"First of all, that is so awesome about the gift. I can't believe it." Elle knows how much I love *Alice's Adventures in Wonderland.* "But you didn't need to say a thing about presents. I'm the one who should be giving you gifts and apologizing."

Elle shrugs. "Right."

I decide that now is a good time to stare at the floor. *Yup. Still there.* "No, it's true. We have bigger things to talk about."

"Like how you dumped Philpot? That was awesome, by the way."

"Nope. Even bigger than that." I set down the dumpling I'd picked up, just to show how serious this particular topic is. "I kissed Knox."

Elle bounces a little on the couch. "You did?"

"Or he kissed me." I squint, thinking back through the experience. "Whatever. It was definitely a mutual thing." I raise my pointer finger. "And it happened twice."

"And?"

I blush my face off. "It was awesome."

Elle rips open a little white box that's filled with mu shu pork. "Details, girlfriend."

"Not until I get a little intel from your side. Anything happen with you and Alec?"

"Nope. Friends without benefits forever."

"Is it because of his magic stuff?" I don't want to come out and say that I guessed Alec is a warden, and Knox confirmed it. That means he can't get married. Which is a little bit of a bummer, but come on? We're seventeen, and no one's worrying about getting hitched now.

"No, it's not that. It's his family."

"Oh." From the little I know of Alec, his family are all creeps. Who ignores it when you get evidence that you're selling stolen stuff? Criminals, that's who.

"*Oh* is right." There's a sadness to her answer that means two things. First, she means this. Second, she's not ready to talk about it anymore at this moment. I've known Elle long enough to realize when I need to be patient.

"Sorry, girlfriend." I offer her the last egg roll, because that's Elle's favorite. She takes it and smiles.

"Thanks."

"Want to hear about my crap day? It's certain to make you feel better."

Elle stuffs the eggroll in her mouth and nods vigorously. There really is nothing like *someone else's* crap life to put your own in perspective.

I lean back on the couch and lace my fingers over my waist. That's my "I'm telling a story, and it's a good one" pose. "Well, it all started because Knox promised to show me the true nature of the Denarii."

"He did?"

"Oh yeah, and boy, it is NOT pretty."

Elle moves her feet up on the couch so she's sitting bird-style. This is her pose when she's super-interested. "Keep going."

Suddenly, twinkling silver lights appear right between us and the opening credits for *Stanger Things*. *Uh oh.* I've seen this before. It happened the last time Colonel Mallory the Magnificent visited me. Sure enough, he comes into view, looking the same as he did last time. Which is basically a graying version Clark Gable from *Gone with the Wind*. The nub of an unlit cigar is held in his teeth.

"Good evening, ladies."

I blink hard, because I'd really convinced myself that the whole "seeing Colonel Mallory" thing was a mirage of some kind. I glance over at Elle. Her eyes are wide with shock, too. In fact, she's so surprised that she's holding some chopsticks of mu shu up to her lips but not putting any actually into her mouth.

"You know," says Colonel Mallory, "in polite society, you'd say good evening."

Elle slowly resets her little white takeout box onto the coffee table. "Not a lot of fairies could get past the wards in my place. That must make you Colonel Mallory the Magnificent."

He bows slightly at the waist. "One and the same."

Elle leaps to her feet. "You bastard! What did you do to my friend?"

Now, I appreciate Elle's protective instincts, but I summoned Colonel Mallory for a reason. I grab Elle's wrist and guide her back down. "I called him here, remember?"

"When you were blabbing on Sixth Avenue?" asks Elle. "I thought you were so stressed out that you were acting crazy."

"I was stressed out, but I really did want to summon Colonel Mallory. You see, he visited me here before."

"Here? In my condo?"

"After Knox dropped me off. I thought it was a mirage, but he said things would be changing—"

Colonel Mallory tips his wide-brimmed black hat. "More specifically, I told Bryar Rose that she would soon be coming into her powers, and therefore, she was in dire need of my expert advice."

"Well, I don't know about powers or anything. But strange stuff has certainly been happening. I do want your advice."

"Advice." Elle glares at Colonel Mallory. "From him."

I shrug. "It's like I told you on Sixth Avenue. Things are going too fast. I need all the perspective I can get."

Elle lowers her voice. "He cursed you, Bry. Why am I the only one of us who's remembering that part?"

"Technically, I did not curse Bryar Rose. I saved her."

Elle flashes him an angry look. "Fairies don't save anyone."

Colonel Mallory chuckles, but there's no humor in the sound. "Bryar Rose seems to think her aunties saved her."

"Oh, her aunties have an angle," says Elle. "Mark my words."

Now it's my turn for my protective instincts to take over. "Come on, Elle. They took me in."

"They had their own self-serving reasons." Elle folds her arms over her chest. "You just don't know what they are yet."

"You've been saying that since we were kids, and we have yet to find any ulterior motive for them to have adopted me."

Colonel Mallory rests his elbow onto the top of the television monitor. "Interesting as this conversation may be, I need to chat with Bryar Rose and you need to go somewhere else."

Elle narrows her eyes. "Dream on. I'm staying."

The edges of Colonel Mallory's mouth curl into a sly grin. "You're powerful, sugar. But not that powerful."

I frown. "What are you talking about?"

"Your best friend here is a fairy, just like me."

My spine stiffens with outrage. "That's impossible! She'd have told me that years ago, if that were true." I turn to face my best friend. "Right?"

But Elle doesn't reply. Instead, she starts staring at her hands. That's not a good sign. In fact, it's a total guilt move if I've ever seen one. The truth hits me like a freight train. "You're a fairy? Really?"

Elle keeps staring at her hands and not answering me. "I'm not leaving Bryar Rose."

Holy crap. From Elle, that's pretty much an admission that she's known all along that she's really a fairy. But why would she hide that from me? From everyone?

Colonel Mallory sighs. "Well, sugar, I warned you." He snaps his fingers, and a cascade of silver dust twinkles around Elle. A second later, Elle yawns, curls up onto the couch like a cat, and falls asleep.

I point at my friend. "You just knocked her out!"

"Sleeping spells are my specialty. But you already knew that, didn't you?"

"Yeah, I noticed the sleeping spell you put on me all my life. Thanks for the reminder." I press my palms against my eyes. This isn't how I pictured this conversation going, at all. In fact, I didn't even picture having this conversation. I lower my hands. "This is a disaster."

Colonel Mallory takes the cigar from his mouth and eyes the unlit tip. "I came here to tell you something important about who you are and what powers you have. And I might do just that. But I might not. Depends if you're ready." He eyes me carefully. "Are you ready, sugar?"

Frustration twists up my back. "Can you be a little more specific?"

"No, and don't try to make me. This is how fairies are, in case you haven't noticed."

I had, in fact, noticed. Fairies are arbitrary, self-serving, and crazy-making in general. I stare at Elle's sleeping form. "Is she going to be okay? Because I'll kill you if you hurt her."

"Oh, she'll be fine." Colonel Mallory sets the nub of the cigar back into the corner of his mouth. "She'll wake up in a day or so." He rubs his palms together. "Now. Back to business. When did you summon me?"

"I thought you were trying to figure out if I'm ready."

"That's exactly what I'm doing, just not in the way you'd expect."

This experience is already very weird. I don't have any compass to judge if this line of questioning is good or bad, so I decide to roll with it. "I spoke your name like an hour ago."

"An hour, that's pretty good. I exist on a different plane of time, sugar. Don't expect me to come running this fast again."

"I'll make a note in my diary." My voice drips with sarcasm. "And I want you to wake up my friend now."

"I'm not doing that." He grins around his cigar. "How much do you know about me?"

"You're a powerful fairy who cast a sleeping curse on me. A few days ago, you said that this spell is actually for my own good."

"That's true. I'm also part shifter."

"You're a werewolf?"

"No, bless your heart." Colonel Mallory snaps his fingers again, and black scales appear on his skin. His eyes become yellow orbs with long reptilian slits. "I'm part dragon."

I try to process this piece of information. "You're part dragon."

"That's right. I'm a fairy lord and a shifter, both." Colonel Mallory snaps his fingers once more, and his skin returns to normal. "Now that was just a partial shift, in case you were wondering. If I wanted to, I could get bigger than this entire brownstone."

"Good to know." *I am so screwed.* Why did I invite this crazy man over for a chat? "You know what? I'm thinking that maybe we're done here."

"Oh, we're far from done. This is only the beginning. You and I will be spending lots of time together."

"Something to look forward to." *Not.*

"Know what's the hardest part of being a dragon shifter?"

"I'm sure you're about to tell me."

"The smells. We're sensitive to them like nobody's business. Everyone has a scent. It can be overwhelming. Intoxicating. Does that ring any bells to you?"

I want to tell him to shut up and glitter his way out of Elle's condo, but I can't. Something about his words knock at the back of my consciousness. *This is important.*

"I can see a few tiny bells ringing away in that pretty little head of yours. Now, reptile shifters soak in their environment. I'm forever too hot or too cold. That's not the way with other breeds, though. Some stay warm all the time."

I grip my elbows. "What are you saying?"

"Something important. But you're not ready to hear it yet. If you were, then you'd be hounding me for the truth. Instead, I'm shoving it at you."

I roll my eyes. *This is such a fairy way of acting.* If you let them, they'll talk riddles at you for hours. "Out with it, already."

"All right, if you insist. You, Bryar Rose, are part werewolf."

Relief washes through me. "Oh, my stars. You really had me going there. I am not part werewolf."

"Yes, you are, sugar. That's why I saved you. I know what it's like to be part shifter. I couldn't stand by and watch someone strip away your animal. They wanted to take even more than that, to be sure. So I stepped in to help. Kept your animal alive with a special spell. It puts you to sleep any time your feral side tries to rise. Now, how's that for incredible?"

It's official. Our conversation has crossed the line from stupid to ridiculous. "So, I'm part shifter. Good to know."

"You don't believe me."

"You think?" I grab another dumpling from the table. "Look, I've had a long day. Everything's been one disaster after another. I actually asked you here to see if you could provide some useful information. Like maybe a few tips on how to stop the Denarii."

"Not my area of expertise, sugar."

"So you say. But instead of giving me anything useful, you tell me lies about being part werewolf? I'm a Sleeping Beauty template. Look at yourself. You're a part dragon who cast a sleeping spell on me. That's my template. Sleeping Beauty. No werewolves."

"You're not a Sleeping Beauty life template."

"I'm not, eh?"

"That's right, sugar. You're something else entirely. That's what I *really* came here to talk to you about. But you're acting mad as a March hare, and we haven't even gotten past the fact that you're part werewolf yet. I'm afraid this really isn't a good use of my time."

Silver dust starts to sparkle around him. *Crap!* Colonel Mallory is using fairy magic to glimmer his ass out of here. Even though I haven't exactly welcomed this conversation, I didn't mean for him to leave. *Maybe.* My mind is a mess of questions. The biggest one of which is why I feel panicked that he's going. The outline of his body is fading. "No, wait! Stop!"

"You're not ready, sugar. Call me again when you are. I'll try to get to you as soon as I can."

With that, Colonel Mallory vanishes entirely.

I run my arms through the airspace where Colonel Mallory once stood. Nothing.

Damn. That visit wasn't too helpful. I slump back onto the couch again. Beside me, Elle snores away.

Be positive. Elle will wake up soon, and you can resume your original plan of girl-talk. When it comes to scheming, Elle is a pro. She'll figure something out in no time.

My official phone rings. I scan the screen, and sure enough, it's my aunties. I'd put the call through to voicemail, but they know where I am. At least, if I pick up, I have a shot at them staying at our penthouse. Not sure if I could handle them coming over to Elle's. I take the call. "Hello?"

Like always, my aunties have me on speakerphone and are all talking at once. I catch the phrases "worried about you" and "poor Philpot."

Lauralei's voice out-shouts the rest. In my mind, I can imagine her elbowing everyone aside as she presses the receiver to her thin lips. "Tomorrow should have been your wedding day."

At those words, I remember Reggie's last song in the basement of LeCharme.

"Bye, sigh, pretty little cry, your wedding day is when you DIE."

"I'll never marry Philpot. I told him today that I never wanted to see him again."

"You don't mean that," says Lauralei.

I grit my teeth. For a second, I debate about telling them off. However, my logical side points out that facing down my aunties is a big deal. If I lay into them now, they'll just crack out their magic and transport over here. Then, what will I do? Sure, they aren't strong enough to transport into Elle's condo itself, but they'll hang out by the door all night. I'll be stuck here listening to them while Elle sleeps.

No, I need to do this in baby steps.

And my first step is to just get them off the phone. This time, I won't even use any games.

"I don't want to talk to you right now." With that, I hit the End Call button and turn off my phone. *Yes!* I just shut down my aunties without even telling an elaborate lie. That's awesome.

For the time being, my aunties may be dealt with, but everything else comes into nasty focus. I mean, talking to Colonel Mallory only made things worse. I'm part werewolf? What a load. And Elle has mega-fairy powers that she's been holding back from me? That bit seems true, considering Elle's recent confession. It's also totally depressing, though.

161

I stare down at Elle. Colonel Mallory said he cast a harmless sleeping spell on her, but how am I to know what's really at work? Maybe Alec can help. I start to search for Elle's phone, since she's the only one with his number. Of course, you can never find someone's phone when you're actually looking for it. I'm about to start tearing the condo apart when a knock sounds on the door.

No doubt, that's my aunties. *Crap.* Sure, I've never hung up on them before, but I thought it would take more than that to make them transport over here. It's not like they have a ton of magic to toss around. My stomach twists with disgust. I'm sure they're here to lecture me about my lack of respect.

I check the clock. That was sure fast. They must have used magic to get over here. "I know it's you, aunties. I'm not opening the door."

After that, the pounding continues for ten minutes solid. This is standard auntie procedure. Usually, I give in around the two-minute mark, but tonight? I do a really good job of ignoring it.

"You can pound all you want. I won't open up."

There, that's telling them.

Perfect silence follows. A thrill of excitement zings through my limbs. Did I really wait them out? Did I set a boundary, and they actually paid attention? I'm tempted to scan the hallway and find out for myself.

I keep staring at the closed door. More silence ensues. They really are gone, and I need to see the evidence that they left.

Hey, what's the worst that can happen?

I step up to the door, undo all the locks, and open it a crack. But the hallway is not empty. And it's not my aunties who are out there, either. It's not even Knox.

Philpot is here.

"Forget it, loser. We are broken up." I start to close the door in his face, but he slides his shiny Cole Haan-covered foot right in the way. He moves so fast, his body is a blur. What's up with that?

Philpot peers over my shoulder. "I see you're alone."

"Elle is here."

"She's not the one I'm worried about."

"What's that supposed to mean?" Did he expect me to be here with Knox or Colonel Mallory? As soon as the question pops into my mind, I dismiss it. This is Philpot being Philpot, that's all.

"I can't have you hanging around with other men, especially not a werewolf. It's just too dangerous."

I shove on the door with my shoulder, trying to jam it shut. Philpot is way stronger than I thought he'd be.

Why did I think it was a good idea to open the door?

At some point, you'd think I'd just call it quits on making any decisions today because my luck is zero. "Go home, Philpot."

"Knox told you what you really are, didn't he? You know you're part werewolf."

His words freeze me as good as any spell. "What did you say?" In my mind, I repeat what's now becoming my favorite mantra. *I'm not a werewolf. I'm not a werewolf.*

"So you *do* know. Or at least, you suspect the truth. I'm sorry, Bryar Rose. I'd hoped it wouldn't come to this." With a burst of strength, Philpot forces his way inside.

Now, I really wish that I had at least one of our phones handy. Instead, I can only glare at Philpot. "Get out. Now."

Philpot reaches into his pocket. "This room reeks of magic. What have you and Elle been up to?" He spies her on the couch. "Oh, my. You told the truth. Elle is here, after all. But your little friend appears to be under a sleeping spell. Uh-oh. She's not doing well, either."

A weight of dread settles into my stomach. "How do you know that?"

"To me, her skin appears to be sparkling with green light. Don't you see it?"

What? Green? That sounds like bad news.

I rush over to Elle, quickly checking her exposed skin. "Nothing looks wrong. I don't know what you're talking ab—"

Suddenly, a white handkerchief is jammed over my mouth. An acidic scent fills my lungs. The fabric is drugged. White splotches take over my vision while my legs turn watery beneath me. Two thoughts repeat through my mind as my consciousness fades.

Philpot is knocking me out.

Just when I thought it couldn't get worse.

CHAPTER SEVENTEEN
KNOX

I follow the darkened sidewalk that leads to Elle's condo. With every step, my mind whirs through what I'll say to Bry. How do you convince someone that they're a werewolf and need to shift immediately?

Not easily.

I'm still obsessing over that question when the familiar outline of Elle's building appears on my right. The way it looks has changed, though. I stop. The main door hangs cockeyed and open on its frame.

That's wrong. Way wrong.

No one leaves a door open in the city. Not unless they have a death wish. The residents in this building would have the thing Super Glued shut if they knew. Which means someone just broke in.

My senses go on alert. Someone just broke into Elle's building. My protective instincts go into overdrive. Whoever it was, they could still be here.

My wolf paces inside me. *"Danger. Mate."*

"We don't know that, buddy. People break into buildings all the time. This is New York. The crooks are probably long gone, and with someone else's stuff." Still, I speed inside and rush up the stairs to Elle's place. My heartbeat pulses double-time in my chest.

I pause at the hallway that leads to Elle's condo. Her door is wide open. I take in a deep breath, looking for any familiar scents. There's Bryar Rose's scent of cinnamon, honey, and sunshine, along with that nasty cologne that Philpot wears.

What's that freak doing here?

I rush inside Elle's place. It isn't huge, so it's easy to see that Bry isn't here. Elle is sacked out on the couch. There's another scent in the air here. It's acidic and sweet, all at once. I know I've come across this aroma before, but I just can't place it.

Well, whatever's going on, I don't like it.

I grip Elle by the shoulders. "It's me. Knox. Wake up."

She doesn't flinch, let alone open her eyes.

I've hung around Alec long enough to know when someone's been knocked out with a spell. I whip out my cell and dial his number. Alec picks up on the first ring.

"What's up, man? I'm on level twelve of my new game, and so help me, if you make me lose a life, I will hunt you down."

"I'm at Elle's place. The door was wide open. Bry isn't here, and Elle's knocked out on the couch. I think something's wrong."

"So, make her some coffee. She'll perk up."

Coffee? Clearly, Alec isn't getting the sense of urgency here. "I wouldn't call you if that's all it was. Elle's under a major spell. I tried waking her up, but it's no use, so poof your ass over here right now. Elle needs to tell us what happened to Bryar Rose."

"Got it. I'll be right there." I'm glad to hear that Alec has his future CEO voice on. It means he knows this is serious and will show up ASAP.

Sure enough, a reddish haze appears by the door. Within a few seconds, the light solidifies into the shape of Alec. He raises his right hand, which still glows from whatever magical jewels are in there. *Whoa.* I've never seen Alec cast a transporter spell this quickly before.

The moment Alec fully appears, he tosses the now-darkened diamonds into the pocket of his suit coat. Alec has a whole system for which pockets go with which magical jewels. All the blackened gems end up in his left pocket.

He doesn't waste any time with hellos. "Where's Elle?"

"On the couch."

Alec rushes over to her side. The guy looks totally freaked. His normally strategically messed-up hair just looks like a rat's nest after the magical transport. He kneels beside Elle and reaches into an inside pocket of his suit jacket. When he pulls his hand out again, his fist holds emeralds. Some gemstones and crystals naturally soak up power, like a battery. Alec can pull that energy out and turn it into magic. Now, emeralds carry power for spell-breaking. I've only ever seen him use one or two small stones before. But this time, he's pulled out three gems the size of golf balls. My buddy means business.

Alec closes his eyes and raises his hand. The gemstones now glow red inside his palm. No matter what the stone, wizard magic always shines red.

The stones keep glowing brighter, but that's it. Nothing else happens.

Alec opens his hand again and stares at the now-darkened stones. "What the hell? That should have broken the spell easy."

"Who can even cast a spell that strong?"

"I don't know." Alec reaches into another pocket of his jacket and pulls out a huge blue sapphire.

"You sure you want to use that?" Alec has been dragging that stone around for years. It's a super-powerful, all-purpose gem, the kind you only use in case of major emergency. I finger the black opal claw that I wear on a chain around my neck. This gem is the same kind of super-powerful stone, only it's to help me escape from wizards. Either way, these aren't things that you use lightly.

Alec closes his eyes once more. A flash of red light shows through the fingers on his closed fist. The illumination becomes brighter and brighter until the entire condo is bathed in crimson. An ear-piercing crack fills the air as the sapphire breaks inside

Alec's palm. It blackens and turns into soot. Bits of dust float through his fingers and onto the floor.

Damn. Alec just used up all the power in that sapphire to cast his spell…and nothing happened. Elle is still asleep. I've never seen anything like it.

Bile creeps up my throat. If someone was powerful enough to do this to Elle, what happened to Bry?

Finally, Elle's eyes flutter open. I exhale. At least, my friend's magic is still working.

"Alec?" she asks. "What are you doing here?"

He scoops her up into his arms. "You scared me to death, Elle. Knox came by just like he promised. He found your door open, you asleep, and Bryar Rose gone, so—"

Elle breaks free from his hold and stands. "Bry is gone?" She doesn't wait for an answer. Instead, Elle stalks around the condo. She even quickly scales up the ladder to the loft. "Bry is gone. What happened to her?"

I step forward. "We were hoping you could tell us."

"All I know is that Colonel Mallory the Magnificent came by."

My voice lowers to a growl. "The fairy who cursed her?"

"He may have cast a curse on her, but I think he meant it to be helpful."

"Never trust a fairy."

Elle and Alec exchange a long look. There's a whole conversation in that stare, and I think back to how cagey Alec has been about whatever the hell is going on with him and Elle. I take a deeper whiff of Elle's scent.

In a flash, I know at least part of the story. "You're fae, aren't you?"

Elle nods. "I always told Bry I was human." She sighs. "That's why I could tell Colonel Mallory was speaking the truth. Call it a sixth sense for my people. We can mislead humans, but it's harder between fairies."

"So where is Bry?"

Elle shakes her head. "I don't know."

I stalk around the small apartment. That scent of sickly-sweet acid hits my nostrils again. Suddenly, I remember what it is. "Someone used a knock-out drug on Bry." My blood heats with rage. "My money is on Philpot. His stench is all over this place." I round on Elle. "How did he get in here? You're a fairy. Don't you have protection spells on this place?"

"I do, but if Bry opened the door for him, then they wouldn't have worked."

I narrow my eyes. "Great. Just great."

Alec steps between us. "Look. This is getting us nowhere. Let me cast a tracer spell on Bry." He focuses on Elle. "Do you have something of hers I can use?"

"Sure." Elle rushes up the ladder to her loft and comes down holding a scarf. "Bry left this here. Will this work?"

Alec turns the silk over in his hands. "Yeah, this ought to do it." While holding the scarf in his left, Alec reaches into yet another hidden pocket in his jacket and pulls out a small white crystal. He grips the stone in his right hand and closes his eyes. A small flash of light glows inside his palm. If you didn't know to look for it, you might have missed the whole thing. Alec opens his eyes once more. "I have bad news."

I can't help the angry edge in my voice. "Don't tell me she's hurt."

"Bryar Rose is fine. But Philpot took her to a conversion zone in the Adirondacks."

His words send my inner wolf into a frenzy. *"Save mate! Save mate!"* I'm not too far behind him either. Conversion zones are bad news.

Elle frowns. "A conversion zone. What's that?"

"It's where they take humans and turn them into Denarii," explains Alec.

"So, why do you both act like that's a bad thing?" asks Elle. "The Denarii who run our group seem nice enough. Mostly."

I could go easy on Elle, but we don't have time for that. "Let me put it to you plainly. Denarii—I mean, the real Denarii—are actually a cross between mummies and zombies. Bry will either get turned into a monster or eaten for lunch."

Elle rolls her eyes. "Mummies and zombies? No way. I con people for a living, and even *I* don't believe that story."

Right. This is what happens any time we have to explain the true nature of Denarii. It's also why Alec and I keep Reggie around. He saves us days of convincing and disbelief.

I decide to try a different approach. "Look, how about I boil this down? Philpot has kidnapped Bry. The place where he's got her is a magically guarded compound near the mountains. Alec and I have been trying to sneak in for years without success. Now, either you'll help us, or you'll get out of the way, because we *are* going after her." I don't need to ask Alec if he's going along. That's a given.

Elle's intelligent gaze flickers between Alec and me. "Fine. I'm convinced. And what about Philpot?"

"I didn't sense anything strange about him," says Alec. "And I checked. I don't like people making a scene in my family's building. Either he's a master wizard, or he's a regular human."

I sniff. *There's no way Philpot is a master wizard.* The guy is too big of a loser. "My guess is that Philpot is one of the human stooges the Denarii employ from time to time. You'd be amazed what people will do for money."

"Actually, I wouldn't be surprised at all." Elle chuckles, but there's no humor in it. "Who's driving?"

Alec stands behind her, points at her head, and mouths four words: *I love this girl.*

I lift my brows. The reply is out there without my even needing to say it. *You love this girl?*

Alec waves me off. "It's a figure of speech."

Obviously, Elle hears that one. She turns around to scope out Alec. "Are you two having a conversation over my head without me?"

I shrug. "Yeah. We do that kind of thing all the time."

"Well, you can do it in the car from now on, because we're leaving."

Alec heads toward the door. "I have the perfect vehicle for this occasion, too."

"Cool. I'm calling shotgun." Elle pulls up the couch cushions until she finds her phone. After that, she starts speed-typing on the thing. "I also have some friends in low places who owe me a few favors. I'm calling them in."

"Thanks, Elle." Alec turns to me. "I have some special gems and spells I can bring along as well. What about you and werewolf friends?"

"I've got a few surprises up my sleeve."

I pull out my own phone and hit the number for Lucky's. Ready or not, I'm talking to Azizi. I need his special brand of help right now.

No matter what comes, I'll free Bry. And after that, I *will* save her wolf. Anything else is simply unthinkable.

CHAPTER EIGHTEEN
BRYAR ROSE

I don't know how long I've been sleeping, but it's the gross taste in my mouth that wakes me up.

Ugh. It's like I gargled medicine and aftershave.

I slowly blink my eyes open. *Huh.* I'm lying atop a double bed inside a round hotel room. Gray paint peels off the walls. A moth-eaten carpet covers the floor. The windows are all cracked and dirty, so I can't see outside. That said, the light itself is bright, and insects are chirping away outside. It must be late afternoon.

I moan and press my palms to my eyes. Late afternoon? That means I've been passed out all night, and it's now Saturday. My birthday. I should not be in a crappy hotel room today. And how exactly did I get here, anyway? The last thing I remember, Philpot shoved a handkerchief over my mouth. He must have knocked me out and brought me…where? To a broken-down hotel room that's somehow round?

I'd say that's totally weird, but this is my life, after all. Strange stuff sticks to me like toilet paper to a shoe. I sit upright, and that's when I see it.

I'm dressed in a red toga. *What the WHAT?*

The dress loops over my shoulder and ties around my waist. Sure, it's ankle length, but it's the kind of thing you wear to a prom, not to sleep. Fear tightens up my ribcage. There aren't a lot of reasons to dress me this way. None of them is good.

There's a knock at the rickety door. "May I come in?" The voice is female, overly bright, and somewhat familiar.

"Sure." Not like I have a lot of choices here.

The door swings open with a long creak, and through it steps someone I never thought I'd see again. At least, not while she was still alive.

It's Blanche, the girl who went missing from my Magicorum Teen Therapy Group.

She's wearing a version of the outfit Madame Grimoire always favored: an A-line dress in sky blue with a pillbox hat and white gloves.

My mouth seems to move on its own. "You're alive."

"Of course I am, silly. I'm Denarii now." She exhales a dreamy sigh. "Perfected." In some ways, Blanche looks the same as she did in group: pale skin, black hair, and red lips. Only, now she looks like someone made a wax model of her. Her skin has no pores or imperfections anymore...more like a mannequin than a person.

Just like Philpot.

Damn. Blanche is a Denarii. And now she looks too perfect to be real.

Can Philpot be one, too?

I want to face-palm myself. Of course, he's one of the Denarii. Only, Philpot's personality was so flawed, I never really focused on the perfection of his face. And he brought me here. Not good.

I work hard to stop myself from shaking. "Where am I?"

"I would've thought that was obvious."

"It isn't."

"It must be those silly drugs we gave you. They can make you downright addle-brained."

Addle-brained? What is she, eighty?

I speak super-slowly. "Where am I, Blanche?"

"You're in the Thornhill Arms hotel, of course."

"Right. Of course." My voice is super-sarcastic, and I don't care. "I'm in the creepy abandoned hotel that overlooks Elle's cabin."

"We all know what you did to Madame Grimoire, by the way. That was very naughty."

I pick at the filmy layers of my skirts. "Why am I here, Blanche?"

"I dressed you while you were passed out. I hope you like it."

"I don't like it, and that wasn't an answer to my question." Blanche was always like this in group, too. It took ten follow-up questions to get her to answer anything.

Blanche blinks a lot and tries to look innocent. "Whatever do you mean?"

"Why am I here? Are you planning to…" I can't bring myself to say the words.

"To what?"

"Roast me for dinner or something?"

"We eat all our meat raw."

"So you *are* going to kill me." I gesture down at the dress. "This dress is just…what? The equivalent of putting those little chef hats on the stumps of turkey legs?"

"Don't be such a silly-nilly. Come on outside, and Jules will explain everything to you."

"Jules." Reggie told me about this guy. He's the leader of the Denarii. And that means I'm in deep trouble. "He wants to talk to me?"

"Of course." Blanche pushes the door open. "Let's go down the stairs. Jules is waiting for you in the courtyard."

"Oh." I glance toward the windows, but they are all too cracked and dirty to see outside. But now that I know I'm in the Thornhill Arms, I have a better idea of my whereabouts. The old hotel was built to look like a fake castle. It even has two stucco towers. Since my room is round and the windows are super-thin, I'm guessing I'm in one of those tower rooms.

I scan the space around me, looking for any kind of weapon. Nothing.

Blanche stands by the open door. "We really shouldn't keep Jules waiting."

My mind races through options for escape. This hotel is so rundown I'm bound to find something I can use as a weapon. I just need to get out of this room and look around. Heading downstairs to the courtyard seems as good an idea as any. "Sure, lead the way."

Blanche starts down a winding staircase. The steps are rickety and filled with cobwebs. Sadly, there isn't anything around that can be used as a weapon. Someone took the time to take down the light fixtures and handrails...all stuff that could be used in a fight. Even the carpet's been pulled up and all the nails removed.

With every turn downward, I look for a door or window. There aren't any. Every possible exit has been nailed down tight. I do hear rustling sounds beyond the walls, though. "Are we the only people here?"

"There are Denarii in residence."

Any bit of information could be useful. "How many are here?"

"I'm sure I don't know. Denarii just follow Jules around. I don't waste my time with the rank and file. You and me..." She glances over her shoulder and grins. "We're special."

Oh no. They really did scoop out her brains, because what she's saying now? It's nothing less than mindless. "Glad to hear it, Blanche. Do we have to visit Jules right this second? Can't you give me a tour of the hotel or anything?" I force on a smile. "I'd love to catch up."

"Why, I'd love that, too. There's so much to talk about as well. But later. You see, Jules would be sorely disappointed if you kept him waiting." She reaches the bottom of the winding staircase and sets her hand on a levered door. "Here we are. Jules is just past this door."

The walls seem to press in on me. Silver spots appear in my vision. My limbs turn shaky. Something rattles inside the deepest well of my being. It's that damned lockbox from Colonel Mallory. Whatever is in there, it's trying to escape.

No, no, no. I can't have an episode now.

"You didn't by any chance get my inhaler, did you?"

"Silly me, I do have it." Blanche pulls the small device from the pocket of her skirt and hands it over. "Now take your medicine like a good little girl and go see Jules."

I uncap the device, take a few puffs, and reset the inhaler into the folds of fabric at my waist. This dress doesn't seem to have pockets, so it's the best I can do.

"Good work," says Blanche happily. "Jules wanted you to do that."

Well, if Jules wanted me to take my meds, it can't be a good idea. I remember how Knox freaked out when he scented my inhaler. I make a mental note to ask him about that later on. You know, if I ever escape here alive.

"Come along, now." Blanche pushes open the door. Bright beams of sunlight blind me for a moment before I adjust. "Jules is waiting."

"I got that, thanks." I step out onto the courtyard. It's a huge square space lined with gray flagstones. On one side, there's the hotel itself, the Thornhill Arms. On the other three sides of the square space, there stand walls made of thorny branches. It's like a hedgerow maze, only with no way out. Even worse, all the walls glitter with silver light. I've seen the same effect on the plants Auntie Mirabelle grows in our penthouse.

They're enchanted with fairy magic.

Blanche extends her arm across the courtyard. "And there's our beloved leader, Jules."

I follow her gesture. At the far end of the flagstone yard stands a lone figure. Although his back is facing us, I can tell that he's tall and strong with a full head of brown hair. Somehow, I expected an old and withered version of Julius Caesar. How come he looks young and hot? I shiver, realizing the answer. It's just what Reggie said. Jules has been fed well. Gross.

Jules is also wearing modern clothing, which is another shocker. Namely, he's dressed up in a modern military uniform that's blue and has shoulder epaulettes. A long red sash crosses his chest to tie at his waistline. And atop his head, there sits a thin golden crown. *He's dressed like a Prince.* The thought makes my skin prickle into gooseflesh.

Oh, no.

I'm trapped in a castle that's protected by magical thorns. Unless I take my medicine, I'll fall into an enchanted sleep. And I'm about to meet some dude named Jules who's decided to dress up like royalty. Worst of all, it's getting close to sunset on my eighteenth birthday, the exact time when I'm supposed to wed my dream man.

This is the Sleeping Beauty template, and it sucks.

I scope out the flagstone yard. There's definitely no easy means of escape. Those thorns will kill me in two seconds flat. That said, I do have one last shot at freedom. Sure, it's a slim chance, but I have to give it a try, so I set my hand by my mouth. "I summon thee, Colonel Mallory the Magnificent!"

Blanche titters. "He can't help you here. No one can." She lowers her voice. "Take my advice. Whatever Jules tell you to do, you do it. Although his plan must be obvious by now."

"Yeah, I got it." A little bit of bile creeps up my throat. "Yuck."

And that's when my memory clicks in. The red toga dress. In ancient Rome, brides always wore red togas on their wedding day. This isn't just the Sleeping Beauty template; it's the big final scene of that story.

I'm here to marry an evil zombie version of Julius Caesar.

My life has officially reached rock bottom.

But then, I underestimate how low I have yet to fall because Jules turns, and I recognize his face immediately.

It's Philpot.

Philpot the Turd is actually the evil leader of the organ-eating Denarii, and I'm about to marry him on my eighteenth birthday, just like my aunties always wanted.

Blanche steps closer to whisper in my ear. "I heard rumors that you can fight. But whatever battle skills you think you have, you're nothing compared to Jules. You're weak, Bryar Rose. Incomplete. He can help you."

With that, Blanche sets off my rebel-reflex yet again. I straighten my shoulders and glare at him with everything I've got. "No, I'm stronger than you can imagine. All of you are underestimating me."

It's a total lie, but Blanche's mouth falls open with surprise. *Good.* At least, she's buying my story. I make a mental note to thank Elle later. All her lessons in conning and bluffing your way out of trouble are paying off. I can almost hear her in my head.

"Keep up the con until you can escape."

In this case, the con is pretending I have a way out of here… until I find one that could actually work. Lifting my chin, I flip my hair over my shoulder and sashay toward Jules with a hip-swish that says I can handle anything. It's not the best plan I've ever had, but right now? It's the only chance I've got.

CHAPTER NINETEEN
KNOX

My inner wolf growls in my head. *"Find mate. Save mate."*

He's wrong about the "mate" part. Still, when it comes to finding and saving Bryar Rose, my wolf and I are definitely on the same page. For the last hour, I've been trying to get past this forest of thorns and reach Bryar Rose. Alec and Elle stand nearby.

It took the three of us all night—along with a ton of wizard spells—to find out where Philpot took Bryar Rose. But we did it. She's not far from this very spot, in a place called the Thornhill Arms hotel.

So far, so good.

About two hours ago, Alec cast a transport spell for all three of us to come here. We couldn't get right into the hotel itself—it's shielded with too much magic. Instead, we landed beside the boundary between this enchanted thorn forest and some regular woods. Since then, we've been pacing along the borderline, trying find a break in the thorns. All you need is one path through magic like this, and you can get through. But whoever cast these thorns is a master. We haven't found a single break.

I stare at the black and twisted branches. The thorns here are razor-sharp and enchanted to attack anyone who enters the forest. An hour ago, I stuck my hand in, and my palm got skewered. Sure, I have the shifter power to self-heal, but even then, I can only handle so much.

Elle and Alec step closer. They're both wearing jeans, T-shirts, and hiking boots. Of course, Alec is also sporting a suit coat that's packed with tons of pockets for his gemstones. He thinks that wizards who carry around man-bags of jewels look like losers. I have to agree with him on that one. Also, it advertises who you are, which isn't too clever either.

I stare greedily at the thorns.

Sure, those things look killer. But they're what's keeping me away from Bry. She needs help, right? I've got to do something. Maybe I should just jump in and trust my powers of healing. Anything's better than standing around. Besides, when I stuck my hand in before, I was in human form. What's the point of being a warden if I don't test my limits every so often?

Alec steps up to my side. "I know what you're thinking." He lets out one of his long-suffering sighs. "I don't like this, Knox." Still, I know Alec's sighing routine. He won't stop me.

"Look, I'm going in. That's not up for discussion. You can watch my back or take off."

He sighs again. "You know I've got you." His face looks pale, though. Between casting all those spells to find Bryar Rose and bringing us here, my friend is wiped out. A small part of me says that if things get tough, he might not be able to heal me.

I decide that little part is wrong. Time is running out. By sunset, Bryar Rose will lose her wolf. Some things are simply worth taking a risk. I give Alec a playful punch on the shoulder. "Thanks, man."

Elle steps closer to Alec. "Can't we talk him out of this?"

A muscle jumps along Alec's jaw. "No. Trust me."

"Don't worry. Everything will be fine." Now that the decision is in motion, I can't wait to get started. Setting my hands at the waistline of my leather pants, I prepare to strip.

Alec sets his hands on Elle's shoulders and turns her away from the "Naked Knox Show." *Whatever.* If she's going to hang with Alec and me, she'll eventually see my junk. It's just how life goes when you're a shifter.

The moment I'm bare, my wolf bursts through my flesh. It's like being torn apart from the inside out. Agony explodes inside me. My bones crack, and muscles snap. Fur replaces skin as my hands change into claws. It's over in a heartbeat, which is some kind of record for me.

The moment my transformation's done, I leap straight into the wall of thorns. My claws rip through the thick branches. There are too many of them though. Faster than I can tear them apart, the branches loop around me from head to toe. Thorns spike through my hide and stab me in a hundred places at once. Pain radiates everywhere.

A moment later, I'm surrounded in red light. I'd know that particular shade anywhere. Alec is casting a spell. The branches loosen from my body. The thorns retract from my skin. Elle grabs my back paws and hauls me out of the wall of thorns. I look like a bloody pincushion. At least I'm alive.

But I'm no closer to Bry.

Alec leans down beside me. His face looks pale. Black circles droop under his eyes. "That was close. I almost lost you."

I get that he's bummed, but I'm too busy healing to care right now. My fur is pretty much soaked in blood. Changing back will hurt like hell, but it's the best way to get cleaned up and healed so we can keep on looking. Glancing over at Elle, I chuff out a low breath. That's all the warning she's getting that I'm about to transform into a naked dude.

Alec's been around me enough that he knows exactly what happens next. He leaps to Elle's side and angles her away from me once more. My body slowly starts turning back into a human. Every snap of bone and tear of skin is excruciating. Still, it's better than running about as a blood-soaked wolf. Within a few minutes, I'm back to my regular human self, only fully healed and dressed. Only, recovering from those thorns took a toll on my inner magic.

Normally, I'd rest for a few hours before going on. That won't happen today, though.

Bry still needs my help.

A faint shimmer of silver dust fills the air. Someone is coming, and that someone is definitely a fairy.

Alec and I exchange a confused look. "Anyone expecting fairies?" I ask.

"Not me." Alec turns to Elle. "How about you? Could that be one of Bryar Rose's aunties?"

My mouth thins to an angry line. I don't know much about Bry's aunties, but they seem to be far too concerned with her marrying that Philpot for my taste. Having them around will not be helpful.

"I doubt it," says Elle. "Bry's aunties aren't powerful enough to transport here. And even if they could, they're three self-centered skanks. They'd never bother."

I smirk. "No, what do you really think?"

The glitter comes into focus. A human outline appears, and whoever this is, it's definitely a guy. Elle pops her hand over her mouth. "I know this fairy. It's Colonel Mallory the Magnificent."

I'm not thrilled about this news, but Elle said that this fairy dude might actually want to help Bry. At this point, I'll take any aid we can get.

The fairy dust finally congeals into what looks like an older version of Clark Gable. He wears a black suit, white shirt, and wide-brimmed hat.

"Colonel Mallory the Magnificent, at your service." He sets his hands on his hips and surveys the wall of thorns. "I see you're having the same troubles that I am. Can't seem to get through to Bryar Rose."

I eye him carefully. He seems legit, but you never know with fairies. They always have an agenda. "Why are you looking for Bry?"

"You seem to have an interest in my girl." He gives me one of those sly Southern smiles.

I make sure my eyes glow golden, just so he knows who he's dealing with. "Answer the question, fae."

"I never cursed Bryar Rose, if that's what y'all are thinking. I saved her. And if you needed any further proof, it would be in the fact that I'm standing on *this side* of the thorn forest. So, let's get down to it. Have you found any breaks in the magic?"

"No," says Elle. "And we've been looking for hours." Her shoulders slump. "You haven't found a way through either, I'm guessing."

"That would be no, sugar. I've cast about every spell I can think of today, but whoever did the thorns in this here forest, they used the power of a hundred fairies. I couldn't break through, and for me, that's really something. Even worse, they cast a spell against dragon shifters. I consider that downright rude."

"So they knew you might be coming." If anything, that fact confirms this Colonel Mallory guy is legit. I'm starting to wonder if Jules himself had a hand in abducting Bry. This kind of scheming around fairy tale themes is classic for him.

Colonel Mallory taps his temple. "We need to come up with another plan, children. I'm afraid that means leaving here for a time. We need more power."

"No way. I'm a strong werewolf. Alec brought a bunch of gemstones. And Elle has a fairy-seed gun." It's a beauty, too. The thing shoots off enchanted seeds that turn into nasty killer plants. As fairy magic goes, it's one of the few inventions they have that adjusts to modern technology.

"I hate to be the bearer of bad tidings, but we need to go back to the city and get more magical help."

"We already called in a ton of favors," I say. "Alec got his hands on some super-powerful gems. Elle got herself a special gun. I asked Azizi to send an army of weres."

Colonel Mallory sighs. "And how did that work out for y'all? From where I stand, we're no closer to Bryar Rose." He taps his nose with his pointer finger. "And I smell blood in the air."

"I tried to pass the thorn forest in were form. It didn't go well."

"Now, you did that without wizard protection—that would be your trouble. I know for a fact that this young man—" he points to Alec— "knows some powerful wizards. They could cast some better protections for you than gems can provide. Also, having all them weres drive out here? Not too subtle. You'd also do better to have extra sets of hands to cast transport spells. That means more wizards, my friend."

I can't help but notice he isn't suggesting we find more fairies. At least, that part of his plan makes sense.

"Colonel Mallory may have a point." Alec turns to me. "You already made a pact to muster the wolves. At least, this will get them here faster. And we can transport in the best from around the world."

Azizi was thrilled when I asked for his help with Bry. He's been dying to get me to lead the werewolves. He'd never force me, though. But when the pack shows up and helps me with Bry, I'll be indebted to all of them. They'll howl for me to be their alpha.

Colonel Mallory holds up his stub of a cigar, takes in a deep breath, and exhales a bit of flame onto the tip. He takes a few deep puffs from the smoke, his eyes lost in thought. "Sorry, son. I'm afraid our best bet is to return to the city forthwith. I can transport y'all, if you like."

All eyes focus on me. An electric anticipation hangs in the air. I know they're waiting for me to make the final call here. Do we leave Bryar Rose? I rake my hands through my hair.

I want to believe there's something else we can do, but I can't think of a damned thing. "Fine, we'll go back to the city."

This is the right thing to do, so why do I feel like howling with rage? We could bribe the wizards and summon werewolves in a matter of hours. Or it could be days—weeks, even—before we can return with enough power to break into Thornhill Arms.

Please, let Bryar Rose still be here.

CHAPTER TWENTY
BRYAR ROSE

Tossing my long brown hair over my shoulder, I stride across the flagstone patio. With every step, my heart pounds harder. My brain tries to wrap itself around what's happening, but can't. This situation is so extreme it just doesn't seem real.

Last night, I was kidnapped.

Now, I'm walking over to Jules, the leader of the Denarii.

But he's really Philpot, my fake ex-boyfriend.

Nope, still doesn't seem real.

I steal a quick glance over my shoulder at the Thornhill Arms hotel behind me. I've never seen it up close before. From this angle, the place looks boxy and cheap in a faux-medieval kind of way. Gray stucco covers the exterior, and jagged moldings line the roof. And of course, there's a tower on either side of the building. I shiver. How many times did I look at this place from Elle's cabin, never suspecting what was really going on here? Some of Elle's old advice echoes through my head.

"Focus on the con. Take stock of your surroundings."

Good idea. Scanning left and right, I check out the borders of the square courtyard. Towering walls of thorns line every side. My breath catches. Wow, those thorns sure look deadly. There's definitely no way to escape through them.

I keep walking toward Philpot, who stands on the opposite side of the courtyard wearing a blue military uniform of some kind and the sickest, most smug grin you can ever imagine. It's like the Grinch on crack. I fight the urge to gag.

"We've never been properly introduced. I'm Jules." He offers his hand. I ignore it.

Rage heats my veins. *He's doing fancypants introductions now? Really?*

I pause beside him. "I'm Bryar Rose, and this is over."

Sure, this guy looks like Philpot, but he's stopped playing the dumbass. Now, his black eyes shine with an evil intellect. The muscles of his face look tight, as if he's barely holding in his rage. It's hard to believe that Philpot and Jules are one and the same person.

But they are.

Jules narrows his eyes into slits. "Is that false bravado I hear?"

"I'm not kidding. I'm leaving. Now." Spinning about, I march back toward the hotel doorway. *Push the con; that's what Elle always says.* Who knows? Maybe I'll be able to stroll right out on home.

Jules moves so quickly, I hardly see him do it. A heartbeat later, he's standing in my path. "But you can't leave. This is all for you...my Princely attire...this hotel...our upcoming wedding. I've watched you for years, patiently waiting for this moment. You aren't walking away until I've had my say."

Now, there was a lot about that speech that I didn't like. To begin with, the fact that he still thinks we're getting married is creepy beyond belief. And the *"watching you for years"* stuff makes me ill. However, there was one thing he said that I *did* like. The whole part about *"you aren't walking away* until" seems to suggest if I listen to him first, then I can go. That's something I need to nail down.

"Let me get this straight," I say slowly. "If I let you talk to me, then you'll let me leave."

"If you still want to depart."

"Fine." I fold my arms over my chest. "Make it fast."

Jules raises his arm. "Wife!"

A door to the hotel swings open, and Blanche comes racing out across the courtyard. She skitters to a stop beside us. "Yes, my husband?"

"Tell Bryar Rose your story."

My back teeth lock with frustration. This is starting to feel like one of those "sharing moment" speeches that Madame would force out of us in group therapy. Sure, Blanche will say something different this time, but I have no illusions. These speeches all end the same way. Somehow, I'm always the big loser in this story.

Blanche clasps her hands under her chin. "Once upon a time, I was a failure, just like you."

Here it comes.

"Really?" I ask. "Because from where I'm standing, only one of us has internal organs right now. I'm considering that a *win* in the Bryar Rose column."

A muscle twitches by Jules' eye. "You said you would listen."

I raise my hands, palms forward. "Fine. Go on."

"But with the help of Jules, I was finally able to live out my dream of the Snow White fairy tale life template. I live in a huge house. I have tons of servants."

"I'm guessing they're all dead though, right?" I bob my head. "Just checking."

"They're not dead. They're Denarii. And most of all, I have married my handsome Prince. You don't have to be a loser anymore, either. With our help, you can finally succeed. You can live out the Sleeping Beauty life template."

"Look, I'm doing fine."

"Don't lie to us." Jules' voice turns tight with rage. "You're a complete waste."

"Is speech-time over? Because I've heard what you have to say, and I'm still unconvinced."

Blanche shakes her head. "Don't you understand? The Denarii are the top of the food chain, even over the Magicorum."

I remember Knox's scars. He got those by fighting Jules and his minions. "I'm sure that's what you like to think, but in reality, the Magicorum are the only ones stopping you from turning all humans into dinner."

A smug gleam shines in Jules' eyes. "It's true. Most Denarii dine on human flesh. Not me. Magicorum is the meal I prefer."

That little tidbit of nasty takes a moment to sink in. I never heard before that the Denarii ever saw the Magicorum as a meal. I thought the Magicorum fought the Denarii, and so the Denarii hunted them right back. "That's not how I heard it."

Jules' stern face softens with a smile. "I allow the Magicorum to think they are rebel fighters. It keeps their spirits up and makes them easier to control. Every hunter ultimately works to control their prey's population, don't you think?"

That makes a sickening amount of sense, actually. Which is all the more reason to cut this conversation short.

I raise my pointer finger. "For the record, I'm still not convinced."

Blanche grabs Jules' sleeve. "Can I tell her, darling?"

"Of course, pet."

Blanche turns to me. "You're a member of the Magicorum. That means you aren't just a meal to Jules. You'll be one of his brides. You can be dinner, or you can live out the fairy tale dream. I'm here to tell you it's better than you could ever imagine." She smiles that 1950s smile, the one that says, *I'm in a cigarette ad, and smoking isn't gross or anything.*

Well, smoking is gross, and this conversation is over.

My lessons in martial arts flicker through my mind's eye. I picture three different ways I could take this guy down. I firm up my footing. "You want to kill me? I won't be easy to harvest."

"And I've no desire to kill you. Bryar Rose, you are special. That's why I created the Philpot identity in the first place. It wasn't easy, pretending to be such a stupid sod. Not to mention the hassle of working with your aunties for so many years."

In this situation, you'd think the fact that I'm about to get eaten by a cannibal zombie Julius Caesar would keep me focused, but those words throw me for a loop. "You've been working with my aunties?"

"Of course. But the terms of our arrangement are confidential, I'm afraid. You'll have to ask them about it directly."

I try to get back into battle stance, but my head isn't there yet. "You're lying."

Jules waves his hand dismissively. "I don't get involved in family squabbles. The important thing is this. I'm very careful about my diet. Based on what I eat, I've been able to gain magical powers over the years."

"We're back to eating my brains. Got it."

"No, silly girl. I'm not asking to eat your brains. I'm inviting you to become one of the Denarii and my bride."

His words send chills over my skin. If I hadn't puffed a ton of meds a few minutes ago, I'm sure I'd be having an episode right now. "We already covered this. No. Never."

"Don't be too rash. Colonel Mallory can't save you here—yes, I know his role in your life. No one will ever get past the thorns to help you escape. And please try to think on this for a moment. You're being offered the chance of a lifetime…of many lifetimes, in fact. As a Denarii, you will know power like you never imagined. And you'll be tied to me, the greatest Denarii of them all."

Blanche blinks so furiously I think she's having an aneurysm. "It's so marvelous, Bryar Rose. We'll be sister wives and everything!"

I pinch the bridge of my nose. "No means no, Jules."

"How can you refuse? Look at Blanche. Is she not eternally beautiful? Does she not seem blissfully happy?"

I can't believe what I'm hearing. "Happy? I knew one of your Denarii ladies. Madame Grimoire. She ended up roasted in the remains of my friend Elle's cabin. Not exactly my definition of a happy ending."

"Madame Grimoire is a poor example," says Jules. "She got what she deserved. Madame was supposed to observe you, not attack. But she became obsessed with you."

My eyes widen. "Me?"

189

"Well, Madame Grimoire wasn't a sister wife," says Blanche. "She was just a worker bee. But she always wanted a place at Jules' side. You see, once you start dreaming about animals from ancient Egypt, that means you're chosen to be a sister wife."

My mouth falls open. "My dreams with the golden jackal."

"Yes, and I had a dream about falcons. Both are from ancient Egypt!"

"I got that part now, thanks."

"Well, don't feel badly. Madame had always been the jealous type, even if you didn't have a special dream. It cost us some very fine recruits in the past."

"Cost us recruits." His words sear through my memories. So that's what the Teen Therapy Group was really about. "Blanche, did you get recruited from the group?"

"Of course. It was the high point of my life. Thank-you, dear husband."

"You're welcome, my love." Jules gives Blanche a benevolent pat on the shoulder and turns to me. "So, are you ready to willingly join us?"

"Let me get this straight. You're completely done explaining this to me?"

"Yes. I should think it's impossible to refuse."

"You're wrong. I refuse. Good-bye." I walk away as quickly as possible, but Jules grabs my wrist.

"Stop. You're joining us anyway."

I pull against his grip, but the guy's hands feel like they are made of steel. "I thought this was my choice."

"It's not. I lied."

My training comes back to me in a flash. I elbow Jules in the diaphragm and stomp on his instep. Once he loses balance and breath, I flip him over onto his back. He lands on the flagstone with a thud. Leaping forward, I land on his chest and jab for his throat. Taking out someone's larynx is the fastest way to kill them, after all. I'm not looking for a big battle here. I just want Jules out of the picture.

What Jules does next happens so fast, it's hard to keep up. From his left hand sprouts a thorn-covered branch. It quickly winds about my wrists, binding my hands in front of me. In his right, Jules grips a large red stone. The gem glows with crimson light as the flagstone beneath me crumbles. I lose my footing as I tumble into the earth. Before I know it, I'm waist-deep in solid rock. I wiggle my arms. My hands are tied in front of me. The bindings on my wrists hold firm, while bottom half of my body is solidly encased in earth and stone.

I'm trapped.

Jules' features lengthen, his mouth turning into a wolf's snout that's lined with pointed teeth. His eyes glow with golden light. The silver glow of fairy dust surrounds his body like a sparkling cloud. And the red light of wizard magic glows on his palms.

All three kinds of magic...all in one man. And he's trying to kill me.

My vision starts to blur. I can picture the lockbox deep inside me. It's made of wood, and its exterior is carved with runes. The lid rumbles as whatever's inside tries to break free. Colonel Mallory called it my power. I call it my curse.

Another episode is about to hit me. *No, not now.* Jules just showed that he has mastered all three kinds of magic—shifter, warlock, and fairy. I'm now embedded half-way into the ground and at his mercy. If I'm lucky, he'll kill me outright. If I'm not, then he'll transform me into a monster just like him.

Meanwhile, Blanche bobs on the balls of her feet and claps with glee. It's like she's a six-year-old who's about to get her first pony. Somehow, that's the worst part of all.

As horrible as things seemed before, they take on a new level of terror. I twist in my bindings. I'm still wrapped in the thorny branches with my body embedded waist-high into the ground. My skin sheens with sweat as I do the only thing that's left to me now.

Scream my head off.

CHAPTER TWENTY-ONE
KNOX

Pursing his lips, Colonel Mallory sizes me up from head to toe, like I'm a sketchy-looking cabbie who offered him a ride in an unmarked taxi. Before speaking again, he does the same to Elle and Alec. "If I'm transporting y'all back to the city, you need to stand a little closer." He grins a white-toothed smile. "I don't bite."

"He bite," says my inner wolf.

"I'm sure he does," I reply in my mind. *"We'll be careful when we go with him."*

"No go. Stay with mate."

I hold in a growl. Leaving the forest is hard enough without my inner wolf giving me crap.

Elle and Alec move into a smaller huddle. I'm sure they're thrilled for any excuse to get closer. Colonel Mallory tips his hat in their direction. "That's fine." He turns to me. "You coming along?"

I don't move an inch. Part of me knows that leaving is the best thing for Bry, but I just can't do it. "I'm thinking about it."

"Well, son. In that case, you can get your own self back to the city. We're leaving." Colonel Mallory raises his arms. A cloud of silver fairy dust appears.

My best friend reaches out for me. "It's not too late. Transport spells take a little while. Move closer. Come with us."

Elle fixes me with a serious look. "You know I wouldn't go unless I was absolutely certain this is best for Bry."

Elle has these huge blue eyes, and right now, they're looking all weepy and sincere. I feel like a total ass. After all, my friends are only trying to do the right thing. Me hanging back just makes it harder. I take a step toward them, ready to join the group and transport back to Manhattan. That's when I hear it.

Bryar Rose is screaming.

"Stop transporting," I say. "You hear that?" She screams again. "It's Bry."

Colonel Mallory lowers his arms, and the silver dust fades. "Are you certain?"

"My wolf hearing is never wrong. Someone's hurting her."

Colonel Mallory shakes his head. "All the more reason for us to go. There's nothing we can do here."

I pound my fist onto my leg. *There must be something.*

Elle gives me those watery eyes again. "Knox, I know how you feel. Believe me. But waiting here does not help her."

I round on Colonel Mallory. "You said you were looking for a break in the thorns. What if you could make one?"

"Even I don't have that kind of magic, son."

An idea starts to form. It's crazy, but it's worth a try. "What if you had help; could you cast something else?"

"Depends on the help."

"What about Elle?"

"Well, now." Colonel Mallory sets his hands in his pockets and rolls back on his heels. "That's a possibility. Miss Elle is a very powerful fairy indeed." He focuses on Elle. "You ever cast a spell?"

"No."

"Didn't even bring one silver particle of fairy dust to life?"

"If I did, my stepfamily would find me in a heartbeat. You don't know what Blackaverre went through to get me out of that house. I'd never risk it." She hugs her elbows. "Now I don't know if I could. I'm willing to try, though. Anything for Bry." She lifts her chin. "Would this spell be hard?"

Colonel Mallory's face creases into a sympathetic smile. "Incredibly. The only spell that could help us here is a magical link. Essentially, you and I would merge our powers to break the enchantment on these thorns. It's as simple as holding hands."

Alec frowns. "You'll cast at the same time?"

"Not really, son. We'd stay separate people, but for the purposes of the spell, our magic would emanate from the same person."

"That's not possible," says Alec.

"Not for wizards." Colonel Mallory shrugs. "But a few fairies can do it."

"A few fairies?" The way Alec asks the question, I can tell that he's absolutely not convinced.

"Fine, *I'm* the only one who can do it."

I get that Alec is skeptical, but Bry is off somewhere screaming. "So you've done this before?"

"Absolutely not," says Colonel Mallory. "It's just a theory. But it would certainly require a fairy whose power and experience matches mine." He turns to Elle. "There's no doubt in my mind. You've got the natural power, sugar."

"But not the experience." Elle scrubs her hands over her face. "So, casting this linking spell is impossible."

"Don't worry, sugar. With enough practice, you'll be able to cast someday. Your soul knows what to do, even if your mind doesn't."

Colonel Mallory's words echo through my mind.

Her soul knows.

I round on Alec. "Back at the LeCharme offices, you cast a spell on Bry. You spoke to her soul. Can you do that to Elle?"

Alec frowns. "It's dangerous to do it with her standing right here. Remember the frog?" He makes an exploding noise and moves his hands apart. "He said they'd need to hold hands."

"A fairy is not a frog," says Colonel Mallory. "A soul spell would be safe."

I turn to Colonel Mallory. "So if he cast the soul spell, you two could link?"

"Why, we most certainly could." He purses his lips. "That is, if your friend can really cast a spell like that. Not too many wizards have that kind of power these days."

"He can cast it."

Alec pales. "I can do it, but I won't. Besides, Elle wouldn't let me cast that spell on her. She'll block it."

"No, I won't. Like I said before, if it helps Bryar Rose, I'll do anything."

"It's a safe spell to cast if you're miles away. But this close?" Alec points to Colonel Mallory. "I don't care what he said about fairies and frogs. It could kill you."

Elle pales. "Did you hear that scream? If we don't get over there now, Bry will die."

Alec pinches the bridge of his nose. "Not doing it."

"Now, children," says Colonel Mallory. "Let me get this straight. This boy here can cast a senior-level soul speak? How's that possible exactly?"

I look to Alec. It's not my place to share his secrets. Unfortunately, Alec isn't talking.

"Son, don't make me cast on you."

A muscle ticks in Alec's jawline. "I'm a warden for witches and warlocks." I notice that Colonel Mallory is the only person surprised by this news. Elle must already have known. *Interesting.*

Colonel Mallory's silver eyes light up. "Are you now? Well, in that case, get casting."

"No. I can't risk Elle."

Everything about Colonel Mallory turns deadly serious. "And I won't risk Bryar Rose. You're no match for me, son. Don't try."

Elle gently rests her hands over Alec's. "You worry about me getting hurt? Well, it would kill me to see my friend die. Do this for me. Please."

Alec opens his mouth as if ready to argue. I'm tempted to punch him in the face until he agrees, but before I get the chance, Alec nods and steps away. "I'll do it. But I hate this idea."

"Thanks, man," I say.

In reply, Alec only glares in my direction. I get that he's pissed, but I can't worry about that now. Bry is in serious trouble.

With that thought, Bryar Rose's screams sound once more. Every muscle in my body gets tense. I want to transform into my wolf so badly, it hurts. It doesn't matter that my thinking mind knows I'll get skewered the moment I leap into the thorns. My animal-self wants to protect what's mine.

Mine.

The word ricochets around my soul. *Mine.* My wolf always thought Bryar Rose was his mate. When exactly did I get the same ideas?

Bry's face appears in my mind. I picture her intelligent blue eyes, luscious pink mouth, and delicate features. I shiver, remembering the touch of her slim fingers along my scars. This girl is a crazy combination of strength and sweetness. She can give a gentle kiss as easily as a swift kick. That girl owns me, body and soul. I'll never allow anything bad to happen to her.

Which brings me back to the present moment. I turn to Colonel Mallory. For whatever reason, he's as invested in Bryar Rose as I am. "You got everything you need to get started, Colonel?"

"Almost." Colonel Mallory waves Elle over. "Take my hand, sugar."

In this situation, some folks might whine or cower. Not Elle. She straightens her back and strolls right over to Colonel Mallory's side. I can smell the sour tang of extreme fear on her. It only makes her strength all the more impressive.

"Good friend for mate," says my wolf.

"Yeah, she's strong." I don't bother correcting my wolf about the whole mate thing. After all, I have bigger worries. Did I just sign Elle up for a suicide mission? What if this doesn't work?

Alex reaches into the pocket of his sport coat and pulls out a handful of red gems. Closing his eyes, he raises his arm. The gems cupped inside his palm glow with red light. Alec opens his hand. The gems cascade from his palm and multiply until they take the shape of Elle. Only, while the real Elle is made from flesh and bone, this version is created entirely from glittering jewels. The Ruby-Elle scans the scene. Without speaking a word, she walks over to Colonel Mallory and takes his other hand.

Now, it's one thing to know that someone's soul knows how to use magic without their mind being in on the game. It's another to see it in practice. The look of absolute calm on the ruby version of Elle is beautiful and upsetting, all at once.

It's as if she knows she's about to die.

The moment Ruby-Elle takes Colonel Mallory's hand, a flare of red light shines around the living Elle. For a moment, she's lit up like a Christmas tree. Alec's magic is really kicking in now. The brightness disappears, and Elle hunches over in pain. I wince. I've had Alec zap me before, and it can really sting. That level of magic has to hurt like nobody's business. Alec rushes to Elle and scoops her into his arms.

"I'm so sorry. I didn't want to do this to you." My best friend may have looked pale before, but now he appears positively bloodless. I've never seen him cast so many major spells in one day. I don't know how much longer the guy can hold out.

"Alec." Elle slumps against his shoulder, her eyes rolling back into her head.

This situation sucks. My best friend is in pain. Elle's hurting too. Hell, she might even be dying. But most of all, I can't stop replaying Bry's screams in my mind. If this magic doesn't work, what will happen to her?

Colonel Mallory and Ruby-Elle raise their joined hands. The gemstones in Ruby-Elle's body glow brighter. Silver fairy dust surrounds Colonel Mallory. Within seconds, the dust begins to glow with a crimson light. My breath catches.

Their magic is linking up, just like Colonel Mallory said it would. This spell might actually work.

The fairy dust begins to swirl into a smaller and smaller sphere. Soon, it's the size of a grenade that's made of both silver and red light. Colonel Mallory and Ruby-Elle share a look before speaking a single word in unison:

"Now!"

The small orb of light zooms off into the thorn forest. The brightness slams forward in a straight line, cutting its way through the wall of thorny branches. After that, it disappears. Have all my hopes gone with it? The branches don't look changed at all, and the light of the spell is gone.

Maybe something more is supposed to happen. All I need is patience.

I clench and unclench my fists, trying to release some nervous energy. Finally, I can't take it anymore. "Did that do it, Colonel?"

"I don't think so, son." Colonel Mallory turns to Alec. "You can release her now."

Alec snaps his fingers, and the ruby version of Elle collapses into a cascade of blackened gemstones. The living Elle curls up with pain. Alec holds her more tightly against his chest. Her body goes slack.

I rush up to Elle and rest my fingers on her throat.

Alec's face is tight with fear. "Is she all right?"

I know a dead body when I see one. Thankfully, Elle isn't one of them. "She's alive. She needs some healing spells, though."

"I have gems back at LeCharme that will do it." Alec addresses Colonel Mallory. "Take us there."

I set my hand on Colonel Mallory's shoulder. "Not yet, man. You should wait. Maybe the spell needs more time."

"I'm afraid not, son. It's over. If the spell were going to work, we'd have known by now."

His words feel like a death sentence for Bry. If we abandon her now, we may never find her again. "You can't know that for sure. Have you ever cast with someone's soul before?"

"That's beside the point. We're heading to the city for help, and that's final."

My thinking self knows this is sane, but my animal side will have none of it. Every instinct I have tells me not to leave. "I won't go with you."

Inside my mind, my wolf grunts in agreement. *"No leave mate."*
I give my wolf a mental high-five. *"Damn right, buddy."*

Alec shakes his head. "You and your furry instincts. Your kind could learn something from wizards. Give logic a try."

Right. Not sure I'd say that wizards use logic. It's more like keeping a list of grudges against rival families. At least, we werewolves fight, and then it's over.

"Go take care of Elle. I'm staying right here." I focus on Colonel Mallory. "Can you transport them? I don't think Alec could handle another casting right now."

"Oh, I can do it." Colonel Mallory inspects Alec. "You look like hell in a handbasket."

"You don't look too nice yourself," says Alec. My friend has a point. Colonel Mallory's tan skin seems almost green. Whatever that casting did, it certainly took something out of him as well.

Elle opens her eyes a crack. "Did it work?" Her voice is barely a whisper.

"Not yet, sugar. But we'll figure out something." Colonel Mallory steps closer to Elle and Alec while raising his arms. A cloud of silvery fairy dust forms around all three of them. It seems to take forever for the dust to grow thick and then fade away. Once it's gone, so are Elle, Alec, and Colonel Mallory.

The thorn forest seems extra-quiet without them here. The sound of my own breathing becomes deafening. I shake my head. What kind of person have I become? I'm waiting around for a miracle while my friends are hurt.

"Wait for mate. Protect mate."

"Don't worry, buddy. We'll stay here."

Suddenly, red and silver light flickers from within the wall of thorns. I pause, my heart beating at double speed. Smoke fills the air. Before me, the wall of thorns combusts from the inside out. Flames lick along the rope-like branches until there's enough room for one man to walk through.

Or in my case, for one wolf to run.

Relief and adrenaline pump through me in equal measure. *The spell worked.* I don't even bother stripping off my clothes. In a single burst of power, I transform into my wolf and take off down the thorny path. Bry's scent grows stronger.

She's here.

She's alive.

And I'm setting her free if it's the last thing I ever do.

CHAPTER TWENTY-TWO
BRYAR ROSE

I'm trapped.

That thought rings through my mind, over and over. Panic zings through my nervous system. *This is too awful to be real.* Jules just cast a spell on me. Now I'm embedded waist-deep in the hotel courtyard. Thin cords of thorn-covered branches wrap around my wrists. And that's not even the worst part.

He also used all three kinds of magic: fairy, shifter, and wizard.

I shake my head. It was enough of a shock to learn that Philpot was actually Jules, the secret leader of the evil Denarii. Those creeps are super-strong and can live for thousands of years. Pretty scary, but that should be the limit of their superpowers, right? I mean, they're not supposed to wield any magic, let alone master all three kinds. A chill runs up my neck.

Yet that's exactly what Jules did. Every cell in my body vibrates with terror. *I have to get out of here.*

Trouble is, I'm still stuck waist-deep in a courtyard. Beneath the ground, jagged stones shove into my lower back and legs. I wiggle against my confinement. A few of the rocks shift against me. It's a start, but getting out of here will be a huge pain. Any time I move, the sharp stones cut into my skin. *Yowch.*

I won't give up, though. Elle's advice rings through my head. "*When you get into trouble, don't lose your cool.*" I slap on what I hope is a confident face.

I can do this. I can get out of here.

Jules kneels in front of me. He's totally returned to his non-werewolf look. "How are you feeling, Bryar Rose?" The smarminess is back as well, it seems.

Somehow, I manage to keep looking calm. *Go, me.* "I'm fine, Jules. Just waiting around, plotting my revenge."

"You won't break my magic." The words come out as more of a question, though.

Awesome.

Jules totally thinks I can escape. My pulse speeds up with this news. Maybe he suspects that I have help coming...or even a weapon hidden in a pocket somewhere. Whatever it is, I'm going to act like I have a plan. Another classic piece of Elle's advice rings through my head.

"*Act like you can do anything, then work the con until you're free.*"

I crank up my sass a notch. "You don't seem so sure of yourself."

"I'm positive." He still doesn't sound it, though.

Yes.

Blanche steps closer. "You're about to remove her organs, am I right?"

"I will transform her into my wife."

Oh, he totally thinks that he's removing my organs. Yuck.

I glare at Blanche. "Back off."

Blanche doesn't move an inch, though. "May I have a single bite, my husband? I know that normally, only *you* can feast on the Magicorum. Still, I thought you might make an exception. After all, I dressed her so prettily." She smiles so wide I'm surprised she doesn't get a face cramp.

"Hey, Blanchey-baby. Over here." She grudgingly flicks her gaze in my direction. "This whole situation is bad enough without you planning on how to divide up bites of my organs. Back off."

"My future wife is right. Your question is disrespectful." Jules gestures toward the hotel. "You may go now."

Blanche puffs out her lower lip. She still isn't leaving, though. "You like her more than you like me. I'm the lead wife. All I wanted was a bite."

In a flash, Jules moves to stand in front of Blanche. He grips her jaw in his hand. "No one feasts on the Magicorum except for me. Do we understand each other?" Blanche nods, but Jules still doesn't release her chin. "Want to join the other Denarii? Fancy being hungry all the time? Little food? No new clothes?" Blanche shakes her head. Tears line her eyes.

If she hadn't just asked to eat some of my brains, I might even feel sorry for her.

"Then go." Jules sets Blanche loose. She picks up her skirts and races for the hotel like her life depended on it. And let's face it; it probably does. I scan the building carefully. Bodies shift in the shadows.

Huh. When I stepped down from the tower, Blanche said there were some others rustling around. Elle always says to get your captor talking. The Denarii hiding in the Thornhill Arms is as good a topic as any.

"How many of your Denarii are here?" Underground, I shift enough that my leg breaks loose. My pulse picks up speed. I can almost taste my freedom.

Jules stands with his back to me as he scans the broken windows. He shrugs. "I really wouldn't know."

Something about his answer just smells rotten to me. "Come on. You know perfectly well how many Denarii follow you around. In fact, I bet you work hard to hide their actual numbers."

"Please. I can't remember every meal." Jules swings around to face me again. A predatory look gleams in his dark eyes. "Those animals are not like my wives. When I consume your physical form, the essence of your energy sears into my very soul."

Wow. Is that ever a gross thought.

"I'm not marrying you. Or sharing essences. Whatever."

"We'll see about that." He kneels before me once more. "You're nothing without me. On your own, you'd have no chance to realize your fairy tale life template. Look what I have done for you. A Prince. A castle. Thorns. You're about to be perfect." He pulls a few gems from his pocket. Inside his fist, the stones flare with red light.

My throat tightens with fear. I know what that brightness means. *Wizard magic.*

When the light disappears, Jules now holds a long knife in his right hand. The blade glows with magical power. At that sight, I strain all the harder to get free. I kick against the underground stones and try to yank my wrists free. The thorns slice into my skin.

"This is such a shame, my love." He gestures between us. "This isn't how I'd wished our nuptials would occur. I had such plans to woo you. You were *so close* to falling in love with me."

"You're delusional."

"Then that werewolf forced my hand, as the saying goes. He stole you from me. I had to kidnap you."

"Really? Has anyone else told you that you're a crap listener? I was not falling for you."

"Did that beast tell you that he's my greatest foe? He's a terrorist dog who hunts down my people."

Keep him talking, Bryar Rose. My right leg is now propped onto a rock shelf of some kind. As long as I keep my upper body still, Jules shouldn't suspect a thing. I firm up my footing. This could be the very leverage I need to push my way out. A bead of sweat trickles down my cheek, but somehow, I keep my voice calm. "Knox mentioned that he hunts Denarii. But calling him a terrorist? I don't think so. In my opinion, Knox is more of an exterminator."

Jules laughs, which wasn't the reaction I was hoping for. "You'll change your mind soon enough. Just wait until he's hunting you."

His words prickle my skin. What if Jules *does* succeed? Then Knox would totally try to kill me. A sickly feeling settles into my stomach as I realize the truth. If I became a Denarii, I'd *want* Knox to end my life. Running around like Blanche or Madame isn't my idea of fun.

Muscles flex in Jules' neck. The subject of Knox really seems to bug him. "That dog knows far too much about me. Knox has foiled me in the past, but now I have finally bested him." Jules' mouth winds into a nasty grin. "He thinks I'm the nonthreatening Philpot. It's just the advantage I need to kill off the furry freak."

I gasp as the news slams into me. Jules has been planning more than forcing me to marry him. He wants Knox dead, too. How did everything get so horrible? I've just handed Knox over to Jules on a silver platter. Shaking my head, I force myself to get organized again. *Think, think, think.* What would Elle do?

She'd work a con.

I slap on a smarmy smile that's worthy of Jules himself. "Keep telling yourself that, honey bunches. Knox already has you figured out."

A flicker of unease moves across Jules' face. "We'll see." Rising to stand, he turns to face the wall of thorns. The way he glares off into the woods, you'd think Jules expects Knox to leap out at any second.

Long moments pass. Nothing happens. Worry becomes almost a palpable thing in the air. My skin turns slick with sweat.

All of a sudden, groans sound from the hotel. Glancing over, I find hundreds of people staring out the grubby windows to the courtyard. But they aren't people, actually. They're Denarii. Their skeletal frames and gray skin are a clear giveaway. Plus, some of them have the classic scar lines on their skin—the sign of their organs having been removed. I shiver. These Denarii wear everything from flapper gowns to medieval tunics. And even though their outfits may be different, they share one thing in common.

All of them are staring straight at me. It's like I'm a yummy steak dinner, and they're definitely not vegetarian.

I kick at the stones by my legs. Some of the rocks move. The grinding of stones echoes across the yard. Jules rounds on me. "What's going on?"

A plan appears in my mind. I decide to call it my "Get the Denarii to Make Lots of Noise So I Can Wiggle out from Being Trapped Half Underground without Jules Hearing Me" scheme.

No, that isn't the best name in the universe, but I'm under a lot of stress right now.

I angle my head toward the hotel and scream my lungs out. "Come and get it, guys! I'm delicious!"

The Denarii go berserk. Their groans grow into hungry roars. Jules turns to face them and drops the whole *what's going on* thing. I could clap for joy, but my hands are still bound up with thorny branches, so that will have to wait for a bit.

Jules glares at his followers. "Stand your ground. She is not for you."

I yell even louder. "He's lying—bite me already! I've got lots of yummy, yummy organs!"

Jules turns back toward me. *Uh-oh.* He raises his right hand. This time, a purple stone is grasped in his fist. Crap, that's another wizard's gem. Maybe I pushed him too far.

I shake my head. *Nah. Elle says you can never push the bad guy too hard.*

The gem in Jules' hand flares with red light as he casts another spell. More silver dust encircles his arm. He did this once before, and I know what comes next.

Thorns.

Sure enough, a thorny branch whips out from Jules' hand and whirls toward me. The prickly wood loops around my head and mouth, acting as a gag. I can't say another word. At least, not right now.

Meanwhile, the Denarii keep up their yelling, so I guess I have that going for me. I only need them to keep up the noise long enough for me to break out of the ground. Hopefully, by the time I'm free, I'll have thought up a part two to this plan.

Jules stares at me, his thin lips winding into a smile. "Now, that's better." The Denarii let out another hungry roar. This one is the loudest yet. Jules raises his arm. "I told you to be silent!" He goes on and on about obedience to his awesomeness. *Whatever.* All I care about is that he's distracted and I can try to escape.

I wiggle my right leg free. *Yes!* Firming up my footing, I press my body upward. My muscles tremble from the effort. Leaning forward, I try to hook the nails on my left hand into the court-yard stones. It isn't easy since both wrists are bound together, but I finally get a decent hold. After that, I strain and shove my way out. The courtyard stones grind as they separate. From where I'm trapped half underground, the sound seems incredibly loud. Good thing the Denarii are still screaming their heads off and not listening to Jules.

I press myself upward even harder. Around me, the flagstone floor shatters with some ear-splitting crackling noises.

Oh, damn.

I risk a look in Jules' direction. He's stopped lecturing his Denarii and now glares directly at me. His angular features almost vibrate with rage. "It seems I can't leave you unattended for even a moment, Bryar Rose. It's time you learned to obey me." He raises his left hand. The magical dagger gleams in his grasp. My breathing turns shallow.

Jules stalks over to stand before me. Little by little, he lowers himself to his knees. His head is so close I can feel his heated breath rush over my face.

No, no, no.

"You should have been a good girl, Bryar Rose. I wouldn't have made this hurt so much." Gripping the blade with both of his fists, Jules raises his dagger high. Late afternoon light gleams off his blade. Every cell in my body seems to freeze.

I try to whisper the word "please," but my speech gets mangled by the thorny gag in my mouth. Instead, all I can manage is a muffled cry.

Suddenly, an ear-piercing howl shatters the quiet. The sound is far away, but it's clearly a wolf. Hope sparks in my chest. I've only heard that particular sound once before, during the fight with Madame at Elle's cabin. There's no mistaking who made it.

Knox.

This realization spins through my mind. *Knox is coming.* I'm not sure whether to be relieved or worried out of my skull. It all comes down to one scary fact. Knox doesn't know that Jules can wield magic. Sure, I pretended to Jules that Knox was onto him, but in reality? Knox will think that Philpot has captured me, and he thinks Philpot is a powerless loser.

Now that I'm thinking about it, the whole situation definitely makes me worried.

Jules pauses, his blade still held high. "That werewolf of yours is coming. He wants to ruin everything again. I won't allow it." He turns to face the wall of thorns. I know an opportunity when I see it, and I won't waste a thing.

Now's my chance.

I press even harder against my confinement. Pain screams across my skin as I heave past thorns and stone. I grit my teeth and focus on getting free. It's one thing for me to lose my life. But if Knox tries to save me, Jules will surely kill him.

Somehow, that thought is far worse.

Firming up my grip on the flagstone courtyard, I haul myself out of the ground. One of the larger, broken stones has a blade-like edge. It gives me an idea how to get rid of the branches that are tied around my wrists. Using the sharp stone, I saw my hands free and remove the gag from my mouth.

I glance over to Jules. He's still staring at the part of the woods where Knox's cry sounded. Clearly, he's decided that Knox is the bigger worry. Not that I'm complaining. It's the perfect time to attack.

I race over to Jules and grab his shoulder, forcing him to bend over at the waist. After that, I knee him in the gut. There's a satisfying "oof" noise as he hunches forward and collapses onto his knees. Clearly, the creep wasn't expecting an assault.

His mistake.

While Jules is crouched over, I grab his wrist—the one that's holding the dagger. Spinning about, I twist Jules' arm behind his back, pressing his wrist so high, he has no choice but to drop his weapon.

I catch the magical dagger midair and set the blade against his throat. Before I get a chance to slice, Jules moves so quickly, his body is nothing but a blur as he delivers a counterpunch to my chest. All the air gets shoved out of my lungs. I fold my arms over my stomach and try to suck in oxygen.

Jules stares at me like I'm a malfunctioning piece of machinery. "How very frustrating you are, Bryar Rose. I keep explaining how this works to you, and you keep failing." Jules raises his arms. A small cloud of silver fairy dust surrounds each of his hands.

With all my willpower, I try to force myself to run or fight. All I can do is try to suck in more air. That punch had supernatural strength behind it. I'm not running anywhere for a few more seconds, and Jules knows it.

"You are a Sleeping Beauty life template. I am your Prince."

All my life, I'd never questioned that I really was a Sleeping Beauty life template. Suddenly, the idea presses in around me like a straightjacket. I want nothing more than to be free of it, whatever that means.

I'm able to heave out a single word through my gasps. "No."

"I beg to differ." Jules lowers his hands. The small silver clouds of fairy dust come hurtling toward me. They slam into my stomach with the power of fists. I fall backward. The fairy dust transforms into more thorny branches, which wind about my entire torso. I collapse onto my knees. Even more thorny brambles encircle my ankles.

I can't move. Again.

Jules stalks over to me. "You are a Sleeping Beauty life template." He yanks on a line of thorns by my shoulder. "My thorns have you."

My arms are pinned to my sides—and the branches cover me from shoulder to waist—but one thing hasn't changed.

I still have a hold on that dagger.

Another howl sounds from the thorn forest. *Knox is still coming. I'm not giving up yet.*

CHAPTER TWENTY-THREE
KNOX

As a man, I'm a pretty good runner. But when I'm in wolf form, like now? I haul ass so fast, most humans only see a blur. And at this moment, my speed is key. To save Bryar Rose, I need to race in quickly and fight even faster. I make a silent vow.

Philpot, you will pay for this.

I speed along a thin path through the thorn forest—it's the one Elle and Colonel Mallory created with their spell. Walls of thorny branches tower on either side of me. High above, the sky is only a sliver of blue. It's almost sunset.

Damn. Bry has to release her wolf before sundown today.

My wolf grumbles inside my head. *"No let mate's wolf die."*

"I'm with you, buddy."

As I race along, my wolf-sharp hearing picks up a man's voice. It's too low to make out the exact words, but the tone is unmistakable.

It's Philpot.

What a tool that guy is. Who would have thought that someone like him would grab Bry? Some small part of me wonders if

Philpot could be more than what he seems, but I quickly dismiss it. Bry has known Philpot for years. He'd have to be some kind of mastermind to hide another identity for that long.

A deep growl of rage reverberates through my chest. Even if Philpot is a total loser, he's still trying to hurt Bry. I push myself to even faster speeds.

Hold on. I'm almost there.

I scan the trail ahead. Shadows play across the walls of twisted branches. That can only mean one thing. I'm nearing the end of the thorn forest. Adrenaline courses through me. I'm aware of a new scent—it's the perfect mixture of cinnamon, honey, and sunshine.

It's Bry.

Fresh adrenaline hits my bloodstream. I take another turn on the trail. Suddenly, a column of light appears before me, marking the end of the passageway.

So close.

I leap through the break in the wall and onto a huge courtyard. The Thornhill Arms stands nearby. A square courtyard stretches before the old hotel. Sure enough, Philpot is here, and he's got Bryar Rose kneeling before him. Her entire torso is wound up in thorny branches. The coppery tang of her blood fills the air. My muscles tighten with rage.

My wolf howls inside my head. *"Save mate. Kill man."*

"I'm with you, bud. We'll set her free. But first, we need to take Philpot down."

My senses hum with excitement. Philpot is a total lightweight. This'll be fun.

Philpot keeps his back to me while he leans over Bry. He's whispering something in her ear, but that loser doesn't deserve to share her airspace.

I'm moving in.

Leaning back on my haunches, I jump high and land squarely on Philpot's back. It knocks the wind out of him, which is perfect. My claws dig into his shoulders. Philpot's face is squished against the stone ground. It's a good look on him.

"You keep interfering between me and my fiancée," says Philpot. "That must end."

For a human, he seems way too calm. I can't even catch a whiff of fear. That's strange, but at this point, I'm too jacked up on rage to care.

As a rule, I don't speak in my wolf form. But there are some situations where rules are meant to be broken. "Set her loose."

Philpot reaches into his pocket. It's a move I've seen a hundred times before from Alec. But Philpot wouldn't have any use for wizardry, would he? I mean, Bryar Rose would have told me if the guy wielded magic. And sure, Philpot could have hired a wizard to make a pendant like mine, but those stones are super-rare.

Bry's voice echoes from behind me. "Be careful! Philpot is really Jules. He can wield all three types of magic."

Her words smell like truth and terror. The realization hits me like a fist. *This is Jules, the leader of the Denarii.* The man I've hunted for most of my lifetime. And now, after hundreds of dead ends and failed attempts, I finally have the man under my claws.

I dig my talons in deeper. A mixture of rage and satisfaction heats my chest. "Why, hello, Jules. Strange outfit you're wearing. Dressed up for something special?"

"Get off of me this instant!"

He twists under my claws. These things are long as knives and pin him in place.

"I hear you have some magical powers to show me. Let's see them." The guy could only do fairy or wizard magic if he could move his arms. That's not happening. And I'm pumping so much alpha power at the man, there's no way he could shift right now.

"Bryar Rose is crazy. I found her like this and was trying to free her."

"Every word you speak reeks of lies."

All of a sudden, Jules explodes into his wolf form. I'm knocked backward.

What the HELL?

For a moment, I can only stare at Jules' wolf. His animal is huge, but that's not what really shocks me. Jules' coat is a patchwork of different shades and lengths of fur. It's like he's sewn together many different wolves into one. Bry's words ricochet through my mind.

He can wield all three types of magic.

My mind races through this information. Denarii have no magic. The few times we've run across a wizard or fairy who was turned into Denarii, their powers were totally gone. And even then, Denarii only consume regular humans, as a rule. But suppose Jules went after Magicorum?

My stomach twists. If Jules ate the flesh of the Magicorum, he might gain some of their powers.

It's possible.

I stare at the patchwork of fur on Jules' wolf. Rage heats my bloodstream.

It's more than possible. *That's exactly what Jules did.*

Sometimes when I'm in my wolf form, I can be a little slower at logic. But at this moment, there's no hiding the truth. Jules has been consuming Magicorum. He's been gaining our powers. And that means the Denarii haven't been trying to wipe us out. They've been harvesting us for Jules.

Wolf-Jules lunges toward me. His speed is whip-fast, but his movements are jumpy and uncoordinated. I can almost picture all the wolves he's consumed as they fight it out for dominance inside him. He must not spend a lot of time in this form.

Good to know.

Wolf-Jules keeps speeding toward me. At the last moment, I growl and feint to one side. Wolf-Jules scrambles to stop himself.

"Having trouble controlling your animal?" I lower my voice. "Or should I say, animals?"

Wolf-Jules lets out a rumbling growl that explodes into a series of ear-splitting barks. I wince, hearing how his voice is that of a hundred wolves crying out at once. "Don't worry. It always takes a little magic to get them under control." A cloud of silver fairy dust appears around Wolf-Jules' body. Pulses of red light appear inside the silver cloud. That settles it.

He's using all three kinds of magic, just like Bryar Rose said.

Wolf-Jules barks once more. The sound is almost deafening, especially to my wolf's hearing. It's also more unified. He's getting his wolves under control.

Everything just got a lot tougher.

Wolf-Jules sniffs the air, and I know he can scent out my concern. "You're afraid, warden for shifters. And well you should be. I will destroy you. There's no escape."

"*No escape.*"

Those two words echo through my mind. I think about the onyx pendant that hangs about my throat, even in wolf form. I can use it to escape any wizard. Sure, the magic isn't supposed to kill anyone. That said, as long as the spell includes my escaping, I'm sure I can throw a little death into the mix.

And Jules definitely needs to die.

Out of the corner of my eye, I see Bry shifting against the thorny cords that bind her. A glint of metal shines by her side. She's got a weapon. *That's my girl.* The blade shimmers as it saws away. A second later, she manages to get her arm free as well.

"*Smart mate,*" says my wolf.

Jules' attention is fixed on me, and I like it that way. If he sees Bry, he'll just trap her again. And Bry must get away. I raise my voice. "Your threats are nothing. You're weak."

"I'm the greatest warrior in history." I scent the tang of his wounded ego from across the courtyard.

"You're not a coward? Then prove it. Fight me in your wolf form. Make it a fair battle." I tilt my head. "Or do you know you'd never win?"

Jules' snout stretches into a wolfy grin. "Of course, I'll agree to that. Just us two." His words reek of a lie, but he's said enough to enter into a magical agreement.

"Agreed."

"And to the death," I add. "Neither of us can shift from our wolf forms or leave this courtyard until one of us is dead."

"I'd expect nothing else."

"Then I hereby activate the magic in this stone." As incantations go, it's pretty short. But Alec didn't want to give me a ton of words to remember to start the spell. A blaze of red light erupts from the pendant around my neck. "It is done."

"The little wizard cast that for you." Jules' face twists into a snarl. "After I kill you, I'll hunt him down next. And I'll bring Bryar Rose along to watch. We'll kiss over his corpse."

With that, all rational thought leaves my head. Jules kidnapped Bry, and now he's threatening Alec? Pure animal rage courses through me.

The man is going down. Now.

CHAPTER TWENTY-FOUR
BRYAR ROSE

Remember when I thought my life hit rock bottom? That place is a citadel of awesome compared to where I am now. To recap: a zombie king named Jules just tied me up with thorny branches because I'm a Sleeping Beauty life template.

I shift under my bindings. As ropes go, these branches are pretty loose. That's the good part. The awful side is that these things encircle me from shoulder to waist. Plus, another loop of them goes around my ankles—that's what keeps me kneeling here. *Fun times.* And sure, the thorns scratch me all over, but that's not why I'm in pain right now.

No, it's the scene before me that *really* hurts.

Across the courtyard, Wolf-Knox and Wolf-Jules pace around each other and snarl. Every growl sends a shiver down my neck. The two of them will start fighting any second now. And since Knox cast a spell? One of them must die before they can leave the courtyard.

Please, don't let it be Knox.

At least, I still have my dagger. In all the commotion of Knox's arrival, Jules didn't take it away from me. I grip the weapon more tightly, angling the blade until it touches the bottom branch. After that, I saw the dagger back and forth until—SNAP—the branch breaks in two. I freeze.

That snapping sound was crazy loud. I glance over to Wolf-Knox and Wolf-Jules. Did they notice anything?

Nope, they're too busy growling at each other. Lucky me.

I saw away again. A second branch breaks. *Yes!*

At the same time, Wolf-Knox lunges at Wolf-Jules. After that, both of them move so quickly, I can only see a blur of claws, fangs, and fur. Low growls echo through the air. The ground shakes as bodies slam against the courtyard stones. The metallic smell of blood fills the air.

Knox could be hurt. I have to get free and help him.

Moving furiously, I slice through even more of the branches. Finally, enough break so that I can fully move my arms. Twisting about, I cut through the loop of branches around my ankles and hop to my feet.

I'm free again.

There's no time to celebrate, though. The battle is heating up.

Wolf-Knox bites Wolf-Jules in the throat. The coppery smell of blood grows even stronger. With a whip-fast motion, Wolf-Knox slams Wolf-Jules' skull onto the courtyard stones. A high-pitched crack echoes through the air.

That must be Wolf-Jules' skull breaking. *Couldn't happen to a nicer guy.*

An eerie silence follows. The air turns still. Behind me in the hotel, even the Denarii have stopped their constant grumbling. Now, they're all just looking out the windows and staring silently at Wolf-Jules. He still isn't moving.

Hope sparks in my chest. *Can Jules really be dead?*

With a whimper, Wolf-Knox limps toward me. His once-sleek black fur is torn and bloody. My breath catches. *That looks bad.* Even more blood drips from his muzzle. Hitching up my skirts, I race over to his side. My heart pounds so hard, it slams against my chest. Knox is only a few feet away when he collapses onto the ground. A crimson pool quickly forms around him.

More blood. This is terrible.

I kneel beside Wolf-Knox and scan his injuries. Great swaths of fur have been ripped from his beautiful black coat. In some places, I can even see exposed muscle and bone. I stifle a gasp. With every breath, his lungs gurgle and heave.

Angling my body, I glance over to Wolf-Jules. Already the tears in his patchwork fur are knitting back together. He's healing up at shifter-speed.

We don't have much time.

I gently stroke Wolf-Knox's neck. "What can I do to help?"

"Run from here." Wolf-Knox's voice is so low I can hardly hear him. "Never come back."

My blood turns cold. "But you'll die."

"One of us has to. That's what the spell demands. I'm too hurt. I can't even heal myself anymore. You must escape while you still can."

My mouth falls open with shock. Knox will die here? I can't accept that. I *won't* accept that. Closing my eyes, I think through everything I saw when Knox cast the spell with Jules. There must be some way around this spell.

An idea appears. Wizard power comes from enchanted stones. I stare at the onyx pendant from Alec, which still hangs on a silver chain about his neck.

Maybe if I take the pendant, then I'll take the spell on myself as well. I stare at the dagger in my fist. *I'm healthy, and I have a weapon. If I take on the spell, I can kill Jules.*

I set my dagger down. Sliding both hands along Wolf-Knox's neck, I reach for the chain's clasp.

Knox flinches. "No. If you take the stone, you must fight Jules."

I unclasp the pendant. "That's exactly what I want."

A few yards away, Wolf-Jules rolls over and moans. From this new angle, I can see an indentation in his head—it's a flat spot from where Knox pounded him onto the courtyard. That's one serious injury. Unfortunately, his skull is already starting to heal.

Jules will wake up again and soon.

"My mind is made up, Knox. I'm taking the stone and fighting."

I reclasp the pendant around my neck. The moment the pendant touches my skin, power slams into my body. Red light dances around me. *Wizard magic.* For a moment, it flares even more brightly. After that, it disappears.

My fingers brush the pendant. "The spell is on me now." I scoop up the dagger and rise to stand. "I'm ready."

The moment the words leave my lips, I feel an untamed desire to defend Knox. A fierce sense of determination pulses through me.

All of a sudden, silver specks of light appear in my vision. My limbs turn loose and sluggish. The very air seems to press in around me. The old lockbox rattles inside my soul.

Oh, no. I'm having another episode.

I pull out my inhaler from where I hid it in the folds of my dress by my toga belt. For a second, I can only stare at the device on my palm. I know I need my medicine, but something about it just feels wrong.

Wolf-Knox raises his head. "Don't take that." He looks to the sky and exhales a rattling breath. "There's not much time before sunset, either. Damn."

I stare at the inhaler on my palm. It's clenched in my left hand while the dagger is still held in my right. "What's in my medicine, Knox?"

Across the courtyard, Wolf-Jules tries to get up. His forelegs are too shaky, though. He collapses again. I scan his head. It's about halfway healed.

"Please, what's wrong?"

"Your dagger is nothing compared to a werewolf. And that medicine stops your wolf."

My breath catches. "My what?"

Knox lifts his muzzle to meet my gaze. Even that effort strains him. "Colonel Mallory put you under a Slumber Beast spell. Whenever you start to shift, it makes you freeze and fall asleep. That inhaler has Predator's Bane. It makes any were take human form. Once you're human, the Slumber Beast spell stops."

I try to process that news. It doesn't make sense. I've spent too many years being told I'm powerless. The words of my aunties play in an endless loop in my head. I'm weak, human, and a total failure. "No, that's not right." My voice is barely a whisper.

I think about the lockbox in my chest. Colonel Mallory said that he placed it there and I had magic. Was he talking about the Slumber Beast spell?

Across the courtyard, Wolf-Jules groans and tries to rise again. His legs are wobbly, but he's making progress. His head looks almost fully healed. I check Knox's wounds. They don't look better at all. I've heard about this kind of thing—it happens when werewolves are close to death.

I stare between the weapon in my left hand and the inhaler in my right. Worry squeezes my temples. *I have to make the right decision.* "Taking the medicine will keep me awake so I can fight."

"No, your best chance is to battle as a werewolf. And you do have a wolf inside you. I'm positive."

With those words, my world splits in two. On one side, there's everything I've known until now. On the other side, there's Knox's answer to my question. "How do you know this?"

"Because you're my mate."

"No, that can't be right." But even as the words leave my mouth, part of my soul knows that it's the truth. *I am Knox's mate.* He's the one who's haunted my dreams for years. Our connection has always been there. And the moment I saw him in Alec's office, some part of me recognized him.

The lockbox inside my soul starts to shift. The internal walls press in more tightly around something inside.

Something that isn't human.

Could that be my wolf? Or perhaps even more?

A short distance away, Wolf-Jules gets back on all four paws. He tosses his head, the motion reminding me of someone who's waking up from a deep sleep. *This is it.*

"You are my mate," says Knox. "And we werewolves don't bond outside of our own kind and potency. That means you're at least as strong as I am. You can easily take down Jules."

His words rattle around my mind. If I'm Knox's mate, then I'm a werewolf. "If I'm only as strong as you are, why are you so sure I can defeat Jules?"

Knox's eyes gleam with golden light. "I've felt the power in your soul. Back in LeCharme, I reached out to your wolf. It was after Philpot left, remember?"

"Yes, there was a surge of power between us."

"That wasn't shifter power. It was something else. I don't know what it is, but I can tell you this. You're stronger than I am. You're stronger than Jules. You can face this fight and win. But first, you must set your wolf loose."

Maybe this is all a lie, but it's the best shot I have to win. I drop my inhaler. "Whatever your plan is, I'm on board."

"I'm an alpha and your mate. That means I can help release your wolf. Just keep looking into my eyes. This may feel like it takes a long time, but only a few seconds will actually pass. Are you with me?"

"I am."

Knox and I lock gazes. Instantly, the world seems to freeze. I feel Knox's power move through my veins. It's like an electrical charge that whips through my very soul. The energy calls to me, over and over. It demands one thing.

I must release my wolf.

Suddenly the courtyard, Knox, and Jules all disappear. Instead, I find I'm trapped inside a lockbox made of wood. On instinct, I know exactly what's happened.

I've taken on my wolf's point of view.

Now, I'm witnessing everything as she does, and she's trapped inside a container of magic that's been implanted in my soul.

I spin about, scanning my prison. Wooden walls surround me. Every panel bears long grooves—marks that must have been made from my clawing and trying to get out. Magic keeps me confined, but Knox's power calls to me, urging me to scale past the barriers and escape. Looking up, I see the box's wooden lid is closed.

Not for long.

With all my strength, I leap up toward the box's lid. As I move, colored lights begin flashing all around me: red, gold, and silver. My human mind knows those represent the three different shades of magic, but my human mind isn't in charge now. Instead, I'm mainly thinking with my wolf's brain, and all she can focus on is escape. Her limbs—my limbs—are huge, covered in white fur and end in paws the size of dinner plates.

I jump higher this time. The warmth of Knox's power urges me on. I get so close my front paws scratch the lid.

Then a chill sets in to my bones. *Knox's power is fading.* Panic heightens all my senses. My wolf knows there's only one reason why Knox would leave us.

He's dying.

Leaning back on my haunches, I jump again and again in a frenzy of action. The wood slams into my bones; the deep grooves scrape across my fur. But no matter how hard I try, I can't scale the wall. I don't even get close to the lid anymore.

The connection with Knox snaps. I shiver with icy fear. A heart-beat later, I find myself back on the courtyard outside the hotel. The sun has almost disappeared on the horizon. Wolf-Knox lies beside me, his eyes closed and chest barely moving.

Wolf-Jules glares at us from a few yards away. "He tried to awaken your wolf, didn't he? Well, it's too late now. Your animal is gone."

My eyes widen. What had Scarlett said in that Magicorum Teen Group so long ago? You must awaken your wolf by sundown on your eighteenth birthday, or you'll lose your animal forever. I search my soul again, frantically looking for my inner wolf. It was so easy to find her a moment ago. But now? I feel nothing.

My heart sinks. Jules is right. My aunties are right. Even Madame Grimoire was right. I'm a failed Sleeping Beauty template. Nothing more.

Golden light shimmers in Wolf-Jules' eyes as he transforms back into his human state. Since I took on the spell from Knox, Jules can change forms now. I'd be disgusted by the fact that he's naked, but I'm too worried about Knox to care. I rise to stand, placing my body between Jules and Wolf-Knox. The dagger is gripped firmly in my fist.

"Spell or no spell, you'll never touch Knox."

"We'll see."

Jules is only a few feet away when I attack. Rushing forward, I raise my dagger high. Jules lifts his hand, and red light glows across his palm. My weapon flies out of my own grip and into Jules' hand. A satisfied gleam shines in his dark eyes as he raises his blade high. "Say good-bye to Knox."

"No!" I rush forward, trying to stop him.

But Jules moves with super-human speed. I've barely taken a half-step when he plunges the blade deep into Wolf-Knox's chest. Jules pulls the dagger free and turns to me. "You're next."

The world seems to freeze as I stare at Wolf-Knox. He isn't moving at all. This can't be true.

Knox is dead. Jules killed him.

With that realization, something deep inside of me snaps. It's my wolf. She's back and howling for her lost alpha. An instinct I've never known before takes over my entire body. Golden light clouds my vision. My bones crack and realign. Fur bursts out across my skin. My teeth lengthen into fangs.

I become a wolf.

Power streams through my limbs. I see the last curve of the sun touch the horizon line. The sun hadn't fully set. My wolf was still alive. And now, she's free.

Knox, I will avenge you.

With a great growl, I leap up at Jules. My massive paws knock him onto his back. Before we even hit the ground, I've locked my teeth onto the pink flesh of his throat. Warm blood flows into my mouth.

Jules' body transforms beneath me. Within the span of a heartbeat, he turns back into a massive wolf. I lose my grip on his throat and fall backward.

Wolf-Jules charges at me. My wolf instincts take over as I latch my teeth onto the back of his hind leg, chomping hard enough to break bone. Wolf-Jules retaliates by kicking me with such force, I go sliding across the courtyard.

I quickly right myself to stand again. Wolf-Jules transforms back into his human form. He rests all his weight on his left foot. Blood streams down his right leg. He turns to the hotel. "Denarii! Come!"

The doors swing open. Denarii race toward the courtyard, but slam against an invisible barrier. They can't cross the threshold.

I lift my muzzle, showing off the pendant. "I wear this now. As long as I'm alive, you can't call anyone else out to help you."

"So it would seem." Jules sneers. "But you can't change who carries a spell and not change some of the rules. I'm sure you noticed how I used wizard magic to take back my dagger."

The dagger. My fur stands on end. *Jules did use magic to reclaim it. And we were able to change forms from wolf to humans, too.*

Jules raises his hand. Clouds of silver fairy dust appear around his fingers. "You needed to say the full incantation for the spell to take hold. Not that it will do you any good now."

A lead weight of dread settles into my stomach. Jules is going to cast another fairy spell on me. When it comes to me, there's only one spell that Jules likes.

Those stupid thorns.

Jules lowers his hands, and the two bands of silver smoke stream out from his palms and head right at me. This time, one slams into my muzzle while the other hits my spine. Both instantly transform into more thorny branches, and these cords are the thickest ones yet, with heavy spikes that pierce my skin. I'm wrapped from snout to tail like a mummy. A cord even loops through my mouth to stop me from speaking.

I shiver with panic. What made me think I could fight Jules, even as a wolf? I writhe under the thorny bindings, but this time, they're super-tight. The branches don't even give an inch.

It's over. I've lost.

Jules limps closer until he looms over me. "This is the last time I'll say this, Bryar Rose. You are a Sleeping Beauty template. Nothing more. And now, you *will* spend eternity as my obedient wife."

At these words, an odd sense of calm washes over me. I've spent my life being told who I am and what I can do. Now, I have precious seconds left to live. The last action I take on this earth will be as the person I want to become, not who I've been told I am.

And who do I want to be? Someone with power.

I'm desperate, so I try something I've never done before. I seek out that lockbox of power Colonel Mallory set into my soul. Minutes ago, I saw the colored lights of magic inside that container: shifter, wizard, and fairy.

I need all of that power now.

I picture the lockbox in my mind's eye—it's a square of dark wood that's covered in runes. Colored light peeps out along the seams. My wolf was set free from there. More magic still lies inside.

With all my focus, I order that container to break wide open. In my head, I see the box rattle on its hinges. Cracks form along the seams. Beams of silver, gold, and red light pulse through the thin cracks in its exterior. The lockbox in my soul rattles more fiercely than ever before.

After that, it bursts open.

The lid rips off. Light pours out. Strength enters my limbs. I shake off the thorny branches like they were tissue paper. A new kind of power licks across my fur, connecting me with energies that I never knew existed. Multicolored lights pulse around me in a cloud. Fresh energy courses through my soul.

This is what has been locked up inside me all this time.

It's all three kinds of magic.

Some small corner of my mind cries out that this situation is impossible. I'm regular Bryar Rose, that's all. I shove those thoughts aside. Somehow these powers got inside me. At this point, it doesn't really matter *how* it happened. All I know is that the magic is here, and I *will* use it.

"You can't wield this power," says Jules. "Stop before you kill yourself."

His words smell rancid. On instinct, I know that he's lying. "Think I can't handle this power? Watch me."

I focus on the cloud of colored magic that encircles me. I imagine the energy flowing into the flagstones that cover the ground.

As soon as the thought crosses my mind, the magic heeds my wishes and streams around Jules' feet. The courtyard stones glow with a mixture of red, silver, and golden light.

I bare my teeth and command the magic further. "Take him!"

Branches lined with thorns burst out from under the glowing stones. For a moment, they hover upright, reminding me of a circle of massive rattlesnakes getting ready to strike.

And they attack.

The branches loop around Jules, wrapping him up like a mummy. It's the same way I was confined just a few minutes ago. Jules no longer looks like a man but a humanoid cocoon of wooden thorns. Everything is silent for a few seconds. I stay on alert, knowing Jules may launch a counterstrike.

Multicolored lights flash out between the breaks in the branches. Jules breaks free. This time, he's back to his wolf form. He howls, and his voice sounds like a hundred werewolves calling at once. I let out a low snarl. I saw this happen before, when Jules first fought Knox. He said it took him some magic to get all the souls inside him under control. Why would Jules need to get them under control again?

A ghostly version of a wolf appears by Jules' side. It's grey with deep black pits for eyes. Another appears. Then a third.

That's when I realize the truth. Jules isn't getting the other wolves inside him under control. He's setting them loose. All the spirits that Jules has consumed over the years...they're now being released to fight me. And I can't leave the courtyard until the battle is done.

A hundred spirit wolves stand around Jules. Then ghostly witches and wizards appear. All of them wear dark cloaks and angry faces. Spirits of fairies fill the skies, their wings unfurled and unmoving. They stare at me with hollowed-out eyes.

Wolf-Jules tenses his muscles. "Attack!"

Thousands of angry spirits fly at me at once. The wolves chomp onto my legs. The fairies tear at my ears and rip at my tail. The witches and wizards carry daggers that they plunge into my chest. I scan my limbs, looking for the damage. There is none. My body is whole. That reality doesn't stop their attacks from hurting, just as if each one were really happening.

And that's when I realize what they're doing.

They're tearing apart my soul.

Jules stalks closer, his paws clacking against the stone ground. "Hurts, doesn't it? Not pleasant to have your spirit destroyed. You should have settled for giving me your body."

I crumple onto my knees. The pain is like nothing I've ever felt. A thousand bites, slices, and tears overwhelm me at once.

I turn my focus inward, back to that lockbox of power. It's still there and strong.

Jules is wrong. They didn't destroy my soul.

Arching my neck, I let loose the mother of all howls. The sound is deafening. The forest shakes. Windows in the hotel crash inward. Colored lights surround me. The flashes of brightness expand. Soon a shifting cloud of red, gold, and silver brightness covers the courtyard. The spirits hover in place, their hollow eyes locked on me. I'm not sure what those gazes mean, but they look surprisingly like hope.

There's one figure who isn't frozen by the mist. Jules returns to his human form, his hands balled into fists. "I'll kill you, Bryar Rose."

Rage heats my bloodstream. This man is evil, through and through. All of a sudden, it's crystal clear what this has always been about. My power. It's why Jules wanted to consume my abilities in the first place. It's why Colonel Mallory hid my powers with this lockbox and Slumber Beast spell. It's why my aunties pretended I was human and weak. There's no doubt in my mind. The source of all my pain has been Jules. And I'm not the only one he's hurt. These many tortured souls hover around me now, and I know they're asking for release.

The worst of all his crimes is that Jules killed Knox. I pace at the courtyard floor, my wolf body rippling with fury. I turn to face Jules head on. "This is over. Now."

The lights flare more brightly than ever before. All the spirits in the clouds fade away, smiling as they vanish. That's not what happens to Jules, though. He's still in human form as the colored lights enter his body. Brightness erupts under skin and turns into fire. The flames engulf him. Within seconds, Jules is nothing but a small pile of ashes. With him, the colored lights vanish as well.

Jules is dead. Did I really kill him with magic?

I suppose I did. But what does that mean? I shake my head. The answer to that question lies in the *Book of Magic*. Until it's fully translated, there isn't much I can do. I already know what my abilities bring, and it's nothing good. From my aunties to Philpot, my otherworldly gifts have only attracted trouble. Even worse, those I love are getting targeted too.

I make a solemn vow.

Until I fully understand my magic, I will never speak of it to another soul. No one saw what happened today. No one needs to know. Besides, I have more important things to worry about right now, like getting out of here with Knox's body.

Behind me, Knox moans softly. Every nerve ending in my body goes on alert. He's still alive? I quickly return to my human form, which means I'm totally naked. Fortunately, Jules' old military coat lies nearby, so I quickly put it on and kneel beside Wolf-Knox. "You're alive." I kiss the top of his head. "I'll get you out of here. Don't worry." I scan his wounds. No improvement.

I check the pockets of Jules' coat, hoping to find a cell phone or car key. There's nothing. I scan the old hotel. Maybe there are some sheets in there or a cot that I could use to roll Knox to safety. It's not much of a plan, but it could work.

Suddenly, hundreds of Denarii come pouring out of the hotel and onto the courtyard. They're in different kinds of dress. Some modern. Some in togas. Others wear ratty wigs and tattered long coats. All of them are filthy. They have the sunken-in cheekbones and gray skin that you'd expect from a pack of zombies.

These are Jules' Denarii. They couldn't leave the hotel before because I was still alive and the spell was in action.

Well, Jules must definitely be dead now, because a whole zombie army is coming for us. To add insult to injury, Blanche is leading the group. She holds a kitchen cleaver in her right hand and has bloodlust in her eyes. Clearly, she still wants a bite of me. Actually, looking at her greedy face, I think she wants more than just one bite.

Closing my eyes, I focus on the lockbox of magic inside my soul. I opened it before; I can do it again. I order the container to release its power.

Nothing happens.

"Come on!" I try again, but it's the same result. Zero magic. I can still feel the energy inside me, but I can't make it come out. And the Denarii are closing in.

Guess I'll have to go with Plan B.

I pick up Jules' dagger from the flagstones. Somehow in all the craziness, this one thing survived. It's not much, but it's what I've got. I move into a battle stance. All my lessons in self-defense tick through my mind. I can take down five or ten of these guys, easy. After that, I'll wing it. This is a bizarre situation, after all. Who knows what's possible? A voice sounds in my head.

"*Protect our mate.*" From the bottom of my soul, I know my wolf is speaking to me in my mind.

I reply. "*I will.*"

As the Denarii close in, I have a grim but satisfying thought. And if I should fail here, at least I'll go down at my alpha's side.

No, at my mate's side.

This isn't the ending to any fairy tale template, but I'm not sure I want to follow someone else's path anymore.

This time, the choice is mine.

⤙

CHAPTER TWENTY-FIVE
KNOX

Damn, every part of my body hurts.

I force my eyes open a crack. What I see is almost more painful. Bry stands before me in some kind of military jacket. Her body is covered in scratches. A long knife is gripped in her fist.

And hundreds of Denarii are racing right for us.

But that doesn't make any sense. The only way the Denarii in the hotel could be released is if Jules or Bry were dead. And I'm certainly breathing, which means Bryar Rose must have taken down Jules. I passed out after the dick jammed a knife in my ribs.

"Strong mate. Strong cubs."

Leave it to my inner wolf to focus on cubs at this moment.

I try to get back on all fours, but with two back legs broken, even trying to set some weight on them kills me. I grit my teeth. There must be enough shifter healing left in me so that I can die on my feet by my mate. I groan and push up onto my front paws. After that, I freeze.

A strange shadow just passed through the shadows from the rising moon.

I smile. I've only seen shadows like that once before. It's a dragon.

Colonel Mallory is here.

A cool sense of relief moves through me. We've got some serious help in this fight. Now that a path was cut through the forest, it must have weakened the magic enough to let Colonel Mallory through. And dragons can do a lot of damage. Maybe not take down an entire army of the undead solo, but I'll take all the help I can get.

A low hum echoes above my head. That's the dragon's fire starter. Seconds later, a shaft of flames cuts a circle around Bry and me. The Denarii howl and hang back. They don't run away, though.

Their mistake.

Bry shields her eyes and watches Colonel Mallory swoop across the sky. He's a massive black dragon with red spikes along his spine. Another hum sounds before he blasts a wide path through the thorn forest. Looks like they did more than weaken the magic there; they figured out how to blow it away.

Bry firms up her grip on the dagger and stares at the Denarii army. They now stand in a circle around us. With Colonel Mallory's dragon off frying the forest, they've started to inch in closer.

"What's Colonel Mallory doing?" asks Bry. "We need him here."

The Denarii move even closer. There are women in long gowns, men in top hats, and even a few Roman soldiers. They all look like hell warmed over. Literally.

I force myself to fully stand. Pain spikes through my back limbs, making it hard to think. What I could really use is Alec and one of his healing spells. It doesn't look like that's happening anytime soon, though. I raise my head and howl.

"I'll kill you if you step closer." It's a total lie, but the Denarii don't know that.

"And I've got your back." Bry's words send a welcome jolt of warmth through me. I can picture her beside me, wearing that ridiculous military jacket that hangs down to her knees, gripping a small dagger against hundreds of walking mummies. *She's perfect.*

My wolf pipes up inside my head. *"Protect mate."*

"*I'm trying, buddy.*"

The Denarii move even closer. They growl and reach for us. It's like something out of a bad zombie movie, only this is real. Moving as one unit, they leap at us. Teeth bite into my fur; hands claw at my back. Bry lets out a battle yell.

That's when the stones of the courtyard start vibrating beneath us. Someone's coming.

The moment one of the Denarii touch Bry, I lose my damn mind. Adrenaline pumps through my system. Maybe a little magic, too. I leap into battle and sink my claws into the Denarii, tearing them off her.

That's when the pack arrives.

Thousands of werewolves crest over the horizon of the now burned-down forest. So that's what Colonel Mallory was up to—clearing a path for a werewolf army. Azizi leads the charge and looks happy as I've ever seen him. He's wanted me to become alpha of alphas for ages. If I live through this, I'll owe all these wolves anything, and alpha of alphas is what they want. At this moment, I'm so happy to see them, nothing else matters.

The horde of werewolves pours onto the courtyard and tears into the Denarii. The undead who were attacking me and Bry get torn to shreds. For the first time in hours, I take in a relieved breath. My body decides to call it quits on me, though. I hit a massive adrenaline crash and collapse onto the ground. Bryar Rose kneels beside me.

Azizi trots closer. "Guard Bryar Rose! Destroy the Denarii!" Dozens of wolves fan out around Bry and me, creating a protective circle. It's one of the best things I've seen in years.

With sure steps, Azizi approaches me. There's the mother of all smug grins on his face. "We saved you."

"Close. If you see Alec, send him my way."

Az turns to Bry. "You must be Knox's mate."

I wince. I'm almost dead, but this conversation makes me shudder. How can Azizi be pushing the mate thing right now? Bry just shifted for the first time.

"My mate?" Bry grins. "My wolf thinks so; that's for certain."

My brows lift. *Her wolf thinks so?* This is about the best news I've heard in forever.

Alec steps into our circle. "I see I have to save your lazy ass again, Knox." Per usual, he looks perfect in some kind of modified black body armor. I'm sure the stuff is tricked out with more pockets than you'd believe.

Alec is here at last. I could kiss him, too. The bastard.

I'd say something smartass to Alec about showing up late, but I'm just too happy to see him. Plus, my back legs hurt like you wouldn't believe.

Bry folds her arms over her chest and glares at Alec. "Save his lazy ass? Stop being sarcastic and help him. He's really hurt."

Alec kneels beside me. Sure enough, he zips open the top of his black body armor and checks the hidden pockets. He takes way too long fishing around for my taste. "Hmm." Alec eyes my wounds. "You look like you're healing up just fine."

Bry Rose leans over me. "You are getting better. You weren't before."

Alec gives me a sly look. "Got any good news lately?"

"Zip it and heal me. My back legs are broken." Alec knows damn well that mated pairs get a boost in all kinds of power, including healing. He's just being a dick. "Fix me fast before you have to re-break my legs again."

"Fine. Baby." Alec kneels before me and raises his fist. Red light shines inside his palm. A chill surrounds me as the magic sets in. My bones straighten and mend. Open wounds close up on their own. Within a few seconds, I'm back to my regular self.

"Thanks, man."

"Any time."

Bry scans the courtyard. "Where is Elle? Is she with you?"

"Oh, yes." Alec gestures across the square, where Elle is wearing black body armor and shooting Denarii with some kind of fairy gun. I know the fairy part because the bullets drop right before their target where they expand into massive Venus flytraps, eat their prey whole, and vanish into thin air. A total fairy spell if I ever saw one.

One Denarii girl with black hair and pale skin keeps screaming that she's in charge and the rest of the Denarii aren't allowed to retreat. Something about her seems familiar, but I can't quite place it. Also, something about that chick says trouble to me. The rest of the Denarii look like crap, but this girl is dressed perfectly.

I look to Alec. "I don't like the look of that one."

"We better go in and help Elle," says Alec.

"Yeah."

Bry chuckles. "Don't worry about Elle. She's got this."

Sure enough, Elle is having the time of her life. She faces off with the Denarii chick, who's holding a cleaver high. "Hey, Blanche. Haven't seen you since group."

"You biiiiiiiiitch!" the Denarii girl—who I guess is named Blanche—races toward Elle like a deranged sushi chef.

I don't care what Bry says, I don't stand around when someone's being attacked. Neither can Alec. He and I rush to jump in, but Elle's too fast for us. She aims the gun straight at Blanche and pulls the trigger. A seed impacts on the ground right at Blanche's feet. A heartbeat later, a twelve-foot-tall Venus flytrap appears, opens its huge maw wide, and gulps down the girl and her meat cleaver in one swallow. After that, a flash of silver fairy dust surrounds the plant, and it's back to being a seed again.

Whoa. That Blanche chick is toast.

Bry winks. "Blanche and Elle never did get along in group."

"Why do I not even want to know what that means?" asks Alec.

I scratch my neck. "What I don't want to know is how she got hold of a fairy-seed gun." That stuff is way illegal.

"Don't ask," says Bry. "It's really the only way to go."

Alec reaches into his pocket and pulls out another handful of gems. "You two should go. We'll stay and clean up."

Colonel Mallory swoops by in his dragon form while he fries up a line of Denarii. There aren't too many left now. I look to Bry. "What do you think?"

"I've had enough excitement for one day."

"We'll take off. Can you conjure us something else to wear?"

Alec searches in his pockets. "I've got lots of body armor gems in here. Does that work?"

"It's fine." I don't usually talk in my wolf form, and it's giving me a headache. "You should turn away, Bryar Rose."

She blushes, which is about the highest compliment I can pay her right now. After everything that's happened today, my girl turns red at the thought of seeing me naked.

"Not just girl," complains my inner wolf. *"Mate."*

"Look, that's her decision. She needs to understand the full story before she commits."

"No story. Magic says mate. Bryar Rose mate."

"And the fact that she could die if we go through a mating ceremony?"

My wolf pauses. *"We talk."*

"Good."

Closing my eyes, I pull in the magic to start my shift. After fighting Jules, this kind of pain feels like nothing. My body snaps and realigns until I'm naked and human again. Alec pulls out some more gems, shiny onyx ones this time. He lights them up, and then, Bry and I are wearing fitted body armor. It's black and pretty badass.

I give him a bro punch on the shoulder. "Thanks, man."

"Is it okay to turn around?" Bry gestures to a pack of Denarii that are getting Venus flytrapped by Elle. "This view isn't too great."

"Yeah."

Bry turns back around. She looks so much better without that torn-up jacket on. Makes me feel all warm inside. "You look good."

"Alec healed my cuts, too."

"That's another one *you both* owe me," says Alec.

Elle now saunters in. She spins her firearm on her index finger. "I love this gun." She spies Bry and squeals. It's a girl-thing with lots of yelling. It's also really cute. Not that I'd ever admit that out loud.

Elle wraps Bry in a big hug. "You're okay!"

"I am. Thanks for coming to help. We were cutting it pretty close at the end."

Elle clasps Bry's hands. "So, I have good news and bad news. What do you want first?"

"Bad news."

Elle taps her chin. "Nah, I'll start with the good news."

I give Alec a sly look. *Is this girl made for him or what?*

Bry narrows her eyes. "Okay, shoot."

"Colonel Mallory just barbecued the last of the Denarii."

"Cool." I move to stand closer to Bryar Rose. Somehow, I feel like the bad news will affect her deeply.

"The bad news is that your aunties are burning up every phone I have."

Bry slips her hand into mine. "Considering the day we've lived through, that's not too bad."

Elle winces. "They're threatening to use magic to locate you and transport to wherever you are."

Bry groans. "Okay, that's bad."

"I've been trying to stall them, but they won't believe anything I say." Elle's eyes widen with sympathy. "And you know what's tonight, right?"

Bry groans again, only louder. "My birthday party with Queen Nyxa."

A jolt of shock moves through me. I may be a werewolf, but even I've heard stories about Queen Nyxa. "She's a psycho."

Bry rubs her neck. "All fairies are a little crazy."

I give her hand a gentle squeeze. "This one's off the charts. She rules the Summer Court. Likes asking impossible riddles and killing anyone who can't answer."

"She comes every year for my birthday."

Bry trembles underneath my touch. It makes me want to destroy anyone who's making her afraid. Right now, that means I want to go after her damned aunties.

My wolf thinks the same thing. He growls inside my head. *"Protect mate. Save mate."*

"I couldn't agree more, bud."

"Give us a minute, guys." I guide Bry away from Elle and Alec. They aren't the type to snoop, but still. What I have to say needs some privacy. When I speak, I keep my voice low. "Look, I know you've had a hell of a day, but it's about to get a lot worse."

She sighs, and the sound tears through my heart. "I can't handle anything else right now."

"You've got to. I hate to say this, but I think your aunties were in league with Jules."

Bry shivers even more. "He said something like that."

"What happened to him, anyway?" Bry won't even look at me. I'm pretty sure she killed him, but there were no signs of a body. Something strange went down; that's for sure. "Do you want to talk about it?"

She shakes her head. "I want to read some papyri about it. Until I know things for certain, it's best for everyone if I stay quiet."

"Whatever you want." I press my forehead to hers. The connection feels comforting. A long pause follows before Bry speaks again.

"I think Jules somehow got me as a baby. Before he could kill me, Colonel Mallory gave me this curse. It protected me until my eighteenth birthday, so Jules gave me to my aunties to raise until then."

I nod. "That would explain a lot."

"Tonight isn't a birthday party. It's a wedding reception for me and Philpot. I mean, Jules."

My eyes narrow. "So, if you walk into that penthouse without Jules, you could be walking into a fight. They wanted you married to Jules. Who knows what they'll do when they find out the truth?"

"Right." Bry's brows dip into a V shape. I'm learning her faces, and this one means she's thinking things through. She's quiet for almost a full minute before she straightens her spine and speaks in a steady and confident voice. "I have had it with that damned Sleeping Beauty template. I want it all over with, forever. That means my aunties need to drop it, too."

I grin. "That's the spirit." She's even stopped shivering. That's a great sign.

My wolf prances around in my soul. His voice is almost a croon, the guy's so happy. *Strong mate. Good mate. OUR mate.*

I hate to crush him, but we don't know that. *"Patience, buddy. The ceremony alone would kill her. And even if it didn't, Bry probably deserves better than us."*

"Bryar Rose mate." My wolf says that last bit with a huffy tone. I can sense him curling up into a corner to sulk.

Much as I hate for my wolf to be bummed out, there's other stuff to focus on. Like how Bryar Rose is going to end this situation with her aunties. "Tell me what you need. I can help."

"The party doesn't officially start until midnight." Bryar Rose scans the horizon. "It's a little past sunset. If I get over there early, I can confront my aunties without having to deal with a fairy queen at the same time."

"Good plan." I kiss her temple. "When do we leave?"

All of a sudden, Bry won't meet my gaze anymore. "I think it's better if I go alone."

That's not an option.

I wind my arm around her waist and pull her against me. Damn, she feels good. "I'm going with you, end of story. And if you sneak off, I'll find you."

Bry half smiles. "I thought you didn't want to be a stalker."

"I changed my mind. And Alec here will help." I cup my hand by my mouth. "Will you transport me anywhere Bry is going tonight?"

"Even if it's dangerous?" adds Bry.

Alec shoots me a thumbs-up. "Absolutely. It's bro code."

Elle steps up closer. "I know I shouldn't have been eavesdropping, but I couldn't help it. It's a big risk for me to go with you to confront your aunties, especially with Queen Nyxa there." All the color drains from Elle's face. Whatever happened with her and the fairy world, it must have been pretty nasty. "So if Knox doesn't go with you, then I'll stalk you too."

Bry frowns, but I can tell she's not really angry. "You guys aren't making it easy on me."

I lean in and nuzzle her ear. It's unnecessary, but it sure feels good. "Don't make me go alpha on you again. I can just order you to take me."

She laughs, and I like that about her, too. "You can try, but I'm pretty sure I could alpha you one better."

And the great thing is, Bry probably could. Sure, she needs a lot more practice with her animal side, but she'll get there. I inhale her scent and smile. When it comes to a mate, you want someone with the skills to make both of you better. Bry's perfect.

"Wait a second." Elle's mouth falls open. "You're a werewolf?" She pokes Bryar Rose in the shoulder. "Why didn't you tell me?"

Bry sets her fists on her hips. "Look who's talking. You're a fairy, and you didn't tell me." She rounds on me. "And I don't want to talk about werewolf stuff right now. We need to confront my aunties." Her mouth quivers. "About you know, everything."

Now, I can't help but notice how she said "we" have to go confront her aunties. Those three ladies have known for years that Bryar Rose is really a werewolf. They better answer her questions straight up, or I swear, I will go werewolf on their bony asses.

I give Bry a gentle squeeze. "I'm ready when you are."

"Okay, then."

I point to Alec. "You got us covered?"

Alec reaches into yet another pocket. "I suppose that means you want transport spells as well?"

"Please," says Bry. She shoots a quick look at Elle, who has her arms folded across her chest and is staring at the hotel like it's her job. If this were me and Alec, we'd just fight it out until we were too bloody to care anymore. But girls have their ways of doing stuff, too. I don't judge.

Alec raises his fist. Red light glows inside his palm. "Ready or not, here you go."

A column of red light surrounds us as Bry and I disappear. We're off for another battle. Only this one, I'm actually looking forward to.

CHAPTER TWENTY-SIX
BRYAR ROSE

After Alec starts the transport spell, my skin tingles with wizard magic. I've never traveled by magic before. On reflex, I step closer to Knox. He tightens his grip on my waist, pulling me against his side. His body is warm, firm, and comforting. I lean into his touch. It's been a crazy day.

The next thing I know, Knox and I stand somewhere that is most definitely not my aunties' penthouse.

I frown. "Did something go wrong with Alec's spell?"

"Nah." Knox's voice is deep and calm. "Alec brought us to my place. He can only send us to spots that he's seen before, and he doesn't know your aunties."

"He could send us to LeCharme."

"And we'd appear right in the middle of his office or something? He's worked hard to hide that he's a wizard." Knox rolls his eyes. "You know how humans can get."

"I've seen it." Last month, I saw some fae get mobbed on the sidewalk for casting a minor spell. Everyone wanted to take a pic and get their autograph. It was creepy.

Now that I know we weren't delivered to the wrong place, I scan Knox's apartment. It's somewhere between a man-cave and a bunker. The place is large and open with lots of exposed concrete and black leather. He's got a massive screen and couch set up for movies and a whole gaming station against one wall, along with a wall rack that's filled with all sorts of magical weapons.

I gesture to his wall-o'-guns. "Is that legal?"

"Mostly. Alec knows people who know people. And most of the time, I keep the weapons out of sight." Knox enters a code into the keypad by the door, and the gun display slides into the wall, only to get covered up by a huge painting of the Manhattan skyline.

"That's pretty slick."

"Wait until you see the guns. Most of those are specifically built to kill Denarii."

Kill Denarii. In my mind, I once again see the image of Jules turning into ash. A shiver twists up my spine. Within the span of a heartbeat, Knox is standing at my side. "What's wrong? You smell confused and frightened."

"I'm fine."

Knox isn't buying it. He stares at the weapons for a moment and then looks back to me. "How did Jules die?"

"I can't tell you that. Not now anyway." I swallow. "I thought you were dead, Knox. I can't do anything to put you at risk again. And until I know what's really going on, that's all details will do. Put you at risk."

Knox pulls me into a warm hug. "I'm a big, bad wolf, you know. I'm not afraid of a little risk."

I nuzzle into his chest. "I know."

"But you tell me when you're ready, yeah?"

"When I'm ready." *And I'm not sure I'll ever be ready.*

His hug is awesome, but if I stay in it, I'll do something crazy like tell him everything. So, I step away and finish sizing up the apartment. There are no less than three different hallways lined with doors. For New York, this place is massive.

"You live here all on your own?"

"Yeah." Knox steps over to the window. "We're in the LeCharme building. Alec and I have this understanding. I rent this place from him." Knox makes little quotation marks with his fingers when he says, "rent." "And then, he can bring his lady friends over when he wants. Sometimes, he'll have parties here, too. The place has five bedrooms."

Wow. Alec is a major player.

"So what happens when a lady friend comes back and says she forgot her scarf or something?"

Knox chuckles. "That's where I earn my rent."

I pull on the neck of my body armor. This stuff looks cool, but Kevlar isn't exactly comfy. "You don't have anything I could change into, do you? This stuff is uncomfortable, and besides, the conversation will be tough enough without having it in body armor."

"People do leave stuff around after the parties. I tell the cleaners to wash it up and leave it in the last bedroom on the right." He gestures down the hallway. "You might find something in there."

"Thanks."

He hitches his thumb over his shoulder. "My room is down this way. I'll change as well, and then we can grab a cab, okay?"

"Perfect. I know we have time until midnight, but sometimes Queen Nyxa shows up early. The sooner we get there, the better."

"Cool." Knox grips the body armor at his waist. A prickle of awareness moves over my skin. Yet again, Knox is going to strip down naked near me. We've only kissed twice, but the nakedness has happened three times. Not that I'm keeping track or something. My face starts to heat. I definitely don't want him to see me blush again, so I speed my way to the last bedroom on the right. Like the rest of the place, it's decorated in bare concrete and black furniture. The closet is massive and filled with clothes.

Mostly girl stuff.

A lot of it is ball gowns and cocktail dresses. Some are torn straight up the front. I slide past those hangers with extra speed. Alec is a nice guy and all, but there are some things about him that I just don't want to know.

My breath catches. Unless Knox has been at all these parties, too?

I push the thought aside. I've been doing that a lot today, and I think I'm getting pretty good at it. I soon find some clean leggings and a long sweater. It's a little more casual than my aunties are used to, but it's certainly better than body armor. I run a brush through my hair and scheme my head off.

The more I think about it, the more having Knox along is an awesome idea, especially if Queen Nyxa is there. I know just how to bring them all to their knees. It's not very mature of me, but once I'm finished fixing my face, I rub my hands together and say, "Mwah hah hah" at the mirror.

Aunties, here I come.

I step out of the room. Knox is already standing by the door. He's back in black leather pants and a dark T-shirt. With his black hair and ice-blue eyes, he looks like a rock star. My heart does this strange fluttery thing in my chest. I try to ignore that too, but it's not so easy.

Knox looks up as I approach. "You look great. I've got a cab waiting downstairs."

"I think I know how to confront my aunties."

"I'm game."

So, I share my plan. My pulse speeds up as I explain things, mostly because the plan involves Knox waiting outside my auntie's door, and I know he's a protective type. But he's totally down with the scheme and even calls me a genius. One of these days, I'll stop blushing my face off when he compliments me.

Knox takes my hand as we leave the LeCharme building. He keeps holding it in the cab and when we get out at my aunties' building. He even holds my hand while we take the elevator to my aunties' penthouse. A dozen questions run through my mind at once. Does this mean that we're still mated? I know next to nothing about werewolf culture. Being mated is a big deal, but I'm not sure you can hold someone to a proclamation made while they were about to be killed by a sociopath undead mummy-zombie.

My chest tightens. Suddenly, it's like I can't pull in enough breath.

I gesture to the door. "This is it."

Knox cups my face with his hands. "You're nervous."

I nod quickly. *Yes, yes, yes.*

"About your aunties or me?"

There's no point lying to a werewolf. "Both."

"Bry, you've got nothing to worry about when it comes to us, yeah?"

I start babbling again and am totally powerless to stop it. "But there were all those dresses in your apartment, and lots of them were torn. You must have gone to some of those parties." I realize I'm speaking so fast, all my words tumble together. Still can't stop myself, though. "Just because you said you were my mate in a battle doesn't mean you have to stick to it. And sure, you were my first kiss, but that doesn't mean—"

"Whoa. Stop right there. Believe me, you've nothing to worry about when it comes to us." He leans in and gently brushes his lips across mine. "We'll talk more later, yeah?"

"Yeah."

Knox takes in a deep breath. "Now, you smell more settled. You ready for this?"

"As I'll ever be." Actually, I'm totally not ready for this conversation. I've spent a lot of my precious prep-time worrying about how Jules got turned into charcoal and what's happening between Knox and me.

Denial much?

Now, I have to face my aunties—and possibly the most powerful fairy queen of them all—and confront them about scheming with Jules. *Oh, well.* Maybe it was best to avoid those thoughts until now. Just starting to contemplate that level of betrayal, I want to race back into the elevator and never see them again.

Best to just get this over with. I straighten my shoulders and push the intercom buzzer.

Mirabelle's voice crackles over the intercom by the door. "Just come in, whoever you are. The door's open, and the party's started." I can hear voices babbling and music blaring at full volume. The intercom goes silent.

I close my eyes and focus. I've always had good hearing, but after I had my first shift with Jules, it seems like everything is super-loud. And now, I need that skill more than ever before. From what I heard over the intercom, the party is in full swing, and it isn't even midnight yet. What I need to know now is if a certain fairy is in attendance. There will be no way to miss her voice if she is.

A nasal screech echoes through the door. "And yet again, I win another battle of riddles!" An odd chorus of voices breaks out into cheers. The sound is a mix between a growl and the twitter of birds. *Those are definitely fairies.*

My stomach drops to my toes. *And Queen Nyxa is with them. Damn.*

I press my hands to my face and force my breathing to slow. *This is a disaster.* The whole reason we sped over here was to avoid seeing Nyxa in the first place.

Knox moves to stand at my side. He whispers in my ear. "The queen is there, yeah?"

"Yup." I make sure to pop the "p" on the "Yup."

"No worries. We're fine. You planned for this, and your scheme is brilliant. Now, I'll just wait out here and listen for you to call my name." He tugs on his ear. "Wolf hearing, right? This will work."

I grip my hands tightly at my waist. "Or we could run. I've always wanted an assumed identity." As the words leave my mouth, I realize I'm definitely half serious.

"Not a chance. You just fought Jules and a few hundred undead losers."

I raise my pointer finger. "I'm not really sure how he died." For some reason, it feels very important to make that point clear.

"I got that. But you still won. And you can do this, too. I believe in you."

With those words, I'm ready to pull up my big-girl panties and face things head-on. I grip the handle and push open the door.

I step down the small entrance hallway and into the main living room. It's like stepping into a funky chic high-end department store circa 1960. We have these egg-shaped chairs and fur-covered couches. The lamps remind me of silver spiders. The rugs are beyond plush. Oh yes, and everything is in different shades of green, yellow, and pink. That's all the work of Lauralei and Fanna, of course.

The place is packed with partygoers. All of them are fae. There are tall willowy types with blue skin and limbs as thin as reeds. Young curvy types with pink skin and wings to match. And little pixies zip around the air with their bright green bodies, dark wings, and pointed teeth. They all join a frenzy of movement they like to call dancing. I think of it more as a magical mosh pit. The scent of dandelion wine hits me smack in the face. *Yipes.* Fairies get absolutely toasted on anything to do with dandelions. And based on the number of glasses filled with yellow liquid in this room? These fairies are all well on their way to being plastered.

Lauralei and Fanna stand in the center of the room in their matching yellow Chanel suits, sipping their yellow drinks from wide martini glasses. Today, they remind me of a cross between flamingoes and Big Bird. Mirabelle waits nearby in another red muu muu thing. And in the center of this trio stands Queen Nyxa. She's hard to miss, considering how she's seven feet tall with orange skin and moss-green hair. A crown of bluebells sits atop her head. The flowers are the same shade as her floor-length gown and over-large eyes. The moment I set foot in the living room, her gaze locks on me.

"Bryar Rose." When the queen addresses me, the entire chamber falls silent. "You have arrived."

"Yes." I'm pretty happy with how calm and level my voice sounds now. "And I have great news for you all."

My aunties grin from ear to ear. Mirabelle bobs happily on the balls of her feet, a movement that makes her muu muu puff out into a muffin shape.

They think they know what my news is. But they have no idea.

Lauralei steps forward and raises her glass. "Let me guess. You have fulfilled your—"

"No!" I'm even happier with my loud exclamation here, because it shuts Lauralei right up. "I want to announce this news in a special way…by holding a battle of riddles with Queen Nyxa."

The smiles melt away from all three of my aunties. "What?" asks Lauralei. "I forbid it."

Nyxa rounds on Lauralei. "Who are you to forbid me anything?" She grins so sweetly, you'd hardly think she was the kind of fairy who killed servants for fun. But she is. "I should very much like to engage Bryar Rose in a battle of riddles."

I curtsy. "Thank-you."

"What is the prize?" asks Nyxa slowly.

"The winner can request any boon she wants of the other, and I'll go first."

Please, let me go first.

"Absolutely not. I am queen here, and I set the rules. I shall ask you first." She taps her chin with one long orange finger. "Let me think…"

My heart starts beating so loudly, I can actually hear my pulse in my ears. I've watched Nyxa play these riddle games for years. Usually, she always starts off with an easy question. Otherwise, she says the game is over too quickly.

"I have it." Nyxa claps her hands. "Why is a raven like a writing desk?"

I could cheer, I am so excited for this question. It's a real stumper, but not for me. It's from *Alice's Adventures in Wonderland*, after all. I give Nyxa my best grin. "Ask the Mad Hatter."

Now, I'm not a hundred percent sure that's the right answer, but based on how Nyxa is gritting her teeth right now? I'm pretty sure I nailed it. "Fine," she says quickly. "Ask your question."

I swallow past the knot of worry in my throat. Nyxa is a massively powerful fairy, and this is a huge gamble. She won't like losing. "Who has my heart?"

Nyxa tips her head back and laughs. "Why, that's easy. Jules, the leader of the Denarii. I'm sure he's captured it both in the metaphorical and physical sense by now, yes?" She makes a slurping noise as she drinks, which is number one, unnecessary and number two, totally disgusting.

"Not exactly." I pull back the wide neckline of my sweater to show the unmarked skin on my shoulder. "As you can see, my heart is still where it's always been." I cup my hand by my mouth. "Knox, we're ready for you now."

The door slams open, and Knox strides into the room. He's all messy black hair, leather pants, big boots, and attitude. I've always noted how his presence fills up a room. Now, I'm thinking that's his alpha warden vibe. Even though the room is filled with obnoxious fairies, suddenly it's like there is only him and me. I can't help it; I stare at his full mouth. Dark bristle lines his chin. I want nothing more than to rub my fingertips over his skin.

Knox's eyes glow golden with werewolf power. An electric sense of connection seems to fill the air between us. Before I know what's happening, his heavy arms are around me, and he's pulled me against his firm body. I don't need any more invitation than that. I lean in and kiss him, hard.

I don't know how long things go on like that, but no one says a word. Eventually, Knox breaks the kiss. "When you told me about your plan, you didn't say the exact words of your riddle." He leans his forehead against mine. "Is that true?"

"Yes, Knox. You hold my loving heart." I can't stop smiling like a fool.

"Glad to hear it. You have mine too, yeah?"

"Yeah."

Nyxa's voice takes on a nasal shriek. "Where is Jules? It's this thing's eighteenth birthday." She points a long finger at me. Evidently, I'm considered a "thing" in her vocabulary. "She was supposed to marry Jules! What's going on?"

I fold my arms over my chest. "That's the precise question I was going to ask my aunties. Jules is dead. I will never marry him."

"What?" ask my aunties in unison.

"And since I won the battle of riddles, I will now name my prize. From now on, my aunties must tell me the truth. Make it happen, Nyxa."

Nyxa sniffs. "Fairies don't lie."

"You don't tell the *full* truth, either."

Nyxa fans her chest with her hand. "This party is boring me to death. I should be going. In fact, it's beyond time everyone left."

"But what about my wish?"

"I'll grant it...someday. Come find me, and we'll talk." She raises her arms, and the room fills with the silver light of fairy dust. When the air clears, the only ones left are my aunties, Knox, and me.

Go find her? Finding fairies is impossible unless they want to be found or you have their real name and can summon them. Leave it to a fairy to weasel out of a bargain.

My aunties stalk toward me, and they do not look happy. Moving in unison, they all raise their arms and summon fairy dust to them. My body freezes with fear. My aunties don't crack out magic often, but when they do? Look out.

I straighten my back and firm up my resolve. After all, this was the situation I'd hoped for in the first place, right? That my aunties would be here alone so I could confront them? Getting Nyxa out of the way was just phase one of my plan.

But now that I see my aunties conjuring up magic against Knox and me? I think about all the times they wiped my nose and changed my diapers. They conjured me dinners and tucked me in at night.

Now that it comes to it, I don't know if I can fight them, after all.

My aunties lower their arms. Long, thin branches burst out of the floor and wrap around Knox.

Not me. Knox.

The thorns dig into his skin. The copper scent of blood fills the air. Rage corkscrews up my spine.

"Jules can't be dead!" Lauralei is shrieking now. "It's all this werewolf's fault. He's lying to her."

Suddenly, different memories fill my mind. Mirabelle telling me I'm a failure and worthless. Fanna handing me Predator's Bane and making me thank her for it. Lauralei inviting me to a birthday party to celebrate my own murder.

And now? Torturing my mate. What little shred of affection I kept for these three ladies vanishes under the fires of my rage.

A voice roars with rage inside my head. *"Attack!"* It's my wolf speaking to me again.

Once again, I agree with her.

Before I know what's happening, my wolf form tears out of my body. It's agony as my limbs realign. Sinews tear, and bone stretches. My great white wolf faces down my aunties. My muzzle trembles as I snarl with rage. "Set. Him. Loose."

I don't know what surprises them more—the fact that I'm a wolf or that I talk. Either way, the three of them only stare dumbfounded at me. I stalk over to Knox. The thorny branches they've tied him with have silver bark. Something about it is forcing him to stay in his human form. I raise my front paw, claws extended. With a flash of talons, I slice through the cords that bind him.

Knox steps free. Within seconds, his own wolf bursts from his skin. His eyes flare with golden light as he approaches my aunties. "That wasn't smart."

"He t-t-t-alks," stutters Mirabelle.

"They both talk," adds Fanna.

Lauralei raises her arms. "We need more thorns, I see." A fresh cloud of fairy dust sparkles around her hands.

Fresh fury courses through my veins. If I live to be a thousand, I never want to see those damned Sleeping Beauty thorns again. I reach deep within me to the place where Colonel Mallory locked up my magic. This time, I do find it.

So I set it loose.

Leaning back my head, I let out a howl. Silver fairy dust surrounds my entire wolf, growing thicker and stronger as my howl grows. Knox adds his voice into the mix, and I can feel his alpha power giving me hope and strength. By the time I finish my howl, the mist is so thick, it's almost a liquid. I lower my head, and the fairy dust speeds off to my aunties, growing larger as it flies forward.

My magic slams into my aunties, knocking them onto their backs. I lower my voice to a rumble. I have no idea how to cast a spell, but I know what I want to happen here. "No more magic for you."

The fairy dust I sent over encompasses the three women, twisting round their bodies like small cyclones. Within seconds, their skin begins to glow. Somehow, I know that's their power—their fairy dust—being drawn out of them. Their bodies shine more and more brightly until the room is bathed in silver light.

After that, the light disappears. From the bottom of my soul, I know their powers are gone as well.

Lauralei scrambles to sit upright. She raises her hands, staring at them like she's never seen them before. Her voice comes out a rough whisper. "What did you do to my powers?"

"I can't pull any fairy dust," whines Fanna.

"Nor me," adds Mirabelle.

Knox gives me a quick look. I still don't know him too well, but I can tell that he's wondering what I did to their powers, too.

I wish I knew. I reach into my soul to find my lockbox of power, and it's closed down tightly once more. Why can I access it sometimes but not others? I shake my head. There must be some kind of logic to it, but that's something to wonder about another day. Preferably when I have a fully translated *Book of Magic* in front of me.

Right now, I have to deal with my aunties.

Still in my wolf form, I stalk up to Lauralei. "I want some questions answered."

Lauralei's face creases into a simpering smile. "You wouldn't hurt your aunties, would you?"

Wolf-Knox stalks forward. "She might not, but I definitely will. Answer her questions." All three of my aunties gasp in terror. I'm not sure what it says about me as a person, but I find it a super-satisfying sight.

Lauralei quickly recovers, though. The next thing I see, she's done gasping and is lifting her chin instead. "Never."

Mirabelle scrambles to stand. "I'll answer."

"Don't you dare," scolds Lauralei.

I stalk around them slowly. "Listen to me closely. I know Philpot was really Jules, the leader of the evil Denarii. You set me up to become his zombie bride."

Lauralei pales. "Don't talk nonsense." I must be getting more werewolf-y, because I can smell her lie like it was last week's garbage.

"I'm not playing this game anymore. You're going to tell me what happened with Jules, why you did it, and who my parents really are. Otherwise, things are going to get ugly."

Wolf-Knox scrapes the floor with his four-inch long claws. "Give me an excuse to make it ugly. Please."

Mirabelle waddles forward. "Jules approached us years ago. He asked us to do little things in exchange for magical tokens. Then, he said he had one last favor to ask of us before he gave us fairy magic beyond our wildest dreams. We didn't have a lot of power to begin with. That lured us in."

Mirabelle's words smell like truth. Even more importantly, they fit with what I know of Jules. He was always trying to put together deals, even when he was pretending to be a hedge fund manager.

"Go on," orders Knox.

"When we agreed to this final deal with Jules, we had no idea that he would bring us a baby. All the other favors were finished in an hour or so."

Mirabelle's words knock the breath out of me. No wonder Lauralei and Fanna acted like I was such a burden. They were expecting a few hours of work in return for a ton of magical power. Instead, they got almost eighteen years of me. A sour feeling settles into my stomach. There's nothing like knowing you're unwanted to ruin your day.

Wolf-Knox turns to me. He tilts his head with sympathy. "You don't have to do this now, you know."

"No, I need the truth. Keep talking, Mirabelle."

Lauralei throws up her arms. "Shut your mouth, this instant. Mirabelle, if you tell Bryar Rose even one more word, then Jules will find you. He'll come after all of us!"

Mirabelle huffs out a frustrated breath. "Don't you get it? We're talking about the deal between us and Jules. Should that be able to happen? He had those wizards and fairies cast about a dozen silencer spells on us."

Lauralei's face pales. "No. I suppose it shouldn't."

"You know what that means. Jules is dead. That's why Bryar Rose is here and we can even discuss these things. There are no more excuses now. And she's shifted into her werewolf form. There's no point pretending." Mirabelle turns to me. "What else do you want to know?"

I feel like a kid set loose in a candy store. All my life, I wondered who my parents really were. In fact, I dreamed up identities for them as regular humans. There's no question what I want to know first. "Who are my parents?"

"You're half werewolf," answers Mirabelle. "That's all we know. Jules dropped you off with instructions to give you Predator's Bane. Although, considering the spell you just cast, I'd guess your other half is fairy."

Wolf-Knox steps closer. "Half?"

Tension tightens up my neck. "Is that a bad thing?"

"No, it's just..." Wolf-Knox bobs his head. "You're really power-ful to be half were. I could be alpha of all alphas if I wanted to, and my wolf chose you."

Lauralei grins. "Alpha of all alphas?"

"And our Bryar Rose is your mate?" asks Fanna.

"It's a pleasure to meet you," says Lauralei. "Apologies for our rude greeting before, Mister...?"

"Knox. His name is Knox." *I can't believe this.* Now that Jules is dead, they're sucking up to the next most powerful person in the room.

And that's never going to be me. At least, not in their eyes. I'll always be some weak foundling they were saddled with. "I have one more question for you. Colonel Mallory the Magnificent says he saved my wolf. What do you know about that?"

"Colonel Mallory? Seriously?" Lauralei waves her hands. "You're dating an alpha, but let's not put on airs. I doubt Colonel

Mallory the Magnificent would have taken an interest in your existence."

"Enough, Lauralei." Mirabelle focuses on me. "Jules once said something about Colonel Mallory slipping away from him before Jules could finish him."

Before he could finish him as a meal of dragon power, more likely.

"I think I know what happened." Knox's wolf-voice is low and soothing. "If Colonel Mallory was held in the same place where Jules was keeping you as a baby, maybe he ran across you there. Jules has tough prisons, but I bet Colonel Mallory could break free. He might have cast the Slumber Beast spell on you there." Knox tilts his head and gives me a meaningful look. I know what he's thinking.

And maybe cast another spell as well. There's no question what spell that would be either: the lockbox in my soul.

I chuff out a breath. "I really want to talk to Colonel Mallory."

"Good luck," says Mirabelle. "He shows when he shows."

Lauralei rounds on Knox. "Our Bryar Rose really knows the great Colonel Mallory the Magnificent?"

"I'm right here, Lauralei. And I already said I know Colonel Mallory." I make a point to turn toward Mirabelle. "Thank-you for answering my questions." I look to Knox. Now that all the excitement is over, I feel like a balloon that's been deflated. All I want to do is go home. "Look, the computer in my bedroom has IP telephony. If I call Alec, do you think he would...?"

"He would. And while you do that, I'll wait here and keep an eye on your aunties."

"Thanks." I pad off in my wolf form into my room, transform back to a human, get dressed, and call Elle. It's the same thing as contacting Alec anyway. In short order, Alec casts some spells so Knox is dressed and we're both back in his apartment.

Once I'm safe inside his place, I launch right into a crying jag. Knox doesn't say a word. He simply directs me to his bedroom and tucks me under the covers. I've never been in a guy's room before, but with Knox? It feels natural and safe to be in his personal den. The place is warm and comfy with lots of earth colors and leather.

Once I'm snuggled under the covers, Knox slides in beside me while keeping his own body over the covers. As I fall asleep, his fingertips brush through my hair, and his low voice whispers, "You did so well, Bryar Rose. I'm proud of you."

And to those words of comfort, I drift off to sleep.

CHAPTER TWENTY-SEVEN
BRYAR ROSE

For a totally crap day, my night was filled with some pretty amazing dreams. Believe it or not, they all happened in the LeCharme elevator. This time around, the place felt quaint instead of old and creepy. And best of all? Knox was there, guiding me into kiss after blissful kiss. And since this was all a dream, we never had any awkward stuff like neck cramps or our teeth knocking together.

As dreams go, it was pretty awesome.

Sure, a few times I caught a wolf in the corner of my vision, but I ignored it, and the animal went away. That pretty much sums up my whole attitude toward my werewolf side at this moment. It's there. It exists. But until I understand what is really happening to me, I'm not ready to fully embrace that side of myself. Who knows what that could mean?

When I wake up, I find that I'm still lying in Knox's bed. After waking up in a strange tower yesterday, I can't even begin to say how amazing it is to awaken the same place you fell asleep. The only negative is that I'm alone on the mattress. Knox himself isn't cuddling me anymore. Not to be a whiny baby, but it's a bummer. Even though Knox was atop the covers and everything, having him so close still made me feel so much warmer.

The good news is that Knox is still here. He's snoozing away in a nearby armchair with his head lolled forward, arms folded, and legs kicked out in front of him. It doesn't look too comfortable.

Knox opens his right eye. "Morning, Bry."

"I didn't mean to wake you up."

"Don't worry about it. It's my wolf. The slightest movement and he's alert." Knox stretches, and since he's still wearing his rock star pants and fitted T-shirt, I'm really enjoying the view. Knox is ripped.

I realize I've been staring for too long, so I decide to turn my mind to something useful. "I'd like to go back to the LeCharme Building. I really want to get a head start on those papyri."

"It's Sunday. Maybe you should take a day off from magic stuff."

My mind blanks. "And do what?"

"I have an idea." His mouth winds into a wolfy grin. "You up for some fun?"

Fun. Me. And with a hot guy. This is really happening.

I do my best to try and act cool. "Sure, fun. I'm into you." I smack my own head. *Way to play it cool.* "I mean, I'm into it. Having fun. That part." *Shut up, mouth.*

"Good." Knox nods to a door in the back of the room. "There's a private bath in there. Should have shampoo and all that girly stuff. I tell the staff to keep it stocked."

He stands and stretches again. This time, his T-shirt pulls up enough that I can see a sliver of bare skin along his belly. Knox catches me staring and gives me one of those sly smiles where his eyes crinkle up.

My stomach goes woozy. "I'll just get ready then."

"Sure. I need to let Alec and Elle know you're up."

My mouth falls open. "They're both here?"

"They came by last night to check on you. Alec has some master plan for us and the papyri, and Elle..." He tilts his head. "She feels really bad about lying to you."

"What lie is she worried about this time?" Elle's a con artist, for crying out loud. She lies for a living. Still, it's all for a good cause, so I try not to get caught up in it.

"The lie of omission. Not telling you she's one of the fae."

"Oh, *that* lie." For some reason, waking up in the tower was less upsetting than confronting my best friend about her major lie of omission. Part of me wants to scream at her for an hour, minimum. But another part wants to trust her. Elle has covered my back more times than I can count. It's against girl code to freak out before she's told me her side of the story. And considering she came over last night, she definitely wants to tell her side.

I debate about going out right now to chat with Elle, but that's the moment my stomach decides to growl at a volume that could break the sound barrier. I quickly set my hands on my stomach. "I need a shower and some food before I deal with Elle. Do you think you could let her know?"

"Sure thing, Bry." He winks. "Besides, I need to shower, too. Mine is just on the other side of the wall from yours."

"Oh." Knox will be naked on the other side of the wall from me. That's a lot of information. *Not that I'm complaining.*

"See you in the kitchen." He saunters out of the room, and it's like the energy level plummets or something. That must be his alpha wolf energy. It sure is magnetic, but I need to steer clear of it. I have some big decisions to make, like where I'm going to live and how I'll earn money for stuff like food. I can't let my mate attraction to Knox distract my focus.

Whatever happens next, I will never let my werewolf side dictate my life. It's just a condition; that's all. In fact, the more I think about it, the more I think that my normal life as a regular human could be closer now than ever before.

⁂

About an hour later, we're all hanging in the kitchen: Elle, Alec, Knox, and me. Like the rest of Knox's place, the kitchen has bare-cement walls, black furniture, and wood floors. We're all dressed in jeans and sweats, except for Alec who's always wearing his ever-present sport coat packed with jewels.

Elle sits across from me at a black granite high-top table. Her shoulders are slumped, and she won't even look at me.

"Elle."

"Hmm?"

I lower my voice a little. "Elle."

"What?" She still won't look at me, though. I turn to Knox. "Can you guys give us a second?"

Knox gives me one of those chin-nods that only hot guys can get away with.

Alec looks ready to burst with excitement. He beams his most winning surfer-boy smile. "Are you sure? I have some amazing news."

"Come on, Captain Excitement." Knox gives him a playful punch on the shoulder. "I'll show you my new gaming console."

Alec heaves out a dramatic sigh. "If we must, we must."

Once they finally leave the kitchen, I take the barstool next to Elle's. "Can we talk now?"

"I feel terrible."

"Elle. Give me your eyes."

At last, Elle looks up. Her huge blue eyes are watery. "I didn't tell you I was a fairy. That's the same as lying. I'm so sorry."

I raise my hand, palm forward. "Did you have a good reason to keep the truth form me?"

Elle nods.

"And did that reason have something to do with your stepfamily?"

"Yes."

"There's more to it, isn't there? You have to keep other things from me because of them."

Her voice cracks. "I'm so sorry."

"Stop torturing yourself. I understand."

"You do?"

"How many times have you had my back when thing were crap? I trust you enough to know that you'll tell me when you can."

"I don't believe this. So you're not mad?"

"Well, I'm not thrilled about the situation, but that's not your fault. Come on. You just faced down a zombie army for me, and yet, you're moping around some dude's kitchen because your crazy stepfamily is making your life hell? We got this, girlfriend." I offer her my fist to bump. "Team?"

She bumps me back. "Team."

Leaning over, I give Elle a major hug. You know the kind. We're laughing a little bit while rocking from side to side. Elle's the best.

Alec marches into the kitchen. "You ready for my news?"

Knox follows him. "That's just rude, man. They were doing their girl-thing in here."

Elle breaks the hug, sits back, and pats the tears from under her eyes. "No, we're good. Right, Bry?"

"Absolutely." Elle and I share a smile. I really am super-lucky to have a best friend like her. We're about to hug again when Alec steps between us. It should be a rude move, but Alec looks so excited, it's hard to be upset with him.

"Hold on," says Alec. "Wait until you hear what I've been up to this morning."

Knox rubs his neck and yawns. "Besides hanging in my kitchen and making a ton of calls?"

Alec rolls his eyes. "It's my kitchen, technically."

Elle turns to me. Her bright smile is back, which is great to see. "Alec has been on the phone for hours." She lowers her voice to a hush. "He's working on some secret project."

Alec leans his elbow against the counter in another classic menswear catalog pose. "My news is about West Lake Prep."

His words send my pulse into high gear. It feels like a million years ago that I was sitting in a basement with Madame, dealing with her crazy in the far-fetched hope that I could maybe-possibly get into this school.

"What about it?" I ask.

"I got you in. I got you all in." Alec beams. "Isn't that great?"

No one jumps for joy. Sure, it's awesome that I got into the school, but that still leaves a ton of questions out there. Like how

I'll pay for school and where I'll live. Both of which Alec promised to cover at one time or another, but I'm not sure it's a great idea to go from relying on my aunties to relying on Alec.

Alec narrows his eyes. "I can't help but notice the lack of excitement here." And he has a point. Elle looks freaked. Knox looks wary. And me? Cautiously optimistic.

"Look, I appreciate what you're offering, but I just walked out on my aunties. I need to find a job before I worry about anything else."

"And that's the beauty of the whole thing. I'm starting an Egyptian Studies club. You'll be doing the same work you were doing on your internship: putting the papyri back together. We still need to find the fountain that's the source of all magic. And to get that job done, the same deal applies. You'll get a salary and an apartment. I've even gotten you a scholarship. How's that for amazing?"

I scrub my hands over my face. "It's super-generous, Alec. I just don't feel right taking you up on it. It's like I'm taking advantage of you or something."

Alec rolls his eyes again. "Please. The benefit is all mine. The Magicorum have been trying to translate those papyri for thousands of years. You've made more progress than we ever have. You'd be doing me a favor."

"That's nice of you to say, but a job, scholarship, and a place to live?"

"Don't forget your salary."

"That makes it worse, Alec. Now I *really* feel like I'm taking advantage."

Alec's face turns serious. "Your help is worth even more than all that. You know I'm a warden, right?"

"I guessed."

"And you know what that means?"

"Out of all your people, you have the most power over wizard magic."

"There's more to it than that." Alec sighs. "Wardens are supposed to guard the fountain of magic, but it was lost thousands of years ago. Now, we have no clue where it is. As long as that thing's hidden, we can't get married. Our spouses die."

I gasp. "What about all those girls you date at parties?"

"Knox told you about that, eh?" Alec glares in Knox's direction. "Casual hookups don't count. It's getting married that causes the trouble. You may not think I'm a serious person, but I do want a wife and family someday." His gaze flickers to Elle. "If you find the fountain, then all the wardens can have families and a future. That hasn't happened for thousands of years. I don't have a shot unless you help me. So, will you help me?"

When Alec puts it that way, I feel like a total creep for turning him down. "Sure, Alec. I'll help you."

Alec's million-watt smile returns. "I've got the best apartment picked out for you, too." He rubs his palms together and turns to Knox. "So you're going?"

Elle frowns. "Why wouldn't Knox want to go?"

A muscle twitches along Knox's neck. "There are a lot of were-wolves at West Lake. Some want me to lead them. Others want to fight me for dominance. It's a total pain in my ass. That's why I've been taking online classes."

"Wait a second." I hold up my pointer finger. "Madame said that West Lake was all humans."

Alec chuckles. "What Madame didn't know is a lot. Folks at West Lake act like regular humans, but they aren't regular at all." He focuses on Knox once more. "What do you say?"

Knox fixes me with a look so intense, I'm glad I'm sitting down, or I might get wobbly. "If Bry is there, then I'm in."

My chest warms. *He's going to West Lake Prep for me...even if it's actually a school full of crazy Magicorum.*

"Excellent. Bry and Knox are a go." Alec rounds on Elle. "And how about you?"

Elle shakes her head. "I have to avoid any kind of typical school. If my stepfamily found out where I was, it would be terrible. I'm really better off on the streets."

Suddenly, the thought of going to West Lake Prep without Elle seems like an awful idea. I'm about to say just that when Alec steps in.

"I've thought about that already." Alec smirks. "After pulling in some favors with a few especially shady characters, I've gotten you a new identity, Miss Evelyn LeCharme."

Elle's eyes widen. "LeCharme?"

"You're my long-lost cousin. And by long-lost, I mean that the Le Charme family is shocked to discover that our dearly departed— and incredibly randy—old Uncle Aaron had yet another illegitimate child with a Las Vegas showgirl."

Elle is trying to keep a straight face, but I can tell she loves this idea. "So I'm a bastardess?"

"A Vegas showgirl bastardess. That's very exalted company." He bobs his eyebrows. "And you'll be doing me a favor." He lowers his voice. "Bry seems rather shady. I think she'll get more work done if you keep an eye on her."

"So it's all about the papyri?" asks Elle.

"What else?" These two are such flirts, this could go on for hours.

Knox seems to feel the same way I do. He pointedly checks his watch. "What do you say, Elle?"

"It's tempting."

"Clearly, I need to sweeten the deal. And the apartment next to this one has tons of extra space. You and Bry can live here. Commute together. Save on groceries and maid service, that kind of thing."

Knox shakes his head. "And then they'll be at your beck and call, too."

Alec winks. "That never occurred to me at all."

"Watch the scheming there, mastermind." Knox turns to me. "Are you cool with that? I know the apartment Alec is talking about. The place is still under construction, but it's huge. You and Elle will have your own rooms."

It's a good question. *Am I cool with all this?* Moving into an apartment next to Knox is certainly intimidating, but it would have its good points, too. And living with Elle would be awesome.

What am I thinking? Of course, I'm cool with it. The whole thing is amazing. It's everything I've wanted.

I shoot a thumbs-up. "I'm in."

Alec beams. "I knew you'd love my plan."

"Wait a second," says Knox. "We haven't covered all the details yet." He steps closer. "Remember when I said there was some stuff we needed to talk about?"

"You and me?" I ask.

"Yeah."

The hair on my neck stands on end. Somehow, I don't think I'll like this conversation. "I remember."

"Before you commit to Alec's offer here, you need to know the full story."

Alec pulls out a barstool and sits down. "This is going to be interesting."

"No, it's not." Knox points toward the door. "Why don't you show Elle her new apartment? Bry and I need to talk."

"I thought we could make microwave s'mores and hang out," says Alec. "I'm sure you want my opinion on whatever it is you think is preventing my plan here."

"Out. Seriously. Before I set loose my wolf on you."

Alec offers Elle his arm. "My lady?"

She sets her hand on his forearm. "Sir."

Their gazes lock as they walk away. In fact, I'm not sure how the two of them don't slam into a wall. They certainly aren't looking where they're going.

Funny the things that stick in your mind when you're about to get bad news.

At last, I hear the far-off snick of the door shutting. I try to keep my features level, but my voice comes out at least two octaves too high. "What's going on?"

"You remember how Alec said he's a warden?"

"Sure."

"I'm a warden, too."

"Yeah. I guessed that, remember?"

"Well, what Alec said about a wife and kids. I want that too. Only, werewolves don't get married. We have a mating ceremony. After that, we can have cubs." He tilts his head and winces. "My wolf really wants to have cubs."

Sure, this is problem for a long-term relationship. However, I see a super-easy solution. "This is fine."

"Really?" Knox frowns. "Because Alec undersold the process a little there. Finding the fountain isn't enough. It needs to be active, too." He takes my hands in his. "That said, I want you to know something. I trust you, Bry. I trust *us*. We'll figure it out, one way or another. The important thing is that we're together."

"I see this as a nonissue, really."

Knox's features tighten. "Why?"

"Because I don't have to embrace my wolf side. I can act like a regular human, and so can you. We don't need to worry about mating ceremonies and cubs. Like last night? I dreamed I saw my wolf like five different times. I just ignored her, and she went away."

"You did, huh." Knox doesn't seem at all happy about my plan here, which doesn't make any sense. Maybe I just need to explain things more clearly.

"I'm not really all that magical. I'm a regular girl, mostly. We can just act like two regular humans and take every day as it comes. What do you think?" The more I talk about it, the more I love this idea.

Knox stares at me for a long time. His ice-blue eyes turn super-intense. I'd worry that he's about to go wolf on me, but his irises aren't gold. Finally, he speaks. And what he says almost makes me fall out of my chair.

"How did Jules die?"

"I don't know," I say quickly. "That is, I don't remember."

"Which one is it? You don't know…or you don't remember?"

"Okay, I know I sound really sketchy. I'm just not ready to talk about it."

"But you're certain you don't have a lot of magic."

Something inside me snaps. I press my palms to my eyes. "Honestly, I don't know what I am, Knox. I don't know who my parents are. I have no clue what my real powers might be. The whole situation is a mess. I'm best off keeping everything on a human level. Come to think of it, that whole West Lake Prep thing is a bad idea." I scrub my hands over my face. "I don't want to be Magicorum."

He steps closer. "I'm Magicorum."

"And you've been amazing. It's just that the rest of it—my aunties, Jules, the battle—it's pretty much been a nightmare. Can't we pretend to be human, just for a little while?"

"That's not how it works with werewolves."

A lead weight settles onto my shoulders. "I see."

"Being Magicorum isn't all horrible, you know."

"I get it. I've really liked our time together." Sure, I'd love to hang with Knox as a werewolf, but the more I think about it, the more it seems like a bad idea. What if I open the lockbox again and blow away lower Manhattan by mistake?

"That's not what I mean. Can I show you something? We'll have to ride my bike to get there."

I worry my lower lip with my teeth. "What are we doing to do, exactly?"

"Have some fun, that's all." Knox offers me his hand. "What do you say?"

Knox looks so handsome and hopeful, there's only one answer I can give him. I set my palm on his. "Yes."

Once we're done having fun, we can get back to this conversation about living a normal human life. That's all I've ever wanted in the past. I'm sure it's all I want for my future.

Definitely.

Maybe.

Possibly.

Oh, crap. I really have no idea.

Being around Knox makes everything a lot more confusing.

CHAPTER TWENTY-EIGHT
KNOX

I ride my Harley along Route 87. Bryar Rose cuddles up behind me. I won't lie; feeling her pressing against me is like a drug. Right now, my inner wolf is about as contented as he gets. I'm right there with him, too.

Bryar Rose and I left my apartment about an hour ago, so it's late morning now. I heave in a deep breath. Damn, I love the tang of clean air in my lungs. This is one of those summer days that makes New York the best place in the world. Bright sun. No wind. Sky so blue, it hurts to look at it. Tall trees lining the road, the branches heavy with emerald leaves.

Perfect day for a ride.

Leaning slightly on my bike, I veer around a nasty dip in the asphalt. At this point, that's a reflex move. I drive this strip of highway so much I've got a mental map of every pothole, slope, and uneven patch. Hell, I even notice new roadkill. All in all, I've toured Route 87 thousands of times, but never with a girl on my bike.

Turns out, Bry is the exception to every rule.

My smile widens. I haven't told Bry yet, but we're going to Bear Mountain. The place is a kind of shifter preserve. In other words, it's a safe zone where folks who can't take the city can get a run. Az gave me the land years ago. I've always let any shifter use it. Mostly it's wolves who stop by, though. And so long as they don't over-hunt the wildlife and leave the tourists alone, I got no problems with them. A sinking feeling sets into my gut.

That's all about to change.

For years, the other weres have been pushing me to let them build some cabins on the mountainside. A real pack-living experience, that's what they want. In the past, I've always told them to forget it. Hell, they were lucky I let them run around on my property.

But now that they saved my ass with Jules? I might have to let them build a cabin or two. Of course, I would never actually live out here with them. Pack life is one long party, and that's not for me. Unless it involves killing Denarii or hanging with Bry, I'm not interested.

I shake my head. *This is all Azizi's doing.* For as long as I've known him, Az has wanted me to take my place as alpha of alphas. The old fart's been sitting around, waiting for an opportunity to lock me in. And the battle with Jules was his chance. He called in every nearby pack to help me out, and now I'm indebted to all of them.

Ah, well. Something to worry about another day.

I change lanes, which means tipping the bike. As we shift, Bry grips my abs more tightly. *Nice.* Truth be told, that move is quickly becoming my favorite part of riding with Bry. Hell, it might now be my fave part of riding, period.

I follow a familiar pattern of turn-offs that lead to ever thinner and more remote roadways. Soon, we reach an isolated stretch of forest divided by a thin path for my bike. We park in a small shed. Not much in here but a few tools for repairs and an emergency stash of clothes. I let people use this too, as long as they put stuff back like they found it.

Bry slips off my bike and looks around. She gives me a shy smile. "This place smells like you."

"The shed? I keep some stuff here."

"No, everywhere. Ever since we got off the highway." A blush crawls up her cheeks. "That's weird of me to say, right?"

"Not at all. This is my territory. It should smell like me."

"So you do what? Pee on the bushes?"

"Yeah. Among other things." Bry has a lot to learn about shifter life. It will be fun to teach her.

"How much land do you have, exactly?"

"Five thousand acres, give or take. I own all of Bear Mountain, pretty much."

"What happened to the bears?"

"A buddy of mine kicked them out. Same guy who gave me the land."

"Azizi?"

"How d'you know about him?"

"He introduced himself at the fight with Jules."

"That smooth talker. I forgot he sniffed you out. Yeah, Azizi kicked out the werebears and gave me the land. He won't tell me any of the story, though, but that's classic Az for you. Now the place still has the name, but it's pretty much Wolf Mountain. Shifters come here a lot." I slip my hands into the pockets of my jeans. Sometimes, being around Bry makes me feel like I'm twelve again. "Wanna go for a run?"

"Oh, I didn't bring jogging shoes."

She looks so wide-eyed and worried I just want to kiss her again. But this isn't about making out. I brought Bry here so she could discover the nicer sides of being in the Magicorum. "I meant as wolves."

"Oh." She bites her bottom lip a little, and the urge to kiss her comes back even stronger. I'll need to turn wolf soon, or I won't be able to restrain myself.

"No, you're good. Before the fight with Jules, I didn't even feel your wolf before."

My wolf begins chanting in my head. *"I knew mate! I knew mate!"*

I clear my throat. "Correction. My inner wolf knew who you were right away, but I couldn't sense anything. Normally, I get that stuff right away."

"But you sense my wolf now?"

"Yeah. Constantly."

Bry exhales a long breath. "So, you want to run as wolves."

"That's right." I have to work hard not to show how much I want this. If Bry wants to shift and run, that's great. But it should be her choice, first and foremost.

Bry laces her hands behind her neck and looks away. *Damn.* I bet she's going to take a pass.

"Run with mate! Run with mate!"

Crap. I should never have said that stuff out loud. Now, my wolf if going to freak if we try to get back on the bike.

At last, Bry turns to me again. "Okay, I'll do it."

I can't stop myself from grinning. "You sure?"

"Positive." She pulls at the neckline of her sweater. "Do I have to take this off?"

"Not if you don't want to. I have plenty of sweats and stuff in the shed. Changing into random clothes is a basic part of shifter life. I have caches of stuff hidden all over the property."

"Good to know." She's trembling a little, but trying to look cool.

"Strong mate," says my inner wolf.

"I know."

"So, how do we start? The last time I did this, it was pretty much instinct. I'm not really sure how to do it on demand."

"I can help there. I'll set my hand on your neck, like this." I palm the soft skin on her nape. She shivers again, but I can smell a different scent on the air. She's excited, too.

"Are you giving me your alpha mojo?"

"A little."

I guide us closer until only a few inches separate our bodies. "Now, look into my eyes." Our gazes lock, and I tap into my alpha power. A warm wave of magic rolls down my arm and into Bry. I keep my voice low and gentle. "Come to me. Show me your wolf."

A crackle of magic zooms across my skin as Bry's power answers mine. Her bones instantly start to snap and reform. Fur sprouts on her skin. Claws appear on her hands and feet. Her wolf tears right through her clothes. Within a few seconds, she's transformed into the most beautiful white wolf I've ever seen.

Her blue eyes lock with mine. "That wasn't so bad. Thanks."

I shake my head. "I still can't believe that you can talk."

She tilts her head. "Doesn't everyone?"

"No. It's a rare gift to talk in your wolf form. Only wolves I knew who could do it were me and Az." I step back and soak in the beauty of her all-white fur, strong muscles, and bright blue eyes. "I shouldn't be surprised that you can, though."

It's on the tip of my tongue to ask what happened with Jules again. That guy could totally talk in his wolf form, which is another sign of how powerful he was. But I shrug it off. That's a conversation for another day. It's enough for Bry to just have a good run as a wolf; we can worry about the rest later. I quickly shift into my own wolf form. Normally, the change hurts like hell. For some reason, the transformation doesn't pain me too much today. Maybe I'm just excited to run with my mate. We are pack animals, after all.

I round on Bry. Seeing her animal through my wolf's vision is a totally new experience. Every strand of fur, scent of sunshine, and flicker of light in her eyes…they all become more intense. The desire to run and explore becomes almost overwhelming.

I take a few steps backward. Wolf-Bry still watches me with her bright blue gaze. "Are you ready to run?" I ask. "Just take a few steps. Start off slowly and—"

All of a sudden, Bry leaps into the air and takes off like flash into the woods. I watch her scamper away. *She's unbelievable.* Most wolves freak out after their first change. A lot of them spend at least an hour sitting around and sniffing at the grass. But with Bry? Once again, every rule goes out the window.

"We find best mate," says my inner wolf.

"That's right, buddy."

271

"*Mate has secrets, though. Even ones she doesn't know.*"

For my wolf, that's some serious contemplative thought. "*I understand. That's all part of being mates, right? We'll figure it out.*"

"*No lose mate.*"

"*Never, bud.*"

Bry's scent is still strong, so I jump into the forest and take after her trail. Wolf or man, my heart has never felt so full.

CHAPTER TWENTY-NINE
BRYAR ROSE

I am a wolf.

And it's mind-blowingly awesome.

I run through the woods, the soft earth tickling the pads on my feet. Tiny breezes caress my fur. All my senses feel crazy-intense. The forest appears with incredible detail down to the last leaf, bug, and blade of grass. And the scents! There are so many, it's hard to keep track. I inhale the gamey waft of rabbit, lemony tang from dandelions, and the green smell of fresh soil. Another aroma enters into the mix as well: it's a mixture of sandalwood and musk. My pulse quickens.

That's Knox.

He's following me.

Fresh energy pours into my muscles. Instinct urges me to run faster. *Another wolf is here.*

Race.

Evade.

Leap.

I rush faster through the trees, dodging one trunk after the next. Wolf-Knox is getting closer. I fake a right turn, but veer left at the last second and leap over a thin stream. A thud sounds behind me as Knox follows my movements with ease.

My combat training comes back to me. *If evasive moves don't work, try to win with brute force.*

For me, that means all-out running.

A grassy field opens to my right. I take off in that direction and run so hard, my legs ache. The drumroll of Knox's paws grows fainter behind me. Triumph makes my body feel weightless.

I am a wolf. I'm unstoppable.

I risk a quick glance over my shoulder, and that's a big mistake. The movement slows me down enough that Knox closes the gap between us. His massive black body leaps into the air and tackles me onto the grass.

We roll around for a while. Knox growls, but somehow I know it's a playful tone. He nips at my neck and slows his movements. I heave in slow breaths and just exist. *What a moment.* The sun warms my fur. Knox nuzzles against me. Green grass cradles us both.

I don't know how it exactly happens, but the next thing I know, Knox and I have changed back into humans. Some part of me thinks I should be shocked, but I can't muster up the emotion. Being with Knox simply feels natural, whatever the form. Maybe it has something to do with being mates.

We lay side by side, facing each other. Knox's ice-blue eyes shine with a reverent glow as he gently brushes the hair off my cheek. When he speaks, his voice is a gentle whisper. "Do you want to change back into your wolf?"

"Not yet."

"Good." He gaze stays locked with mine.

"Does this happen a lot?"

Knox lets out a rumbling chuckle. "Changing into a human without consciously wishing it? Can't say I've ever had that happen before." His blue eyes flare with golden light. "I'm not complaining, though."

"Me neither." I lean in closer until our lips meet. If I thought our first kiss was intense, it's nothing compared to this time. My inner wolf rouses.

"Mate." Her voice sounds rusty inside my head. Still, there's a fierceness and eloquence to her that I wouldn't expect. *"He's our mate."*

Before I can think of a reply, Knox breaks the kiss. "Did I convince you?"

It takes me a moment to realize he asked me a question. Those kisses were so good they drained my mind of any rational thought. "What did you say?"

"Did I convince you?" The knowing look in his ice-blue eyes tells me that Knox realizes exactly what his kisses do to me. "You wanted both of us to act human. I brought you here to show you that embracing the Magicorum can become the greatest adventure of our lives." Knox brushes the backs of his fingers up my jawline. "Did it work?"

All of a sudden, being this exposed doesn't feel so comfortable. "I've loved running in my wolf form, but being a human is safer, you know? I know the rules there. I know who I am."

Knox frowns. "You know that pack of lies your aunties fed you. There's no need for you to hide as a human. I mean that. Bry, you're the most beautiful and powerful person I know."

My soul trembles at those words. "Keep telling me that. One of these days I might just believe it."

"You've got a deal." He cups my face in his hands. "And there's something else I want you to know, too. We'll find that fountain and activate it, together. I won't let the fact that I'm a warden stop us from having the choice of a full future together, if that's what you want."

My inner wolf paces inside me. *"Of course, we want cubs with him. Say that. Now."*

I close my eyes. "Shut up, I'm trying to have a conversation."

"Is your wolf talking to you?"

I reopen my eyes. A blush heats my cheeks. "Oops. Did I just say that out loud?"

"Yeah. It's okay. Mine talks to me all the time. It's not something most wolves do, you know. Lucky us." He grins. "I'd like to show you the view from my favorite mountain. Want to run there? I'll warn you though, it's pretty steep."

"I'd love to go."

Changing back into our wolf forms only takes a matter of seconds. It hardly stings at all. I wonder if that's another side effect of changing beside my mate, but there's no time to hang around and wonder.

Knox nudges me in the shoulder with his muzzle. He wants to run. And with every fiber of my soul, I want the same thing. We race back toward the trees.

And here, in the woods, with Knox at my side, a few thoughts keep echoing through my heart, drowning out years of hurtful words from my aunties.

I am Magicorum.

And I am strong enough to face the future, whatever it holds.

Together, Knox and I race toward the mountaintop. And what could be a tough journey becomes all things simple and joyful.

The End

The adventure continues with Shifters and Glyphs, Book 2 in the Fairy Tales of the Magicorum

Also from author Christina Bauer:
The best selling paranormal romance series, *Angelbound*

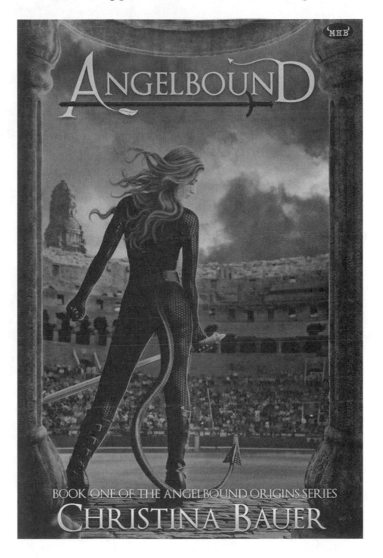

Also from author Christina Bauer:
The dark fantasy romance series, *Beholder*

Also from author Christina Bauer:
The snarky dystopian novel, *Dimension Drift*

Also from Monster House Books,
The urban fantasy romance series, *Circuit Fae*

ACKNOWLEDGEMENTS

To begin with, I'd like to acknowledge my super-secret (about to be not-so-secret) list of what makes for a kick-ass chick in a kick-ass story. I use this list to write *Wolves & Roses,* and well, everything. It's also the standard I hold up in my reading as well.

Now, you may be aware of the Bechdel test to see if a story meets a standard for feminism. Basically, it asks if the story has two female characters with names, do they talk to each other, and do they talk about something other than guys? When I first heard it, I thought that most stories probably met that criteria. They don't. And as I started to write more, I started to read more. Over time, I got even pickier about what kind of stories I liked (don't we all?), and I like me a book with kick-ass chicks.

Without further ado, here are my rules of kick-ass chick-ness:

The least you can do is throw a shoe. In a story about kick-ass chicks, you can't have someone cowering in a corner while someone else fights the big bad. The very least you can do is yell, "Go get 'em" or chuck your stiletto into the battle. And honestly? In real life, no one wants to go into the battle of life with someone they have to protect twenty-four/seven. Or if they do, you might want to get them a psychiatric evaluation. I love stories where the good folks fight the big bads together (more on that later).

He offered her the world; she said she had her own. I love world building. If the story is built around a world that is focused on our heroine's love interest, that's fine. However, the heroine also needs to have her own something-something going on that she's passionate about. It can be raising a family, working at a diner, making crafts in the garage, or mastering a superpower that saves the universe. I don't care as long as it's hers.

Being an active participant in your own superpower. Speaking of superpowers, I love a story where the heroine has one...but with one caveat: she has to choose to work her ass off to develop it. Here's why. As women, society gives us a lot of power for just blossoming into young womanhood (at least, that's what they called looking grown up and sexy when I was a teen). There's a ton of emphasis on beauty, and youth is the most important kind of beauty.

Pro tip: Actually, there are four kinds of beauty—heart, mind, soul, and body—and only one of them gets worse as you age, no matter what you do. I wrote a series of books (BEHOLDER) about a world where all four types of beauty were valued equally.

Okay, back to the physical beauty thing and choosing to own your superpower. To me, kick-ass chicks work for more than the physical. A kick-ass chick grits her teeth and makes a conscious choice to develop her mind, heart, and soul. You don't grit your teeth to choose to develop physical beauty. That's more bowing down under the overwhelming crush of society telling you that's what's important. All of which is why I like stories where someone has to make a conscious choice to develop or abandon their power. As a storyteller, I find it more interesting.

Physical attraction and anger. My experience of growing up was that proper women didn't have either of these emotions. Today, I like telling stories where the heroine must deal with both of these emotions, especially as a young adult. I wrote a whole series about this (ANGELBOUND) around this topic.

You plus me equals "we." I also like stories where the hero and heroine fit together and create something altogether new and positive between them. Sure, this can be a new sense of obsession and seeing each other as a drug, but a little of that goes a long way. Kick-ass chicks in kick-ass relationships hook up with someone where they make their significant other a better person for being in their lives, and vice versa. I love it if there is something between them—like magic or battle strategies—where they create a physical manifestation of that "we." This can also be done with children, too. For me, I like to see the "we" manifest before the kiddos start.

Okay. So, that's my list of kick-ass chick-ness. It's behind all the stuff I write as well as what I read. My reviews are all on my Goodreads account, and I read about a book a day on average. With that preamble behind me, I'd like to get to the important stuff: showing my heartfelt appreciation to everyone who made this book possible.

To begin with, I would like to send a massive thank-you out to my readers. The second I posted that I was writing *Wolves & Roses*, you hopped online and told me how excited you were for this story. All that enthusiasm kept me going through long nights and extra revisions. You are awesome.

Next, I must bow down to the amazing folks at INscribe Digital, who move mountains and make it look easy. This includes the wonderful Kelly Peterson, Stephanie Gomes, Allison Davis, and Larry Norton. You all are totes awesome. Also, a big welcome to the new team at IPG; I look forward to getting to know you all!

Behind the scenes is a team of crazies who keep me writing and happy. Top of the list is my kick-ass editor, Genevieve Iseult Eldredge. It's been a joy to work with you, and I can't wait to see what the future holds.

Best for last. Huge and heartfelt thanks to my husband and son. None of this would be possible without you. First and last, you're the best.

Christina Bauer thinks that fantasy books are like bacon: they just make life better. All of which is why she writes romance novels that feature demons, dragons, wizards, witches, elves, elementals, and a bunch of random stuff that she brainstorms while riding the Boston T. Oh, and she includes lots of humor and kick-ass chicks, too. Christina lives in Newton, Massachusetts, with her husband, son, and semi-insane golden retriever, Ruby.

List of Publications
By Christina Bauer

ANGELBOUND ORIGINS SERIES
(YA Urban Fantasy)
1. Angelbound
2. Scala
3. Acca
4. Thrax
5. The Dark Lands (Fall 2018)
6. Armageddon (Already here, long story!)

ANGELBOUND OFFSPRING SERIES
(YA Urban Fantasy)
1. Maxon
2. Portia
3. Zinnia (Fall 2019)

BEHOLDER
(YA Epic Dark Fantasy)
1. Cursed
2. Concealed
3. Cherished
4. Crowned

FAIRY TALES OF THE MAGICORUM
(YA Urban Fantasy)
1. Wolves and Roses (Fall 2017)
2. Shifters and Glyphs (Fall 2018)

DIMENSION DRIFT
(YA Urban Fantasy)
1. Prequel (Spring 2018)
2. Dimension Drift (Fall 2018)
3. ECHO Academy (Spring 2019)